FULL STORY INSIDE

Steve Horsfall

ISBN   ISBN 978-1-4092-1124-2

Cover Art: **Steve Horsfall**

For Vera Tonner and Rose Horsfall

Also by Steve Horsfall

You Are Here   ISBN 1-84401-305-7

Follow the exploits of four thirtysomething friends (Dave, Gavin, Phil and Tony) as they venture on holiday to Crete. For all of them, life will never be the same again.

'The perfect book to read on the beach or when just lounging in the garden.'

It's Cold Outside   ISBN 1-84728-233-4

It's Christmas and a diverse group of Brits find themselves snowbound in Lapland and have no choice but to work together to survive. It is time for them to learn who they really are.

'This is a Christmas story with a difference.'

Do You Believe What You Read?

1

Harkness Goes For A Bung – Senior government minister James Harkness has resigned following allegations of receiving donations from wealthy party sponsors which he subsequently invested in a private business enterprise. Crooked Harkness was exposed by The Globe's very own award winning undercover investigative reporter 'The Mole'.

Harkness has always proclaimed his innocence, stating that the donations were erroneously misplaced by a third party. (Full Story Inside)

Richard Kay folded the day's copy of best selling national newspaper 'The Globe' and flung it across a paper strewn desk.

"Whoa," junior colleague Alex Hart pulled away his polystyrene cup of black coffee just in time as the paper landed close by.

"Sorry mate", Richard chuckled, "serves you right though for buying that rag. Call yourself a bloody journalist."

"Why do you read it if it's so crap?" Alex opened the paper in front of him, perusing the full colour spread on how The Globe had orchestrated the downfall of the corrupt government minister.

"The cover story was enough mate," Richard switched on his PC to review his own news copy.

Richard and Alex held respective positions as senior and junior journalist on the weekly local newspaper 'The Dartcombe Herald'

"Don't knock The Mole bro'," Alex was nodding as he read the first hand account of how The Mole had trapped and then exposed James Harkness. "The man is the pinnacle, the king."

"Stop slobbering," Richard gave a hard stare, "I just hope you never meet this superhero as you'd probably explode from so much gushing. Mind you, is it a man or is it a woman. Who is that masked…person?"

"I despair of you Rich, seriously." Alex switched on his own PC, "I mean you've been working on this rag for over twenty years covering such hard hitting stories of village fetes, lost pets and vandalised schools. Did you never want to progress? Never want to move on to the nationals and write some real news?"

Richard looked on with silent scorn.

Alex held up a hand before stating sarcastically "although last week's article on the bus stop's planning permission rumpus did deserve a much wider audience."

"Look you cocky git," Richard stood up and wagged his finger at his young naive colleague. "I have pride in what I do and after twenty years I'm still learning my trade. You guys think you know it all in five minutes so if you want to go and work for a daily scandal sheet, then fucking go. See what you become. See if you can live with yourself. Me, I always sleep at night and I'll give you an example of why. Some fifteen years ago when you were still kicking a ball in the school yard, we had this young girl found dead in St

Thomas's graveyard. Turned out she was running across the graveyard to take a shortcut home as she was late. She simply tripped, tearing her dress in the process, and banged her head on a headstone. The blow killed her and she wasn't discovered until the next morning. Anyway, the police at first viewed the death as suspicious because the two mourners who found the girl had moved the body. So they called a press conference and the national press descended like hyenas. I asked the first question in terms of what line of enquiry the police were taking. Next up was some hack from your beloved Globe. As the young girl's grief stricken parents sat close by, the scum honed in on the ripped dress and asked question after question about the lass's sexual history. He implied she was some kind of whore and the police could not really comment or defend the girl. The stories he wrote as exclusives made me want to puke, with headlines like 'Ghoul sought after sex ritual death'. Even when the truth unfolded there was no retraction or apology. The Globe just moved on to another target. So yes mate, I'm very happy in what I'm doing."

Alex grimaced slightly as he silently returned to his work. A tensed and red faced Richard did likewise.

Approximately two miles from the cramped Dartcombe Herald office, eighty year old Marjorie Ball almost scurried along an uneven rural pathway. She was en-route for the village post office about half a mile from her home. Marjorie held her coat collar tight around her neck to keep out a very cold March wind and filled her mind with thoughts of spring, when the countryside around her would once again be in colourful bloom. Rather than continue to follow the winding village road, Marjorie decided to take a short cut along by the river. She nearly turned back when the swollen river banks came into view, but the path was mainly dry and Marjorie was running late. Marjorie's pace naturally picked up as she moved along in solitude. The clouds above were darkening by the minute and the cold wind now bit even harder by the water's edge. It was almost nine am but it felt like dusk. The lights of the village shops glared into view through the gloom and Marjorie sighed with relief as spots of cold rain began to fall.

The river flowed as a torrent, stirring up the silt from the bed below to produce murky and dirty water. Marjorie thought of how she would walk her grandchildren here in the summer and they would gaze down at the small fish in the crystal clear water. Now large dislodged branches from the trees that lined the banks formed a continual flotilla of debris. The larger logs of wood even looked like small animals. Marjorie shivered as she pondered the fact that rats might be present. Marjorie had a rat phobia. In fact she had a phobia of all rodents.

It was just as Marjorie reached the steps that would take her away from the river and closer to shelter from the now incessant rain that she glanced back at the swirling cloudy water. A very large black log floated by. Marjorie looked away and then curiously peeked back. The log was almost static and going around slowly in circles on the spot, somehow resisting the harsh flow of the river. Marjorie stared hard as the river flipped the log in the air. As it came to land Marjorie's face contorted in instant horror as her squinting eyes honed in on a bloated blue face of a young man. Instantly cupping a hand over her chattering mouth, Marjorie moved as fast as her arthritic legs would carry her through the hard rain, unable to scream and desperate to find help and shelter.

2

Jane Coker felt unusually nervous as she breezily made her away around the London backstreets. Even the combined smell of fried breakfasts, croissants and bagels that wafted through the chilled March air could not overcome the butterflies that knotted her stomach.

Jane had always been so confident in everything she had ever done. That confidence had made her the star student on her journalist post grad. That confidence made it easy to then take two years out and travel the world. On her return, Jane Coker had no qualms about applying for a job at the UK's leading national newspaper, The Globe. Her confidence meant that the interview was a formality.

On this, her first day at The Globe, Jane Coker felt nervous and she did not know why.

"OK children, settle down," Chief Editor Paul Langmead flapped his hands like a teacher as The Globe's main boardroom filled with all of the paper's principle journalists. Jane Coker sat quietly as a couple of wide boys gabbled incessantly with strong cockney accents behind her. Jane could feel their eyes burning into her arse as they openly weighed up the new office totty. Jane had hardly been introduced to her buddy writer when she was given a strong and bitter plastic cup of coffee and ushered to the boardroom for the weekly editorial review. She was now trying to profile buddy writer in her mind as nobody else made any effort to introduce themselves. Buddy writer was a greasy late forty something, whose paunch of a stomach ensured his cheap white shirt never stayed tucked into his brown polyester trousers. Even his loosened stained tie was made of polyester.

Buddy writer, or Iain Baxter to give his real name, had dumped Jane in a chair as soon as they had arrived in the boardroom and gone off to talk to some geeky looking colleagues.

"Right then," Paul Langmead now thumped hard on the polished oak table and raised his voice louder. After a few persistent mumbles the room fell silent. "Thank you," Langmead continued, "now I hope you all feel suitably invigorated on this wonderful Monday morning. I hope you all learnt from last week's botch of a meeting. I remind you that our goal is to constantly come up with fresh and challenging ideas. Our motto people, if the news does not happen then let us make it happen. That's why our market share increased to seventy-eight percent last month. Any more sessions like last Monday and we'll end up going south. Do you get me?"

A disgruntled murmur filled the room.

"OK let's have some quality people," Langmead yelled as a large plasma screen descended from the ceiling. A stern looking female typist sat nearby ready to record themes and ideas in lights for all to see.

"Sports idol," a balding fat looking man shouted out. "A sort of pop idol for young sports stars and The Globe sponsors it and tracks the progress of the winner."

The words 'Sports Idol' flashed up on the screen.

"Nah," was the sheep like chorus as grown men and women gave the idea a childlike thumbs down. A line was scored through the words on the screen and a cartoon turkey waddled into view to signify that the idea was no good.

"PC city," another older journalist cried out. "A national review to find the most politically correct city in the UK. A good excuse to slate the bastards who are killing our traditions."

The suggestion went the same way as 'Sports Idol' and so it went on, with the appearance of relentless turkeys on the screen, even after some of the more original ideas had at least triggered the odd debate. Langmead shook his head, tugged at his already loosened tie, and checked the time. "Nearly out of luck folks. Another crap Monday."

"Come off it Langmead," a very fat ginger haired hack sat next to the Chief Editor snarled. "Whatever we come up with is always going to be the support act. The Globe should be renamed The Mole because that is all it is about now. Whatever the Mole does is the main feature period. The Globe doesn't fucking need real journalists."

"Does that mean we can discount you from the Mole sweepstake Gregson," a heckler yelled from the back of the room.

"Shit, I had a tenner on him," the sarcastic cry brought a roar of laughter around the room.

"Fuck off," Gregson growled. "I tell you what, I come from an era when you went out and reported the news. There was a skill in it. Now it's all fucking showbiz and no talent. The Mole is really the Weasel."

A loud single hand clap echoed around the oak panelled room. Jane Coker turned her head towards the source of the applause. A small group of young writers moved away from the door to leave one man standing alone. He stood out immediately in an extremely expensive Italian suit, contrasting to the cheap high street apparel on those who flanked him. Jane Coker became very aware as she gazed around the room that there were very few female journalists in the room. She suddenly felt self-conscious.

"From the heart Mr Gregson, from the heart. I like that," the new arrival walked forward. He was Mediterranean in appearance, with combed back slick black hair and tanned skin. Jane now recognised him from the media. It was The Globe's multi billionaire owner, Arturo Tabb.

"Mr Tabb, what a pleasant surprise," Langmead stuttered and grovelled. "I'm sorry about that. You know how these open and honest sessions can get."

Tabb held up a hand to silence his Chief Editor, "let's get back to basics." He spoke with the utmost calm. "To contradict Mr Gregson, The Globe does need to evolve. It needs to stay fresh and ahead of the game. The Mole achieves notoriety by staying ahead of the game. Learn from that my friends or end up like Gregson here, over the hill and way out of time. A fucking dinosaur."

A red faced Gregson stormed out of the room bumping his way past several junior colleagues as he went.

Tabb now took Langmead's place at the head of the table. "I've been stood listening to this crap for twenty minutes now, has-been hacks full of wind and bluster. A waste of my time and I'm paying wages for this shit. Let's try a different approach." Tabb stared straight at Jane, who instantly shivered with the attention. "Young lady, I think you must be new. The giveaway is that you are far prettier and fresh faced than anyone else in here."

Jane now blushed to match her bright red skirt and jacket and flicked back her long blonde hair before finding composure.

"Young lady, your name please," Tabb asked softly.

"Jane...Jane Coker," she answered timidly.

"OK Jane Coker, It's your big moment." Tabb walked over and placed a hand on Jane's right shoulder, "give me a feature idea."

Jane shuddered slightly, partly from being put in the spotlight and partly because of Tabb's slimy demeanour. An awkward silence followed as all the eyes in the room trained on Jane. A few mumbled but audible sniggers could be heard as some wallowed in the new girl's embarrassment. Jane's mind spun idea after idea like a fruit machine rotating a combination of shapes. Suddenly an idea stuck.

"Um, a regional focus," Jane coughed and spoke louder. "You could have a weekly feature on a UK town or city, picked at random each time. The idea would be that a journalist would visit the nominated location undercover and write a column. Warts and all, beyond the mundane local press. The Globe could bring notoriety to the suburbs."

The words 'Local Review' flashed up on the plasma screen. Another awkward silence followed.

"What do we think?" Tabb smarmily looked around the crowded room.

"Nah," sneered one short long haired hack, "boring and ridiculous.

"Actually," a pretty female journalist spoke up, "I think it would work. All those cities and towns out there would be wondering if they were next on the list, not knowing who the undercover journalist was or what they would write about. The chance for lots of controversy, which we all know sells."

"Anything else Miss Davenport," Tabb seemed impressed as he gesticulated towards the smartly dressed brunette.

"Yes I think the writer should be a woman," Miss Davenport spoke with the utmost confidence, which impressed Jane. "Assuming that our other great undercover reporter is a man, this would bring a nice balance."

"Never assume anything my dear," Tabb scoffed. "Assumption is the biggest mistake you can make in life. Anyway I happen to agree with you on all accounts in respect of Miss Coker's idea."

Tabb then simply left the room with Langmead in tow as the plasma screen flashed a visual thumbs-up.

"Like the new girl, who's she buddied with?" Tabb growled at Langmead as they left the room.

"Iain Baxter," Langmead replied.

"Slimeball Baxter, fuck off," Tabb snapped. "Put her with Davenport and let them work on the new feature idea together."

"Yes sir," Langmead almost bowed as Tabb headed for the revolving doors at the building's exit.

Tabb turned back. "Oh and Langmead, make sure Gregson clears his desk within the hour." Tabb then left swiftly.

"Yes," Langmead mumbled to himself. "Would you like me to thank him for his thirty years dedicated service?" He spoke rhetorically with heavy sarcasm.

3

Alex Hart was bored. It was only 10am and he could not get motivated. To make matters worse Richard Kay was eagerly tapping away at his keyboard, humming loudly with the odd interruption for an audible sigh as he reviewed his copy like it was a masterpiece. The Editor, Dan Goodman, had finally trudged in some ten minutes ago and shut himself in his office after exchanging a grunted greeting with Richard. There was no disguising the fact that Richard hated Dan and it appeared that the feeling was mutual. Alex wondered if Richard liked anyone.

"Richard," Dan had ventured out of his office before midday, which was far from usual. He hardly even stepped out for a toilet break most mornings and would call people in if he wanted something.

"Yeah," Richard stayed focussed on his screen.

"I need you to go out, there's been an incident near Bagley Bridge." Dan now stood next to Richard's chair.

"What sort of incident?" Richard finally looked up at his boss.

"The body of a young lad has been found floating in the river. Looks like an accident but we need to get someone down there." Dan turned to go.

"Send the kid," was Richard's instant reaction. "He's looking for excitement and I'm busy."

"OK," Dan did not question the suggestion. "Alex, get yourself down there."

Within minutes Alex was driving his battered old Vauxhall towards the scene, curious to know what had occurred whilst feeling saddened that someone had died. The local radio station reported that an incident had taken place at Bagley Bridge and that emergency services were at the scene. Just as the DJ announced that traffic was building up in the area, Alex slowed to a standstill in a queue that stretched for some distance. In frustration Alex pulled over and decided it would be quicker to proceed on foot. Soon he was jogging past the static cars with adrenalin pumping more than ever.

Just as Alex reached the bridge a young policewoman greeted him. "Sorry sir you'll have to take a different route," the cop said rigidly.

Beyond the policewoman Alex could see that the steps down to the river had been cordoned off with bright yellow tape. Two police cars and an ambulance masked any activity.

"Press," Alex held up his ID and felt really important.

"Just a second," the policewoman tutted before speaking into her radio. "Sir I have a gentleman from the press here. The Dartcombe Herald."

"OK let him through," was the quick and simple response.

As Alex walked towards the police cars he felt nervous beyond belief. Maybe Richard was right, at least people rarely died at village fetes.

"Hey son, who are you then?" A uniformed policeman appeared from behind a police car. "Where's grumpy fatboy?"

"Sorry?" Alex walked up to the officer brandishing his press pass once again. Alex noted the Sergeant's stripes on the fifty something officer's immaculate uniform.

The Sergeant brushed the pass away, "I take it you work with fatboy Kay. I suppose he's now too fat to get off his arse these days."

"Um, Richard...yeah." Alex took out a notebook as the rain started to fall, "what can you tell me Sergeant?"

"Not a lot. A young lad barely twenty was found floating in the river by a local biddy this morning. She's still in shock somewhere, drinking lots of tea." The Sergeant rubbed rain from his face as Alex tried to take notes. "We think it might be a local lad who was reported missing last night. Can't confirm that until his parents have ID'd the body."

"What do you think happened?" Alex asked as he looked over the Sergeant's shoulder. In the background two plain clothed policemen were consulting as two medics carried the covered body on a stretcher to the waiting ambulance. A pathologist ushered them on.

"Well, off the record, it looks like the lad got pissed and fell in the water last night. Simple as that. If it's our missing lad then he was a student. Probably had a snakebite too many." The Sergeant almost scoffed, "don't quote me on that though."

"No I assume that's just conjecture," Alex stated as he wrote.

"Whatever," the Sergeant muttered, "give me your card son and I'll keep you posted."

The emergency vehicles were soon on their way as Alex began walking back to his car. "Shit, not much of a story there," he said to himself as the heavens suddenly opened.

4

"Paula Davenport, pleased to meet you," Jane Coker was greeted by her new buddy writer.

"Jane Coker, likewise," Jane shook her elegant colleague's hand.

"Let's grab a coffee and get to know each other," Paula grabbed her coat and ushered Jane to do the same. "Luigi's is just around the corner and offers the best cappuccino and selection of pastries in the area. My treat."

Jane did not object, warming to her co-worker immediately. She was certainly a vast improvement on the first slimeball that was assigned to her. It was nice to escape the stuffy offices of The Globe and find a haven at Luigi's. The upmarket café reminded Jane of Central Perk in the sitcom 'Friends' and Paula was proven to be right about the fare on offer.

"OK, here we are," Paula crossed her stunning legs as she sat back in a comfy sofa. Jane smiled as she noticed a few male customers gawking nearby. "So Jane Coker, tell me about yourself and then I'll fill you in on The Globe. I would prefer to do it over a bottle of Chablis but it's far too early even for me."

Jane gave Paula a quick summary of her academic background and brief highlights of her world travels.

"So that's how you ended up at The Globe," Paula sipped at her cappuccino. "Sounds like you've packed a lot into a very young life. I like that."

"How about you Paula, what's your background?" Jane was genuinely curious about her mentor's past.

"Nowhere near as exciting as yours," Paula chuckled to herself. "Pretty much a school drop out who managed to scrape a work experience job on my local rag. Actually found I was quite good at writing and journalism seemed as good a job as any. Went back to college, passed some exams, and then worked my way around the glamour mag circuit. Had a nasty fall-out with the editor of one glossy and got the boot. She then proceeded to make my name mud so I tried newspapers. Got interviewed by two lecherous bastards at The Globe and I've now been working here for five years."

"Why are there so few females writers here?" Jane enquired.

"You noticed," Paula smiled. "The Globe has always been a bit of a boy's club. Langmead once said to me that the trouble with women is that somewhere deep inside they always have a heart. A conscience basically. With The Globe you have to be prepared to scrape the depths and then sleep at night."

Jane shook herself, "sounds horrible. What sort of outfit have I joined?"

"Don't worry babe, us token women are just here for the softer side. To lighten up the paper's hard hitting approach. Two provisos for the job; one you can actually write your name and two you look bloody hot. Welcome to your prime role as office eye candy."

"Shit, sexist bastards," Jane was annoyed, "but what about The Mole? Some say it could be a woman."

"It's not, believe me it's a man," Paula confirmed quickly.

"You've met him…you know who he is?" Jane was now excited.

"No," Paula hesitated, "but I have inadvertently spoken to him on the phone. Time to give you a little warning."

Jane's mind was reeling, "go on."

"Arturo Tabb," Paula stated blankly. "Have as little to do with him as you can. He is a dangerous man to know and once he's got you in his web there's no escape. I like you Jane so stay clear."

"I don't think I'm senior enough for him to bother with," Jane gave a nervous laugh.

Paula leant forward, looking extremely stern. "Tabb picked you out today. Whilst we've been chatting one of his underlings will have compiled a complete dossier on you at Tabb's request. It will have every little detail of your short life. If you have any skeletons in the closet or any weaknesses then beware. He already knows more about you than I do from our short chat. If you were a man then any previous indiscretion or weak point would be found and available to be exploited, wherever and whenever. If you are a woman then he's going to want to own you and shag you whenever he wants. Tabb likes to control everything and everyone."

"Scary," Jane nodded, "don't tell me he's shagged you?"

Paula did not reply.

"My god, he has. This place is unreal." Jane then pointed straight at Paula, "that's how you spoke to The Mole."

"You really are a smart girl," Paula got up to go. "He was in the shower and I cheekily answered the phone. Nearly lost my job and more besides, but at the end of the day Tabb likes shagging me. He says he has no weakness but I may be just that."

Jane followed Paula out of the café imagining her as some glorified call girl whilst wondering what hold Tabb must have over her and the fact that it must be something really horrible. She shuddered at the thought of having sex with the slimy Tabb, single minded in the fact that she would rather die.

5

Monday had passed more quickly than usual for Alex Hart after his impromptu dash to the scene of a local death. Now he was back at his desk and writing up more mundane copy for the Thursday edition of the Dartcombe Herald. Alex had made a few notes following his discussion with the police sergeant but at the moment the story read nothing more than 'local man drowns in river'. Editor Dan Goodman had reserved a front page slot for the item as it was big news versus the tale of the old lady who had tripped on an uneven pavement outside the local hypermarket. The old dear's swollen knee had been pushed on to page five.

"Hello fatboy," a semi familiar voice broke Alex's concentration.

The Police Sergeant who Alex had met earlier was shaking Richard Kay's hand. He was no longer in uniform.

"TA, how are you mate?" Richard beamed as if he had found some long lost friend.

"Fine…and still not as fat as you fatboy," the Sergeant grabbed at Richard's sizeable paunch.

"Fuck off," was all Richard could manage in reply. "What you doing here anyway?"

"Double header mate," the Sergeant moved over towards Alex, "come to take you out for a beer to fill that gut of yours and also to talk to your kid here."

Alex also felt like telling TA to fuck off for calling him a kid but instead said nothing.

"Kid," the Sergeant stood next to Alex, who ground his teeth at a repeat of the insult. "I've got something for you. It's no great scoop but a chance to write a nice piece for the Herald. I'm sure you're better than old fatboy over there."

"What is it Sergeant?" Alex was now intrigued.

"Just call me TA kid, everybody does," the Sergeant pulled an envelope from his inside jacket pocket.

"Why TA?" Alex enquired as he was handed the envelope.

"Because the twat thinks he's a soldier," Richard answered the question. "Only trouble is that the army wouldn't have him so he joined the police. Then he spent every bloody weekend going training with the TA. Never married because he was never around to meet women…either that or he's gay."

"Oh yes that's quite right," the Sergeant put on a camp voice, "and I want your lardy arse tonight Kay."

"Um," Alex coughed loudly, "Sergeant…TA, what's in the envelope?"

"Bloody well open it, call yourself an investigative reporter," the Sergeant boomed.

Alex did so and found it contained a slip of paper, which read:

Martin Gardner Aged 20

17 The Mill

Bagley
Tel: 01745 217865

"It's the young lad who we pulled out of the river this morning. Turned out it was our missing student. His dad identified him," the Sergeant solemnly confirmed.

"Thanks, I'll incorporate it in my story," Alex stated with a feeling of anti-climax.

"That's not all. His mum wants you to write a full spread on the lad. A sort of tribute. I said I'd get you to call her," the Sergeant tapped the phone number shown at the bottom of the paper. "You can call the mum on that number. OK?"

"Yeah sure," Alex was now a little more inspired.

As Richard and the Sergeant headed for a local pub, Alex went to tell Dan Goodman of the development.

"Come in Al," Dan said with a warm smile. His office was a cluttered mess and always had been. Alex had to remove a pile of papers from a chair to sit down.

Alex filled Dan in on the Sergeant's request.

"That will be nice," Dan nodded. "Good chance for you to write something different Al. One for the portfolio."

Dan was always referring to the portfolio and the need for Alex to build up some quality features. He was eager for Alex to succeed and reach a level that Dan had never managed to attain himself. Unlike Richard, Dan had wanted to go to the top. He craved to be a celebrated writer. Despite rising to the position of editor at a top daily city newspaper, Dan Goodman was to go no further. The arrival of new vibrant bosses saw Dan labelled as old school and he was soon banished to a rural outpost.

"Al, I like you. I can see lot of me in you," Dan invoked a father-son style chat. "Don't waste your talent. Don't end up sad and twisted like Richard out there. Take a chance. Always take a chance. View nothing at face value and always question. Consider the facts from every angle and make sure you grab your audience in whatever you write about."

"Thanks Dan," Alex felt a bit uneasy, "although it does get a bit difficult to spice up the Dartcombe carnival or Bagley fete each year."

Dan let out a very forced laugh. "Point taken, but make this piece a good one OK. A fitting tribute to a tragedy but it could be your meal ticket if a national includes it."

As Alex went to leave the office, Dan switched on a small portable TV sitting on the corner of his desk.

"Al, come and see this," Dan called out. Alex reluctantly returned. He was hungry and eager to go home.

"Look at this guy," Dan pointed at the small badly tuned screen. Arturo Tabb was being interviewed on an early evening chat show.

"That's Arturo Tabb," Dan stated like he was some sort of hero. "This man is the guru of modern journalism. He built up a multi billion media empire form scratch. I got his autobiography for Christmas. It's called 'I Am The News'. I tell you the man is a genius."

On the screen the middle aged blonde TV interviewer giggled and blushed as Tabb teased and flirted with her.

"You see Fiona, I'm just a cuddly bear really. So my staff tell me. I'm living proof that journalists can be nice guys. I can't even bring myself to kill a woodlouse let alone ruin a good person. The rule is simple; if you're a bad person in the spotlight then my paper will sort you out. If you are innocent and law abiding, you have nothing to worry about. Tabb's words tailed off as he momentarily stared with wide eyes and a static grin into the main camera. The programme made way for a commercial break.

As Dan continued to gush, Alex felt strangely haunted by Tabb's beaming face.

6

Jane Coker was relieved that her first day was nearly over. After the initial excitement of the morning Jane had been assigned to review potential incoming stories for the main news desk. This basically entailed answering the phones and reading emails. Jane felt like she was now working in a call centre. Paula had been called away to cover a suicide on the underground.

"Hi Jane, sorry about that," Paula whipped off her coat and sat down with a sigh. "A messy business but just some loser who couldn't take being dumped by an Essex girl with a nose ring and dire highlights."

"Does the job make you like that?" Jane said slightly agog. "So cynical and hard nosed."

"If you get involved you've had it my dear," Paula poured herself a stewed black coffee. "It's just like that whole doctor patient thing."

"Wow and that's how I'm going to be," Jane was wondering if she should have just gone for a job on a glossy women's magazine.

"You'll be fine," Paula asserted, "anyway I bumped into Langmead and he wants me and you out on the road tomorrow. So where are we going? Somewhere nice for our first assignment I fancy."

"I haven't given it a thought," Jane confessed, "I just thought we would be sent somewhere."

"Vicky, where's that place you go on your hols to every year?" Paula shouted over to a middle aged secretary using the photocopier.

"Dartcombe," Vicky answered without looking up. "It's divine. So quiet and peaceful compared to the grime and grind of London."

As Vicky left the room Paula smiled mischievously. "Dartcombe it is then. Give me your address and directions and I'll pick you up sometime tomorrow morning. I'll get us booked into a nice hotel. We'll play it that we are two best mates down for a pamper weekend." Paula winked.

"Yeah fine, so it's as simple as that?" Jane felt elated that she would not have to come into the office for a while.

"Oh yes, quiet and peaceful to quote our Vicky," Paula clapped her hands together. "I like a challenge."

Paula told Jane to go home and that she would do a little bit of research on the idyllic Dartcombe.

Jane felt very tired as she headed for the underground, sparing a thought for the spurned lover who had killed himself down the same track that very day. Jane just missed the departing tube train as she sauntered onto the platform. As the train moved away a large billboard poster on the other side of the track came into view. The huge image of Arturo Tabb looked down, advertising his recently published autobiography which had been top of the book chart for four months. The words 'I Am The News' were emblazoned across the bottom of the poster as Tabb smugly pointed at himself. Jane cursed the fact that she could not escape from Tabb even outside of work.

7

Disgraced Comic Ends It All - Des Banner, the award winning comedian and former TV star has taken his own life. Suicide was confirmed by a police spokesman last night after the troubled celebrity was found slumped in his fume filled car by ex-wife Cindy Smith. Des Banner's career was riding high until he was exposed as a cocaine addict and sexual pervert by The Globe's very own premier reporter, The Mole. Banner, 51, saw his earning potential collapse after the scandal. He was forced to sell his home and tried unsuccessfully to start a new career as an agent (Full Story Inside).

"I used to quite like him," Jane Coker perused the front page of Tuesday's edition of The Globe as she nibbled on a slice of toast. "Just shows you that these stars put on a façade and behind it all who knows who or what they really are."

"A little naive Jane," Paula Davenport scanned her eyes around Jane's cramped kitchen as she clung to a steaming mug of coffee. "Sorry I'm really early by the way. Thought we could make an early start and didn't think I would find your place so quickly."

"That's fine, although I think my other half was a bit surprised to hear you banging on the door. I left him in bed. He has a really dossy job running the local gym." Jane blushed as she remembered how Paula had interrupted the early stages of a farewell shag. Surprised did not really cover it. Furious was closer to the truth. "Anyway, why am I naïve?"

"Because you obviously believe what you read. Just because it says it on the page does not mean it's true," Paula winced at the bitter taste of instant coffee in the cracked mug.

"Why, you don't think The Globe makes things up do you?" Jane scoffed.

"Maybe, maybe not," Paula stood up, "come on. Go and give your man a quick snog and let's get going. I'll fill you in on my background research to Dartcombe as we go."

Jane did not bother waking her snoring boyfriend but instead left him a hastily scribbled note before grabbing her travel bag and running out to Paula's classy Mazda MX. Paula revved the engine of the 2 litre two seater car and pressed hard on the accelerator before Jane could even fasten her seatbelt.

"Nice car," Jane commented, "very flash."

"Oh yes journalism does have its perks," Paula selected Lilly Allen's 'Alright Still' on her multi changer CD player. "OK Dartcombe. On the surface an ordinary, and therefore dull, west country rural retreat. It has a few small villages nearby full of retired folk whilst Dartcombe's purpose in life seems to be to cater for holidaymakers. The townsfolk lead simple lives and no doubt are really simple yokels. No real crime rates to worry about apart from the odd burglary and the annual arrival of travelling pikeys. Having said that some young student fell in the river and drowned yesterday. As I said, simple yokels who can't even stay on dry land.

"Great, sounds like a laugh a minute," Jane gripped hard on her seat as she began to feel queasy from Paula's incessantly fast driving. "I take it there's not a lot of wealth in this town?"

"Actually there's a few mansions around acting as country retreats for a number of hotshot city dealers," Paula nodded along to the music. "Also there is the national headquarters of IBEX electronics about fifteen miles away. It's mainly a data centre employing low calibre programmers and gap year call centre staff."

"So we've got our work cut out." Jane pondered. "Will people want to read about the UK's dullest town?"

"Never heard of dramatic license?" Paula sniggered. "You'll be surprised how many people actually believe what they read."

Jane realised quickly that Paula was jibing her. She closed her eyes as she thought about the challenges of her new career, and partly in fear as Paula fired the Mazda up to 100 mph as they joined the motorway.

8

Alex Hart was starting to feel like a real writer. He had tentatively called the parents of Martin Gardner first thing that morning. Mr Gardner had answered the phone and Alex had put on his most sympathetic voice to gain empathy.

He calmly explained that the article would need to be written today in order to make this week's edition. After consultation with his wife, Mr Gardner was sure that it would be a fitting tribute.

As he drove towards the Gardner's cottage on the outskirts of Bagley, Alex was trying to play out in his mind what kind of man the late Martin Gardener had been. One thing was for certain, even if he was some wild ASBO thug who drowned kittens, the Dartcombe Herald would only portray an ordinary boy next door. Local papers could not afford to offend the small communities that they served.

The cottage was easy to find. It was picture perfect for a classic English village, complete with thatched roof, small timber windows and surrounded by a pristine garden, even in March. Most of the curtains were drawn as Alex walked up the cobbled path and then gently knocked on the front door. Mr Gardner answered, forcing a slight smile as a greeting and welcomed Alex in. He was smartly dressed, including a shirt and tie. His wife was sat solemnly in the lounge clutching a thick photo album. She too looked very smart wearing an old fashioned, but posh, frock. Thankfully the curtains were not drawn and so Alex did not have to sit in semi darkness.

Mr Gardner left to make some tea as Mrs Gardner tearfully picked up some pictures of Martin as a toddler and one in his senior school uniform. Alex could not help but think that he looked like a geek, reinforced by his most recent portrait hanging over the fireplace. He looked like he weighed about eight stone, wore thick rimmed glasses and had slicked back greasy brown hair. The only difference between his school photo and the latest photo was that the uniform had been replaced by some dreadful brown sweatshirt.

The sad facts were that Martin was an only child who had never had many friends, enjoyed any sports or ever had a girlfriend. He was academic and was taking a gap year before going to university. His passion had been computers and he had been working at IBEX Electronics to boost his savings.

"Thank you," Alex said as he finished his tea. "I can certainly put a fitting tribute together for Martin with what you've given me."

In truth Alex was thinking he could have written most of the copy from just seeing the unfortunate Martin's picture. He was about to call it a day as Mrs Gardner began to sob, when an instinct pressed him to ask a little more about the death.

"I really know that this is not easy," Alex thought hard as to how he could put his questions tactfully. "…but Martin's death seems so tragic. So unnecessary. Did he often walk home by the river?"

"No," Mr Gardner spoke up, "that's the odd thing. Our Martin was scared of his own shadow. He even slept with the light on if he watched something scary on TV. So I just don't know why he went by the river. I mean he would normally call me and I would gladly go and pick him up from the pub. I'm a teetotaller you see. Always sober and available."

Alex's head was suddenly reeling, "did you tell the police this information?"
"Yes, but they did not deem it important and said it was sadly just an accident. Said that he'd had a lot to drink and that when people have a lot to drink they lose inhibition, sense and fear," Mr Gardner sounded like he was quoting a well intentioned police view.

"Who did Martin normally go to the pub with?" Alex asked with more assurance.

Mrs Gardner answered, "that will be young Stephen Howard. He's been Martin's pal since school. They are very alike. Stephen works at IBEX too and was also going to the same university as Martin in September."

"The police did speak to Stephen." Mr Gardner intervened. "Said he was distraught and could hardly speak. Stephen went home earlier than Martin so could not say if he got really drunk and why he went down by the river."

"So he left Martin drinking alone?" Alex felt like a policeman.

"Yes it would appear so," Mr Gardner shrugged, "maybe Martin started reading a book, had a few more pints and forgot the time."

"And got paralytic in the process, I don't think" Alex mumbled to himself. Alex thanked the Gardners for their time and got up to leave.

"Oh and one more thing you might want to mention in your paper," Mr Gardner held up his hand. "We're going to sell Martin's things after the funeral. His bike, DVD's etc. It's just too painful keeping them and we thought that we could raise some money to build a proper and fitting memorial. Something that we can visit to think of him. A nice arbour in the garden with a plaque is the idea."

"Good luck," Alex nodded gently whilst thinking how all people deal with grief in different ways.

As Alex drove away from the Gardner's cottage he had one thing on his mind; time to talk to Stephen Howard.

9

The rain clouds gathered above as Paula Davenport's Mazda glided down the narrow hedge lined country lane. A small rusting white sign showed that Dartcombe was 2 miles away.

Jane Coker was ironically starting to long for home comforts as she looked out on a dreary moor in the late morning gloom. Jane could not understand why but suddenly she had a bad feeling about this assignment, and inner sense of foreboding. She decided to put it down to the weather. Jane had travelled the world and never felt the slightest bit homesick and yet a trip of just over a hundred miles had her dreaming of London. Maybe sitting behind a desk in The Globe's office was not such a bad idea after all. At least Paula seemed to have remained in good spirits.

"So," Jane decided to break a lull in the conversation that had lasted some twenty minutes. "You were saying last night that you had spoken to The Mole. How did you know it was him?"

"How do you mean?" Paula shrugged her shoulders and maintained her concentration on the road as the rain began to fall.

"Well I'm sure he didn't just say hi my name's The Mole, is Mister Tabb in?" Jane replied cuttingly.

Paula smirked, "good point, there's no fooling you. A bright career beckons."

"Well?" Jane was getting irritated as the weather darkened her mood.

"Well," Paula paused, "as I say I was at Tabb's house. He was taking a shower and the phone kept ringing in the study. I was curious…I am a journalist after all. Part of me thought it might be another woman that Tabb had his claws into. I was half hoping for an ally of sorts. Anyway this gruff voice barks out 'I want to speak to Tabb'. I asked who was calling and he just said an old friend. I said I would get Tabb and he just said 'sweet'. I remember it clearly."

"So how do you know it was The Mole?" Jane scrunched her face, "are you just guessing?"

"No," Paula said sharply, "firstly Tabb had an eppy when I told him there was an old friend on the phone. He screamed that I had no right to go into his study. He smashed me against the wall and put his hands around my neck. He squeezed so hard and went so red in the face that I thought I was dead. As I said he likes shagging me and a murder could finish his career, so he eventually came to his senses and let go."

"Shit, I would have got out of there and called the police," Jane stroked her own neck at the thought of the attack.

"As I said, once Tabb has you there's nowhere to run and hide," Paula bit her lip hard as she drove the Mazda past the ornate sign that welcomed visitors to Dartcombe.

"Wow, he must have some really big hold over you," Jane was now even more worried as she looked out at the small quaint shops and houses in the heart of Dartcombe. "So that was your final deduction, it had to be The Mole."

"No that was not all," Paul confessed. "I mean I was really shaken but my curiosity was stronger than ever. Next to Tabb's study is a small kitchen which I was able to sneak into and sufficiently eavesdrop on his conversation. It became one hundred percent clear that it was our man. He talked about the government minister, Harkness, and what a good job had been done. A week later that was The Globe's front page."

"Bloody hell, have you told anyone about this?" Jane's mind was a whirl.

"No," replied Paula sharply, "I've been waiting to tell someone but could trust nobody at The Globe. I feel I can confide in you, unless of course you're a Tabb spy and I'll be dead by the end of the week."

"You make it all sound so sinister," Jane was relieved that they had arrived at the hotel.

"It is, believe me it is." Paula parked the car as the heavens opened again. "and there's more."

"What?" Jane looked genuinely scared.

Paula turned to face Jane looking extremely serious, "you must not repeat this or anything I have told you. For your own life's sake as well as mine."

"OK I promise," Jane was already thinking about quitting her new job.

"The thing is that Tabb and The Mole are working on something really big, massive in fact. In Tabb's words 'something that will shake British society to its core'. That's all I really know apart from the fact that Tabb kept referring to some sort of list. That seemed to be the key to whatever scheme they are working on."

"Bloody hell," Jane was intrigued, "I look forward to that one breaking, or do I?"

Paula looked really concerned, "oh and one more thing. There was something vaguely familiar about The Mole's voice. I've been racking my brain since that night but can't suss it. I think I might actually have met our mystery man."

Paula and Jane swiftly retrieved their travel bags from the car boot and ran through the rain into the hotel reception. Jane felt she was part of some surreal dream. Life had been so simple last week and now this.

10

Alex Hart had not found it difficult to persuade Dan Goodman that the article on Martin Gardner would look really polished with some quotes from best buddy Stephen Howard. Alex had quickly written and submitted the framework of the front page story, along with a selection of photos provided by Mrs Gardner. The unexpected difficulty was finding Stephen Howard. Stephen Howard had reported in sick for his job at IBEX but also did not appear to be home at the address supplied by Mrs Gardner. Alex was resigned to heading back to the office and facing the extremely grumpy Richard Kay. Grumpier than ever because he was covering Alex's work whilst, in Richard's words, he was out on some jolly. Proper fieldwork was how Dan Goodman corrected him.

Alex decided to give the Gardners one more call under the premise that he was concerned about Stephen's wellbeing. Mrs Gardner did not question the motive and came up with a suggestion of an old fisherman's hut by the river, which Martin and Stephen used as a den when they were younger.

Alex parked his car and made his way on foot to the hut. He vaguely recollected spotting the hut on summer walks but had never given it a second thought before. The path was muddy and slippery as the rain persisted as a constant drizzle. Alex tightened his raincoat around him, totally aware that nobody else was savouring the delights of a lunchtime walk in the vicinity. He was just thinking that there would be little hope of finding Stephen when he spotted the dark weather beaten hut several yards ahead. Crouched in front of the hut and staring into the river, oblivious to the rain, was a tall gangly man. He was wearing a baggy blue sweatshirt and jeans, whilst his coat was lying on the floor nearby. He was soaked through.

"Stephen," Alex had walked up behind the crumpled figure completely unnoticed. The man suddenly jerked up as if given an electric shock.

"No…no, please don't hurt me," the man's face contorted as he sobbed openly.

Alex held out a reassuring hand, "I'm not here to harm you. Please let's get you somewhere warm and dry. You are Stephen Howard, yes?"

"Yes," Stephen was trembling from a mixture of cold and fear. "Who are you? You're not one of them?"

Alex reassured Stephen that he was not there to harm him and managed to lead him back to the warmth of his car. The offer of taking Stephen home to dry off was met with more hysterical crying and so Alex had no choice but to take him back to his own flat. Stephen continually stared out of the window without uttering a word as Alex sped home.

Despite a few odd looks from several neighbours, Alex led Stephen into his flat. He gave him some old clothes and a towel and ran him a hot bath. As he brewed some tea Alex pondered on the facts before him. This was going to be a very different interview to the one that he had anticipated.

Stephen emerged from the bathroom in a more composed state, whilst looking ridiculous as a tall man in undersized clothes.

"Here you go mate, get that down you." Alex handed Stephen a large mug of tea, "so let's start at the beginning.

Stephen's face looked haunted as he visibly checked that nobody else was in the room. "It's been a nightmare and my best friend is dead, that's the long and short of it."

Alex leant forward, "are you saying that Martin's death was not an accident?"

"Well spotted," Stephen said with a hint of bitterness and sarcasm, "and now you know that be careful who you tell. I'm already a dead man walking and so could you be."

"Who did it? Who's after you Stephen?" Alex probed softly.

"I don't know," Stephen shook his head and stared wide eyed at the floor. "All I know is they, whoever they are, killed my mate and I reckon I'm next."

"OK," Alex sat back to think, "so the big question is why did they, whoever they are, kill Martin? What did he do to piss them off?"

"I can tell you what I know but they will get to you if you try and do anything. There's no escape," Stephen looked petrified.

"I'll have to take that chance," Alex shuddered a little inside, "I guess I'm already in deep."

"Right," Stephen sat up with a more confident air, ready to release a burden. "Myself and Martin both had jobs at IBEX. It was just an easy job really and a chance to earn some dosh before going to Uni. It was great working at IBEX, like a busman's holiday. We both love computers and we just had to answer the phone and help users who didn't know one end of the computer from another. You felt like a god showing the light to hundreds of computer illiterates. We got a nice bit of pay and could get pissed. There was even some nice totty to ogle at in the flesh rather than on the net."

"Was it IBEX? Are they the killers?" Alex's mind was whirring with a local conspiracy theory.

"No," Stephen laughed, "people at IBEX are a good laugh. And they are massive, serving so many companies. They would have nothing to gain from murder. No the problem started with Martin. He had this addiction, to find a better word. Hacking, he loved hacking. On a computer he was brilliant and so hacking into other sites and files was a piece of piss to him. He loved the challenge. I play Su-Doku, Martin hacked. When he was feeling really evil he would create an email virus and destroy a company's whole system. He was so good that he always created a smokescreen and never got caught. A pure genius."

"Nice," Alex curled his upper lip as his respect for the late Martin Gardner diminished.

"Anyway we used to have a good laugh about it over a pint. Martin would fill me in on what he'd managed to hack into. He used to download some really juicy stuff, everything from HR files like sexual harassment cases to porno pictures taken in someone's front room. It was a scream. That was until a couple of weeks ago."

"What happened a couple of weeks ago?" Alex said in eager anticipation.

"Well," Stephen hesitated as he thought back. "I remember it clearly. We met in the pub, the Pullman Arms, after work as usual. I always got there first as Martin was usually stuck on a computer somewhere. Anyway he turned up even later than usual and he was as white as a sheet. Absolutely bricking himself. It turned out that he'd hacked into some personal computer the night before. He downloaded some files, like he always did, but said they looked really dull. Probably why he did not mention them before but he hadn't even properly looked at them. Anyway he suddenly gets this email from the computer owner. Totally out of the blue and like how did they track him down? It just said 'you've been a naughty boy Martin'. Knew his name, the lot. Then when he'd read the mail it just deleted itself and then another would arrive. 'What shall we do with you Martin?' it said. This just went on and on, teasing. Martin just sat there taking in each message, unable to reply or comprehend what was going on. This guy had more nouse than him and he wanted to demonstrate it. After about ten short sharp messages came the final one. It just said 'time to die' in bold red letters that trickled like blood and disappeared."

"Wow, and this is what Martin told you?" Alex smiled in disbelief. "You don't think that he was having you on? A joke?"

"No, no way," Stephen dismissed the very notion. "I knew Martin really well. He was so scared. Anyway he kept a low profile for a while and didn't even touch his computer at home. Just went to work as normal. Everything seemed fine until Martin was called to the manager's office at IBEX last Friday. He came out smiling and was really chuffed. It turned out some government agency guy had spoken to him. Said he knew all about his hacking history and about the threatening emails. The guy assured him that he would be protected and that he was keen to tap into Martins computer skills. Said that it would be worth big money. When the guy asked if anyone else knew about the incident he told him about me. The guy wanted to know if I was good with computers too and Martin bigged me up. Anyway this guy had to go somewhere but said he would meet Martin and me for a drink on Sunday night to talk about a job offer."

"Sunday night? Why Sunday?" Alex queried.

"Yeah I thought that was odd at the time but he apparently played the whole undercover walls have ears spy bit." Stephen shrugged his shoulders, "Martin has every James Bond DVD so loved all that. So we met this guy on Sunday. He was well creepy. Quite an old guy with an army haircut, a crew-cut. He was dressed in black trousers and a black jumper and looked quite sinister. He did buy us loads of drinks but said he was teetotal. He said very little apart from the fact that we were very lucky he had got to us as we had pissed off some nasty people. I was not enjoying it at all as he kept asking me what I thought about what Martin had found and if I had told anyone else. I told him I hadn't seen what Martin had found and not told anyone else. Eventually he tells me that he needs some time alone with Martin to talk about a top secret job. He gave me a tenner to get a taxi home."

Alex jumped in as Stephen paused, "and that's the last time you saw Martin alive?"

"Yes," Stephen hung his head again, "and there was something else."

"What?" Alex almost snapped.

"When I got back from the pub I was pretty drunk, so I went on the computer. Wanted to look at some porn. It was then it happened. I got the same sort of emails as Martin. The first said 'you know too much' and it went on and on just like Martin had described. The last one said simply 'time for you to die 2', with the number like a text."

"Shit and was there no sender's address?" Alex asked.

"No, the sender's field was blank," Stephen bit his lower lip. "So there you have it, Martin's dead, I'm next and then it's probably you."

"Cheers for that thought," Alex did feel slightly worried. "So do you think this guy in the pub killed Martin? Did he give a name?"

"Yes and no," Stephen replied. "Bloody obvious he killed him and said he could not give a name for security reasons. We called him M for a laugh, like in James Bond."

"Why did you not go and tell the police all of this?" Alex was curious.

"I was going to but then I got this call on my mobile. This gruff voice said I still had a chance to live if I met with him. He said that the police were in his pocket. He could even have me arrested; frame me for something horrible like kiddie porn. I was disgusted. He told me to go to work as normal and he would find me," Stephen began to sob again.

"But you didn't go to work did you?" Alex stated.

"No I went to hide. Stayed in a hotel last night, then I kept thinking he was on to me. I was paranoid so I went down to the hut. Then I didn't know what to do. I just lost it." Stephen was shaking uncontrollably.

"And that's when I found you," Alex pondered the facts before him. "OK best you stay here for now, until we can find help or get you away from Dartcombe. I need to think what to do next. I wish I knew what Martin found on that computer. It has to be the key."

"He did copy the files on his computer back home," Stephen confirmed.

Alex smiled briefly before grimacing, "the Gardners. The bastards are sure to go after them."

Alex jumped up and grabbed the phone whilst retrieving the slip of paper that TA had given him with the Gardner's contact details. After what seemed like an age, Mr Gardner answered the phone. At least he was OK.

Alex thought quickly, "um I was thinking about your intention to sell some of Martin's belongings. I might be able to offer you a good price for his computer and donate it to a good cause."

"Shit," Alex cupped the mouthpiece with his hand as he shouted to the side before recovering his composure. "Oh well sorry to bother you."

"Well the good news is that I think the Gardners are now safe," Alex sat back down. "A special policeman, in Mr Gardner's words, arrived yesterday afternoon and removed Martin's computer and all his software. Sounds like our man M."

"The thing is," Stephen smirked, "Martin used to stash all his dodgy files in a secret place in his room. I doubt M's intelligence stretches that far."

"And you know where this secret place is?" Alex stood up again.

"Oh yes indeed," Stephen smiled with a newfound calmness almost revelling in the situation.

11

Jane Coker was pleased to have had some time to herself in the hotel room, able to wallow in the comfort of her own personal space. Paula had insisted on separate rooms in the extremely plush five star hotel. In her own words it was in case she got lucky. That suited Jane fine. It gave her the opportunity to chill out and think things through. A chance to try and make some logic of the world she had now become part of. The net result of a hot bath and an afternoon nap brought an inner calmness but still more questions than answers. Jane had never been a quitter but if this all got too much she would simply have to walk.

Jane was awoken from a semi doze by the sharp trill ring of the telephone by her bed. Paula cheerfully announced that Jane had fifteen minutes to meet her in reception and told her not to bring a coat. After quickly making herself presentable, Jane sighed heavily as she looked back at the luxurious room. Onwards and upwards she thought before confidently opening the door and striding into the corridor.

Paula was already in reception and grinning like a Cheshire cat. She was far from inconspicuous in her role as undercover reporter but rather the epitome of style in a short black skirt and lilac blouse. Her long shapely bare legs had caught the attention of most of the male hotel staff. The concierge was trying his luck and visibly flirting with the stunning brunette guest.

"Jane darling, there you are." Paula put on a greatly exaggerated posh voice as she walked across the foyer.

"Hi Paula," Jane mumbled like a second rate actress unsure of her part.

"Oh Darren this is my best friend in the world. The one that I was telling you about," Paula addressed the concierge.

"Hi Jane, I'm so pleased to meet you," Darren said smoothly as he reached out and kissed Jane's hand.

"Anyway I shall have to see you later as me and Jane are off to be pampered," Paula grabbed Jane's right arm and led her past the reception desk.

"Ladies," Darren almost took a bow as he suggestively winked at Paula.

As they scurried down the corridor Jane scowled at Paula, "what is going on?"

Paula was trying not to laugh, betrayed by the odd infectious giggle. "Oh Jane this is going to be the best assignment ever."

Jane stopped and stood still, "so now what?"

"OK, here's the plan," Paula was still laughing as if she was drunk. "Firstly I have made it abundantly clear in this hotel that me and you are bezzie friends, down here for a real pamper weekend. The first stage is to go to the beauty salon for a massage, pedicure, manicure and haircut. All on expense of course and all in the line of duty. Because as any girl will tell you, the best place to find out about any local gossip is to go to the hairdressers."

"Fair enough," Jane was not going to complain, "and was there a second part to the plan?"

"Yes," Paula ran her tongue over her upper lip, "if all else fails I will be shagging the concierge, who also knows everything there is to know. The fact that he's called Darren is outweighed by his incredible good looks."

Jane certainly enjoyed the initial beauty treatments but the therapists were far from forthcoming with any juicy Dartcombe gossip. Paula did not seem bothered. Feeling relaxed, and a little guilty, Jane joined her brazen colleague in the hairdressing salon. They were the only patrons and were tended to by two loud and bubbly women; Kate and Bridget.

"So what's Dartcombe really like?" Paula loudly announced after sharing a few rude jokes with the over tanned Bridget. "Is it the quiet sleepy town it appears to be?"

Bridget flung back her mop of brown permed hair and laughed raucously, "don't be deceived my dear. One long orgy in Dartcombe, a bloody swinger's paradise. They're all at it"

"Really," Paula sounded really interested.

"Oh yes lots of landed gentry round here you see. All after a bit they are. I had this old boy in here once come in for a cut. He says can you give me a blowjob? And I says you what? He says sorry love I mean a blow dry. So I say you'd better make up your mind as I'll need to adjust the chair." Bridget exploded into a grating hyena-like laugh, with Kate joining her as a chorus.

"I think The Mole can sleep easy if that is our best news item," Jane whispered as an aside. "Let me have a go."

"Bad business with that young lad," Jane now spoke up, "the one who drowned the other day."

"Yes terrible," Bridget's mood changed dramatically. "A nice boy and his parents are lovely. None of us can believe it. My fella was drinking down the pub with him the night he died. Reckons he caught the eye of some sugar daddy who kept buying him drinks. Young Martin wasn't complaining and probably none the wiser. My mate Val reckons it was all sexual and that there's a cover-up now to protect the tourist business. Men like that should have them cut off. It's reckoned that they paid off the Gardners but I can't believe that."

"The young lad, Martin, was he gay?" Jane asked.

"Who knows love," Bridget shrugged her shoulders. "Never had a girlfriend on his arm but then he was always in love with that computer of his. Had a best mate, Stephen, who was just the same. Maybe he was his boyfriend all along. He's gone missing right enough, a broken heart probably."

"What his friend Stephen has gone missing? Jane looked over at Paula as if to say we might have something.

"Yes by all accounts his mum and dad are beside themselves," Bridget nonchalantly admired the hairstyle she had created for Paula.

"See," Paula smiled at Jane as they left the salon with perfectly groomed hairstyles, "there's a start for you and we haven't even left the hotel yet. Well probed by the way. A good juicy titbit that can be moulded nicely. Dartcombe the swinger's paradise whatever your sexual preference. Anything goes with the residents looking for the ultimate thrill. We'll mention no names to protect the innocent and the threat of legal action. They even ask for blowjobs at the local hairdressers." Paula winked.

"I can see I'm going to have to lose any scruples I may have to keep up with you," Jane said nervously.

"Don't go that far, don't ever become me. I am not your ideal role model," Paula seemed deadly serious before adding with a more jovial lilt "drink?" Jane nodded, she needed a glass of wine right now.

12

Alex Hart chaperoned the gangly Stephen Howard out of his apartment block as if he feared a sniper was trained to pick him off at any moment. Fortunately his coat had dried sufficiently for Stephen to wear to mask the tight, small and tatty clothes he had borrowed. The pair sighed in relief as they reached the relative safety of Alex's battered old Vauxhall. Almost on cue the rain began to pound the car's roof as the dark sky produced yet another shower.

Once Alex had realised that there was a good chance that he could get his hands on the files that could hold the key to the murder of Martin Gardner, he did not hesitate to act. Alex knew he was in danger whichever way he turned so it made no sense to do nothing, His mind was spinning and he needed to make sense of recent events. If he could find a solution it could mean glory and salvation. On the other hand he could end up dead. So Alex had called the Gardners yet again. The story this time was that he wanted to bring Stephen over to spend some time to reflect; a chance to be at one with Martin and say goodbye. The idea was that he could do this by spending some time alone in Martin's room. It was a request in haste but Mr Gardner thought it was a wonderful idea. And so Alex and Stephen were on their way to the Gardner's cottage with the perfect opportunity to retrieve Martin's hoarded and hidden files, carefully secreted in a box behind a piece of false skirting board.

Just as Alex was about to knock on the Gardener's door he received a call on his mobile from Richard Kay, wanting to know when he was going to get his sorry arse back to work. Alex almost felt like filling Richard in on the recent series of events but resisted. He curtly told him that he was working on a lead, which was no lie, before disconnecting and powering down. Mr Gardner once again welcomed Alex into his home and then hugged the bowed disconsolate figure of Stephen, who sobbed openly.

Stephen somehow managed to resist Mrs Gardner's attempts to relieve him of his coat, fearing that he might arouse some suspicion with his ridiculous attire and that he would lose the advantage of the large deep pockets in which to store Martin's collection of disks.

Mrs Gardener made Alex a very milky cup of coffee whilst Stephen went upstairs to find solace in Martin's bedroom.

"Why do you think the special police were so interested in Martin's computer?" Mr Gardener asked Alex.

Alex shrugged, "not sure on that one. Did the policeman not give you any indication why they were taking it away?"

"No they just said it was standard police procedure," Mr Gardner replied, "very odd though."

"Did he show you his badge? I just wondered which department he worked for." Alex tried to hide the cup of sickly coffee behind a strategic plant pot.

"No," Mr Gardner thought hard, "TA...sorry Sergeant Etheridge called me on the phone and said to expect his visit. Because he was part of a special force I was not to mention it to anyone. He said they just wanted to check his files to make sure it was not suicide or that Martin was in any trouble. The policeman specialised in computers. All routine and there was nothing to worry about. Not heard anything since."

Alex opened his mouth wide in shock, "what did the policeman look like?"

"He reminded me of that man who used to be on the telly in the chocolate adverts," Mrs Gardner jumped in. "You know, all in black clothing from head to toe. He was quite stocky though with a good old fashioned close crop haircut."

 It was at that moment that Stephen entered the room, "thank you very much Mr and Mrs Gardner. That has really helped me." Stephen slyly turned to Alex and tapped his bulging right coat pocket to show that he had the goods. Alex once again paid his condolences to the Gardners and swept Stephen back out into the rain and then hastily to the shelter of the car.

"Shit," Alex placed his head down hard on the steering wheel, "what the fuck is going on?"

"Hey chill mate, I've got the goods," Stephen once again tapped his pocket.

"No that's good but there's been a development," Alex looked sternly at Stephen. "How well do you know Sergeant Etheridge or to use his nickname, TA?"

"Oh very well, he's always been a policeman around here. He's a good laugh and well into the army stuff, hence his nickname." Stephen smiled with a genuine sincerity.

"Well it looks like our friendly local copper is connected to Martin's murderer. God knows how and what this all means but that voice on your phone that said they had the police in their pocket would not appear to be lying." Alex nervously looked out of the window at the pouring rain.

"Don't be crazy, how does that all work out?" Stephen laughed.

"We need to look at those files to hopefully find the answer, but the truth is that we now have a connection between TA and your man M. Further to that it was TA that pressed me into covering this. Why?" Alex started up the car, "the only explanation is that I could do the donkey work. Lead them to you and any other unturned stones. Well I'm here now and we need to find a safe haven and fucking fast."

Alex was shaking slightly as he drove his Vauxhall down the murky and bendy country road that linked Bagley and Dartcombe. His was the only vehicle on the road, which somehow made him feel even more vulnerable. Stephen in comparison now seemed the calmer of the two, reflecting the old adage of a problem shared.

Throughout the journey Alex was constantly checking his rear-view mirror. It could only have been a matter of seconds from one glance to the next when Alex's eye spotted something. Through the dirty back windscreen Alex could just make out a black car moving up to his tail. Just as he cursed the driver for not having his lights on in the gloom, the car's headlights flashed into full beam. Alex winced from the extra bright light that was maintained. He registered that the car was a sturdy black Mercedes just as it picked up speed, almost touching the Vauxhall's back bumper. Alex reacted by pressing harder on the accelerator.

"What's the matter?" Stephen sensed Alex's nervousness.

"I think we have company," Alex yelled, "we have been found."

Within seconds the Vauxhall jolted sharply as the Mercedes rammed it from the rear. Alex managed to recover the car's trajectory by steering hard. He pressed firmly on the accelerator but the Mercedes had too much power. After another attempt to ram Alex's car, the chasing driver swerved the car to the other side of the road, accelerating to come alongside its prey.

Alex glanced over but the windows of the Mercedes were completely blacked out. He knew what was coming and could not think how to avoid it. Confirmation came as the mystery driver slammed his tank of a car into the side of Alex's flimsy old banger. Despite Alex's best effort to steer back into his foe, the Vauxhall shunted and swerved to the side of the road, the passenger side wheels skidding on the muddy summit of the bank that ran parallel to the tarmac. The bank itself dropped some fifty feet to the small river below. The attacker's objective was plain to see.

Alex sighed with momentary relief as he managed to regain some meaningful tread on the road and steal a slight advantage on his foe. The Mercedes had skidded in the effort to skittle its prey and also needed to regain a degree of balance. However it did not take long for the sinister looking vehicle to make up ground and move alongside the recently dented Vauxhall. Alex braced himself for another hit but luck was on his side as a van headed towards them. Sharply the Mercedes driver applied his brakes and skidded into the slipstream of the Vauxhall. The van flashed its headlights and sounded its horn as it missed the oncoming Mercedes by a matter of inches.

"How the fuck do I get out of this?" Alex screamed.

Stephen was in a state of shock, pushing back hard into his seat as he braced in readiness for a crash. "I don't know," he said with a tremble, "think we're dead. I'm sorry, it's all my fault."

The Mercedes had once again pulled alongside Alex's car primed to attack. Alex pushed the Vauxhall's small engine to its capacity, focussing hard on the road ahead. He knew the route so well and it was that knowledge that was about to save his life. Just as the reinforced Mercedes swerved to knock him off the road, Alex slammed on the brakes. He timed it to perfection, thanking the heavens that he had recently had the car's brake pads replaced. The Mercedes spun at ninety degrees as its back wheels clamped on to the slippery and muddy bank on the road's edge. Alex shot the Vauxhall to the right across the road and up a partially concealed single track. As he did so the Mercedes went into a wheel spin, unable to move forward and continue its pursuit. Fortune was on Alex's side as he darted the car around several bends before taking another small track towards an old disused factory. The Mercedes was now back on the road and powering up the initial track to renew the chase.

Alex moved swiftly out of sight to the rear of the derelict building that had once proudly produced exquisite pottery. The cottage industry had long since died as production moved to China. Alex stopped the car and said a little prayer to himself, which was duly answered as the Mercedes glided past the factory turn off and on towards the coast.

Within minutes Alex manoeuvred the Vauxhall onto a second track that ran back towards Bagley. The uneven surface made for a bumpy ride as Alex moved with a speed that tested his car's suspension. The track led back down to the narrow single track road that had offered the initial escape route. With several checks in his rear-view mirror, Alex moved back down to the Dartcombe to Bagley road. The scene of the recent and very real stock car assault.

There was no sign of the Mercedes as Alex headed towards Dartcombe. With relief he reached the welcoming flickering lights of the town within minutes. Alex knew he had to dump the car as soon as possible and get to a place where they would be amongst crowds. He made a course for the local hypermarket.

As Alex parked the car in the crowded car park he felt a big sense of relief. There was something immensely comforting about the hustle and bustle of the shoppers going about their routine business. To Alex it was a jolt of much needed mundane reality in his now surreal world.

Alex and Stephen almost jumped out of the car and strode purposefully towards the bright light of the hypermarket. Alex looked back at his battered car, wondering if he would ever get to drive it again. Several hundred yards away the black Mercedes glided past the hypermarket entrance and on into Dartcombe.

Almost in a trance, Alex led Stephen to the café situated at the back of the shop floor. They found a table in the corner of the café by the window and purchased two cups of strong coffee.

"Fuck," was all that Alex could say. He thought hard about his next move.

"We could try and get abroad," was Stephen's suggestion.

"And be on the run forever, no thanks." Alex dismissed the idea, "I'm going to call work." Alex retrieved his mobile and powered it on. He had several voice-messages and texts but ignored them all. Instead he called Dan Goodman.

"Dan, it's Alex," Alex held the handset tight to his ear; "I think I'm in trouble. I also think I'm on the verge of uncovering something big."

Alex listened as his editor spoke and then his jaw dropped in shock. "Oh my god, that's just not true. Dan, I'm being framed; you've got to believe me. Wherever this story leads I think it's going to blow my portfolio apart. We could be talking Woodward and Bernstein here."

After another short interlude Alex just simply said "thanks" and clicked the phone off. "Well," Alex turned back to Stephen, "we're in it up to our necks mate and it's just getting worse. The police have a warrant for our arrest after good old Sergeant Etheridge unmasked us as burglars. Apparently we stole many items of substantial value from the Gardner's home. We have been painted as the lowest of the low."

"Fuck…oh fuck, we're doomed." Stephen buried his head in his hands, "they control everything."

"Luckily Dan is no fool. Richard would shop me straight away but Dan has been waiting all his life for a story like this. When I mentioned the Watergate journalists I'm pretty certain he got an erection on the spot. He told me just to keep him posted."

"Where do we go now?" Stephen looked around, "we can't stay here all night."

"I know, but we can't go back to mine and I don't fancy sleeping rough." Alex looked for inspiration, "OK I've got a really good mate who's Deputy Manager at The Combe, the big five star hotel on the other side of town. He's managed to pull strings before and get me a room when they are not fully booked. It could be our only hope, unless the police have got an APB out on us, which I think would be a bit extreme for a couple of chance burglars."

"Yeah OK, whatever," Stephen readily agreed.

Alex called his friend, Julian, and after a general chat easily persuaded him to get him a room. Julian would meet him by the delivery door at the back of the hotel in keeping with the routine when Alex had done this previously. On those occasions it had been for a romantic liaison when Alex had pulled and wanted to offer the lucky lady something more than his dingy flat. Explaining Stephen was not on the agenda. He would have to smuggle him in.

"Let's go," Alex stood up, "it's a bit of a walk but at least the rain has stopped. I dare not use the car. Let's go and get some rest and then decide what to do next, i.e. how we can get to view the late Martin Gardner's key to this bloody mess."

Stephen felt his pocket to ensure the disks were still there and then followed Alex out into the night.

13

Arturo Tabb sat alone behind a large oak desk in his office at The Globe HQ. The vast room was mainly in darkness save for the arc of light beaming from a desk lamp, which illuminated the desk top but barely stretched to the ornate oak panels on the office wall. The blinds were drawn to shut out the stormy London weather. Tabb felt at ease in darkness alone with his thoughts and plans. He picked up a file marked 'Jane Coker' and scanned it quickly with a frown. Tabb could not find what he was looking for, and he had already read the file several times. No skeletons in the closet. Not yet.

Tabb threw Jane's file across the desk and it landed on top of another file of the same colour. Almost simultaneously the old fashioned red phone by Tabb's right hand rang with loud clarity.

"Tell me," Tabb barked into the mouthpiece before listening with real intensity. After a couple of minutes his face turned even sterner and he thumped down hard on the desk in anger. "Eliminate the problem tonight. The list is nearly complete and we have no room for distraction. No mess, no loose ends. Do you follow?"

Tabb placed the phone down and reached out for Jane Coker's file. He placed it to one side and instead picked up the file beneath. It was labelled 'Alex Hart'.

14

Alex Hart had led Stephen Howard through the Dartcombe backstreets en-route to The Combe Hotel. Progress was slow but more importantly uneventful, apart from a very nervy moment when Stephen mistook a speeding boy racer for the returning sinister Mercedes. Eventually the very grand Combe Hotel came into view. Alex and Stephen casually made their way to the back of the hotel and waited in the deserted beer garden. In a few months the garden would be packed at the height of summer but tonight it was conveniently empty. Nearby a few members of the catering staff enjoyed a cigarette and a joke at the rear of the kitchen.

Alex called his mate Julian via the speed dial on his mobile. "Jules, hi mate I'm here. Listen the bird I'm with is really nervous. Can I come and grab the key and then sneak her in. She's taken a bit of persuading mate. Well shy but worth it if you know what I mean." Alex crossed his fingers as he listened, "cheers mate. Owe you again."

"Right wait here until I signal you," Alex turned to Stephen, "we've got to get this right or…god knows what."

Alex crept over to an almost concealed back door, obscured from the kitchen staff by a tall hedge. Stephen peered over a bush as the door creaked open. A very smartly dressed man slapped Alex on the back and handed something to him. He then disappeared as Alex took a few steps forward and beckoned Stephen over. Stephen stealthily made his way over and was ushered quickly into a small dark corridor.

"Quickly," Alex almost shouted, his heart pumping. He led Stephen to a service lift, where he entered a code on the side panel. Once inside the lift Alex selected the seventh floor whilst he nervously flicked an electronic room key around in his left hand. When the doors opened again, Alex pulled Stephen out on to a stairwell. After a quick glance through a fire door window he moved on into a lushly decorated landing. Alex quickened his pace even more until he found room 720, as dictated by Julian. Nobody had spotted them.

Relief then turned to frustration as Alex could not get the electronic key to register. "Jules, don't do this to me you twat," Alex fumbled the key and dropped it as his nerves took over. He then heard voices from around the corner.

Stephen calmly picked up the key and slotted it. After a couple of seconds the light on the lock turned from red to green. Stephen turned the handle and the door clicked open.

"You have to give these things time." Stephen smirked as they strode into the luxurious suite.

Alex went straight over to the mini bar. Julian had scavenged a few alcoholic miniatures for him as usual. He grabbed a small single malt whiskey and swigged straight from the bottle. "Mate, I was sure we would get sussed. Just wasn't sure how I was going to explain to Julian about my apparent change in sexual preference."

"Am I not good enough for you then," Stephen mocked as he selected a small bottle of vodka. "I guess you're a bit of a shagmeister then. More girls than you know what to do with. Jammy bastard."

"I do OK and nothing jammy about it," Alex started to calm down.

"Well, not that I like to admit it, but I have still to savour the delights of a woman. And maybe now I never will," Stephen bowed his head.

"Don't go all morbid on me. Losing your cherry is the least of your worries at this very moment." Alex walked over to the television and switched it on, "this room buys us a little time but we must be gone before breakfast or Julian will be in trouble."

"What can we do but rest," Stephen lay back on one of the two double beds.

"You rest; I'm going to see if I can get a laptop. The Herald's office is only a few streets away. Everyone would have gone home by now and I have a key," Alex held it up as if supplying proof. "The sooner we look at those files the better."

"Don't you think that's dangerous?" Stephen was nervous again, "what if you're spotted?"

"I best not be then," Alex walked over to the door, "don't let anyone in. I'll have the key so will not need to knock. Just chill, watch TV, have a drink. I'll nab some food on the way back."

Stephen just nodded as Alex swiftly disappeared from the room. He then settled back and turned up the volume on the television. Arturo Tabb was being interviewed on the news on the subject of press intrusion.

"Of course my newspaper, The Globe, adheres to strict moral standards and I will not tolerate this modern distasteful fascination for witch-hunt and constant scrutiny."

"But surely that is a double standard," the young naïve reporter interjected, "I mean The Globe does have a history of destroying people's careers."

Tabb visibly scowled, "people ruin their own careers by their own actions my boy. We simply report it."

Tabb left the deflated and belittled reporter standing in the rain as he made his way into a tall grey building.

Stephen Howard was asleep.

15

Jane Coker switched off the television with a small huff after viewing Tabb's little party piece. She decided to venture down to the hotel restaurant rather than eat alone in her room. Paula had taken up Darren the Concierge's kind offer to show her a good time amongst Dartcombe's swinging night life. So Jane had an evening to herself; the plan was a nice meal with a bottle of wine and then an early night. Jane had dutifully called home but her boyfriend was out. Probably still at the gym Jane thought as she closed the door behind her. It was then that she was nearly knocked off her feet by a rushing male guest.

"I'm sorry," the clumsy man said as Jane caught her breath.

"No problem," Jane beamed a false smile before staring hard at the man. "Oh my god…um, Alex."

"Jane…Jane Coker," Alex Hart stood still and slowly wagged his finger at Jane as she stood next to the door of room 725. "It must be three years at least, wow. What are you doing here?"

"Oh just having a pamper break with a friend," Jane blushed, "and yes it is three years. It was that writer's conference in Birmingham."

"How could I forget," Alex grinned cheekily, "I did try and contact you but to no avail."

"Well, we all move on," Jane blushed even more heavily as she remembered a very drunken one night stand. "So what are you doing here?"

"I live here," was Alex's simple reply, "and work here. On the Dartcombe Herald. Are you still writing?"

"I keep my hand in," Jane did not want to betray her undercover role. "But I've mainly been travelling for a couple of years."

"Look I've actually got to go. Very late for a meeting but we should try and catch up. Are you here for a while?" Alex turned to go, remembering what he was meant to be doing.

"Yes, just a couple of nights. Call me and we'll go for a drink. Room seven two five," Jane pointed to the number on the door.

"Will do," Alex turned on his heels as he held up a hand to say goodbye. He too visibly remembered the one night stand after a booze filled writer's conference. All he needed to do now was sort out the mess he had got himself into and he had the reward of a hot date. Simple.

16

Alex semi jogged around the Dartcombe backstreets clutching his invaluable key to the Herald's offices. He had moved swiftly through The Combe's reception area, thankfully avoiding any contact with Julian, the Deputy Manager. Any sort of questioning would be difficult to cover in that instance. Alex felt out of breath when he finally reached his destination, betraying the nervous energy and effort involved in getting from A to B. But now he was at the Herald's office and, after a few anxious glances over his shoulder, he went in and deactivated the alarm instantly by keying in the four digit code. 2211 for 22nd November, the day that England won the Rugby World Cup in 2003. Richard had come up with that one.

Alex crept past the empty Sales office and into the Editorial office. He chose not to switch on any lights just in case it was noticed outside. He quickly located his trusted laptop locked in Alex's own designated cupboard. Before leaving he decided to scribble Dan Goodman a quick note.

Dan – Thanks for your faith in me, I will not let you down. Should find out more tonight as to what this is all about. Will contact you soon if hopefully still alive. Alex H.

PS needed the laptop in case you wondered where it had gone.

Alex secreted the note inside the copy of Arturo Tabb's biography lying on Dan Goodman's desk, placing it within the pages that Dan had bookmarked. The smarmy face of Arturo Tabb looked up at him from the cover, with the words 'I Am The News' emblazoned beneath.

With the laptop safely in his possession, Alex reset the alarm and made his way back to the hotel. He felt more assured as he strode through The Combe's car park, determined to avoid Julian once more and get back to the safety of the room. It was as he strolled past a line of expensive looking cars that his confidence was dealt a shattering blow. Parked under the full beam of a lamppost was a dark black Mercedes. Alex stopped in his tracks. Although the windows were blacked out, he was sure there was nobody inside. Alex noticed a slight dent on the passenger side in the reinforced front door. There was no question in his mind that this was the car that had tried to run him off the road earlier. If the driver was not inside the car then he, or could it be she, had to be inside the hotel. They knew what Alex looked like but he had no idea who his foe was. Alex could avoid Julian but what if the driver was in reception.

Alex suddenly thought of Stephen. What if they had already got to him? Without a second thought he sprinted into reception and moved across to the lifts without looking up. He did not even notice Julian chatting to a porter. Julian however did see him.

Once again Alex could not operate the electronic door key to the room, adding to the tension. Abruptly the handle clicked down and the door opened.

"You really are shit with these things," a beaming Stephen announced.

"Thank god," Alex barged his way in and shut the door behind him. "Listen, I've just seen the Mercedes that attacked us earlier. It's in the car park which means they are ridiculously fucking close."

The colour drained from Stephen's face as he looked over at the door, half expecting it to be kicked in at any moment. "Do you think they followed you?"

"No," Alex said quickly, "I was really careful outside. Whether they spotted me in the hotel is another matter, although I got to the room without being followed. Only Julian knows where we are and he would not betray me."

There was a loud knock at the door. Alex and Stephen froze on the spot before Alex placed the laptop on the bed and crept over to the door. He looked through the peephole and with some relief saw an agitated looking Julian shuffling from foot to foot. Alex slowly opened the door and stepped out into the corridor, shutting it behind him.

"What the fuck are you doing Al?" Julian said angrily. "You're meant to keep a low profile. A room to shag in, that's all. So what's with the appearance in reception? You'll get me fucking sacked."

"Sorry Jules," Alex thought quickly, "the bird was feeling really hungry so I just popped to the local shop." Alex remembered that he was actually meant to pick up some food.

"And so why did you have a laptop?" Julian had spotted the distinctive blue case that Alex had been carrying.

"Um, got it from the car," Alex replied, "hid the food inside so as not to arouse suspicion.

"Fucking hell," Julian was still agitated, "look next time, if there is a next time, just call me on the mobile yeah. I will sort it. Never do that shit again." Julian started to walk away, "I hope she's fucking worth it."

Alex sighed with relief and knocked gently on the door. Stephen let him back into the room.

"I think it is way past time that we looked at those disks," Alex flung open the laptop case and pulled out a silver laptop. Stephen placed the disks down on the bed as Alex powered up the slick machine.

"Right which one do we go for?" Alex scattered the disks with his hand. Each had a different indelible pen marking.

"Let me see, they should all be labelled chronologically. He used to write the dates backwards like the Americans." Stephen picked up a CD to demonstrate, " see 1307, that is the 30th January this year."

"So what date are we looking for?" Alex browsed all the number in front of him.

"I'm just trying to think," Stephen thought back. "I met him in the Pullman on a Thursday. It was the 22nd of Feb and he downloaded the stuff on the Monday, the19th that was it. We need to find 2197."

"OK got it," Alex picked up a disk, "mind you it says 2197A."

"Ah I know what that is," Stephen rummaged through the remaining disks and pulled out another. "See 2197B. He must have done a lot of hacking that night."

"Well let's try both and see what we find," Alex took Stephen's disk and placed it in the CD-Rom tray.

Within a few seconds the words 'Password Required' flashed up on the screen.

"Please god tell me you know what it is?" Alex was flustered.

"Sort of," Stephen puckered his lips.

"Sort of?" Alex repeated in disbelief.

"Well Martin was a bit sad and obvious when it came to passwords," Stephen moved over to the keyboard. "Being a bit of a Trekkie he always chose a character name from Star Trek. Only trouble is we need to think about whether it was original series, Next Generation, Deep Space Nine, Voyager or Enterprise."

Alex fell back on the bed, resigned in defeat. "Well don't ask me unless it's Captain Kirk or Spock."

"Well luckily I'm a bit of a Star Trek fan myself," Stephen started to punch in some character names.

"And still a virgin. What are the chances eh?" Alex said sarcastically.

"I'll ignore that hurtful comment," Stephen carried on regardless.

After almost fifteen minutes of increasing levels of exasperated tutting and loud keyboard tapping, Stephen finally was victorious. "Got it. The little bugger, it was an obvious one in the end. Rand as in Janice Rand."

"Who's she?" Alex joined Stephen at the laptop looking bewildered.

"The blond bit of totty in the original series," Stephen smiled whilst almost licking his lips.

"What have we got?" Alex ignored the Start Trek quip.

"As expected, some files. Although not many; there must be a lot on 2197A to use up that disk."

"Fuck, do you think we chose the wrong one?" Alex could hardly stomach a repeat of the password game.

"Yes I'd say so. These just look like jpegs, videos and photos. Nothing incriminating on the surface. Aye aye," Stephen pointed at the screen where two very unattractive middle-aged women were dancing naked in a dingy lounge.

"Lovely," Alex said unimpressed, "Let's see if we can crack the other file. Hardly think that two old bags justify murder."

Stephen loaded disk 2197A and began the password elimination process again. After half an hour he was still trying, whilst Alex was almost asleep on the bed.

"Fucking fuck I just can't get this one," Stephen jumped up in annoyance.

"What…uh?" Alex snapped out of his semi slumber. "No joy eh. Have you tried Rand again? Maybe it's the same password for both."

"Duh, hadn't thought of that," Stephen stated sarcastically, "I just can't think of any more characters. Trust the git to get one over on me. He'd be pissing himself if he was still alive."

"Come on Stephen, don't give up. There must be a logical way to crack this," Alex slapped his companion on the back.

"My word that's worth a try," Stephen excitedly went back to the keyboard and punched in some letters. "Yes result, we're in."

"What was it?" Alex was both baffled and elated.

"When you said way…Captain Janeway from Star Trek Voyager. I hadn't tried her and lo and behold," Stephen smiled up at Alex. "You're a Trekkie and you did not know it."

"Whatever," Alex shrugged and stared at the small flat screen, "what have we got?"

"A lot of stuff basically," Stephen nodded as he manipulated the integrated mouse. "Seems to be a big bunch of master files. Let's try this one, Sport." Stephen selected the file on the screen and double clicked the mouse. Within the folder were around twenty sub-files. The majority simply had a surname as a title.

"Bloody hell, this is a real mixture. Football stars, Rugby stars, Athletes, Snooker players, the lot," Alex ran his eye down the list. "There are even football teams. Maybe they are an Agent's files?"

"Possibly," Stephen clicked back to another master file, titled Politics. "I suppose politicians have Agents too. Look there's MPs from all parties here."

"Yeah look, Harkness. That must be James Harkness the disgraced MP. The guy The Mole uncovered, have a look at his file." Alex moved forward for a closer look as Stephen double clicked on the file.

The file contained a large number of documents; letters, account statements and company records.

"This is heavy stuff," Alex pushed Stephen from the keyboard. "What I think we have here is the actual damning evidence against Harkness. This is what brought him down. Bloody hell it can't be," Alex clicked back to the Sports file and shook his head in disbelief.

"What is it?" Stephen was baffled.

"Look here we have former Heavyweight Boxing champion Luis Carter. He was a hero of mine until he found a hobby for beating up women out of the ring and then committing rape. His file here contains all of the records and details of those attacks. It was The Mole that exposed him as a drug crazed bully."

"Who is The Mole?" Stephen screwed up his face, "is he like Batman or something?"

Alex laughed, "in a way mate. He is portrayed as good fighting evil. He's a journalist who writes for The Globe and he basically goes around finding celebrities and such like who've done silly or corrupt things and then tells the world about it. Nobody knows what he looks like but I think that Martin has found his way into his research files."

"Maybe there's a picture of him somewhere and that's why he's trying to kill us," Stephen was serious.

"I don't think so, that would be a little far fetched," Alex scoffed as he selected a file titled Celebrity. "Look, Des Banner, the Comedian. He's only just topped himself."

"Oh yeah, I used to like him," there was now recognition from Stephen. "A bit racy," he quoted his often mimicked catchphrase, "although he turned out to be a right perv exposing himself on the Internet and all that."

"Yes and it was The Mole who exposed him for exposing himself, if you know what I mean." Alex clicked back to the master files again.

All the files followed a similar pattern in categorizing dossiers on public figures. However the last file on the disk stood out as different. It had a different coloured font label, red as opposed the deep blue general print. It also appeared to cover no specific group and was simply titled 'The List'.

"What's this one then?" Alex mumbled to himself as he clicked on the file. Within he once again found a large collection of documents, although this time they did not seem collated to target any individual. Instead they were historical in nature focusing on the genealogy of the Royal Family. Alex ran his eyes over numerous parish records and witness accounts dating back to the Sixteenth Century. There was particular focus on the life and times of Mary Queen of Scots, including a number of scanned letters that seemed foreign and illegible. Alex quickly became bored and exited the folder, "looks like a student's history project to me. I hated history at school. I reckon this file if from another source, unless our friend The Mole is studying English History in his spare time.

"So what do we have then?" Stephen sat back on the bed to ponder. "What is there here that really puts our lives in danger?"

"It's got to be the fact that we have The Mole's files," Alex stroked his chin, "his whole image and persona is huge in the world of journalism. He may just fear being unmasked and ruined. Maybe it's The Mole himself that's come after us."

"That's just nuts," Stephen stood up in annoyance, "my mate has been killed and now the murderer's after us because of a few newspaper stories. That's bollocks."

"People have been killed for less," was Alex's only defence before he was interrupted by his mobile phone ringing. "Shit I left it on. It's OK it's Julian," Alex saw Julian's name and number come up on the small display screen. "Jules what's up?" Alex stated confidently. "Well OK, I'll have to be quick though. See you in five, "Alex clicked off the phone and powered it down. "Jules has something for me, says it's really urgent. Don't like the sound of this."

"What will you do?" Stephen was pacing nervously.

"I have no choice but to go and meet him," Alex stood up, "if I don't I may arouse suspicion. I'll be really quick, just stay put. Lock yourself in the bathroom if you're really worried."

Stephen nodded and headed for the bathroom, "just hurry up," he locked the door behind him."

Instinctively Alex unloaded the disk and slipped it into his pocket before heading out of the room. Alex headed back to the service lift and then down to the hotel's rear staff entrance. Julian was waiting near the main door, impatiently tapping his foot and looking extremely agitated.

"What the fuck is going on you twat?" Julian snarled as he menacingly paced towards Alex.

"Uh you tell me," Alex shrugged.

"I mean how many people have you told about our arrangement? You know the score, stay discreet, shag all you like, tidy the room, leave."

"Exactly and that's the way it is," Alex said reassuringly, "I said I was sorry about the scavenging for food, but that was it. I was not going to leave the room again until morning."

"So what's this all about?" Julian shoved a small jiffy bag into Alex's hand as a couple of members of the kitchen staff passed by sharing a joke.

Alex looked down at the package. Written in thick black letters on the front was 'Attention Alex Hart, c/o Julian Hunter'. His baffled look was certainly not an act.

"This is bizarre mate," Alex ripped the envelope open, "do you think it's one of the lads having a laugh?"

Alex emptied the contents into his hand. A single wet shave razor fell out. "Eh?" Alex held the razor up to examine it. There was no blade. "Mate I have no idea what this is about but I'd better get back to the room. I will get to the bottom of this, I promise, and I'm sorry."

Alex charged back to the service lift, his heart pumping hard with fear of the unknown. He had no idea what the significance of the razor was but he sensed trouble. Alex's concern was heightened when he reached the room and found the door slightly ajar. He quickly glanced over his shoulder before barging into the room.

"Stephen are you OK?" Alex shouted as his eyes glanced around the room. He squinted and focussed on the laptop sitting on top of the bed. The bright light of the screen shone in the semi darkness. Alex cautiously moved towards it as he spotted some text. A message had been typed in relatively large font on a Word document. Alex speed read the narrative.

I can no longer take the pain. I have let everyone down and betrayed my best friend. I am now at peace. So sorry – Stephen Howard.

Alex felt an instant wave of nausea as he digested the apparent suicide note. He moved swiftly over to the bathroom. "Stephen are you in there?" he said in desperation before pushing the door. It swung open with ease.

Alex threw his hands up to his mouth with the fear of being sick. Before him was the naked body of Stephen lying prostrate in the bath. His right arm was hanging over the side of the bath above a pool of bright red blood, supplied by a badly gashed wrist. More blood was smeared over Stephen's lifeless pale limp body, drawn from another gash on the left wrist. A single razor blade sat glinting as it rested on Stephen's hairless chest.

Alex flung himself over to the small compact toilet and then threw up violently. His whole body was shaking and he felt on the verge of sobbing. Alex moved over to the sink and turned on the cold tap. He fervently splashed the water onto his face resisting the urge to look back over at Stephen's dead body through fear of fainting.

Alex stared hard into the mirror at his own pale reflection. He stood rigidly still as his ears picked up on faint voices. Hurriedly he moved from the bathroom and back into the bedroom and then crept towards the main door. The voices were now clearly audible through the gap in the partially open door. Two men were talking; Alex eavesdropped.

"Why have we got to wait for Tracy Fox then?" the first voice said, "I mean I'm sure we can handle this."

"That was what I was told," the second voice replied, "the call came into Fox herself. She called me and said we had to meet her here. She'd had a report of a serious incident."

"Strange," voice one chuckled, "I mean for a start this room is unoccupied. I reckon she just wants to prove her authority. It's about time Julian took over but you can tell she sees him as a threat."

"Right you're both here, good," a posh female voice interrupted. "Ah the door's open, well let's go and see what this is all about."

Instinctively Alex jumped into the spacious wardrobe next to the main door and slid the wardrobe door shut behind him. The Hotel Manager, Tracy Fox, led two junior managers into the room. As they walked past the wardrobe Alex swiftly and silently crept out from his hiding place and out into the corridor. He could hear the highly audible reaction of the hotel staff as they discovered Stephen's body. Alex walked at pace away from the room but was startled by the murmur of voices approaching. He stood still and pretended to make a call on his mobile whilst facing the wall. Two more members of staff hurried past him as a tearful and shaking Tracy Fox emerged from the room. Alex moved forwards again, feeling extremely vulnerable. He came alongside room 725, Jane Coker's room. Irrationally he knocked hard on the door and only had to wait a few seconds before a bewildered Jane was stood in front of him. She looked half asleep dressed in a dressing gown. Alex almost barged his way through without explanation. "Hang on," Jane reacted angrily, "what are you doing?" She left the door open in preparation to evict the unwanted guest.

"Jane I need your help," Alex turned towards his old flame as he began to shake and visibly sob.

Jane was stunned at Alex's apparent distressed state. She finally closed the door as more people gathered in the corridor and the commotion grew.

"Sit down," Jane said gently as she beckoned towards an armchair. She then collected a whiskey from the mini-bar and poured it into a glass. "Have this," she handed the single malt to Alex, "and let's hear what this is all about."

After a few sips, Alex began to recount the events of the last two days. Jane listened intently, finding the bulk of the tale highly intriguing whilst baulking at the sinister overtone. It was as Alex explained his theory about The Globe and The Mole from the files on Martin's disk that she became really unnerved and found empathy. This was followed by sickening revulsion at the description of Stephen's supposed suicide. The same Stephen that Bridget the hairdresser had spoken of earlier.

"This is horrible," Jane was now slightly trembling as she went to pour herself a drink. There was a loud knock at the door. Both Alex and Jane froze.

Jane moved over to the door and looked through the peephole. "It's OK, I think; it's just the porter or something." She slowly opened the door, but only slightly to obscure Alex's presence in the room.

"Hello Miss Coker," a cheery voice announced, "I just wanted to apologise for any noise you might hear and hope it does not disturb you. We've had a bit of an incident with a guest in a room down the corridor. Please do not be alarmed as it is all now under control."

Jane curiously peered around the door and down the corridor. She could see a couple of policemen. One of them was chatting to Deputy Manager Julian Hunter. Julian was extremely pale and in shock as the policeman jotted in his notebook.

"No problem, I'm a deep sleeper" Jane smiled and bade the porter "good night."

"Oh my god this is really heavy," Jane marched back into the bedroom, "what are you going to do?"

"I just don't know," Alex replied honestly, "I am going to need to get away from here at some point but not yet."

"Listen Alex I shouldn't tell you this but I work for The Globe," Jane confessed. "I'm here with a colleague, Paula Davenport. We're here to do an undercover warts and all feature on Dartcombe. It's the start of a new editorial series."

"Why Dartcombe?" Alex could think of more glamorous settings for an expose.

"Why not?" Jane shrugged.

"So you know about The Mole. You know how big this could be," Alex felt relieved although slightly suspicious of the coincidence.

"Yes I've started to get really worried about who or what I am working for," Jane admitted, "in fact it's only because you told me about The Mole connection that you're still here. It made it real."

"Otherwise?" Alex enquired.

"Otherwise I would have shopped you to the jolly porter," Jane was serious.

"And I wouldn't blame you. To be honest I do not know who to trust anymore, even you if I'm truthful with your links to The Globe." Alex raised his niggling concern.

"If it helps I only started on Monday and would never hurt a fly," Jane smiled sweetly.

Alex reciprocated the smile and then glanced over at Jane's laptop, "do you want to see the files for yourself?"

"In a word yes," Jane shadowed Alex over to the desk where the laptop was situated. Jane had been surfing the net prior to taking a nap before being interrupted by Alex knocking on the door.

Alex loaded the disk and carefully tapped in the memorized password. He darted amongst the master files and presented all the previously discovered evidence.

"Well there's no denying it," Jane exhaled loudly, "but murder? Just to protect a story. I know journalists can be bastards but…well it's crazy."

"I know, there just has to be more to this. And the facts are that our murderer wants to get his hands on this disk. We know he will not stop at anything and basically kill anyone who gets in his way. It's like holding this disk is a death sentence." Alex stopped talking and looked worryingly at Jane, "I'm sorry; by association I'm now putting you in danger. I will get out of your way as soon as I can and make sure nobody sees me. You can stay clear of this and stay alive."

Jane shivered slightly, "Alex I'm a journalist too. Despite the danger do you think my mind could ever rest without knowing the solution?"

"Thanks I could do with an ally," Alex placed a reassuring hand on Jane's shoulder, "We've just got to make sure we do this right."

"Yep, let's have another look at those files and see if we can crack it from here. Ultimately we hold the trump card right here, we just need to find it." Jane sat down at the desk in a business like fashion and scanned the files. "What's this file? The List?"

"Oh don't worry about that," Alex almost laughed, "our deceased hacker used to download anything he could get his hands on. It looks like he's bunched in some A-Level project with the Mole's files."

Jane ignored the file and instead selected another titled 'Staff'. Within the folder was a consistent list of individual sub files. "Oh my god," Jane exclaimed, "I recognise some of these names. They're members of staff at The Globe. Paul Langmead is the Chief Editor, who according to this likes a bit of S&M on the quiet. Here's another, Iain Baxter, a slimy git. Not a lot on him though apart from the fact that he's a loner with a drink problem."

"Why would The Mole maintain files on his own colleagues?" Alex could not make sense of it.

"My colleague Paula reckons that Arturo Tabb, The Globe's owner, keeps dossiers on all his staff. He likes to be in command of everything, a total control freak. If you have any skeletons in your closet, any sign of weakness, he will hold it over you." Jane continued to peruse the files. "Shit I'd never have thought that after meeting him yesterday. George Snow the macho sport's writer is bi-sexual. Now this one I am really curious about. Jane selected a file titled 'Paula Davenport' as Alex peered over her shoulder.

"I know for a fact that Tabb has some really big hold over Paula," Jane perused the information on her colleague.

"So what we are saying is that Tabb is in on this. He's driving it," Alex could hardly believe his own suggestion. "But why? What does he have to gain? He's rich and famous enough as it is."

"People like Tabb thrive on power. It becomes a drug and they want more and more. They lose sense of reality and just make their own rules." Jane stopped reading and took a deep breath as she looked up at the ceiling, "well it looks like Paula really did get herself in the shit. Look at this," Jane directed Alex back to the screen, "if I'm reading this correctly my learned colleague has something of a criminal past. It appears that she got involved in some sort of drug smuggling exercise in Thailand when she was a teenager. According to this she has two friends still serving time in a Bangkok jail. Paula somehow got away but they must have shopped her as there is still a warrant out for her arrest. The twist is that Paula Davenport is not her real name, it's Tanya Davis. There's even a mug shot and that is definitely Paula."

"Does nobody lead a boring simple life at The Globe?" Alex sniggered.

"Well I do, or did, apart from the odd one night stand, "Jane smiled up at her former sexual partner. "I guess that Tabb, or The Mole, already has a file on me. Just hope you are not in it."

"Are you connected to the Internet?" Alex ignored Jane's remark.

"Yes," Jane clicked over the Internet page.

"I just want to check my hotmail. My editor may try to contact me. For now he's backing me," Alex logged on to a hotmail webpage and signed in to his personal email list. There was a mail from Dan Goodman but it was just a plea for Alex to get to a police station and turn over any evidence. "It's far too late for that," Alex mumbled as he noticed an email from his cousin. It was just a general 'how's it going' note with a couple of jpeg attachments of his cousin's young sons. It made him long for the mundane reality the mail represented.

"Thanks," Alex moved away from his desk.

"What's this?" Jane shouted.

An incoming email popped up on the screen. It simply said 'nowhere to run' before deleting itself.

"Here we go," Alex commented calmly, "this is the scary email bit that Stephen described. About to warn of my impending death no doubt.

A second email appeared; 'you will be found soon'. It quickly deleted itself before a third appeared in quick succession; 'time to die Alex'.

17

DI Jack Parker loved being a detective. It was all he ever wanted to be, a love drawn straight from his childhood and watching old black and white Sherlock Holmes movies in the school holidays. With Basil Rathbone as a role model it was always going to be difficult to find total satisfaction in the modern police force. Working his way up through the ranks, DI Parker had spent most of the time protecting the peace at football matches, breaking up domestic disputes and dealing with drunken youths fighting on a Friday night. No great detective work required there.

Jack Parker had risen to the rank of Detective Inspector through his above and beyond attitude. He did not just look at any given case from one angle but to the full 360 degree approach. DI Parker's attention to detail and the way he left no stone unturned had led his colleagues to nickname him Columbo, after the infamous scruffy TV detective from the Seventies. Parker loved all that and played on his nickname for all it was worth. Some wondered if he was taking it a bit too far, although force dress code had so far ruled out a scruffy raincoat.

Parker had been sent to The Combe Hotel in Dartcombe. A nice drive into the countryside and a chance to get out of the city for once. It was a routine situation he had been told. A gruesome suicide but the local plod would need a hand to tie up a few loose ends. "Just get in and close it out quickly," the DCI had ordered, "the local community will not want any mess or bang goes the summer tourist trade."

The word gruesome certainly summed up the scene. Parker had witnessed a number of corpses over the years, including murder victims, but this had more the look of something out of a horror movie.

"So as you can see just a very sad suicide," local policeman Sergeant Etheridge shrugged. "The lad was really unstable and the death of his best mate obviously sent him over the edge."

"And where does this local journalist fit into all this?" Parker enquired.

"Just a bloody chancer, you know how these journalists can be." The Sergeant dismissed the question.

"Well he was only a local hack wasn't he?" Parker stared curiously at the Sergeant.

"True," the Sergeant thought for a moment, "although apparently he was more than eager to pursue a career with one of the big nationals. Looks like he was trying to create his own story. He led young Stephen on, even got him to steal."

"See that's odd as well," Parker was really puzzled, "you say he nicked a load of computer stuff from the house of his mate, who is also dead. Why would the journalist encourage him to do that?"

"Because he's devious," was the instant answer, "he wanted to make a story out of Martin Gardner's death so he got his best mate to pilfer all his personal computer files. I reckon the lad Stephen realised he'd been conned and then ended it all. Simple as that."

"Mmm," Parker pondered, "but I don't like the fact that he left a suicide note on a computer screen. It means we can't verify if it was him who really left it."

The Sergeant laughed, "there was simply no paper or pens in the room. Just the laptop."

"And you say that the room was set-up by the journalist through a special arrangement?" Parker walked back through to the bedroom as a pathologist completed his work.

"Yes the journalist, Alex Hart, is best mates with the Deputy Manager here, a Julian Hunter. Looks like he did it to try and finish the story. Hunter reckons he thought that Hart had a woman in the room. We're still questioning Hunter down at the station. His career's over."

"And the journalist, Hart?" Parker looked around the room.

"Not located yet but he can't get far. We've already found his car abandoned at the local hypermarket," the Sergeant turned to go.

DI Parker stopped by the door and tried to make sense of it all. The pieces just did not fit. If they did then the journalist was one sick guy. Parker was suspicious. The answer had to be found in the death of Martin Gardner. He would start by interviewing Julian Hunter himself and then take a look at the circumstances around Martin's death.

Jane Coker and Alex Hart continued to trawl through Martin Gardner's pilfered files. They intricately analyzed every bit of information shown but apart from reconfirming the already reported celebrity scandals, there seemed to be nothing of substance.

"All this really proves is how thorough The Mole is," Jane observed. "I mean how does he get all this information? There's company records, police statements, banks statements, psychiatric reports and it goes on and on."

"Extensive network I guess," Alex suggested whilst leaning back to rub his eyes. "I would imagine that he does not acquire all this legally. Maybe that's all this is about. If we turned this disk in would there be enough evidence to bring the mystery reporter out into the open to face trial?"

"No," Jane said instantly, "in a word. There is no proof that these files belong to The Mole. They would need to find this on his hard drive and I'm sure that's been covered. Paula said that Tabb and The Mole were working on something really big. If we have the details here then that is why you are in danger. That is why two people are already dead."

"We need the key," Alex stood up frustrated, "something or somebody to point us in the right direction. What about Paula?"

"Paula," Jane winced, "she confided in me but she's too embroiled with Tabb. I would not feel comfortable trusting her. Not with lives at stake."

"Fair enough, then we have to start somewhere else," Alex closed his eyes as he became overwhelmed by tiredness.

"You forget that there are a lot of people out there looking for you." Jane lay down on the bed, "and I can't really bring people back to the room for interrogation."

"I need sleep," Alex looked down at Jane lying on the bed, "and in the morning we'll work out how to get me out of here. I think we then need to get across to IBEX. This all kicked off there and maybe that's where our key lies."

"Right IBEX it is. I'll think of something to dump Paula for the day and we'll go from there. The hard bit is going to be smuggling you out of here. The police are in residence and you'll be their number one catch." Jane moved over to a cupboard and collected a thick blanket.

"The beauty is that they will assume that I'm long gone. Holing up a few rooms down the corridor is the last thing they will suspect," Alex moved over to help Jane spread the blanket on the floor. "No space in the bed for me then? Top and tail?"

"Nope," Jane threw Alex a pillow and climbed into bed, promptly switching out the lights.

19

"OK Mister Hunter, let's see if we can make some sense of this," DI Parker looked up from some written notes and smiled at Julian Hunter. "I know that you are in a state of shock and I thank you for volunteering to assist in the enquiry."

"Yeah, no problem," Julian was still shaking as he held on to a paper cup of strong coffee with two hands.

"So from reading this statement," Parker held up a single sheet of A4 paper, "we can establish that you are a generous guy. You like to help your mates out now and again by giving them a bit of luxury in a five star hotel. You pull a few strings in your position of responsibility and voila they have an exclusive and expensive shagging den."

Julian nodded in agreement.

"And so one of your best mates is Alex Hart. A local journalist who by all accounts is a good bloke with a keen eye for the ladies."

"Yes that's Alex," Julian confirmed.

"So good guy Alex finds himself in a bit of a hole. He turns to you for help but does not tell you the full story or reason why he needed a room"

"That's correct, he is normally very discreet but this was a disaster from the start," Julian opened up a little more.

"Really," Parker checked the statement, "it looks pretty straightforward here. You get a room for Alex and a young guy ends up dead in it. Is there more to say?"

"Well first of all there was the fact that Alex went out for food, although it was weird that he appeared to smuggle it inside a laptop case. That was obviously a ruse to actually get the laptop in," Julian concluded.

"Nice detective work and spot on," Parker noted the inclusion of the incident in the write-up. "Was there anything else?"

"The package," Julian offered.

"The package" Parker repeated, "What Package?"

"This package arrived at the hotel for Alex care of myself. I was furious and called Alex down to confront him. He looked genuinely baffled and then when he opened it there was a shaving razor inside," Julian lent forward.

"Just a shaving razor?" Parker enquired.

"Yes but the even odder thing was that there was no blade in it. Alex freaked and ran back to the room. The next thing I know is that a guy has been found dead with his wrists slit. Weird, what can it mean?" Julian was hoping to make sense of the recent events for his own sanity.

"Well this certainly puts a new dimension on things, although at the moment I have no answers." Parker held up the statement once again, "why did you not mention this before?"

"I did," Julian instantly replied, "TA, I mean Sergeant Etheridge dismissed it as a sick prank on Alex's part and of no relevance."

Parker could not understand why the local plod would dismiss such a crucial piece of evidence. He thought back to thirty minutes earlier when he advised the Sergeant that he would like to talk to Julian. The Sergeant had suggested quite strongly that he did not need to and acted with real affront as if the ability of the local police force was being questioned. An assurance was given that everything was in the report. The question in Parker's mind was whether Sergeant Etheridge was just stupid and incompetetent or was he deliberately trying to cover something up.

20

Another Bar, Another Brawl – Former World Boxing Champion Luis Carter was involved in a fracas at the trendy Dreams bar in London last night. The police were called after Carter became involved in an altercation with two men who were reportedly goading him in respect of his high profile fall from grace. Luis Carter was exposed by The Mole as a woman beater and a rapist. After spending time in jail he was subsequently spurned by the celebrity circuit that once proudly supported him and he was never to fight professionally again (Full Story Inside)

Jane Coker threw down the day's copy of The Globe on to the bed, still nestled inside the plastic bag in which it had been left hanging on the hotel room door.

"That Boxer has made the front page today," Jane smiled down at Alex still lying on the floor. "They seem to be just hitting old targets when they are already down. I wonder who they are building up to hit next."

"Could be anyone," Alex rose up gingerly from his makeshift bed, "damn I was hoping yesterday was all a bad dream."

"No such luck for either of us," Jane grabbed the blanket and pillow from the floor. "I ordered breakfast in my room before you showed up last night, so you'll have to hide in the bathroom as soon as the knock comes."

"Fine, I'll do some research by reading your newspaper," Alex picked up The Globe. "The thing is that The Globe does do a service by exposing scum like Luis Carter. I don't really care how The Mole gets his information; it's the fact that he wants me dead that pisses me off."

"Just because it says it does not mean it's true. That's all I keep hearing from Paula and I think she's right. Maybe that's what this is all about. It could be that those files provide proof of fabrication."

Before Alex could answer there was a firm knock at the door prompting Jane to point vigorously at the bathroom.

"Morning Miss Coker," a very jolly waiter almost sang as he pushed a small breakfast trolley into the room, "beautiful day today. About time with all this rain we've been having."

"Great I look forward to taking in some nice country air later," Jane waited patiently and calmly as the waiter removed various silver lids to expose a very appetizing cooked breakfast and plentiful rounds of toast. "So all OK with the drama down the corridor last night?"

The cheerful waiter frowned, "horrible business. A lover's tiff from what I can make out. Two guys but the older father figure one has done a runner. All very sad really but don't let it spoil your day."

"I won't," Jane smiled back as she handed over a tip and showed the waiter out.

"A lover's tiff," Alex emerged from the bathroom, "how'd they work that one out?"

"Convenience," Jane offered, "and don't forget just as you should never believe all you read, it can be the same in what you hear."

Jane rationed but ultimately shared her breakfast with Alex after hanging the 'Do Not Disturb' sign on the door. She then phoned Paula who she eventually awoke from a very deep slumber. The suggestion to split up for the day and then reconvene in the evening to compare notes was readily accepted by a badly hungover Paula. The bonus came with Paula's offer to Jane of the use of her car for the day.

"She's one hell of a tart," Jane sniggered as she came off the phone, "although we should be thankful as it works in our favour. Just need to get you out of here now and get over to IBEX."

"More good news on that front," Alex looked up from the laptop he had been studying. "IBEX conduct visitor tours around their site. The main premise is obviously sales."

"Excellent, well I suggest I go on that tour and see what I can find out." Jane had a real enthusiasm for the task, "it will be too risky for you to join me."

"Yeah," Alex reluctantly conceded, "but I think you need to take a look at this."

Jane came over to look at the IBEX webpage.

"Firstly IBEX customers range from Government offices to hospitals to public record offices to the police force. Even the bloody Royal Family relies on them for software advice." Alex gritted his teeth, "a nice hunting ground for The Mole methinks. A whole world of records and information at his fingertips once access had been established."

"But how does The Mole get in?" Does he work at IBEX do you think?" Jane was not convinced.

"Well here's the connection," Alex proudly sat back to allow Jane to see what he had found. On the screen it broke down the principal owners of IBEX, of which the majority share at seventy-four percent was Tabb Enterprises.

21

"So Mr Goodman, from the picture you're giving me, Alex Hart is just a nice bloke and a journalist of great potential." DI Parker looked up at Dan Goodman, Editor of the Dartcombe Herald, as they sat in his office.

"Absolutely," Dan answered without hesitation, "I just know that he would never intentionally use anyone or harm them."

"Surely that goes against what makes a successful journalist? No scruples and all that," Parker challenged.

"Successful maybe, with a price to pay in selling your soul, but not necessarily good," Dan countered. "Alex is a good journalist with a moral code."

"Ha," Richard Kay snarled from his slouched position in the corner of the room.

"You disagree Mr Kay?" Parker raised his eyebrows and smiled at the senior journalist.

"Here's my take on it," Richard was quite animated. "He's basically a good lad but unfortunately he's had his head turned. He wants to join the big boys and be a writer on that rag he reads, The Globe. TA gave him an opportunity to write a human interest story when Martin Gardner died but instead he twisted it and now he's paid a shocking price."

"Who's TA?" Parker asked.

"Sergeant Etheridge, one of your lot," Richard replied.

"How did Sergeant Etheridge give Alex the chance to write a story?" Parker was now highly curious.

"He introduced Alex to Martin's parents. They wanted a fitting tribute written for their son," Dan jumped in. "That's how this all kicked off; that's what led Alex to Stephen. He was Martin's best friend.

"Very odd wanting a tribute written so soon after the death. You would have thought that grief would mask any rational thinking." Parker screwed up his face.

"The Gardners are no ordinary couple," Dan smiled.

"Thank you for your time," Parker shook Dan Goodman's hand as Richard skulked off in the background. "This has been very helpful."

"I'm glad," Dan looked mournful, "listen I know Richard has a bit of a downer on Alex but he is a good lad. Just to let you know, he did tell me he was on to something big. I just have no idea what."

"Yes well I just hope we find Alex soon to find out more," Parker turned to go whilst mumbling under his breath, "before it's too late."

22

It was whilst Jane Coker was on a reconnaissance walk around the hotel that she was presented with an unexpected opportunity. The dual purpose of Jane venturing from the room was to both collect the car key from Paula and to check the situation in terms of the police and staff presence. Room 720 had official crime tape across the doorway and there was a single police officer standing guard. There was no other visible police presence that Jane could spot in the reception area but the unnerving fact was that she had no idea who might be watching. Could The Mole himself be present or the hired assassin looking for Alex? Were they one and the same?

Paula looked as bad as she sounded on the phone and happily handed over the car keys before returning to bed. Jane wondered if she would venture from the room at all and was probably just happy for the rookie to cover.

It was on the way back to the room that Jane instinctively became a thief. She had decided to take the stairs rather than the lift to check out its potential as an escape route. As she passed a row of ground floor rooms, Jane happened to stop by a cleaning trolley. The room door was wide open and a maid was cheerily singing inside as she made the beds. Hanging off the handle of the wardrobe door was a big black overcoat. Without thinking of the consequences Jane simply grabbed the coat and hurried on her way. After climbing the stairs she was able to avoid the guarding policeman by walking anti clockwise around the long square maze corridor.

"See it swamps you. Even I would not recognize you in that if you walked past." Jane had got Alex to put the coat on whilst explaining her thinking.

"It's bloody massive don't you think. I might look even more conspicuous and what if the real owner spots me in it?" Alex was not convinced.

"A chance we have to take, better the owner rather than The Mole. Unless of course they are one and the same. That would be unlucky," Jane smiled. "I suggest we just go as the longer we leave it the more chance there is of the coat owner spotting you."

"I think you're bloody enjoying this," Alex grumbled as he took a deep breath and headed for the door.

Jane led Alex down the stairwell she had just used, avoiding the guarding policeman once more. The maid was just finishing cleaning the room on the ground floor from which Jane had pilfered the coat. Jane ensured that Alex moved past quickly in case the guest had returned. She then beckoned for Alex to cross arms as if they were a loving couple before they headed across the crowded reception area. Alex kept the large lapel collar upright to mask his face and buried his chin deep onto his chest. They finally made it to the main door, although Alex nearly blindly walked into the Bellboy as he courteously opened the door. The couple continued to huddle together as they made their way outside. Relief finally came as Jane clicked the key fob to open the doors of Paula's Mazda. As Alex sat down in the passenger seat he was on the verge of hyperventilating.

Sergeant Etheridge strolled into the Red Rose café with a carefree air about him. He exchanged pleasantries with some of the regular and aged clientele, who always felt more secure in the presence of the long serving community officer in full uniform. Old Joe, the owner, was already handing over an extremely strong cup of tea by the time the Sergeant had reached the serving bar.

The Sergeant made his way over to the corner of the café and sat down on a cheap foam-filled and plastic covered bench. He took a sip of the dark brown tea and sat back.

"No luck I take it," the Sergeant seemed to be talking aloud to himself.

"He's just vanished," a reply came from a stocky man sat at the next table. He was positioned directly behind the Sergeant with his back to him. "For now anyway, he'll turn up."

"And then what? Another bloody mess for me to sort out?" the Sergeant muttered with an angry tone.

"You know the score Etheridge," the mystery man snarled back, "you signed up for this and you've reaped the rewards. The Assignment will soon be on the move and our job is to protect her by keeping The List confidential."

"When I signed up as you so eloquently put it, I was supposed to be assisting in the uncovering of stories in the public interest. Just keep a watchful eye on IBEX and help out a couple of contacts there, and nothing else. I don't know why The Assignment is so special or what this List shows but I do know that two local lads are dead and you're looking to make it three. I now have a bloody suspicious DI on my back to boot."

"You have been well rewarded over the years and well protected. There was always a chance that this day would come and that is why you were recruited. We have strong contacts everywhere and will get the DI off your back," the man said calmly.

"Did Stephen divulge if they had found anything on the disk?" The Sergeant asked, "before you so gracefully killed him."

"I had little time but my guess is that he knew nothing. The journalist has the disk now and he has had time to review it, although he would have to be extremely smart to have worked out why it is significant," the man semi turned to talk to the Sergeant. "However by the weekend it could become absolutely clear. I simply need to get the disk and eliminate the risk. Keep in touch."

The man instantly got up and walked out of the café without any acknowledgment for the Sergeant.

After the grim wet weather of the previous few days there was now a Spring like feel in the air, which coincided nicely with the freedom felt by Alex Hart as Jane Coker drove him away from Dartcombe and into beautiful English countryside. The temptation to put the convertible's roof down was resisted so as not to invite undue attention.

The national headquarters of IBEX communications was a large but aesthetic building, standing alone amongst rolling hills. Constructed from eighty percent glass, the impressive building had the appearance of a colossal greenhouse. The glass reflected the surrounding countryside helping the very modern building to blend in.

"Very nice, I'm quite looking forward to having a look round," Jane parked the Mazda in a small layby on top of the hill that looked down on the IBEX site.

"What are you going to look for?" Alex suddenly felt nervous again.

"Whatever this journalist nose can find," Jane replied with confidence. "Somehow need to cement the link between IBEX and Tabb."

"Good luck and just make sure you call me at the slightest hint of any trouble," Alex held up his mobile before swapping seats with Jane.

Alex drove down to the main entrance, joining a queue of traffic tailing from the main security gate. Getting past the guard posed no problems as Alex calmly explained that he was dropping his girlfriend off for the tour. He was directed towards a dropping-off point near the main entrance.

"I'll be in the area," a worried looking Alex shouted as Jane jumped out and joined the mixed crowd of workers and visitors heading into the building. Jane simply smiled back.

The main IBEX reception area was as plush as Jane had expected. It had more the feel of a lavish hotel than a place of work and the staff seemed very jolly as they scanned their electronic passes in turn. Once the pass had registered, each person would individually walk into a transparent tube that ran from the floor to the ceiling. Two curved doors opened to allow access before closing the worker inside. For a few seconds they were trapped inside before two doors on the other side of the tube opened and they entered the offices. Five identical access tubes lined the main wall to the left of the reception desk. To Jane it was like something out of a science fiction film but to the IBEX staff it had become a commonplace routine.

Jane made her way over to the main desk and spoke to a very glamorous female receptionist. In fact all the receptionists were women and all were equally as glamorous, contrasting with the smart but thuggish looking security guards stood nearby.

"Hi, I called earlier to book on the tour. The name is Ali Rose," Jane provided a false name.

The receptionist checked her computer screen and smiled an acknowledgement as she found Jane's alias name on the list. She got Jane to fill out a simple form before asking her to stand on a big red dot in front of the desk. A digital camera embedded in the back of the woman's PC screen than took Jane's photograph. And within a few minutes she was presented with an electronic security pass. Jane's picture was implanted on the front. "Please display your ID at all times," the receptionist finally spoke as she tugged at the blue ribbon to which the pass was attached, indicating that Jane should wear it around her neck. "If you can take a seat in the waiting area your guide will be along shortly."

Jane moved over to a small seating area, furnished with extremely expensive black sofas, which emitted a strong fresh leather smell. The others in the small touring party ranged from young students looking for a potential employer to old aged pensioners simply on a day out. Jane stood out like a sore thumb.

The sixty something male guide soon arrived and gleefully handed out some information packs on IBEX to the tour party.

"My name is Jason and I will be showing you around our wonderful complex today," the dapper silver haired guide stated almost robotically as he recited his well rehearsed script. "The IBEX customer base is growing extensively everyday and the reason we offer these tours is to show off."

There was a murmured chortle from the group before Jason continued, "sorry just my little joke. I'm afraid there will be plenty more of those. Seriously, we offer these tours to demonstrate how useful and effective our organization can be for you as individuals or for corporations and businesses on a wider and grander scale. You will get a good overview of IBEX hardware and software packages, and we have a fantastic shop here should you wish to buy anything from a personalized mouse pad to a complete computer package. You will also see how we offer invaluable twenty-four hour support to all our customers. If you're interested in a career at IBEX, we will be hearing from our Chief Personnel Officer on what we look for during recruitment. Fancy being a Programmer sir?" Jason picked out a very elderly man in the tour party bringing another polite group chuckle.

"Right let's get underway. A few house rules; you must display your security passes at all times, you must not wander off from the group and please keep any questions for when we are off the shop floor. Follow me and I'll first of all guide you through our rather space age entrance."

Jason led the party over to the tall tubes and explained the simple concept of passing through them. The experience scared two older women witless and it took them a while to recover their composure. After swiftly walking past the company restaurant and leisure facilities, that included a gym and squash courts, Jason began referring to the offices as a campus to further instill the feeling of a happy-go-lucky working environment.

Outside in the main visitor car park, DI Parker had just arrived in his Blue Mondeo. It was his first visit to IBEX and like Jane and Alex before him

Parker was slightly staggered at the sight of the unique complex. He too had to undergo security processing and be presented with a photo ID. Parker was then shown up to the office of Bob Eubank, CEO of IBEX.

Bob Eubank's office incorporated its own small boardroom as well as an adjoining executive bathroom. Parker considered his own cramped and shared office space back at HQ, silently sneering at the huge disparity. Eubank was joined by the Chief Personnel Officer, Julie Ingram, and the main Support Desk Manager, Peter Ashton. The latter was the boss of the late Martin Gardner and Stephen Howard.

"I'm not sure that there is much we can give you," a very posh Eubank spoke for the welcoming committee. "Both lads were good at their jobs and valued team members. From all accounts there was no sign of any external issues and problems with their character, which of course makes all of this even more of a shock."

"And also unusual, which is why I need to investigate further," Parker coolly supped some coffee from a delicate china cup. "Did either Martin or Stephen have any disciplinary issues? I mean you have access to a wealth of information at IBEX. Did they ever exploit that?"

An awkward silence followed before Peter Ashton spoke after getting a nod of approval from Eubank. "We were suspicious of some of Martin's activities. A lot of our Call Centre staff tend to be gap year techies. Very bright but also full of brash mischievousness. We have had a couple of serious fraudulent hackers over the years and Martin did not come into that bracket. Through gossip alone we knew he was taking a look at restricted access sites. However he was very clever and we could never prove it. Stephen on the other hand was too honest and straight laced to break the rules, let alone brag about it like Martin."

"So you turned a blind eye," Parker inferred.

"Not totally," Julie Ingram finally spoke, "we kept a note in his personnel file, which he was aware of under data protection and all that. On the whole his work was excellent and he was loved by the customers."

"Anything else in those files that may be of significance?" Parker nodded at the two blue foolscap files sat in front of Julie Ingram.

"Not really," Ingram flicked through them, "mostly letters or email of thanks from grateful customers. Martin's talent was even spotted by our owners."

"Your owners?" Parker quizzed.

"Tabb Enterprises," Eubank replied, "as in the flamboyant media tycoon Arturo Tabb. He is both owner of IBEX as well as being one of our biggest customers through The Globe newspaper. They have their very own dedicated service team."

"And Martin was part of that team?" Parker concluded.

"No, gap years like Martin were just put on general calls," Ashton confirmed, "the service teams are comprised of dedicated long termers."

"So how did Martin's talent get spotted by The Globe newspaper?" was Parker's obvious question.

"It's a good point," Ashton was puzzled too, "I'm not aware that Martin did any work for The Globe team. It's run by one of my direct reports, Nick Ford, and he's meant to run everything by me. Can I see the file note." Ashton was passed a memo from Martin's file. "Yes well it's very clear they were impressed with him. Nick even arranged for Martin to meet with a Rep from Tabb's to talk about career prospects. He came in just last week, although there's no mention of his name. I will have to ask Nick about this."

"Can we speak to him now?" Parker was insistent.

Eubank immediately picked up the phone and asked for Nick Ford to be summoned. After only a few minutes small talk, Ford knocked on the door and then entered Eubank's office. He was scruffily dressed in old torn jeans and a badly crumpled white shirt.

"Excuse the clobber," Ford smugly declared, "it's always dress down on the shop floor. They force me to put on a tie when I meet clients so I try to keep meetings to a minimum. What can I do for you Officer?"

"Detective Inspector," Parker growled, "and all I would like to know is how did the late Martin Gardner come to the attention of The Globe newspaper?"

"Uh," Ford scratched his unkempt hair and thought hard, "I think I mentioned him. Always liked Martin and he was so hot with computers. Reckon he was wasting his time going to Uni so I put in a word at The Globe. I really sold it to him and he was well chuffed. Stephen tried to talk him out of if so I got a Rep to come down and have a chat."

"Why didn't you tell me about this?" Ashton seemed furious.

"Sorry Guv, I knew you'd be pissed off," Ford carried on smirking.

"So what was the name of the Rep who came to visit?" Parker pressed on.

"I forget actually," was Ford's instant reply, "never met the bloke before."

"Well find out," Eubank snapped aggressively.

"Yeah sure, consider it done," Ford sprung to his feet and swaggered out of the office.

"Sorry about that, it should not take too long to track down our man," Eubank sincerely apologised.

"Yes and you will have to excuse me," Ingram stood up, "I have to go and give a talk to some visitors." She picked up the personnel files and also left the office.

Jane Coker was starting to get bored. The guided tour of IBEX was nothing more than a lecture on the importance of computers coupled with a badly disguised sales pitch. Jason, the Guide, was amiable enough, although his badly delivered jokes at every opportunity were beginning to grate. Jane even noticed the staff wincing nearby as Jason delivered some worn out pun on cue. Her earlier promise to Alex to sniff out some clue to all the mess was beginning to sound very hollow indeed. All the information gathered so far, mainly around the scope of IBEX's operation, could have simply been gleaned from the website.

"Right everyone, we are now about to enter the dark side or HR as it is better known. Human Remains as I call it," Jason scoffed at his own joke yet again before leading the party into a very modern and colourful office. "OK please gather around as I'm going to hand the stage over to our Chief Personnel Officer, Julie Ingram. Julie is renowned for her ability to assess a suitable job candidate within the first ten minutes of interview. She also has great legs."

"Yes thanks Jason," the tall leggy Julie Ingram stepped forward slightly embarrassed by Jason's quip as she sensed the eyes of the tour party honing in on her shapely pins. "I would like to just take a few minutes to tell you a bit about the IBEX recruitment policy should you either have aspirations to work here or should you have any concerns about the staff quality in our support centre."

Jane began to switch off as Ingram went through her spiel. Her eyes wandered around the neat compact office, which had a majority of female staff. As Jane's focus moved back to Ingram she caught sight of her placing two blue files to one side on a nearby desk. The name on the top file was clearly visible in thick black print. It said 'Martin Gardener'. Jane's heart skipped as this was the prize she was after.

As Ingram finished her speech with a large insincere grin, Jane's eyes stayed fixed on the file. Ingram invited questions, to which one school leaver enquired about job application forms. Ingram moved away to collect a form from a nearby collection of colourful papers arranged in various wooden pigeon holes. She had moved away from the files.

"OK thank you very much for your time and I hope you've enjoyed your short stay here at IBEX today. You will have to excuse me now as one of our team is about to leave to have a baby and we're going to have a presentation," Ingram looked over as the rest of the office had gathered around a desk as the far end of the room. A heavily pregnant woman was sat down looking very embarrassed as balloons and ribbons adorned her workstation.

Jason ushered the tour party out as Ingram moved away. Jane knew this was her opportunity as she sneaked over to the files and quickly opened the top one, Martin Gardner's. Her heart was racing as she speed read the memos, notes and appraisals. There seemed to be nothing of great value until Jane's eyes fixed on the words 'The Globe'. She had found the memo written by Nick Ford advising of the newspaper's interest in Martin. It also stated that a Rep had visited Martin at Ford's behest the previous Friday. This was it thought Jane, the connection between Martin and The Globe. His link to Tabb, The Mole and everything. The Rep had to be the murderer and Nick Ford must know his identity.

"Excuse me what do you think you're doing?" a very stern older lady holding a pile of papers confronted Jane.

"Uh," Jane jolted in shock, "I'm sorry I think I got lost from my tour party."

"What's going on?" Ingram had walked over after hearing the commotion.

"Sorry Julie, I was in Jason's tour party. I came back to see you and didn't want to disturb you," Jane announced.

"So what were you doing looking through that private file?" The stern lady would not relent.

"Sorry, I was bored and did not realize it was private," Jane pleaded her innocence as two security guards arrived.

"Escort this lady from the building," was Ingram's snapped response much to Jane's relief. Ingram snatched the files from the desk, angry with herself for leaving them there in the first place.

Jane was frog marched by the two guards and whisked past the dumbstruck Jason and the rest of the tour party. She was taken out into reception via a thick security door, bypassing the futuristic entrance tubes. As Jane was pushed through reception a very serious looking Nick Ford moved to one side and hit the speed dial on his mobile.

"This is IBEX one, we have a problem at base. A female has just been ejected from the building for looking through the Gardner file. She currently has no transport, description as follows; blonde, early twenties, blue suit, small brown handbag. Awaiting transport, repeat awaiting transport." Ford flicked his mobile shut and strolled back towards an entrance tube.

Jane managed to catch her breath amid a noticeable sigh of relief as she stood in the open air. She quickly called Alex on her mobile who in turn promised to pick her up within five minutes.

About a mile away Alex pulled the Mazda out of a layby and headed for IBEX once again. He felt quite sleepy after lounging in the driver's seat listening to Paula's CD collection. The Mazda hit 80mph with ease on the long quiet road and it was not long before Alex spotted the IBEX complex. Just as Alex was able to manoeuvre around the final bend another car was suddenly on his tail, appearing from nowhere. Within a split second it had overtaken him and powered away. Alex gritted his teeth in dismay as he instantly recognised the distinctive black Mercedes that had attacked him and Stephen the night before. He then watched helplessly as it turned left and moved up to the IBEX security gate. Alex knew he had to warn Jane.

"Right but surely it's just coincidence," Jane had taken Alex's call, "you'd better stay put in case he spots you. I'll hang around and see if I can get a glimpse of him. He does not know about me."

Jane rang off with a strong sense of Alex's anxiety as he waited outside the complex. Alex was sure that the mystery man was coming for Jane.

Jane did not have to wait long for the solid black car to glide into view. She watched as it slowly passed the main entrance at which she was standing and parked nearby. Due to the blacked out windows Jane could not get a single glance of the driver or any other of the car's occupants should there have been any. A group of IBEX workers suddenly congregated by the curbside and a small company bus drew up. The workers flashed their ID passes and entered the shuttle bus, chartered at IBEX's expense to take staff into a nearby town. Jane glanced away from the bus queue and back at the Mercedes but it had gone. Slightly panic stricken, Jane stepped forward unsure of her next move. She dare not call Alex for fear of luring him into a trap and now she would have no idea of the mystery man's identity. Instinctively Jane began walking towards the bus. The guards had not taken her ID pass and she saw a chance to slip away. She almost expected to be instantly ejected by the driver but in truth he did not register the sight of the visitor's ID in comparison to the employee IDs that were shown in rapid succession. Jane took a seat by the window at the front of the crowded bus and stared back at the IBEX entrance wondering if the mystery man was amongst those milling around.

The fact was that the Mercedes driver had already spotted his prey on the initial drive by. She stood out instantly from Nick Ford's description. Moving the car out of view, the man had secretly watched Jane board the bus and he was now heading towards her. Nick Ford smiled as he watched from the office above the main concourse.

The bus driver was just about to close the doors, to Jane's relief, when he spotted a bulky figure in a long black trench coat hailing him. The man showed a pass before turning and staring straight at Jane. His square hardened face, complimented by an extreme Crew Cut, sent a chill down Jane's spine. The man's upper lip curled as he sneered before moving down the bus. Jane knew something was wrong as her intuition moved beyond paranoia. As the bus moved away she slyly looked back only to immediately catch the hard stare of the same man sat two rows back. Jane twitched her head back and looked out of the window once more as the bus passed security and out of the complex. She was feeling nauseous but found some comfort in spotting Alex in the Mazda as he acknowledged her in return with a qick wave. As the bus progressed out into the countryside, Alex moved behind in slow pursuit.

25

Arturo Tabb loved winning and always had. Even as a child he had to win at everything from board games to sports to educational prowess. Tabb came first in all that he did and he soon found that made him powerful. Driven to continually succeed he created a media empire from nothing that became the biggest, most powerful and most financially solvent in the world. That was Tabb's goal and that was why he had named his UK newspaper The Globe and subsequently its US sister paper The Planet. He forecast he would be on top of the world by the age of twenty-five and he was quickly proven to be accurate. The trouble for Tabb came when he reached the summit and hit a plateau of boredom. He was so rich that any further financial gain was like a drop in the ocean. He welcomed and craved celebrity but needed much more to satisfy his calculating brain. The answer was found in the art of manipulation and Tabb found he could control people through the power of his newspapers like a puppeteer. He could bring fame and fortune to nonentities whilst destroying others in the public eye on a whim. The majority believed what the newspaper told them and with the ingenious creation of The Mole, Tabb was able to casually pick a target and seal their fate like a scriptwriter on a popular soap opera. The game was fun and Tabb found notoriety as someone to be feared by celebrities and revered by the public.

Tabb was once again sat in his office idly completing a su-doku puzzle from his own newspaper just as he would idly pick a celebrity and concoct a strategy to destroy them. The puzzle was quickly solved and was no longer a real challenge to his shrewd brain. He had also become bored with the general celebrity game. Thanks to the devious Mole and the network of information available it had all become too easy. Tabb had therefore moved on again and devised a more satisfying and high risk plan. A target had been chosen as an ultimate challenge but Tabb knew he would pull it off. He confidently pulled the strings as his plan went into operation and all was fine and working with typical Tabb efficiency. That was until Martin Gardner came on the scene, a nobody who created an unforeseen problem and challenge. Tabb moved swiftly to eradicate the problem; utilizing his network for the very purpose it had been created. Instead the issue grew and could not yet be restrained. The ultimate plan was days away from launch but it was no longer perfection. Tabb hated any form of imperfection and not being in total control. For the first time since early childhood he felt vulnerable.

"Tell me," Tabb growled into the telephone mouthpiece seconds after snatching it from his desk. A smile cracked across his face, "this is good news my friend. We will start to slowly feed the public imagination from tomorrow. The List is about to be revealed." Tabb listened carefully as his smile turned to a scowl, "you must focus on your part of the operation. The problem will soon be eradicated and The Assignment will not be questioned. Your identity is secure and will remain so. You will be greatly rewarded." Tabb replaced the handset and hauntingly stared at a photo on his desk. It was of the Queen handing him an MBE at Buckingham Palace two years earlier.

26

Jane Coker felt extremely stiff with tension as she continually looked out of the bus window. She tried desperately hard to shut out the fact that a potential murderer was sat close by ready to pounce at the right moment. The thought crossed her mind that she had got it all wrong and that the man was no more than an ordinary employee. However her instinct won the day driven by the earlier exchanged glances and the fact that he had not stopped staring at her throughout the whole journey. Jane knew she was safe on a crowded bus but she had to make a move before the bus made its final stop. Secretly, but nervously, Jane sneaked her mobile on to her lap, although she fumbled and almost dropped it as a man opposite roared with laughter and caused her to reactively twitch. With shaking fingers Jane typed a text to Alex who was still tailing the bus in the Mazda. The text read 'Alert man on bus nd 2 gt off wen stp pik me up'. As she sent it Jane sent a little prayer that he would receive it quickly. After a couple of minutes she received a reply, 'ok'.

Jane now kept her eyes fixed on the road ahead and after a few minutes seized her chance. A road sign signified that a parking layby was half a mile ahead. Jane stood up and moved alongside the driver and then visibly clutched her stomach.

"You'll have to sit down love, health and safety and all that," the driver glanced at Jane and then back at the road.

"I'm sorry but I'm going to be really sick. Can you pull over? There is a layby coming up," Jane semi whispered.

"Yeah OK love," the driver instantly agreed fearing the mess he would have to clear up otherwise.

Within seconds the bus pulled over and into the layby as the driver simultaneously released the doors to open.

"Excuse us folks for a few minutes but this young lady is not feeling well," the driver called out to the rest of the bus.

As Jane stepped down from the bus she caught sight of her pursuer moving from his seat. The second that her feet hit the tarmac, Jane broke into a sprint to the back of the bus where with great relief she found the stationary Mazda.

"Go, go," Jane screamed as she jumped into the Mazda's passenger seat.

Alex accelerated away, screeching the tyres through attrition. Jane looked out to see the mystery man cursing loudly and gesticulating with menace, after he had apparently sprinted in pursuit and come to an abrupt halt at the back of the bus.

Alex almost took the car off-road through his effort to get away whilst looking constantly in the rearview mirror for any sign of activity. He would not have been shocked to have seen the bus in hot pursuit as nothing could surprise him any more.

"What the fuck happened?" Alex yelled as he finally pulled out of sight. After a few deep breaths Jane filled him in on recent events.

"Shit that means that number one somebody at IBEX warned our persistent murderer and number two you are now out in the open as another target." Alex turned into a narrow country lane heading for the town of Acarn.

"Well the plusses are that I used a false name and unless that guy saw you he could not have made any connection between us," Jane said with convincing optimism. "On the point of the somebody at IBEX, my money would all be placed on Nick Ford."

Alex drove on for several more miles in relative silence until he reached the small and quaint market town of Acarn. He parked the car in the corner of a convenient and reclusive tourist car park. In need of caffeine he then led Jane to a nearby café.

"Strategy, what do we want to do next?" Alex looked at Jane over the top of his extra large cappuccino.

"We need to somehow get to Nick Ford. We need to know his role and just who is he? What's his connection with Tabb and with Martin and Stephen's murders? Is he in fact The Mole?" Jane summarised.

"That's what we need to do but how do we do it? We can't just drive back to IBEX and ask for a chat with him." Alex was feeling tired and frustrated, "and then on a secondary note we have to think about Mr Murderer. What if he did spot me? He definitely saw the car and we know he was at the Combe last night."

"Let's worry about tonight later and take this a stage at a time," a smile cracked across Jane's face, "I wonder."

Before Alex could question her train of thought Jane had stood up and walked across the café. In the corner was a segregated cyberspace section with pay-as-you-go internet access. Jane had spotted a free monitor and moved in quickly. Alex picked up his cappuccino and followed.

Jane had already logged on to the IBEX site, after initiating payment with her credit card, and was surfing the various menus.

"What are you hoping to find? Nick Ford's home address?" Alex scoffed.

"Aha, almost. How lucky is that?" Jane sat back as she brought up a management profile page. Nick Ford had his very own profile slot, which for the most part detailed his enthusiastic love for IBEX. There was however a small personal reference paragraph which listed one of his hobbies and interests as Snooker. He was apparently a member of the Little Hayford Snooker club.

"Little Hayford, that's only a mile or two down the road," Alex said excitedly. "It's barely a village really but a very small knit community."

"So pretty easy to find out where our Mr Ford lives," Jane smiled up at Alex.

"Oh very easy," Alex smiled back.

After losing the trail, Jane's mystery pursuer had to endure a round trip on the IBEX shuttle bus before returning to the complex. Under the pretence of a business meeting he made his way up to Nick Ford's office.

"Are you sure you don't want to take off that coat?" Nick Ford felt slightly uncomfortable as the hired assassin sat opposite him, cocooned in a thick black trench coat.

"No," was the stern reply.

"That's fine, let's see what we can find," Ford began to tap on his keyboard to search for data. "I tell you what, with that access that Mister Tabb is able to give me there is no hiding place for anybody. Let's start by taking a look at our female snoop and for that we can go to our very own security database. Only Security has access to this database of course…well apart from me." Ford was gabbling with nerves as his guest retained a stony faced silence.

"Here we are, today's visitors," Ford was glad to find something to focus on. "Well according to this her name is Ali Rose, although we will need to check if that is kosher. I'll print off her photo." Ford selected the ID picture taken of Jane earlier and sent it to print before doing some searches on the personal details provided. "Aha it looks like she gave false details, which means she is now an official problem rather than an irritating snoop. Let's take a look and see if we can find out anything from that number plate you clocked during the dramatic rescue." Ford moved to the central vehicle registration site where he once again had approved access that would normally only be given to the registration office staff. "The flash motor belongs to a Paula Davenport from London, so let's see if we can find out more about her and if she is really Ali Rose."

The Assassin continued to sit in silence and showed no emotion, although inside he was irritated by the annoying office boy and his cocky attitude. He appeased his niggle by imagining putting a bullet in the Yuppie's head.

"My word now this is interesting. By searching on Paula Davenport's details I can confirm that she is not our office snoop, so I would deduce the driver of the rescue car. Here's her photo to prove the fact." Ford enlarged Paula's driving licence photo on the screen before sending it to print. "The other startling bit of information is that Ms Davenport is a journalist and works for, wait for it…The Globe."

The Assassin finally sat forward as his brain tried to make sense of what was going on. He always liked to keep his work on a single level; resolve the problem and move on. Now he was not sure of what the problem was and what he needed to eradicate. It was time for guidance.

Arturo Tabb sat staring at his fax machine as it clicked into action and delivered several pages of information from IBEX. His scowl grew as he looked down at the clear black and white pictures of Paula Davenport and Jane Coker. The footnote simply stated that IBEX1 awaited instruction.

"I'm really sorry we could not help you any further," Julie Ingram escorted DI Parker back into the IBEX reception area. "I can assure you that our security reviews are very stringent, so it is highly unusual that we have not been able to pinpoint the Rep from The Globe at the moment. Nick Ford will have the name for you later today."

"Yes that would be really useful," Parker did find it odd that the information was not readily available. His suspicions were now even more aroused over something that the IBEX staff dismissed as insignificant.

"We are all highly shocked by the deaths of Martin and Stephen. They were both so young and suicide seems so pointless for those with their lives ahead of them." Ingram seemed genuinely choked.

"If it was suicide Mrs Ingram," Parker gave his best and well honed Colombo stare, "that's what I am looking to establish."

"This is a whole new world to me Detective and I am sure you have vast experience in such matters. Surely for it to be something more sinister there has to be a motive." Ingram shrugged her shoulders, "if that motive comes out of IBEX, which granted is the main link between the two boys, then believe me we would have some notion of what it was. We pride ourselves on a risk free and secure environment to support our particular customer base. Big Brother is watching all the time. We know the details of everyone whoever enters or leaves and we closely monitor every bit of work undertaken and every phone call that is made or email that is sent or received."

"And yet you cannot confirm to me who visited Martin Gardner in this very building last Friday," Parker made his point before arrogantly strolling towards the exit.

"Detective," Ingram called out, "this may be nothing."

Parker returned to a perplexed looking Ingram, "I like nothing as that is where I normally find the answer."

"A little earlier there was an incident. A woman in an office tour party was caught looking through Martin Gardner's file in the HR office. It was my fault really as I put the bloody thing to one side and forgot about it. I wrote her off as a nosey parker and I still think that's all she really was, but…" Ingram hesitated.

"But you can't be totally sure," Parker finished the sentence for her.

Ingram led Parker over to the cramped security office on the far side of the reception area and requested the ID details of the morning tour party.

"Usual suspects by the look of it," the laddish security guard grinned as he began printing details from the list of visitors designated to the tour party.

"Aye aye, anyone in the PID database?" the guard shouted out to a few other guards sat by a bank of security monitors, which showed transmissions from cameras situated in all areas of the complex. There was no affirmative reply.

"What's the problem Mike?" Ingram was already embarrassed about IBEX's inability to provide the Rep's details and could now sense more problems with the supposedly state-of-the-art and watertight system.

"According to the system here somebody is already viewing the records of one of the visiting party, which is basically impossible as the only access granted is via the terminals in this very room." Mike moved over to double check the other terminals, only to confirm that none were logged on to the database.

"What's the visitor's name?" Ingram asked.

"One Ali Rose," Mike replied as he played around with the system.

"That's the name of our busybody," Ingram confirmed to Parker.

Another security guard entered the office.

"Trevor, just the man," Mike called out, "I need you to override a template so we can view it. This gentleman here is from the police and wants to see a record that for some reason is shown as locked even though nobody in here is viewing it."

Trevor smiled at Parker before taking over at the keyboard from Mike. "Very odd as you say but as head security guard I do thankfully have override capability."

After some speed typing the photo and personal details of Ali Rose appeared on the screen. Just as Parker made a mental note of the information shown a bar appeared at the bottom of the screen. A blue line gradually moved along the bar as Trevor frantically typed. In seconds the word 'Deleted' appeared across the screen and the data had gone. "What the fuck?" was all that Trevor could muster in reaction.

Despite some frantic stabbing at the keyboard to retrieve the file it became obvious that it had gone. According to IBEX records nobody by the name of Ali Rose had visited that day.

As the other security guards gathered around the terminal, Parker made a call on his mobile. "Can you do a check for me on a Ali Rose of Twelve Devonshire Court, Bristol," the detective had easily memorised the address and only had to wait a few minutes for a reply. "Thanks, thought as much," he mumbled before looking over at Ingram, "for Ali Rose read Jane Doe. She provided false details which coupled with her intent in looking through Martin Gardner's file makes her one very suspicious lady."

"Yes I agree," Ingram was visibly aggravated, "damn I wish I'd called you when we first caught her."

"Don't worry, you were not to know," Parker said reassuringly, "but I think we can now say that this case has complexity way beyond apparent suicide." Ingram nodded in agreement.

"I'm sorry about this," Trevor butted in, "we need to have an overhaul of the system as it looks like we have been corrupted."

"Did Nick Ford contact you about a visitor we are trying to identify from last Friday?" Ingram asked.

"Yes," Mike replied, "and there was no record of any such person. We even checked the CCTV footage for the day."

"Somebody is manipulating your system at will. That somebody has technical computer knowledge which should be pretty commonplace within this very building." Parker spoke directly to Ingram, "a lot of trouble to go to over the deaths of two supposedly insignificant employees don't you think? The piece that does not fit is our Jane Doe here. My guess is that she is trying to unravel this mystery as well and if so then I would say her life is in danger. But why is she putting herself at risk and what is her connection? Could you check the CCTV for her picture?" Parker turned to Trevor.

Trevor nodded for Mike to go and check, "I did ask for her actual ID card to be sent down but my dopey guards forgot to take it off her."

"Hey I wonder if she was the lass who did a runner from the shuttle bus," a burly guard shouted over.

"What?" Mike looked puzzled.

"Old Phil who drives the lunchtime shopper bus had this weird incident earlier," the burly guard continued, "he was chugging along when this young lass gets up and says she feels ill. He stops and she gets off and then this flash car picks her up and legs it. I mean what was that all about?"

"Can I speak to Old Phil?" Parker said instantly.

Old Phil was still on site enjoying a coffee in the canteen and it did not take long to track him down.

"So that's about it Officer," Old Phil gave a simple overview of the recent event on his bus. "It was a very flash car with a soft top but the roof was up and I did not see the driver that clearly but I would say it was a bloke."

"How did the other passengers react?" Parker asked as Julie Ingram continued to observe intently.

"Most took no notice to be honest apart from this one bloke," Old Phil thought back, "he almost seemed to run after her. Then afterwards he stayed on my bus all the way back here."

Parker sighed, "sounds like he was after Jane Doe, but why? How did he get on your bus?"

"Showed a pass like all the others. Can't remember his name like but he had a staff pass," Old Phil spluttered.

Parker exchanged glances with Ingram, "if I can get an identikit drawn up from Old Phil's description can we do some checks to see if our man actually works here?"

"Sure," Ingram readily agreed, "this is all getting rather confusing I must say."

"I'd say it was actually becoming clearer in many ways," Parker smiled knowingly. "I think I'd better take another look at Martin Gardner's file and see if I can work out our Jane Doe's next move."

30

Little Hayford did indeed have the appearance of a small idyllic English village as described by Alex Hart. Even in March all the lawns and Gardens looked pristine in keeping with the charming old fashioned cottages that circled the extensive open village green.

Alex slowly cruised the Mazda along the edge of the green, finally having the courage to lower the Convertible's roof and enjoy the unseasonable sunshine.

"Very peaceful and a nice place to live if you like that sort of thing," was Jane Coker's eventual comment.

"And you wouldn't?" Alex asked.

"Always been a city girl me. This would be far too quiet and boring," Jane nodded at a handful of villagers walking aimlessly around the green. "That's probably about the most exciting thing to do here."

"Well that's not true as up there we have a shop and a pub and of course a snooker club," Alex sniggered.

"Of course, just what any dead end country retreat needs," Jane sneered.

Alex pulled over by the small snooker club feeling a little disheartened inside at the prospect that Jane would not be looking to settle down in the area in the near future. That was if he had a future with Jane or even any future at all.

"Right you wait here and leave this to me," Jane said with supreme confidence before applying a little lipstick, flicking her long blonde hair several times and then marching into the compact clubhouse.

Jane returned within a matter of minutes, "OK we need to take a left into a Trin Close, which is just up there." Jane pointed to the end of the road on which the Mazda was parked. "Ford lives in one of the three houses on the Close although the wurzel inside could not remember which one."

"What did you say then? Where does Nick Ford live?" Alex started up the car engine.

"Sort of, I said I was an old girlfriend looking him up. The old guy in there got all hot under the collar as he eyed me up and spilled the beans." Jane threw her head back and felt the cool Spring breeze brush her face, "that will give them something to gossip about around here."

Alex stared at her for a moment in admiration and part lust of her natural beauty triggering a momentary flashback to their night of passion from several years earlier. His concentration on the issue at hand was being distracted by a renewed ardor for Jane.

Trin Close was only a hundred yards down the road and on the edge of the extremely small village. Alex parked the Mazda near the Close entrance and he and Jane proceeded on foot.

"We've now got to try and somehow suss which of these stylish houses belongs to our Mister Ford," Jane scanned the three large detached four bedroom houses with double garages that faced her.

"For the quick solution we can thank our man's ego," Alex pointed over at a large plaque at the entrance to the middle house. On the plaque was written 'Ford's Gaff'.

Alex and Jane ambled up the drive, unsure of their next move before Jane decided to lead the way through a large gate and into the back garden. She suddenly stopped in her tracks as Alex almost walked into the back of her; they could hear voices. Jane peered around the side of the house and could see two middle aged women sat on the lawn enjoying a cigarette. Both were wearing white cleaning aprons.

"Cleaners," Jane whispered before pointing to the side of the house, "the back door is open, follow me."

Jane edged silently along the wall before promptly moving inside the house. Alex followed suit.

"What are we looking for?" Alex continued to whisper with an anxious undertone.

"Not sure until we find it, let's see if there is a study," Jane almost tiptoed up the stairs, slightly in fear of anyone else being in the house. Once upstairs she quickly located the study which housed a very large oak desk with a very modern compact computer terminal perched on top. Jane and Alex began searching around the room for anything of interest. Jane concentrated on a large number of documents housed in a small cabinet.

"This guy seems to keep records of everything," Jane muttered, "which tells you a lot about the man. Obviously well organized, hence the filing system. Obviously comfortably well off as all his bills are paid on time. He likes his clubs, Snooker, Bristol Rovers Fan Club, Jennifer Ellison Fan Club…sad, Dr Who Fan Club…even sadder."

"Hardly crime of the century though and no obvious connection with The Mole," Alex was frustrated as he sifted through some printed Internet pages that just seemed to cover all aspects of computer specifications.

"Well this is interesting as Mister Ford would seem to be more than comfortably well off. We are talking a villa in Ibiza, paid for, an apartment in London, paid for, this house, paid for and apparently there's an eighty grand Aston Martin in the garage and guess what, it's paid for."

"Bloody hell, how much do they pay you at IBEX?" Alex's eyes widened at the thought of having such wealth.

"Not that much I'm sure and if you owned all this outright, why would you need to work and as a Customer Service Manger at that," Jane shook her head gently.

"Who are you? What you doing here?" A female voice rang out loud in broken English.

Jane and Alex looked up to see an irate looking cleaner stood with her hands on her hips at the entrance to the study.

"Police," Alex shouted in improvisation, instantly flicking his press badge before whipping it out of sight. "And you are?"

"I am Mister Ford's cleaner. Why you not tell me before you come in?" The cleaner was not convinced.

"The art of surprise," Alex stated convincingly, "but we have now finished and I am glad to report that Mister Ford will play no further part in our enquiries."

Alex moved quickly passed the cleaner before looking back at Jane, who had not immediately followed him. She now made a move, almost shifting past with her hands behind her back. When the couple got to the stairs they both broke into a sprint and thundered down the steps.

"Hey you come back," the cleaner now shouted having decided that this was definitely not a police raid. The second cleaner emerged from the lounge downstairs as Jane and Alex darted out of the back door and off towards the Mazda.

Alex wasted no time starting up the car as the almost breathless couple settled quickly in their seats.

"Well apart from proving that Nick Ford is almost certainly on the take, I would say we failed in our mission wouldn't you?" Alex maintained a moderate speed as he drove out of the village.

"Not entirely," Jane said coyly before pulling out a small but thick red notebook, "I always say you can learn a lot about someone from their address book."

31

As the first hint of Summer arrived in Southwest England, there was a marked contrast in the Highlands of Scotland. Mid-afternoon brought a thick mist that restricted visibility to a few yards through the damp and eerie air. The lights of a small isolated cottage gave some warming comfort to the scene if anyone should have been venturing across the bleak landscape. Bar the occasional seasoned and hardy fell walker, that was a very rare occurrence indeed.

Inside the cottage two men and a woman sat in the cramped farmhouse kitchen, dominated by the colour and heat of a large open fire.

"Nearly there," a middle aged man stated with a very lilting and light Scottish accent. "I just can't believe how boring this week has been. When Friday comes and we get out of here I'm going to get merrily pissed. Then on Saturday it's straight off to the footie. Gonna see the Jam Tarts and then get even more merrily pissed after they lose yet again."

"What if Saturday comes and the order doesn't?" The second man with a much stronger Scottish accent said gruffly.

"No chance of that, how can anything go wrong now. She is who she is, the evidence is clear and the world will be told," the first man grinned. "A new world for us laddie."

"Well she is becoming a right royal pain in the arse," the woman snapped. "I tell you if it wasn't for the fact of who she is and the money I am getting, I would have had her by now."

"Ach, she's just as bored as the rest of us. The lassie's fine and besides it's good training for being a real royal pain the bum," the first man laughed.

"Aye well I can tell you that I'm getting nervous now," the second man seemed edgy, "we don't know what's happening out there. What if the call never comes? Then what? We have to get her out of here."

"Listen to us, stir crazy and we've been here barely more than a week," the first man scoffed before leaning over the table towards the other man. "Just think about when you are lying on the beach of your choice next week with money to burn and chicks at your beck and call. Makes it all worth it eh?"

The other man reluctantly nodded just as a small servant's bell rang out in the corner of the room.

"Jesus, does her ladyship never give it a break," the woman stood up to go.

"Better make that her highness Mary," the first man chuckled, "start as you mean to go on."

"From next week she can have her own bloody servants," Mary scowled as she left the kitchen.

32

Julie Ingram pondered before picking up the phone on her desk and dialing. "Hi, Detective Parker? This is Julia Ingram from IBEX. I'm sorry to report that our CCTV coverage did not provide any pictures in relation to our snoop or the erstwhile member of staff from the bus. There is something very odd about all this and we will get to the bottom of it. However I did track down some of the passengers from the bus who witnessed the earlier incident. All of them corroborated Old Phil's recollection of events. A couple of them confirmed that the car was a sky blue Mazda Convertible. No registration number I'm afraid, although it would seem it had an 06 plate. We did check it out on the CCTV as well but had no joy. Not much I'm afraid but hopefully of some use."

DI Parker smiled as he switched off his mobile but it was more to do with his liking for the attractive Julie Ingram than any positive headway in the complex jigsaw of a case that he was working on. Now he had just arrived in the village of Little Hayford after hearing about a suspected distraction burglary back at Dartcombe Police Station. The victim was one Nick Ford and that was enough to get the experienced Detective back into his car. He just knew that this was no coincidence.

A Panda car was already parked outside Nick Ford's house and so Parker parked next to it.

"Not sure why you'd be interested in this one sir," Sergeant Etheridge was already outside the house and greeted the DI as he had barely climbed out of his car.

"I could say the same to you Sergeant," Parker retorted, "must be quite serious for you to get involved."

"Shorthanded today, so just decided to lend a hand," was Etheridge's quick response.

"So what do we have?" Parker walked towards the house curious in the fact that the station had seemed full earlier with various constables doing nothing in particular.

"Waste of time as it happens," Etheridge tried to slow his superior down, "couple of chancers who tried their luck and got away with nothing. Sounds like they are from outside of the area and have probably legged it far away by now. They won't show their faces around here again."

Parker made his way into the house with a disgruntled Sergeant Etheridge following behind. The duo were quickly at the crime scene, the study. The two cleaners were still sat in the room.

"Have you taken any prints?" Parker scanned the study.

""No as nothing was taken," Etheridge said with a very matter of fact air.

"Are we sure of that? Where is the homeowner?" Parker smiled at the cleaners.

"Mister Ford is on his way home," the elder cleaner replied, "but the burglars left with nothing. We saw them and they said they were Police, but I not believe them."

"What did they look like?" Parker asked directly.

"One man and one woman, both young. The woman was very pretty with blonde hair and wearing a very nice blue suit. He was actually quite scruffy, wearing a white shirt and brown trousers that were not ironed and he had no shave. Brown hair I remember." The elder cleaner spoke as her co-worker nodded.

"Strange sounding combination for a burglary team," Parker looked over at Etheridge, already linking the description of the woman to that of the IBEX snoop.

"What does your average burglar look like? They unfortunately don't all go around wearing stripy jumpers and carry bags with swag written on them," Etheridge stated through gritted teeth.

"Quite," Parker was silently seething.

"Hello, everything OK up there," the voice of Nick Ford resounded from down the stairs. He soon appeared in the study and reeled in slight shock at seeing DI Parker present. "Oh hello again, surprised to see such a high ranking policeman attending something like this."

"I was in the area Mister Ford and felt I owed you after you were so helpful earlier," Parker glared at Ford.

Ford visibly shuddered, "I am of course flattered but it sounds like I've been a lucky boy and got away with it."

"Did you though?" Parker continued, "I mean what do you think our burglars were looking for in here?"

"Who knows?" Ford shrugged, "petty cash but then I don't keep any in the house. This is a very desirable neighbourhood, which can attract a lot of unwanted attention. The main thing is that the girls are alright." Ford gently patted both his semi-bowed cleaners on their shoulders.

"Do you keep any work records here? From IBEX I mean," Parker persisted.

"No absolutely not, I'd face the sack." Ford replied nervously.

"Right, well I'll leave you in Sergeant Etheridge's more than capable hands to close this one out. Good day ladies," Parker turned and nodded warmly towards the cleaners.

Ford and Etheridge exchanged relieved glances as he left but Parker's brain was working overtime. His suspicions of Etheridge were now absolutely confirmed and Ford's edgy performance had placed him alongside the hapless Sergeant. Just what were they up to? How would Colombo play this one?

"Excuse me," a man's voice broke Parker's concentration, "are you a policeman?"

"Yes, Detective Inspector Parker," Parker flashed his badge, "how can I help you sir?"

The grey haired man in a pin stripe suit pointed at Ford's house, "I heard that Nicks place got turned over. Word travels fast around here. Only three houses and we all use the same cleaning firm."

"Right," Parker was thinking that the man was just a busybody wanting to confirm some gossip. "Nothing to worry about sir as I don't think we will see this lot back again and they did not get away with any loot apparently."

"That is good to hear," continued the man with a very posh accent. "It might be nothing but when I came home earlier there was this flash blue Mazda parked at the entrance to the close. I was just admiring it when this young couple made a right dash for it. They jumped into the car and made off without indicating, a pet hate of mine. Never seen them before and just thought whether they could be our villains."

"Very possibly sir," Parker banked the sighting of the blue Mazda as final confirmation of the fact that this was no ordinary chance burglary.

"Well I took down the registration number," the man handed over a piece of paper on which was written GV06 NHP.

33

Alex Hart parked the Mazda by the side of a small secluded bay. The registration plate sparkled in the sun, displaying the very same number written on the piece of paper handed to DI Parker; GV06 NHP.

"It always looks so peaceful out there, so calming." Alex looked out to sea as waves constantly lapped in and kissed the shore.

"That's great but in the real world we have a job to do," Jane Coker was not in the mood for sightseeing and was busy leafing through Nick Ford's address book.

"What have we got then?" Alex looked over at his pretty blonde companion as she speed read the pages.

"Mostly crap," Jane did not look up, "girlfriends, who he has even given a rating out of ten, the saddo. A lot of website info, but mainly sport, music, shopping and of course porn. Typical single bloke stuff really."

"Hah," Alex tried to sound offended as if to say he was not a typical single bloke.

"Well this is interesting as your friend Sergeant Etheridge is in here," Jane finally looked up.

"That could mean anything. They might just be drinking pals or members of a club," Alex offered.

"Maybe," Jane carried on perusing, "there's quite a few numbers with sort of coded names by them. I could swear that some of these numbers are at The Globe going by the first few digits versus the number I have been given. Something I can check out there."

"Again it might not be anything as he does look after The Globe as a client but the codes do seem odd." Alex looked over Jane's shoulder, "what's all that stuff?"

"Not really sure. The page is titled 'The List' and there seems to be a lot of entries for archive and public records offices. There's contact details for a history professor and a Genealogist, the first based in Edinburgh and the other in London. Do you think he's tracing his family tree?" Jane smiled at Alex as she went to turn the page.

"Wait a minute," Alex rubbed his chin, "oh my god, the disk…on the disk was a file called 'The List'. It was all about the Tudors or something, but definitely historical. I just dismissed it as some sort of history project and unrelated or linked to The Mole's records. But now it all ties up. We couldn't find anything in the other files that we looked at because basically we were looking in the wrong place."

"The answer is always where you least expect it. It's not always the Butler who did it you know." Jane sounded condescending, "where's the disk?"

"Right here," Alex tapped his shirt pocket.

"Let's have another look at that file then," Jane got out of the car to retrieve her laptop from the boot.

Jane rested the slimline computer on her lap and loaded Martin Gardner's disk. She selected 'The List' file, which previously received scant attention. Within the main folder were around thirty separate documents ranging from Parish records of births and deaths to historical testaments of past events and numerous scanned letters. The final document was labeled as 'The Family Tree'.

"Damn this one will not open," Jane was getting an error message as she tried to open the file. "It looks like you need a particular software to get into it. Gedcom, whatever that is, but I obviously don't have it on this computer."

"We need to look at it somehow as it is probably the key. But why? I just can't get my head around the fact that a history project is so important and worth killing for," Alex was beginning to feel extremely tired and jaded.

"As you rightly point out, the family tree has to be the answer. Genealogy can be an extremely sensitive subject and could be the basis of anything from birthright and inheritance through to simply confirming your true nationality or class status. Look at America and all those seeking confirmation from the past that they are of pure Irish descent or of other European stock. The other records go back to Tudor and Stuart times and so somebody is taking a lot of trouble to prove a blood line going back a long way. The question is why and what has prompted Tabb to look into history," Jane shivered, "quite eerie really."

Before Alex could speak, Jane's mobile rang out with a high pitched shrill.

"It's Paula," Jane confirmed.

"Hi, how's the patient," Jane said cheerily into the phone. "Oh just taking a break at the moment but I've had a good day." After a long pause, Jane confirmed "I'm currently outside Dartcombe but can pick you up in an hour" before ringing off.

"What's happened?" Alex was concerned at the gist of the conversation.

"Myself and Paula have been summoned back to London. We have to be in the office for nine tomorrow morning, so Paula wants to head back tonight. Solves the problem of staying at the Combe I suppose," Jane still looked worried.

"Shit do you think you've been sussed?" Alex felt really uncomfortable about the situation.

"Who knows, but at least they didn't just top me in my hotel room this evening. Paula didn't sound too bothered or agitated. What are you going to do? I can't really pull off the whole hitchhiker story," Jane was already feeling apprehensive at parting from Alex.

Alex pushed his forehead on to his clenched fist as he thought things out. "I need to get to London too," was his conclusion. "If you drop me at the train station, I will go from there. I have friends I can stay with and we can touch base up there somehow."

"That's fine, It will be really good if we can stay close," Jane smiled warmly and rested her hand on Alex's thigh.

"Absolutely," Alex felt his heartbeat rise.

"I would put you up myself but my boyfriend would ask too many questions," Jane shrugged.

"Right," Alex now felt very deflated, "can't have that can we." He did his best to mask any disappointment.

"Look I'll take over the driving and you tell me the way. If I take the address book and check out The Globe numbers. If you take the pages regarding 'The List' and see if you can suss out the contact in London and also if you can open that family tree file." Jane moved to get out of the car.

"Sounds like a plan," Alex jumped out of the driver's seat, "and yes I have a techie mate who I can call upon for advice on opening the file."

As Jane drove Alex back to Dartcombe in the bright late afternoon sunshine, he closed his eyes and began to doze. It would have been very easy to have fallen into a deep sleep had Alex's head not been a whir of activity from recounting recent events to thinking through his feelings for Jane. In a short time she had become his soul mate and companion and he needed to protect her through instinct and association, but his feelings were now running beyond friendship. The facts were that she was a past sexual conquest from whom he had moved on very quickly, as good a shag as he could remember it being. It was only the sex that connected them. They were both very drunk and in a party mood and had just ended up in bed together. Alex had chalked off plenty of other one night stands and girlfriends since. Now in the sober reality of the situation they had found themselves in, Alex's view of Jane had gone beyond pure animal lust. They had bonded so well without mentioning their own recent history but the truth was that Jane had a boyfriend. Another fact was that current circumstances were far from ordinary. Staying alive had to be the primary objective and ensuring that he had a future, with or without Jane.

Jane too felt tired as she drove, allowing herself the odd glance at her sleeping companion. That night at the conference was almost a complete drunken blur and Jane had long since blotted out any lingering thoughts about Alex. Then against the odds she had met him again. He was certainly good looking and she quickly made the connection as to why she was such an easy conquest during that carefree celebratory evening. It was in fact her first and only one night stand. Something she had almost dared herself to try; meaningless sex with a stranger who she would never see again. That was how it was meant to work and yet Jane's one night stand had come crashing back into her life, and how. Although Jane had quickly bonded with Alex she had already surmised that he was not really her type. Jane went for men she could intellectually dominate; beefcakes with muscles on their muscles. Her current man was just that, a gym instructor who's mental capacity never stretched beyond shagging, football and aerobic programming. It just made life simple and fun and Jane liked that.

"We're back in Dartcombe, where to sleepy head?" Jane shouted over to her seemingly comatose passenger.

Alex quickly opened his eyes, "just at the end of this road will do it."

Within a couple of minutes Jane was pulling up outside the train station, "are you OK for money?"

"Yeah, I would hope that they are not tracking my debit card or anything," Alex undid his seatbelt and grabbed the oversized coat pilfered from the hotel. "At least this will keep me warm later. I will need to get some new clothes in London."

"And a bath," Jane joked. "Seriously, take care and call me on my mobile if anything comes up."

"Will do and likewise, and I guess I'll see you in London. We can finally somehow resolve this thing," Alex leant over and gave Jane a friendly hug. As Jane drove way, Alex felt very much alone. If it was not for Jane's involvement he would simply have been tempted to flee for his life and leave the whole mess behind. Alex nervously purchased his ticket to London, feeling very much to be the fugitive on the run. Fortunately the next train was only half an hour away meaning he would be out of Dartcombe before very long. After grabbing a chocolate bar and a coffee, Alex made a snap decision to give Dan Goodman a call. He knew he could trust Dan and maybe, just maybe, something may have happened to resolve the issue and clear his name.

Alex's heart was pumping as Dan Goodman's phone rang. "Where are you?" was the gruff and sudden response.

"Dan?" Alex was puzzled.

"Where are you?" the voice repeated, almost drowned out by the railway station announcer.

Alex quickly realized that he was not talking to Dan and rang off. He closed his eyes in frustration wondering why someone else had his phone. A quick glance at the watch showed there was still fifteen minutes until his train arrived. It could not come soon enough.

34

DI Parker did not take long to track down the owner of the blue Mazda once he had returned to Dartcombe Police Station. Finding out it was a journalist intrigued him, especially as she worked for The Globe. If a national newspaper had an interest in events there had to be significance. On the other hand there was a link between the same paper and IBEX and then again to Martin Gardner. Parker had already decided that it was time to head to the capital and visit the offices of The Globe. His plans, however, were quickly thrown into disarray.

Parker had already decided to call it a day and head out of Dartcombe when he nearly ran headlong into his own DCI, Andy Burton.

"Jack, I'm glad I caught you," Burton seemed really downbeat, "there's been something of a development."

"In the Dartcombe case?" Parker was curious as to what could bring his boss down in person rather than just making a straightforward phone call.

"No," Burton seemed quite evasive, "can we go and sit down."

"What's all this about Andy?" Parker found them somewhere to sit.

"The thing is, and being totally blunt, an allegation has been made against you." Burton paused, "a very serious allegation."

"Go on," Parker was almost blithe in his attitude.

"About a year ago you got a result on the Jess Anderson case. Anderson got life when you proved she murdered her young lodger," Burton summarized.

"Well let's just say that evidence has come to light that proves that Anderson could not have committed the crime and even worse that you planted evidence to finish the case."

"You what?" Parker chuckled, "that's just a joke. I knew it was Anderson from the off and the evidence was damning but not planted. I've never had to fit anybody up and never will."

"Jack I believe you," Burton placed a comforting arm on Parker's shoulder, "the trouble is there's going to be a full enquiry and one hell of a media show. You're going to be in the national spotlight and I need to spare you from that. That's why I'm taking you off the Dartcombe case and putting you on garden leave."

"Andy, this case is like no other I've ever seen. It's complex but I can nail it," Parker stared hard at his boss.

"The decision's been made mate and way above my head at that. We have to leave this one to the local plod. I think you've met Sergeant Etheridge. He's a good copper with local knowledge and will close this out, building on the work you've put in," Burton got up to go.

"Andy, Sergeant Etheridge is part of this mess. I'm not quite sure how or why but putting him in charge is like asking a fox to guard a chicken." Parker stated sternly as the reality suddenly hit him of the coincidence and timing of the allegation against him. Had this spider's web of a case claimed another victim?

35

Late afternoon in Dartcombe soon became early evening as the sky darkened and the temperature fell quickly. Alex Hart huddled inside the large padded overcoat and enjoyed its warmth as a light mist gathered beyond the small train station platform on which he was seated. The view before him was flat and in normal daylight offered a rural scene of fields stretching to the horizon. As the mist descended and clung tightly, Alex could barely make out the train track or even his fellow passengers gathered further down the platform.

It was with relief that the announcement came that the train to London was approaching, shortly followed by the powerful engine appearing out of the mist. Only a few passengers got off as Alex made his way onto a central half empty carriage. He scowled inwardly at the fact that it was old rolling stock that did not offer the comfort of the modern hi-tech trains. Alex could hear the loud clumsy doors clattering further down the train as other passengers embarked. He chose a double seat and slumped by the window. Outside the mist had become fog and offered no view at all. Alex was conscious of a handful of other passengers in the carriage as he settled down to try and sleep. At least he would have a real bed that evening having blagged to stay with an old school friend living in Clapham. The cover story was that he had a potential job lined up and just needed somewhere to stay for a couple of nights.

Just as Alex closed his eyes, a piercing whistle sounded to send the train on its way. One passenger just climbed aboard in time and Alex sensed him taking the seat behind. As Alex quickly fell asleep, the Assassin was less than two feet away.

36

"So what did you get up to?" Paula Davenport sat back in the passenger seat of her own Mazda having insisted that Jane Coker drive back to London.
"Went to look at IBEX," Jane thought there was no need to lie, "very interesting place."
"Sounds like Dullsville to me. What was the point?" Paula was still tired and grouchy.
"It was the connection between the lad who drowned and the one who topped himself in the hotel last night. Simple as that, they both worked there," Jane concentrated hard on the road as the fog descended.
"Somebody topped themselves in the hotel? Really? What have I missed?" Paula sat upright.
"Did you not notice all the police in the hotel?," Jane giggled, "and the vividly marked crime scene of course."

"No, shit. To be honest I've been in my room all bloody day. Felt like crap. Worth it though, got totally rat-arsed and shagged all night." Paula sat back once more with a huge smile on her face.

"You're shameless," Jane meant it.

"So what did you find out at IBEX? Was it just such a boring place that the employees top themselves?" Paula was already writing the copy in her head.

"It looks like they were just really good mates. One died tragically and the other could not go on," Jane offered.

"Gay?" Paula sparked up again.

"No, I don't think so," Jane huffed.

"Pity as there would have been some mileage there, but at least we can twist something out of this. Well done you." Paula felt like sleeping again.

"Paula," Jane paused as she thought how to pose her question, "did you know that The Globe is a client of IBEX? In fact Tabb owns it."

"Really," Paula smiled knowingly, "I guess Tabb owns a lot of things and people of course. And yes come to think of it I do call IBEX when I have a computer issue. Did not really connect the two until you said it."

"That's really interesting," Jane decided to press further, "so who at The Globe would deal with IBEX from a computer perspective?"

"Interesting, computers are not interesting. I could go off you Coker, but if you are that way inclined then you will need to talk to Graham Monroe on the fifth floor. If it's not him he will know who it is." Paula looked out into the thick fog, "I'll be glad to get back to civilization."

"Any idea why we had to get back so promptly," Jane said curiously.

"Just routine, a meeting's been called so you have to drop everything and run for home. That's The Globe for you, get used to it." Paula closed her eyes and sat back again to signify that the conversation was over.

Jane sighed heavily as she spared a thought for Alex, hoping he was safe and well.

37

Aided by the constant motion of the train, Alex Hart had fallen into a deep sleep within the soft and enveloping stolen coat. In a state of exhaustion he had not sensed that the Assassin had moved forward and taken the seat next to him. Silently and patiently he waited, diligently checking his watch whilst staring intently at his prey. Soon the moment he had been waiting for arrived. The Train's brakes eased into action as it slowly came to a standstill and the lack of constant movement eased Alex from his slumber. He looked out of the window at the relentless thick fog, assuming that they had stopped at a station. Alex immediately caught sight of a face staring over his shoulder as an image reflected sharply in the window. He knew instantly that it was the Assassin and jolted around to face him.

"Say nothing and stay still," the Assassin snarled within a whisper.

Alex looked down to see the man pointing a semi-concealed pistol at him from under a jumper held on his lap. Alex simply froze in fear as the train came to a complete standstill.

"Right get up and walk in front of me. One move out of place and I'll slug you, get it?" The Assassin backed out of his chair keeping the gun trained on Alex at all times.

Alex slowly stood up, trembling and trying hard to think what to do within his tired and scrambled brain. He led the Assassin down the aisle as the sparse collection of passengers sat minding their own business.

At the end of the carriage the Assassin beckoned for Alex to open the exit door. Alex once again silently cursed the fact that the train was so old and not fitted with automatic locking doors. The freezing cold night air hit him as he stepped down on to the track. Alex realised that they were not at a station and quickly deduced why the train had stopped. They were sat on top of the Darcot Bridge. Alex had been on many journeys that had taken in the infamous local bridge that stood five hundred feet above the Darcot River. It was standard for a train to stop for up to ten minutes on the bridge to allow a southbound engine to pass. The Assassin pushed Alex along the track with the barrel of his pistol jabbing continually. At the end of the high safety barrier the Assassin signalled for Alex to stop. As he looked out into the dense fog, Alex could hear the fast rushing water below. He braced almost expecting a bullet in the back of his head at any second. Just as Alex went to plead for his life he was given a heavy push and fell into immediate freefall through a freezing cold abyss. Alex did not have time to scream as he flung his arms around in desperation, fearing imminent death. Unexpectedly his hand brushed something solid and instinctively he grasped out and then gripped hard. His hand clamped rigidly on to a thick coarse rope, severely jolting his right shoulder before his grip loosened and Alex felt an instant excruciating burn caused by friction as he slid downwards. Somehow Alex found the strength to secure his aching palm around the rope and halt his rapid descent. Now he was left clinging for his life by the strength of one arm and with a biting pain in the same shoulder. Breathing erratically and trembling with a mix of fear and adrenalin, Alex managed to move his other hand across and secure a full two handed grip on the rope.

High above the Assassin looked down into the fog, positive that he had heard the sound of a faint splash as his victim met his death in the water below. He could not see that Alex was still alive and clinging for dear life on the remnants of an old fireman's rope. A rope discarded after a training exercise initiated by the brigade some months ago for the purpose of practicing the retrieval of suicide victims. The Darcot Bridge unfortunately claimed many such victims each year. The Assassin re-boarded the train satisfied that he had at last completed his mission.

As Alex hung perilously below the bridge he could hear and feel the motion of the train as it moved away on its journey. He felt the strain on his muscles as his arms began to tire and so instinctively kicked out his legs to swing the rope. Alex could clearly hear the sound of rushing water below as he began to pick up momentum. He swung blindly through the cold air without any notion of his actual position in relation to the bridge and the river. Just as his arms began to ache with severe pain, Alex felt his left heel clip a solid base. Spurred on he pushed harder and masked any reaction to his overstretched muscles. After a couple of more swings he was able to place both feet firmly on land. Impetus took him out above the river once more but on the return Alex had already made the decision to jump. As his feet hit the side again he instantly threw himself forward, pushing his body flat against the ground. He hit a slope that was several degrees from being vertical, providing enough leeway to stop an immediate fall. With both hands Alex grabbed hard on to a mixture of overgrown turf and overhanging rocks. His hands, already sore from hanging from the coarse rope, strained and cut in the effort to survive. With a final show of strength, Alex clambered upwards before finding respite on a small rock. He sat still for several minutes to catch his breath and rest his throbbing limbs. The thick fog allowed no concept of where Alex was situated but his natural instinct was to move slowly upwards. Thankfully as Alex delicately climbed the slope decreased in gradient and he was able to feel his way to relative safety. As he continued to clamber Alex began to fear that the Assassin would be waiting for him and would simply push him back over the edge. It was at that moment that his foot slid heavily on a damp smooth rock. Reacting quickly, Alex once again scrambled at the vegetation and somehow prevented a dramatic fall towards the rushing water below. Finally he made it to the summit, faintly marked out by the railway crash barrier at the exact point where he had been pushed by the Assassin. Alex wearily slithered back onto a flat surface and could at last find comfort in still being alive.

Even within the padded thickness of his large coat, Alex was shivering. He felt exhausted but knew he could not afford to rest; it was imperative that he fought any fatigue and found focus. After getting to his feet slowly, Alex staggered to the barrier and propped himself up. He was now very conscious of an eerie silence broken only by the odd large bird screeching in the distance. Alex's imagination began to run wild as he felt sure he could make out the sound of some wild animal near by. In his mind a pack of wolves were gathering. Alex focused on Jane and smiled at the thought of retelling his amazing escape at the hands of the Assassin. It was just so far-fetched that would she ever believe him?

Alex began to feel more unsteady on his feet, longing for such home comforts as a hot bath or his own bed. The normally mundane would now be pure luxury at that moment. It was then that he picked up a different sound faintly breaking through the silent night air. Alex strained to listen as the sound grew stronger and into a continuous rumble. He jolted upright at the realisation that a train was approaching.

The roar of the oncoming train's engine got louder by the second until finally it almost deafened the waiting Alex. He now feared that it would simply shoot past and began to prepare to take cover in case he was sucked into the train's wake. The noise then began to subside as the train eased down towards a standstill. Alex was now able to pinpoint the sound of a second train approaching from the north. He smiled knowing that the first train would have to make the customary stop on the bridge.

It was not long before the northbound first train came into view through the persistent fog and stopped next to Alex. He was dwarfed by the powerful engine as it sat majestically on the track. Alex did not hesitate for a second but moved quickly down the line of carriages longing to climb aboard. This time he was cursing the fact that it was a modern train with internal locking electric doors. Safety now seemed so close and yet so far away. The southbound train was getting louder and would pass within minutes leaving Alex stranded once more.

Feeling very frustrated and defeated, Alex moved back towards the front of the train when he sensed a strong smell of tobacco in the still air. Stealthily creeping forward Alex could make out the ghost like silhouette of a refreshment porter enjoying a quick cigarette by the side of the train. Alex now moved quickly, seizing his chance through the fog and with the porter's back turned he boarded the train from the only open door. Once onboard he walked hurriedly down the central aisle of several carriages before finding an isolated single corner seat. Breathing heavily he collapsed in to the chair simultaneously feeling the warmth of the train envelop his cold and tired body. Alex stared down at his hands, which were covered in sores and scabs. A female passenger glanced over at the same time, dismissing the ragged new arrival as a vagrant.

Alex smiled at the woman, "excuse me but where is this train heading?"

"Don't you know?" the woman replied indignantly.

"I've forgotten, I have a problem with remembering," Alex mumbled playing a role of backward ignorance.

"Bristol," the woman snapped before picking up her newspaper to ignore the obvious nutter.

Alex closed his eyes to sleep just as he had done a couple of hours ago on the London train. He would now have to reach the capital on a journey via Bristol. And that was of course if he could avoid or bluff the ticket inspector. For now he did not care and gladly went to sleep as the train moved on.

38

Jane Coker had a very uneventful journey back to London after escaping the West Country fog. Her companion, Paula Davenport, slept most of the way just as she had slept for most of the day. Finally Jane parked the Mazda outside her small two bed terraced house.

"Are you going to be OK to get home?" Jane pushed Paula gently to wake her, "or do you want to stay here tonight?"

"No I'll be fine, no disrespect but I need my own bed tonight," Paula sat up looking remarkably fresh. "Could I just use your loo before I set off?"

Jane led Paula into the cramped house. "Josh are you in?" Jane called out to her boyfriend after noting that all the downstairs lights were on, "Josh?"

Paula smiled, "might be having a bath or something."

"Could be interesting," Jane giggled, "as the bathroom is where our one and only toilet is."

The sound of a creaking bed and shuffling of feet echoed down the stairs as Jane made her way up. As she opened the door to the master bedroom her first sight was of a naked Josh grappling to collect some clothes as a large breasted girl sat equally naked but unmoved on the bed.

"What the fuck is going on?" Jane bellowed.

"Pretty obvious I would say," Paula answered from behind as she looked over Jane's shoulder."

A totally naked Josh held out his hands to plead, "Babe it's not what it seems. Just a bit of fun, you know I get lonely."

"Not the perfect case for the defence," Paula mocked as an irate Jane looked on in continued disbelief.

"I mean why didn't you call to let me know you were coming home," Josh moved forward as if to hug his girlfriend.

"I'm out of here," the naked brunette began to get dressed in the background.

Jane smiled sweetly at Josh before kicking him hard in the groin. As her hapless boyfriend collapsed in a heap on the floor she moved quickly over to her wardrobe. "You stay love; it's me that's out of here. Paula, the bathroom is next door and I'm afraid I'm staying with you tonight."

"No probs," Paula was almost enjoying the whole episode.

Jane hastily gathered some clothes and toiletries whilst ignoring Josh's continued plea for forgiveness. After confirming that she would be back for the rest of her things at the weekend and that the rent was now Josh's problem, Jane promptly left to join Paula in the Mazda once more.

"What a bastard, a total thick bastard," Jane fumed as Paula drove on into London.

"Good looking though," Paula conceded before feeling the effect of Jane's icy stare. "But a bastard as you say. I tell you what though, there would not be many who would mess with you Coker. A timid little girlie you are not."

"Thanks for putting me up," Jane calmed herself.

"That's OK, as if I had any choice. But seriously I look forward to your company." Paula switched on the radio to lighten the mood.

The news came on, 'It would seem that The Globe newspaper is to reveal a sensational world exclusive story this Saturday. The paper's charismatic owner, Arturo Tabb, gave notice that The Mole, his mysterious star reporter, had uncovered a major new scoop that will shock the world. Mister Tabb was presenting a gong at the annual Global Media Awards when he dropped the bombshell with a knowing smile and dig at his rivals. He would not reveal any further details other than that the remaining editions of the paper this week will have some subtle clues. Speculation is already rife amongst the journalist community as to what the storyline will be with the most bizarre prediction being the confirmation of alien life. Now that would be a stretch for The Mole.' The newsreader laughed smugly.

"That's' what we've been called back for then," Paula turned the radio down, "I wonder what the story is. Bound to be an anti climax."

"Yeah I wonder," Jane's mind was snapped back onto recent events in Dartcombe. Her now failed relationship with her ex-boyfriend was small fry to whatever was coming next.

Paula made quick headway to her exclusive apartment in Chelsea. As she parked the Mazda in the street and led Jane up a small flight of steps to the front door a bulky figure moved out of the shadows across the road and stood in the full glare of a nearby lamppost.

"Davenport has arrived home," the Assassin snarled into his mobile, "and you should know that Coker is still with her."

"Excellent," Arturo Tabb replied from his study, "then tomorrow we shall tie up the last loose end. The List is safe and the Assignment can be revealed to the world."

39

Scots Call For Reform Of Monarchy – More than two-thirds of Scots want the Monarchy scrapped. An extensive poll conducted by this newspaper found that most Scots do not want an English Queen as head of state. Questioned on whether Scotland should recognise the authority of the Queen, only 23% back the Monarch. Despite being descended from the Scottish Stuarts, a staggering 61% of Scots no longer acknowledge the line of succession as relevant to modern Scotland. (Full Story Inside).

Jane Coker sat at her desk in The Globe offices flicking through the Thursday edition of the newspaper. Whilst other journalists and media experts would be looking for clues towards the Saturday scoop, Jane had already picked out the insignificant looking paragraph on the Scottish poll, positioned in a small column to the left of the main front page feature about a

US environmental conspiracy theory. The fact that the main feature was written by The Mole would lead the majority to analyse the lead story whilst Jane immediately connected the link between the Royal succession line and the genealogy reviews detailed on Martin Gardner's disk.

Jane's mind was completely focused on solving the complex puzzle behind the recent chain of events in Dartcombe. She had switched off her mobile to avoid the constant bombardment of calls from her now ex-boyfriend, Josh, pleading for forgiveness. Paula Davenport had proven to be a fantastic support, promising Jane that she could stay in her plush apartment for as long as was needed. Jane cynically realized that Paula appreciated the company as she was basically a very lonely person despite her lavish lifestyle. So the new arrangement suited them both. Jane even got a lift to work avoiding the daily grind of travelling on the underground.

After driving Jane to work, Paula had disappeared on a mission to flirt with Chief Editor Paul Langmead to see if she could find out more about the forthcoming world exclusive. In Paula's word, "Langmead has always had the hots for me."

Alone and left to her own devices, Jane decided it was time to call Alex. She initially picked up the phone on her desk to make the call before deciding her mobile was a much safer option. The events of the last couple of days had taught Jane to be extremely cautious about anything concerning The Globe.

After ignoring the stream of voice messages and texts from Josh, Jane hit the speed dial to call Alex. The phone seemed to ring for an age and Jane really began to fear for his safety. Finally she got a grunted response just before the phone was about to click to voicemail.

"Alex, are you OK?" Jane almost whispered as she cupped the phone tight to her ear, "it's Jane."

"Hi, how are you?" Alex struggled to sit up on the extremely uncomfortable futon he had been given to sleep on by his friend.

"Fine," Jane hesitated, "well last night was not the best of my life but that's of no concern right now. The first thing is that I assume you got to London in one piece?"

"I got to London but in one piece is hard to justify," Alex felt the effects of his sore and stiff limbs and the rope burns on his hands after the previous night's life saving exertions.

"Why, did something happen?" Jane was alarmed.

"Yes our friendly Assassin tried to kill me. He was on the train and…it's a long story. He failed so whatever," Alex tried to sound laidback and cool.

"And what about the Assassin?" Jane asked.

"Still out there I'm afraid," Alex almost shuddered at the thought of another encounter with his would-be killer. "Although I guess he now thinks I'm dead, which could be an advantage."

"Listen I'm going to have to be quick," Jane was conscious that Paula could return at any moment. "Tabb made an announcement last night that The

Globe will reveal its biggest ever exclusive on Saturday. He said that there will be clues leading up to it and guess what, today's edition has a piece on the Royal Family and the power of the Monarchy over Scotland. It has to be the clue and something to do with The List. I'm going to try and find out more on the IBEX link with The Globe from this end. Would you be able to get across to that Genealogist in Ford's book?"

"Sure," Alex did not hesitate, "I'm going to borrow some of my mate's clothes, although he was bloody suspicious after I turned up looking a right state last night and without any bags. Had to tell him I'd been mugged which is not that far from the truth."

Jane could hear voices approaching, "look someone's coming. Call me later when you've seen the Genealogist. We will compare notes, stay safe."

Jane clicked the phone off just in time as Paula entered the small office along with a man pushing a refreshment trolley.

"Jane, let me introduce you to Harry the sandwich boy. A cocky letch who tries to chat up every woman in the office." Paula held out a hand to present Harry.

"Charmed my dear," the very chirpy Harry spoke with strong Cockney accent, "and I'll have you know I'm every inch a man and not a boy. Two more things, what you doing tonight? And would you like to try my tuna mayo on brown special?"

"I'm afraid I have a boyfriend and don't like mayo. Sorry but nice to meet you," Jane carried on with her work ignoring Harry, who she concluded was a just a wide boy loser.

"Your loss love on both counts, catch you all later," Harry trundled away with his trolley.

"So are we back with Josh then?" Paula sat down and picked up the day's copy of The Globe.

"No, just a convenient lie to get rid of the creep," Jane did not have the time or patience for any niggling distractions.

"Harry's harmless, nearly even relented and shagged him once," Paula winked.

"What did you find out about the scoop?" Jane moved the conversation on.

"Nothing really, everyone's as much in the dark as we are," Paula quickly thumbed through the paper. "Most guesses are about ecological disaster."

"Based on the lead story, hardly subtle," Jane sneered just as Paula's phone rang.

After a quick telephone conversation, Paula smiled over at Jane. "Looks like we may get the chance to find out more as we have been regally summoned to the office of Arturo Tabb."

Jane bit her lower lip and did not reply. She considered that fact that she would soon be face to face with the architect of the plot that had left two young men dead. Her heart began pumping fast as she felt far from being at ease and totally unsure of how she would approach the meeting. Her discomfort then turned to almost nauseous anxiety as her mind spun with why Tabb might want to see her.

40

Ever since the team codenamed 'The Shadow' had arrived in the remote cottage in the Highlands of Scotland they had been surrounded by an all encompassing and persistent mist. It had now been eight days and none of the party had really seen proper daylight until now. Finally the mist had gone and the sun shone brightly through the small and dirty cottage windows. Despite knowing the finishing line was in sight and the rewards that would come their way, The Shadow team had been pushed to the limit of boredom. If climbing the walls had been an option, any member of the party would have taken it to break the monotonous routine of eating, sleeping and reading. And that was only when they were not at the beck and call of their Assignment, although in truth that role only really fell to Mary.

The two men in the party had been happy to leave Mary to tend to the Assignment for the majority of the time. They bestowed upon her the title of 'Lady in Waiting' and in essence that is what she had become. The elder male would argue that the men were only present to protect the Assignment like bouncers in a nightclub. Whilst they conducted drunken philosophical and sometimes heated debates over a bottle of whiskey, they were in fact working. In the same way that Mary worked as she cooked and waited on the Assignment as well as her own team members. Mary did not really care as at least she was keeping active and busy. She even volunteered to collect the firewood, making time to find her own personal space even if it did mean spending half an hour sat on a rock in the cold air. Mary needed that because although her two male companions were just chauvinistic wasters, the Assignment was a different matter. Mary pitied but did not despise her, although every character trait the young girl possessed wound Mary up. She was arrogant, spoilt and pretentious without any apparent grasp of the real world. "I've never seen a Scottish lass so far up her own arse," Mary snapped to her companions after only two days of the girl's constant demands and opinions. But Mary took it all on the chin and never let the Assignment see that she had got to her.

It was now the final Thursday and the Shadow team knew that if all had gone to plan they would get the order to move south the next day. It could not come soon enough. The provisions had all but gone and the whiskey had all gone. The men were now moaning in stereo at Mary whilst the Assignment had become an unbearable spoilt child. The break in weather at least allowed for some welcome fresh air. The Shadow team gathered by a small loch. As the two men skimmed stones across the water, Mary sat relaxed under the shade of a nearby tree watching the Assignment. Until now Mary had just been doing a job for which she would be ridiculously well paid. Now as she watched the young woman in her care wistfully standing by the water's edge dressed in a long black hooded coat, the enormity of Mary's role finally hit her. Momentarily she had strong doubts about her own future as Mary knew that it lay beyond the country of her birth. Just because she looked after the Assignment did not mean Mary had to believe in her and the fact was that she knew the truth. As Mary looked across the colourful picturesque loch a single tear trickled down her cheek for the secret that she dare not share. In contrast the hooded Assignment smiled knowingly as she caught her reflection in the clear water. Both women were Scottish but one viewed her land with love and affection whilst the other had only thoughts of greed and power.

41

Alex Hart felt revitalized. He was still sore and in physical pain and was having to lodge in an old school friend's cramped London flat, but he felt strangely lifted and optimistic. The phone call from Jane Coker had awoken him from a deep slumber and brought him back to immediate reality. But now he had a mission and he and Jane were part of a team. If they cracked the case and defeated Tabb, fame and fortune beckoned. It also left him intrinsically linked with Jane and even though she had a boyfriend, Alex could not help thinking that she would soon be his. Today Alex Hart was the eternal optimist; to think in any other way would have just destroyed him. Alex's old school friend had already gone to work but had left him a key, a pile of clothes and a note. The latter just confirmed that Alex could use the flat as his own for the few days he was staying.

After taking a bath and shaving the thick stubble from his face, Alex was so grateful to be wearing some clean clothes. His friend, Simon, had even left him some underwear, which the note stated did not have to be returned. Feeling relaxed, Alex settled down in front of Simon's forty-two inch plasma television with a plate piled high with toast. After flicking through the channels he eventually settled on a News channel.

Following a Sport bulletin the lead news story was the announcement by Arturo Tabb of the forthcoming world exclusive in Saturday's edition of The Globe. Alex shivered slightly as the overbearing Tabb was shown delivering his award ceremony speech with a conceited air. The news item then moved on to the growing speculation about the exclusive, including some ludicrous bets being placed by members of the public. One commentator even mischievously suggested that some of these bets were being tactically placed by Globe staff in order to enhance the story's reputation. Little did his laughing colleagues know that he was in fact totally correct.

Alex was about to switch the television off as a collage of small soundbite news items were given screen time. It was then that a familiar face appeared before him.

"I would obviously once again like to pass on my own personal condolences to the parents of Martin Gardner and Stephen Howard. This is a very small community and I know both families very well, as I indeed knew both of the boys. I am glad to report that the result of the investigation into the deaths of Martin and Stephen concluded that no foul play was involved, but this will only bring very small comfort to the bereaved. However we can now officially close this case and allow the respective families to grieve in private."

Sergeant Etheridge spoke with extreme clarity and confidence at the hastily assembled press conference.

"What about the missing journalist, Alex Hart. Are you still looking for him as part of any ongoing enquiry?" A member of the press asked as Alex shuddered, relieved that he was not watching the programme with Simon.

"No, we no longer need to speak to Alex. Although he has been very foolish and his behaviour has been unethical, he has not committed any crime or played any part in either death. I believe Alex has chosen to move away from the area and start afresh." Etheridge punctuated the statement with a conceited smile.

Alex was now fuming as he watched; what the hell was Etheridge implying by referring to any connection with both deaths, even if he had been declared innocent. And was he so smug because he knew or thought that Alex was dead?

The news item moved away from the press conference and flashed up a photograph of DI Parker.

"Sergeant Etheridge of Dartcombe Police concluded the tragic case of the now confirmed double suicide following the sudden removal of Detective Inspector Jack Parker as principal investigating officer. DI Parker is facing charges of corruption relating to the conviction of Jess Anderson for murder last year. The full case against Parker will be presented by Anderson's legal team tomorrow."

Alex switched off the television and headed for the door more determined than ever to solve the riddle of The List and bring the likes of Sergeant Etheridge to justice. It was the very least he owed Stephen Howard and Martin Gardner.

42

"Are you OK?" Paula Davenport glanced over at an anxious looking Jane Coker as the pair took the lift up to the top floor of The Globe building, the location of Arturo Tabb's office.

"Yeah…yeah fine," Jane snapped out of her concerned train of thought. "Don't worry he's harmless really, especially where the ladies are concerned. If you feel frightened then just imagine him naked, that normally diffuses any tension for me." Paula chuckled loudly, "believe me I've seen him naked for real and have had to keep a straight face on every occasion. Should have been an actress me."

Jane returned a nervous smile as the lift reached its destination. The doors opened to reveal a swish oak paneled corridor which led directly to the desk of Arturo Tabb's PA. To Jane the walk up to the office felt like she was moving down a dark tunnel. The walls were adorned with avant-garde artwork, which to the untrained artistic eye looked like no more than non-strategically placed splashes of colour.

"Mister Tabb is expecting you, go right on in," the PA did not even look up from her work.

The even darker interior feel to Tabb's office, which offered very little natural light through the small and shuttered windows, made Jane feel even more uncomfortable. It reminded her of being summoned to the headmaster's office at school, although this was in essence far worse. Tabb was sat at his desk signing some documents and did not look up.

"Mister Tabb, you wanted to see us," Paula's voice trembled.

Jane baulked at the formality of Paula's demeanor considering that she frequently shared a bed with Tabb. She was also very cognisant of Paula's own fear of the man.

"Yes sit down," Tabb said gruffly as he finally looked up and stared hard at his visitors. "Tell me," Tabb said simply.

"What would you like to know?" Paula was now even more nervous.

Tabb intently gazed into space for about a minute before continuing, "about Dartcombe, tell me about Dartcombe."

"Well um, not a lot to tell," Paula continued to be spokeswoman, "we chose it at random for the weekly regional focus story. Very dull place in the main although there was a couple of suicides recently, which will be the main concentration for our article."

"Miss Coker," Tabb gaped straight at Jane, "tell me about IBEX."

Jane felt almost nauseous with fear, "IBEX, what would you like to know?"

Tabb threw a loose file over at Jane containing several photographs. Jane took the file as Paula looked on curiously. Inside were several colour photographs of Jane taken by the IBEX CCTV cameras as well as the mug shot from her temporary ID pass. Another couple of pictures were of Paula's blue Mazda parked in the dropping off area at IBEX. To Jane's' relief the pictures were not clear enough to make out the driver.

"So Jane Coker or should I say Ali Rose, tell me." Tabb leant forward menacingly focusing his wide eyes directly at Jane.

"Yes that is me obviously," Jane gave a nervous cough. "I went to IBEX to see if I could find out anything on the two boys who committed suicide. They both worked there you see. I did use an alias which I am now guessing was silly. I'm sorry."

"No not silly at all really," Tabb sat back and smiled, "so what did you discover on your jaunt to IBEX?"

Jane visibly exhaled, pouting her lips, "nothing really. It looked like a great company to work for and the suicides could not be connected to IBEX in any way. I'm afraid I failed."

"So why the Mission Impossible scene in getting off the company shuttle bus? Why not just get off at the bus stop with everyone else?" Tabb leant forward again.

"I panicked," Jane was not lying, "I got caught checking some files that I should not have seen. I thought that IBEX security were after me."

Tabb nodded aligning Jane's account of events with the report from Nick Ford and the Assassin. "Miss Davenport, why did you allow Miss Coker to take the lead here? It seems that you were nothing but the getaway driver, although a very good one at that."

Jane's heart almost froze as she considered the fact that Paula may deny all knowledge of the events at IBEX.

"Yes," a perplexed Paula looked stunned, "I take full responsibility. It was my idea to go in at the deep end but it obviously backfired."

"Apology accepted," Tabb held up a hand and grinned broadly, "let this be a lesson to you both. Now Langmead has separate assignments for you this morning, so Miss Coker it is in at the deep end again I'm afraid. See if you can swim this time; go." Tabb ushered the two women away.

As a relived Jane stood up her eyes caught sight of a brown folder near Tabb's left elbow. It was labeled 'Alex Hart'.

Jane and Paula maintained an uneasy silence as they walked back down to the lift. As the door shut and enclosed the pair Paula immediately snapped, "What's going on Coker? Who the fuck was driving my car?"

Jane turned to confront her red-faced irate colleague, "we need to talk. Not here and not now, but we need to talk. I've stumbled on to something big and it's time to bring you in on it."

Paula reeled from the response as it was not what she was expecting, "lunchtime, tell me then." The lift doors opened and Paula strode quickly out into the office, completely ignoring Jane.

At the same time Tabb had made a brief phone call, "keep an eye on Jane Coker, I want to know who she meets and anybody she calls."

43

Julie Ingram was angry, both with herself and the world in general. She always thought that she was a good judge of character and yet after bonding quickly with a seemingly bright and honest policeman, Ingram was horrified to see the very same man exposed on national television as devious and crooked. It was all not proven of course but Julie Ingram had always been a believer that there was no smoke without fire. She now felt betrayed and not just by the once charming DI Parker. Ingram had a passion for her job and for the company she had worked for over so many years. Even though the scrutinizing DI Parker was of dubious character, he had still exposed some glaring holes in IBEX's security network and this was where Ingram would vent her anger. Never again would she be so humiliated by having the standards of her beloved employer so badly brought in to question.

Chief Security Officer Andy Oakham had already been pre-warned that Ingram wanted to go through all his standard operating procedures later that morning. This would be followed by a full internal audit and risk assessment. No stone would be left unturned. First, though, Ingram was off to see Nick Ford, a manager she had despised since their very first meeting. In her eyes he was an arrogant and scruffy waster who did nothing to portray the type of corporate image that IBEX stood for. So without warning or invitation, or pre-clearance from Ford's manager, Ingram had stormed down to his office with a clear and assertive strategy in mind. If he did not come up to scratch she would have no hesitation but to make it a more formal HR interview. Ingram was deflated to find that Ford was not in his office and had according to his PA "popped out for a fag." Smoking was another of Ingram's pet hates. She snapped that she would wait in Ford's office for him but was stopped in her tracks by a locked door.

"He always does that, very security conscious is Mister Ford," the PA said with a smile.

"Very good to hear," Ingram replied condescendingly, "do you have a spare key to let me in?"

"I do but Mister Ford would have my guts. I'm not even allowed in on my own." The PA grimaced as if it meant she could not be trusted.

"Well you certainly know who I am," Ingram said sternly before adding, "I'll square it with Mister Ford."

After pondering for a few minutes, the PA reluctantly opened the door. The small office mirrored its owner, untidy and un-corporate. It reminded Ingram of her fifteen year-old son's bedroom. As she paced around Ford's desk she wondered how he kept track of all his paperwork and files. Ingram had seen it so many times before with the customer service staff, all the gift of the gab and superficial front but underneath was a total disregard for procedure. That was why Ford had no idea about the Rep from The Globe as it was already history and the details no doubt buried in one of the many files piled high on his desk. Ingram was already thinking how she was going to have someone go through all his files under the premise of finding that very information. She was sure that they would find more than enough evidence to hang Ford out to dry once and for all. Just as Ingram sat down at Ford's desk she heard a loud high pitched beep. Curiously she got up and followed the direction of the sound, which appeared to come from an obscure cupboard. Without hesitation Ingram opened the door but was not expecting what she found inside.

Ingram had anticipated she would be confronted by a small storage cupboard but instead found another mini office, complete with a desk and a computer. Along side the computer was a printer and fax machine from which the beeping sound had originated. In contrast to the main office, this small room was extremely tidy and uncluttered. Ingram stepped forward and pulled out some papers from the fax tray that had been previously transmitted by Ford. Ingram reeled in shock as she saw the clear images of the previous day's female snoop as well as CCTV photographs of the reported blue Mazda. Baffled and confused she turned her attention to the computer. Ford had not locked his screen. After a quick glance over her shoulder, Ingram opened up the system. She was faced with a comprehensive dossier on DI Parker and the Anderson murder case for which he was facing corruption charges. Ingram felt oddly sick in her stomach but recovered her composure to print the screen contents. She also grabbed the faxed photos and copied them in the main office. With trembling hands Ingram stuffed all the paperwork into her company folder before dropping the original faxed papers on the floor. As she hurriedly scooped them with her heart beating rapidly, Ingram could hear voices. Next door the PA was explaining to Ford that he had an important visitor. Ford subsequently strode into his office to find Ingram standing by the window with her back to him.

"What's up Julie?" Ford had a guilt ridden expression.

Ingram took a deep breath and turned to face Ford, "after the events of yesterday I am undertaking a review of procedures. I need to know how you are progressing with finding the elusive Globe Rep."

"Oh that," Ford nonchalantly moved over to his desk, "to be honest I did not bother looking any further after that cop was exposed as a fraud and the Gardner case then being closed out."

"You've been keeping a close eye on the news then?" Ingram tried to maintain an air of calm.

"Local events and all that, you have to don't you?" Ford winked.

Ingram semi closed her eyes in disgust at the cocky junior manager, "fair enough but I still want to know who our elusive visitor was and so you can start looking again."

"You'll need to square that with Peter Ashton as I've got a to-do list as long as my arm love," Ford logged on to his PC.

"Oh I will and don't ever call me love again," Ingram jabbed her tight index finger aggressively. "Also the case against DI Parker has not yet been proven and until it is we should not jump to any conclusions."

"Believe me he's guilty and will get what's coming to him, just a bloody glory hunter. I mean look how the man tried to make a sinister case out of a straightforward suicide," Ford scoffed. "No wonder he had to go around planting murder weapons to get results."

Ingram had watched the brief TV footage on the news about DI Parker's suspension but she certainly could not recall any mention of planted murder weapons. As Ford returned to his work Ingram left without a word and made a beeline back to her own office. She almost felt breathless on arrival, finding comfort in shutting herself away. Ingram took a close look at the printed DI Parker dossier. It gave a blow by blow account of the Anderson murder case highlighting glaring inaccuracies in the evidence presented by Parker in court. This included a readily dismissed key alibi for Jess Anderson and the fact that the knife used to murder the unfortunate lodger was not found during the initial search of the murder scene, Anderson's lounge. It also stated that the knife perfectly matched the description of one that was purchased by DI Parker two days after the murder and the very day the knife was discovered in the lining of the settee. The dossier even named the shopkeeper who had a receipt to evidence the sale of the weapon.

Ingram shivered in disgust at the account of events as she knew such evidence would never be made so public before a case had been heard. And further to that why did Ford have all this detail? Why did he have all the missing photographs from the security system?

Ingram needed to talk to DI Parker and she still had his mobile number. He answered very quickly with the same suave and sophisticated manner as the day before.

"DI parker, it's Julie Ingram from IBEX," Ingram hesitated.

"Hi," Parker replied with a soft informal tone, "I'm afraid I've been taken off the Gardner and Howard case. All tied up now apparently."

"Yes I've seen the news," Ingram mumbled, "the thing is I need to see you. I've found something here at IBEX, evidence of our snoop but also more alarmingly information about you and the Anderson murder case."

There was a brief silence before Parker spoke seriously, "Julie be careful. The reason I'm off the case is because I was getting close to something and all I can say is it's something big. Without a doubt it centers on IBEX and I believe that Nick Ford is heavily involved. These people, whoever they are, have the power to control and manipulate anything or anyone. They are looking to destroy me and they will certainly look to destroy you if you become a threat."

Ingram had heard enough, "I know Ford is a crook and I can help you fight the charges against you. Whoever these people are as you put it, they must be beaten. Can you meet me in an hour?"

Parker again paused before replying a simple "yes."

"There's a pub on the Dartcombe Moor called The Yokel. I can meet you there at Midday," Ingram knew the pub was mainly for travellers and not too busy in March. It also had great food.

"Yes I know it," Parker replied, "but Julie be careful. Above all make sure you are not followed."

44

Alex Hart had never enjoyed travelling on the London underground and today was no exception. The journey from Clapham to London Bridge had proven tedious and cramped; although it provided Alex with a great deal of time to think about how he would approach the Genealogist listed in Nick Ford's book. Finding his address in reality proved relatively easy and the fact that it was marked as an official business premises by a large blue sign at the front gave Alex more confidence to venture straight in to the grand old building.

Once inside Alex found himself in a plush waiting room not unlike a Harley Street practice. A silver haired lady greeted him from behind her reception desk, "how can I help you?"

"I'm here to see Mister Jameson," Alex replied quoting the name shown in Ford's book under Robert Jameson, Genealogist.

"Do you have an appointment?" the woman was already leafing through a large diary.

"Uh yes the name's Adrian Carter," Alex blatantly lied.

"I'm sorry Mister Carter but I do not seem to have you listed. Was it just a pre-consultation?" The woman looked unperturbed.

"Yes that's correct, I've travelled up from Cornwall especially," Alex faked his disappointment.

"Not to worry, I can just fit you in as I have a cancellation. I will need you to fill in this form," the receptionist handed over as small piece of paper. "I'm afraid you will have to wait for about half an hour."

"No worries," Alex took the form and strolled over to the waiting area.

Feeling very relaxed as he lounged on a soft and deep sofa, Alex even helped himself to a free cup of coffee from a nearby machine before perusing the consultation form. Aside from the required personal details, which Alex faked, the three questions were very basic:

What is the main reason for wanting to trace your Family Tree?

Have you completed any previous research into your Family Tree?

How far back would you like the research to be concentrated?

At the bottom of the form was a statement to the effect of should the client be happy to proceed with the assigned research following the consultation they would be required to sign a contract relative to a fixed fee agreement. A deposit of thirty percent of the agreed invoice would be required within seven days of the consultation coupled with a completed questionnaire on immediate family members.

Alex could understand the appeal of the services offered by Robert Jameson for those unwilling to spend the time and effort to undertake the painstaking research themselves. There was certainly a lot of money in London and it gave the idle rich an opportunity to invest in an obvious status symbol.

"Is he in?" a loud booming male voice distracted Alex from the form. A burly man with a thick black beard had stormed into the reception area. Before the receptionist could speak he simply barged his way into Robert Jameson's office.

"Jameson you're a bloody fraud and I will expose you as such," the man's voice was clearly audible outside of the office. "You are nothing but a Genealogy prostitute determined to drag the profession into the gutter."

A very pale and sheepish young woman scurried out of the office and left the building assuming her consultation with Robert Jameson was over.

"Calm down Brian, you are going to have a seizure if you keep getting so worked up." The calm voice of Robert Jameson contrasted greatly to that of his visitor, "what on earth has upset you?"

"I'll tell you what has bloody upset me," Brian continued in the same blustering loud fashion. "I recently completed a family tree for the Dandell-Carter family but Mrs Dandell-Carter was horrified that her blood line came from simple coal mining stock. So the rich stuck-up cow decides to get a second opinion and trots off to good old Robert Jameson, the Genealogist who never disappoints. And lo and behold Mrs Dandell-Carter is really related to a noble landowner."

"Sounds like you got it wrong Brian," Jameson suggested daring to offer a red rag to a bull.

A loud clattering bang echoed out of the office prompting Alex to finally move over to the office door. Brian was holding his adversary by the throat as he pressed him hard against the wall.

"Mister Jameson, should I call the police?" A very worried looking receptionist stuttered.

"Come on gentlemen, let's try and calm this down," Alex moved into the office.

"Who are you?" Brian barked.

"I'm just a client here for a consultation," Alex replied.

"Ha," Brian shouted, "well this twat will tell you whatever you want to hear. If you fancy being related to Charles Dickens then he'll sort it out for you. What we have here is a master forger."

Jameson was turning a crimson shade of red as Brain's large squeezing hands moved around his windpipe. "Brian please," he gasped.

"Come on Brian, you've made your point, let him go." Alex pleaded.

Reluctantly Brian released Jameson from his grasp, "you've not heard the last of this Jameson. I will expose you as the charlatan that you are." Brian stormed out of the office with a ferocity equal to the one that marked his arrival.

"I'm sorry about that," Jameson loosened his tie and took a few deep breaths to regain composure. "Would you believe we used to be really good friends but then I became very successful and basically he didn't."

"Sure," Alex just nodded.

"Anyway, I believe you're here for a consultation and as my previous appointment has run off, why don't we begin. Please take a seat." Jameson ushered Alex towards a chair.

"Yeah great, although I haven't filled out your form yet," Alex held up the piece of paper.

"No problem let me just grab my notepad and let's see what we can do." Jameson threw the form to one side as if it was of no real importance. "So what are we looking to find out?"

"Uh well I heard from a friend that you had a certain expertise in looking at Tudor and Stuart history and I have a particular interest in that period for a project I'm running," Alex offered confidently.

"Oh yes I would say that I am an expert for that period, without blowing my own trumpet," Jameson smirked as he logged on to his computer. "What is the focus of your project?"

"Kings and Queens really, quite basic," Alex shrugged.

"Well without wishing to do myself out of a job, you can gather a lot of information about such a well documented subject from the Internet." Jameson frowned.

"Right but I want to go in at a new angle. Find something ground breaking and radical to shock my history professor," Alex almost punched the air in determination.

"Believe me it's all been looked at and written about already for that period and I should know." Jameson now patronisingly pouted.

"I heard from my friend that you had uncovered something exciting and that it would be ideal for my project," Alex pressed hard after being stung by Jameson's belittling manner.

"What?" Jameson's expression had become severe, "and just who is your friend? And who are you?"

"Adrian Carter," Alex just about remembered his alibi, "and my friend works at The Globe newspaper."

Jameson instantly stood up, "I am going to have to ask you to leave. I am not interested in taking on this work."

Slightly shocked, Alex got to his feet and felt he best go in light of the abrupt stance taken by Jameson.

"Close the door behind you," Jameson sat back down and blanked his departing guest.

As Alex walked past the reception desk he nodded politely as the old lady before being struck with an idea."Excuse me but just out of interest, who was the burly gentlemen who threatened Mister Jameson earlier?" Alex asked with an over friendly manner.

"Oh that was old Brian Harris, he has a Genealogy practice a few doors down," the receptionist replied. "His bark is worse than his bite really."
"Thank you," Alex turned on his heels.
As Alex left the building, Robert Jameson was making a phone call. "It may be nothing but I think I might just have encountered a problem."

45

Before Jane Coker could meet Paula for lunch and explain what really happened in Dartcombe she had the distraction of her first Globe solo assignment. This had proven to be a mundane trip to the House of Commons to hear a statement from an obscure backbencher on his campaign for more investment in renewable energy. Jane was sure that she was being sent to reconfirm the paper's focus on the environment and therefore continue the red herring story that so many had now latched on to as the forthcoming world exclusive.

Jane worked out that she had just enough time to seek out the paper's main technology contact, Graham Monroe, as cited by Paula. She decided to make a quick visit in person and use her feminine charm. Just as Jane made her way down to Monroe's desk her mobile phone emitted a short sharp jingle to announce the arrival of a text message.

Jameson odd & actd v gilty nothg concrete hv new lead wl upd8 lv Al

Slightly bewildered by the message, Jane decided to wait for the update and sent a short response.

Ok tk care lv J

"Hi you must be Graham," Jane almost fluttered her eyelashes after spotting the very clear desk name plate.

Monroe looked up from his work, instantly blushing as he caught sight of the voluptuous blonde in front of him. He tried to act cool by removing his glasses but ended up squinting heavily as his eyes failed to adjust quickly, "yes…and who might you be?"

"Jane Coker, I'm new around here." Jane sat down on Monroe's desk, deliberately allowing her skirt to hitch up and reveal an extremely shapely pair of legs.

Monroe trembled slightly, "what can I do for you Jane?"

"Well Graham the thing is you come highly recommended by Paula Davenport as someone who could answer a few simple questions for me." Jane nibbled her lower lip suggestively.

"Yes please fire away and I'll see what I can do," Monroe was smitten.

"OK," Jane clicked into a more business like tone, "I'm trying to understand the links between The Globe and IBEX. Do you have much to do with them?"

"Quite a bit, although the staff there are very good and so normally it is just to reconfirm that we are happy with their support desk service. My team tends to deal with the hardware issues but IBEX are really the expert programmers and software experts." Monroe was feeling more inside his comfort zone.

"Makes sense," Jane nodded, "so do you mainly deal with Nick Ford down there?"

"Heard of him but have never spoken to him. How do you know him?" Monroe put his glasses back on.

"I was there recently, at IBEX, and met him. It was just that he mentioned how The Globe had been interested in employing a member of his team and had sent somebody down to interview. The thing was that Nick could not remember who came down from here. Any idea?" Jane slid closer to Monroe.

"No," Monroe shook his head and laughed, "and believe me if it was a techie recruitment I would need to know."

"He did give me a telephone number," Jane pulled out a piece of paper showing the number copied from Ford's book; 0207 718585.

"Not mine I'm afraid but that is definitely a Globe number. Hang on a second, I can do an advanced search on the system." Monroe quickly tapped away at the keyboard, "there you go it's actually the main man's number. Can't say I ever call him myself so no wonder I did not recognise it." Monroe tilted the screen towards Jane. The name Arturo Tabb was emblazoned in thick black letters.

46

Alex Hart had not taken long to walk down the road from Robert Jameson's office to that of his rival, Brian Harris. A sign marked the location of another Genealogy practice, although in contrast it was a flaking white wooden plaque that was partly obscured by a very overgrown front garden. Instead of walking straight into a plush reception area, Alex had to ring the doorbell. Brian Harris himself answered and instantaneously proceeded to stare down from his six foot five frame at his visitor like a teacher observing an unruly pupil.

"Mister Harris," Alex felt extremely unnerved.

"Yes and what can I do for you?" Harris almost spat the words out.

"I was visiting Robert Jameson when you came to see him earlier. I think I need your advice." Alex said with the utmost sincerity.

"Well if I put you off that bloody fraud I'm very happy indeed but I have no time for any appointments this week. I will bid you good day," Harris went to shut the door.

"I have something that will be of real interest to you and I must stress that it is a matter of extreme urgency," Alex shouted and pleaded at the same time.

Harris thought for a minute before relenting and opening the door wide, "ten minutes that's all you have."

Alex followed the large overbearing figure of Brian Harris into the house. The main hall was cluttered with books and papers and the air was filled with dust, prompting Alex to sneeze on several occasions. Harris flung open the door to his study, which was even more swamped with paperwork piled high around a rickety old desk that supported a very old computer terminal.

"What have you got for me young man?" Harris sat down and placed his feet on the desk.

Alex pulled out Martin Gardner's disk, "basically what's on this. It contains a Genealogy project and I'm sure it was researched by Jameson."

"Dodgy?" Harris asked smugly.

"I think so but I'm no expert," Alex confirmed.

"So what's your angle? Why bring it to me? Are you looking to destroy the git?" Harris again spoke with real venom.

"This goes beyond Jameson. People have died because of what is on this disk and I need to know why," Alex replied sharply as he remembered what was at stake.

"I guess we'd better take a look then," Harris held out his hand and took the disk.

After Alex had spelt out the password, Harris promptly moved down to 'The List' folder as he was directed. He speed read and perused a number of the underlying folders and became increasingly excited in the process.

"Any thoughts?" Alex was desperate to know more.

"Oh this is very very interesting young man. And you say this is Jameson's work?" Harris looked up and smiled through his unkempt beard.

"Yes I believe so. I tried to subtly probe him around the subject of the Tudors and Stuarts period but he sussed and kicked me out," Alex shrugged.

Harris let out a booming laugh, "well this really just starts with the Stuarts my friend but it then implies so much more," Harris was still reading a particular file.

"Wow," Alex said in surprise, "although there is one file that I could not open. You need some sort of software."

"Gedcom, well I would not be much of a Genealogist if I did not have that," Harris guffawed as he clicked on the family tree file.

The file revealed a traditional but very long family tree model which Harris quickly scrolled through. "Aha and this is the icing on the cake that confirms what this is all about."

"What does it show, it looks like the Royal Family to me," Alex peered over Harris's shoulder, making out the highlighted famous monarchs throughout history.

"That's what it is young man but the big difference is that this family tree has never been seen publicly before. The shaded part of the diagram where you are focusing shows the bloodline to our current Queen. This other additional unshaded part of the diagram shows another bloodline where someone else is Queen; one Sophie Devine to be precise."

Harris jumped up causing Alex to visibly start. "Let me gather some files as I just need to check a few things. I will then explain exactly what is going on here and just why this information has cost lives."

Alex watched as Harris frantically searched through mounds of paperwork, recklessly flinging discarded documents to one side. "Here we are," Harris announced with glee as he selected a number of bound documents, "come and look at this…sorry what was your name again?"

"Alex," Alex tutted as he looked down at one large sheet of paper that Harris was spreading out on his desk. It was another Royal Family tree.

"Right now if we print out the more extensive family tree from your disk I can explain what all the fuss is about." Harris selected print on the computer screen and then removed a pile of books obscuring his compact printer. After collecting the printed sheets he lay them down by the side of his own less complex version.

"Let's start by explaining this in very simple terms along with a quick history lesson. Like most Genealogists my first love is history and like Jameson I know this period like the back of my hand." Harris was noticeably animated about what he had found. "On my basic and well known family tree if we take a straight as you like line from our lovely current Queen Elizabeth II back to the focus of the document on the disk, Mary Queen of Scots. The bloodline is started by Mary's son, James I, the first of the Stuarts and the first monarch to combine the thrones of England and Scotland. Now if we look at our family tree on the disk we can see a completely alternative line. This diagram shades out the bloodline from beyond James I as incorrect and then suggests an alternative drawn from another offspring of Mary Queen of Scots. Basically it is saying that our current Queen should not be ruling over us but we should now bow down to Queen Sophie as direct descendent of Mary Queen of Scots."

Alex grimaced, "well it's all well and good drawing up a nice picture but who's going to buy it. Can't see the British public saying OK Liz you can get lost now and hand over the keys to Buck Palace to Sophie on your way out."

"Of course," Harris clicked on to one of The List documents on the computer. "But what they can do is instill doubt and then make a case and legal challenge to the rights of the monarchy. You quite rightly picked up on the rough period that these files spotlight from the background research notes, but the key is the scanned letters like this one on then screen. What do you know about the fascinating history of Mary Queen of Scots?"

"She had her head chopped off and Queen Elizabeth I hated her. That's about it really," Alex shrugged.

"Time for that history lesson then. Born in Scotland, Mary became Queen of Scotland when she was only six days old. As Henry VII's great-granddaughter she also had a very strong claim to the English throne. She was meant to marry Henry VIII's son, the future King Edward VI but was instead betrothed to the French King's, Henri II, heir, the Dauphin Francis. This riled Henry VIII and he ordered a number of savage raids on Scotland known as the Rough Wooing. Mary married the Dauphin who became King in 1559 but died a year later. Mary returned to Scotland in 1561, even though she was a Catholic monarch returning to a now very Protestant country. She was however warmly received and eventually married her second cousin Henry, Lord Darnley in 1565. Now this is important because Darnley is supposedly the father of their son, who became James I of England." Harris stopped and grinned broadly at Alex.

"Supposedly, so there is doubt?" Alex queried.

"Let's say that there have always been conspiracy theories. One of the strongest was that James's father was in fact the Earl of Bothwell, who became her husband after Darnley's death. In fact it is always thought that Bothwell murdered or at least participated in the murder of Darnley."

"I'll tell you the modern soap operas have got nothing on this lot," Alex was enjoying the history lesson. "But surely the fact is that Mary was still the mother and that the bloodline was secure whoever the father was?"

"Well another theory that has always been around is that Mary's son actually died at birth and was replaced by another, who took the part of James I. This is supported by the fact that remains of a baby skeleton were found within the walls of Edinburgh Castle in the Eighteenth Century. And that my dear friend is one of the components that our researcher here is looking to confirm."

"How?" Alex almost spluttered.

"As I mentioned this file contains a number of scanned letters, a whole series of them. They are purportedly written by Mary Queen of Scots and Mary Seton, who was one of the Four Maries, all ladies in waiting to Mary Queen of Scots and all called Mary. It was Mary Seton who never married and remained faithful to the Queen throughout her life. She was the most loyal of companions and in the end Mary Queen of Scots almost had to send her away to retire. Now there are a lot of stories abound that Mary Queen of Scots was subjected to rape, even by Bothwell himself. Mind you if so he got his just rewards. He was eventually imprisoned in Denmark and chained to a pillar half his height so that he could not stand upright. He remained there crouching in the dark for ten years and died insane," Harris's booming laugh sounded again.

"And anyway," Alex was beginning to lose patience and wanted to get to the point.

"The thing is that there are many records of letters written by Mary Queen of Scots and what we have on this disk is a collection of letters that have only been written between the Queen and Mary Seton. These letters from the bits I have read give account of how Mary Seton herself was raped and fell pregnant. According to the narrative both Maries were pregnant at the same time. According to this letter on the screen, Mary Queen of Scots did in fact have a still birth and Mary Seton gave birth to a healthy boy on the same day. The statement loud and clear is that James I was not of Royal birth. If these letters are authentic and are to be believed, Mary Queen of Scots bonded with young James as if he was her own and always kept his real mother by her side for as long as was possible."

"So where have these letters come from?" Alex was stunned.

"They were found very recently secreted in a small chapel in Rhiems, France. Mary Seton retired to a convent there and it would appear kept and hid the letters between her and her mistress, which were written whenever the two were apart. The recent discovery of some documents in Rhiems has been quite highly publicised recently. The esteemed Historian Raymond Hilliard was meant to be researching them but then as if by some stroke of nature a fire ravaged the chapel in which they were still kept and the documents were supposedly destroyed."

"Raymond Hilliard," Alex almost shouted, "Fuck." He pulled out Nick Ford's address book, "that's the name in Ford's book. He's based in Edinburgh."

"That will be him, all tying up eh? And just how convenient was that fire?" Harris was really in his element.

"So these letters could be forgeries," Alex deduced.

"Could be but as I say enough to challenge people's thinking because historically it all fits, "Alex clicked up another of the scanned letters. "And now for the second part of the jigsaw and how Sophie Devine fits into all this."

Alex nodded for Harris to continue.

"In June 1567, Mary and her followers were defeated by the Protestants in a totally one-sided affair known as the battle of Carberry Hill. The Queen was imprisoned at Leven Castle and that had a lot to do with her marriage to Bothwell. He fled and she was supposedly pregnant with his child or children I should say, twins in fact. History tells us that they were still born and hastily buried on the island of Lochleven. Shortly afterwards Mary escaped and eventually fled to England where she was later executed in 1587. All fine and dandy of course but our correspondence here talks of the twins surviving and that the whole miscarriage story was just to protect them. From what I read here it was Mary Seton that arranged the safe passage and protection of the children, smuggling them from Leven Castle. It would make sense that such a secret was only shared between the two Maries. There was certainly no mention of this in any of the letters she famously wrote during her imprisonment, so if it's true she played it out extremely well. In fact one of those letters has just sold on EBay of all bloody places for some two thousand pounds."

"I must admit that I can't make head nor tail of the writing," Alex stared intently at the letter showing on Harris's screen.

Harry roared with laughter once more, "young man, although the writing is very neat and clear copperplate it is also in Latin. Mary was known to write in Latin but mostly corresponded in French. I am fluent in Latin, see it is signed 'Tie Virtulis Amica' which means Your Virtuous Friend and then simply Mary R. Also this letter bears the infamous Queen's seal. All looks bloody kosher but let's do a comparison." Harris pulled out another piece of paper which was a scan of a similar looking letter. "This was an actual letter written by Mary Queen of Scots to the President of the Privy Council in 1557. It is also in Latin and bloody well identical in every detail bar what it says. Harris held the scanned original up against the letter on the screen. "The problem is that as far as I know there are no existing letters written by Mary Seton so our friends are on to a winner. Nothing to say it wasn't her."

"So to sum up we are saying that all the recent events and I mean murders are all linked to stopping a newspaper exclusive being rumbled before it can be officially announced." Alex was extremely scornful.

"On the face of it yes," Harris smirked knowingly, "although I think I may have spotted something that might just be the Achilles Heel to all this. It is that I believe they are looking to protect."

"What is it?" Alex asked sharply.

Harris clicked on to a second family tree on the computer. "If we look at this diagram it is all focused on one specific area and that being any distant relatives of Mary Seton. As we know, Mary never married or supposedly had any children but our researchers have meticulously looked at any close ties, no matter how seemingly insignificant. For such a major revelation no chances can be taken that even the smallest detail might find them out. And of great interest to us is that they have noted that all modern relatives of the Seton family have been unearthed and discounted as non-threats. That is all but one; at the bottom of the page our friends have, at the time of print, failed to find one Marie-Claire Magne. She is reportedly a distant relation to Mary Seton via one of Mary's cousins, and they seem awfully concerned about her if the footnote is anything to go by."

"So Marie-Claire whatever is the key that can bring all this crashing down," Alex was still perplexed. "I mean it's hardly bloody obvious to someone like me or Martin Gardner so why not just let it go."

"Well their rationale and concern is proven by the fact that you now know and I reckon if they are still coming after you they are yet to find the elusive Mademoiselle Magne," Harris expressively drummed his hands on the desk.

"And what do you think she knows?" Alex asked curiously.

"Maybe nothing but they can't take that chance," Harris got up quickly, "why don't we pop along and see the illustrious Raymond Hilliard and pump him for information."

"What in Edinburgh?" Alex grimaced.

"Oh no, our famous history professor just happens to be in London for a lecture he's due to deliver tonight. He's staying at the Dorchester." Harris was full of enthusiasm.

As Harris led Alex towards the front door, the Assassin had pulled up outside in a black mini. He peered through the side window and made out the white plaque that marked Brian Harris's Genealogy business. This was the place described by Jameson's Receptionist, and she seemed pretty sure that the mystery client had made his way here. The Assassin was just about to get out of his car when the front door to the Genealogy practice opened and a man matching Harris's description stepped out closely followed by another, who the Assassin could not yet see clearly through the overgrown garden bushes. The two men walked down to a small adjoining garage and Harris flung open the rusting metallic door. He then moved inside and started up a very old brown Austin Allegro. As the car pulled forward the passenger turned around before jumping in. The Assassin was given a clear view, it was Alex Hart. As the Allegro moved on down the road, leaving a thick cloud of exhaust fumes in its wake, the Assassin shifted the black mini into an instant pursuit.

"So do you know this Raymond Hilliard very well?" Alex was already feeling queasy from the bumpy ride offered by a combination of Harris's driving and the Allegro's dubious suspension.

"Yeah, you get to know most of the guys on the circuit. Quiet and unassuming bloke really although I seem to remember tearing into him last time we spoke." Harris missed fourth gear with a crunch.

"Figures," Alex had Harris marked as impatient and very fiery. "So with this whole re-writing of history thing, do you think they can really get away with it?"

"Why not, they would by no means be the first. Hollywood does it all the time," Harris swerved the car away just in time from a jutted curb. "Take a look at good old Captain Bligh and the Mutiny on the Bounty for instance. Bligh was actually one of the best and most considerate seafarers of his day but with relatives of the mutineers finding eventual favour in Tinsel Town, history was totally re-written for the masses. Most modern audiences truly believe that Jon Bon Jovi really captured the Enigma machine during the Second World War. The truth is far duller but no less heroic, so there you have it."

"So who did capture the Enigma machine?" Alex asked, "I mean I know it was not Jon Bon Jovi but it was the Americans."

"I rest my case," Harris looked annoyed, "and take bloody note that it was the Royal Navy young man."

The traffic lights ahead were just turning from green to amber and so Harris looked to accelerate on through but somehow stalled the car instead. There was an immediate impact jolt from the car behind.

"Oh blast," Harris spluttered.

Alex looked out through the back windscreen, "I don't think there will be any damage. It was just a mini; I'll get out and take a quick look."

As Alex got out of the car he instinctively smiled at the driver of the black mini before reeling in shock. He instantly recognised the driver as the man who had thrown him off Darcot Bridge.

"Drive," Alex jumped back into the car and screamed at Harris, who did as ordered and sped through the red light whilst swerving to avoid the oncoming traffic. The black mini followed quickly behind.

Alex looked anxiously over his shoulder as the Assassin stayed in close pursuit, "have we really got any chance of getting away? And how the bloody hell did the git know I was with you?"

"On the first point, it is very difficult to say. I guess we need a stroke of luck," Harris clung tightly to the square steering wheel as the Allegro struggled to maintain a decent speed as it weaved amongst the midday London traffic. "On the second point, I would say that Jameson dobbed you in. Sort of confirms his guilt wouldn't you say."

Alex semi closed his eyes as Harris swerved to fractionally miss a group of tourists crossing the road. Up ahead a large delivery lorry was backing out of a side street causing Harris to initially slow the car down. "This could be our stroke of luck," Harris yelled, "hang on to your hat."

Alex was momentarily baffled as Harris pushed hard on the accelerator and screeched the Allegro up to sixty mph. The lorry was now blocking half the road and still reversing whilst the driver's companion directed the traffic to stop. Alex clung tightly to his seat with both hands as the realisation of Harris's plan became very clear, "Brian you'll never make it, don't risk it," he screamed.

Harris was oblivious to any doubts and maintained the Allegro's strained speed as the lorry moved closer to blocking the entire road. As the speeding car approached, the man directing the traffic shouted and gesticulated for Harris to stop. Just as it looked as if the Allegro was about to plough straight in to the back of the lorry, Harris spun the steering wheel vigorously and took the passenger side wheels on to the curb of a very narrow pavement before accelerating hard once more. A loud crack resounded as the Allegro's wing mirror snapped off after hitting the lorry's tailgate. Somehow Harris managed to squeeze the car through before it could be crushed up against the wall by the vastly bigger and heavier goods vehicle. In his wake the Assassin had no choice but to stab hard at the brake pedal and utilise every ounce of the ABS capability as the Mini came to a screeching halt. It did so with inches to spare as the lorry finally blocked off the entire road.

"Oh yes," Harris cried out with elated joy, "that was incredible. I feel like that Indiana Jones chap."

Alex took a deep breath and checked over his shoulder once more to ensure that the Assassin had not renewed the chase. "Looks like we've definitely lost him. Now what?"

"On to the Dorchester young man and our chat with Raymond Hilliard. I can't wait to find out more and we're not too far away now." Harris began whistling and irritated Alex's already strained nerves.

47

Julie Ingram sat nervously waiting in the Yokel pub constantly sipping at a glass of chilled sparkling mineral water. She had felt a wave of paranoia all morning since the discovery of Nick Ford's illicit office. Ingram had left the IBEX complex early in order to take a non-direct route to the Yokel and thus ensure she was not followed on her way to the lunchtime rendezvous with DI Parker. Now she was sat in the mainly empty lounge bar and Parker was already twenty minutes late. Ingram was starting to fear the worst for the supposedly disgraced policeman and starting to question why she was getting involved and putting herself at risk.

"Mrs Ingram, sorry I'm late," DI Parker's suave dulcet tone broke Ingram from her semi trance.

"Oh please call me Julie," Ingram replied nervously, "can I get you a drink?"

"Let me get you one as it sounds like I owe you," Parker smiled warmly. Ingram did not challenge and Parker soon returned with another glass of mineral water and a pint of real ale. "So Julie, what have you found out?" Parker took a small sip from his beer.

"Let me show you," Ingram reached down to her briefcase and pulled out the file of papers copied in Nick Fords' office. "Take a look at these and let me know what you think."

Parker took the small collection of papers and began to peruse them. As he did so his mouth fell open in disbelief, "where did you get this information?"

"I kind of stole it, although I'm guessing it was already stolen from somewhere else. It was mostly on Nick Ford's computer and those photos, which I think you will notice show our elusive snoop and the now infamous blue Mazda, were in a file on his desk. Ford is basically our security system hacker and it obviously goes so much deeper, I mean he has a hideaway office within his own office. And why is he trying to bring you down if I'm reading this all correctly?" Ingram was now very animated.

"The answer lies in the Gardner and Howard case. Those boys died for a sinister reason," Parker remained calm. "My deduction is that they stumbled on something very big and were both killed as a result. I was obviously getting close to the truth and touched a raw nerve, hence why they want me out of the equation."

"And what about our snoop, where does she fit into all this?" Ingram jabbed at Jane Coker's picture.

"I think, like us, she was also on to them. And I can say with great certainty that her life is in grave danger," Parker was now very frank. "I also surmise that the fugitive journalist Alex Hart is also in the know and that's why they want him too."

"But it was the police that were after him surely," Ingram was puzzled. Parker sat back and sighed heavily, "would you believe that the police, and I mean our jolly local copper Sergeant Etheridge, are all involved in this conspiracy."

"But what is it? What are they protecting that is so valuable that people have been killed?" Ingram raised her voice in anger.

"That I don't know but I have a feeling that our two journalists may have a better idea and I am also guessing they are working together on this. I need to speak to them but I'm now officially on garden leave pending investigation."

"Now we know that they are somehow manipulating the evidence against you, I think we can reinstate the status quo if you have a good enough recollection of the actual events last year." Ingram pointed at the case notes that Ford was viewing.

"Well one thing I am is meticulous," Parker pulled up a briefcase, "in here are all my notes from the case which we can cross reference to the file you have gathered. That's the easy bit, but then how do we set the police records straight?"

Ingram smiled broadly, "oh I have a plan there too. Let's just say that I have some good contacts when it comes to computer whiz kids myself. And whatever Nick Ford can hack into then we will be able to as well."

48

Jane Coker was at first relieved to enter the House of Commons, feeling that she had reached a safe haven and a momentary reprieve from the chaotic recent events. Alex had sent her another short text that stated he was at a hotel waiting to see an Historian who could have all the answers. She could tell he was very excited about a lead but had no clue as to what he had actually found.

The tedium of the Junior Minister's address on renewable energy only drove Jane to mull over the situation with Arturo Tabb and The Globe, causing her to openly fret. The lack of questions from the other journalists in the room proved the stuck-up MP had bored his entire audience. Now Jane was relieved to get out of the place and make her lunchtime meeting with Paula. She just hoped that Paula would agree to help and more importantly not shop Jane and Alex to Tabb.

"Was that not the dullest thing you've ever been to in your life?" A chirpy male voice broke Jane's semi-trance.

"Um yeah, totally," Jane turned to be greeted by a buck toothed young hack.

"David Morgan, London Telegraph," the reporter pointed to his badge that clearly showed his name above an unflattering photograph.

"Jane Coker, The Globe," Jane replied politely.

"The Globe, so can we read anything into your presence vis-à-vis this amazing but currently confidential exclusive?" Morgan almost swaggered in excitement.

"Haven't got a clue," Jane was now keen to end the conversation.

"Well there's somebody you won't want to flash your badge at," Morgan pointed at a suave middle aged man in an expensive grey suit. "That's good old James Harkness, the housewives' favourite until your lot kicked him in the bollocks."

Jane's eyes lit up, "excuse me David but I do actually need to speak to Mister Harkness."

"Mind if I tag along?" Morgan went to follow Jane.

"Yes I do," Jane replied curtly and threw a menacing stare which caused Morgan to immediately back off.

"Mister Harkness," Jane called out quite meekly but loud enough to get the disgraced MP's attention. "Could you spare me a couple of minutes?"

James Harkness at first smiled sweetly before frowning as he spotted Jane's Globe press badge, "and why would I want to speak to you young lady? Your paper has done everything to destroy me."

"Because I know you were framed and I think we can help each other," Jane now spoke firmly and with more confidence. "And just by speaking to you I'm risking my own life," Jane looked cautiously at the people nearby.

Harkness hesitated for a moment, "very well we can use one of my old colleagues' office. I've always been a sucker for the ladies."

Harkness led Jane away from the main atrium towards a small side office. As he did so one of Arturo Tabb's henchmen huddled in a corner to make a call on a mobile phone to his employer.

The office was a small cramped and dusty room with hardly enough room to sit down. Harkness pulled aside two rickety old chairs after removing a pile of papers from each.

"Alright Jane Coker," Harkness read directly from Jane's badge, "what have you got to tell me?"

Jane gave a clear high level summary of the recent events in Dartcombe, including the information that she and Alex had discovered on Martin Gardner's disk which comprised particular focus on Harkness himself.

"Whoa," Harkness was stunned, "when you said you had something I did not really expect all this. I mean murder."

"I know, it's still all quite surreal to me too," Jane reflected, "and it's fair to say that my own life is in real danger. Tabb's already tried to have Alex killed."

"So this disk, do you really think that the files belong to The Mole? Do you know who he is?" Harkness was now really opening up.

"We are positive the files belong to The Mole and everything leads back to Tabb himself, but sadly no I don't know The Mole's actual identity." Jane shrugged with disappointment.

"Where is the disk now? Can I see it?" Harkness was extremely keen to move on the information that could clear his name.

"It's with my friend, Alex Hart, who as I mentioned is another journalist. We both think the murders are linked to a particular file on the disk that supports The Globe's forthcoming world exclusive. Alex is meeting some bigwig Historian this afternoon to try and solve what the file is all about. All I can really tell you is that it is something about the Royal Family." Jane could sense that Harkness was frustrated.

"Jane I need to see that disk. If I can clear my name it will mean I will have more power to solve all of this," Harkness stated with great sincerity.

"Can we meet later as I will need to get Alex to bring the disk over after his meeting with the Historian," Jane was sure she could trust Harkness.

"That will be fine; we can meet at my city apartment. I'll give you the address and it's just around the corner from here. I'll also give you my mobile number," Harkness was already reaching for a pen and a sheet of paper.

Jane felt a pang of caution as Harkness scribbled quickly, "Mister Harkness, if anybody saw you with me today…I'm concerned for your safety."

Harkness chuckled, "please call me James and funnily enough I have the perfect man in mind for my bodyguard. I'll introduce you later."

Jane took the sheet of paper from Harkness and secured it in her briefcase before nodding a goodbye, "I'll call you later."

Felling more assured, Jane strode purposefully back into the main atrium before almost walking headlong into a man.

"Careful my darling, I know I've got an irresistible body but did you really have to hunt me down to the House of Commons?"

Jane immediately recognised Harry the cocky sandwich boy from their earlier introduction at The Globe's offices. "What are you doing here?"

"Now that's not a nice greeting for a future lover," Harry continued with the smarm, "and as you ask the quality of my sandwiches gets me all the best gigs in town, including here."

"Very nice and well done, sorry I can't stop but I'm late for a lunch meeting," Jane looked at her watch before swiftly moving away, "bye."

"Sweet, bye darling," Harry pursed his lips as he admired Jane's swinging hips and shapely legs as she headed for the exit.

49

Alex Hart was feeling agitated as he paced up and down in the Dorchester reception area whilst in comparison Brian Harris was sat calmly nearby. The main reception desk had contacted Raymond Hilliard's room to inform him that two visitors had arrived but he appeared in no rush to welcome them up. After thirty minutes Alex's patience was beginning to wane as he contemplated the fact the Hilliard may have already alerted the Assassin and that he and Harris would soon be sitting ducks.

"Chomping at the bit aren't we," Harris found his young companion's nervous energy amusing. "Come on I think it's time we invited ourselves up to see Hilliard."

Harris leapt up from his chair and moved towards the main lift area as Alex followed quickly on his heels.

"We don't even know which floor he's on let alone which room," Alex pleaded as he followed Harris onto a lift.

"Observation is one of my key strengths young man and one thing I did observe was that the Receptionist selected the Concierge level when she called for Hilliard. We just need to get to that floor and then search out the bugger's room." Harris suddenly scowled as he realized that you needed to insert a specific key in order to reach the Concierge floor, "damn and blast." An elderly couple entered the lift prompting Alex and Harris to move to one side. With a great stroke of fortune the man stabbed a key into the Concierge slot, "which floor?" He asked politely.

"Oh the same," Harris replied whilst suppressing a chortle.

The couple did not question that their fellow lift occupants had no right to travel to the same privileged floor. Harris beckoned for the couple to leave first on reaching their destination before following them out on to a plush and expensively decorated landing. As the couple tottered over to their room Harris whispered, "well that's one we can rule out."

"Yeah great but what do we do now? Knock on every door until we find him?" Alex was still impatient for a quick fix.

"Correction, you knock on every door until we find him," Harris slapped Alex hard on the shoulder. "Hilliard knows me and will not answer if he spots me through the little peephole."

"What's my cover story?" Alex was still unsure.

"Just say you are checking if everything is OK with the room or something. You're the journalist so should be used to wheedling your way in." Harris pushed Alex towards the first door.

Alex played his role well as he knocked on several doors and portrayed a supposed Hotel Manager checking on the guests. Some rooms were unoccupied whilst the people who did answer the door were always keen to keep any conversation to a minimum.

"After my experience in Dartcombe hotels give me the creeps. Not sure if I'll even be able to stay in one again," Alex thought back to Stephen Howard's gruesome death before gently rapping another door with his knuckles. Harris did not reply as he stepped aside of the doorframe once more.

Alex could hear someone moving inside the room before the door slowly opened. A fat balding man in a T-shirt and jeans stood before him, "can I help you?"

Before Alex could speak, Harris had moved into view and pushed the man with some force back into the room before forcing him up against the wall, "Hilliard you twat, we need to talk."

"Subtle as ever Brian," Alex said under his breath before entering and closing the door behind him.

"What do you want Harris?" You're a bloody lunatic," Hilliard spoke breathlessly whilst turning a bright shade of red.

"Tell me about Rhiems and I mean tell me everything," Harris loosened his grip and allowed Hilliard some room to talk.

"Rhiems?" The request had taken Hilliard by surprise, "what about Rhiems?"

"The papers you were asked to review and authenticate in the chapel, what were they?" Harris spoke with restrained calmness.

"I don't understand why you're asking me this and why you deem it so important as to attack me in my hotel room to ask the bloody question." Hilliard was evasive whilst being much more assured, "you could have simply attended my lecture this evening and posed any question you like."

Harris gritted his teeth and squared up face-to-face with Hilliard once more, causing the much smaller man to cower. "Let me put something to you, the documents you were reviewing were apparently destroyed in a fire, correct?"

Hilliard nodded, "that is sadly correct and that is unfortunately the end of it. I was unable to complete my research effectively."

"Although I understand you were sensible enough to take copies of the documents that were found and those copies are now authenticated by your name alone." Harris was moving to the point.

Hilliard rolled his eyes in fear, "how do you know?…I mean who told you? Who is this man with you?"

"So we are getting somewhere," Harris stepped back again and did not introduce the watching Alex. "Let's just say I have seen the copies of the Rhiems documents. The copies either represent one of the greatest historical finds of all time or one of the greatest forgeries and con tricks. Which is it my friend?"

"Listen Harris, I don't like you but stay out of this as it could cost you your life," Hilliard was on the verge of tears as he visibly trembled.

"So it's the con trick then," Harris nodded as if it was formally confirmed.

"Just heed my warning," Hilliard made no denial.

"Don't worry about me as I think my friend and I are in deep enough. Just two questions; one, why are you involved in this and abusing your trusted position?"

"Just drop it," Hilliard was now shouting back, "as of Saturday I will be the most famous and renowned Historian in the world. Pitiful lecture tours will be a thing of the past. And no longer will I just be ignored as some insignificant dull swot. For Physics you think of Newton, for Biology you think of Darwin and now for History people will remember the name of Hilliard."

"But you are already renowned in your field, so what more do you have to prove?" Harris softened his voice.

"Because I want more, I want recognition in all quarters and to find the fame and notoriety I deserve," Hilliard now had a cocky swagger about him. "And believe me my friend there really is nothing you can do to stop me now."

"So I guess we can rule out just doing it for the money then," Harris seemed extremely disappointed as if the financial rewards would have added more credence. "But to quote Lucian, the famous Syrian philosopher, the true Historian should state the facts as they really occurred. You're going against that somewhat."

Hilliard did not reply but tried to move away.

"So I take it you've been working with Robert Jameson on putting this fiction together," Harris would not relent.

"Yes, although he really is in it for the money," Hilliard beamed an ugly toothy smile.

"Pity you have scruples Harris as you could have made a mint instead of dragging your heels in that backstreet practice of yours. And if it means anything I truly believe you're better at your job than Jameson, but as they say nice guys always finish second."

"I'm flattered," Harris replied insincerely as Alex continued to just listen and observe.

"So anyway thanks for coming to see me and please find your own way out," Hilliard beckoned towards the door.

"I still have another question," Harris moved back towards his foe, "what do you know about Marie-Claire Magne?"

The colour immediately drained from Hilliard's' face, "What? How do you know about her? Did Jameson spill the beans?"

"Touched a nerve eh?" Harris moved in for the kill, "well you've just confirmed Marie-Claire's importance. I'm going to find her Hilliard and destroy this whole ridiculous scam and you with it."

Harris now moved to leave, signalling for Alex to follow.

"You can't win Harris," Hilliard shouted in desperation, "even if you find her she may know nothing, and that's if you do find her as she's probably dead."

Harris ignored the shouts and flung open the door only to come face-to-face with the Assassin.

"It's him, it's the killer," Alex screamed as the Assassin's face contorted into an irritated scowl. Without hesitation Harris lurched forward and head butted the Assassin full in the face, sending him reeling before crashing to the floor outside on the landing.

"Run," Harris shouted and stormed off towards the stairwell with Alex close behind.

The Assassin rubbed his blooded nose and regained his senses before clambering up and setting off in pursuit. His anger was building by the second as he crashed down level after level of stairs, aware that his prey was noisily making headway a couple of floors below.

Alex kept up with Harris by relying on sheer nervous energy generated by the fact that the Assassin was not far behind. With relief he reached the basement floor and sprinted through the door kicked open by the rampaging Harris. Relentlessly Harris moved on down the corridor as the Assassin began to close the gap with the elusive pair now firmly in his sight. A few members of the kitchen staff flung themselves to one side of the corridor as the chase continued. Eventually Harris rushed into the kitchen itself, startling the large group of chefs in the process. Harris and Alex continued running down the middle of the large open plan kitchen as the Assassin followed in their wake. It was at that moment that the head chef picked up a large tray of expertly prepared starters only to be unceremoniously barged by the Assassin, causing all of the dishes to clatter on to the floor. The renowned fiery chef immediately reacted and leapt forward to rugby tackle the intruder, sending him crashing to the floor. Meanwhile Alex and Harris had made their escape out of the hotel and were sprinting towards the Allegro that was conveniently parked on a nearby side street.

The kitchen staff joined their head chef and surrounded the Assassin but were soon in retreat as he pulled out a gun and threatened to shoot. Whilst keeping the gun trained on the staff, the Assassin backed away before sprinting out of the kitchen. He kept running out into the street only to see Harris's Allegro speeding away. His own Mini was parked several blocks away.

50

Jane Coker did not bother checking back in at the office after returning from the House of Commons but instead rushed round to Luigi's, where she hoped Paula would still be patiently waiting. Jane had sent a text to say she was running late but had received no acknowledgement. It was therefore with relief that she entered the cozy café to instantly spot her grim looking buddy writer.

"Two more cappuccinos," Paula signalled over to the waitress without a hint of politeness as Jane approached.

"Thank you," Jane said warmly as she took a seat.

"So what's the story hotshot?" Paula vented her anger immediately, "what the fuck's going on?"

Jane took a deep breath as the waitress delivered two large frothing cappuccinos. "Right I'm going to tell you all I know and everything that's happened in the last twenty-four hours."

Paula's stony expression did not alter in the slightest as Jane recounted the events in Dartcombe, including the deaths of Martin Gardner and Stephen Howard and how she had become embroiled in a real life drama following a chance meeting with old flame Alex Hart.

"So you just happened to bump into this former shag of yours and hey presto you're Miss Marple." Paula snapped with extreme sarcasm.

"Listen Paula," Jane retorted gruffly as she decided to bin the nicey-nicey approach, "what I have told you are the facts and the main thing is that people have died all because of our illustrious employer."

"Fine, nice story," Paula shrugged, "good luck with bringing him down because I tell you what girl, you're going to need it."

"Paula we need your help," Jane returned to a soft and sincere tone. "Alex is piecing it all together in terms of this global exclusive and I've now secured support in high places, but you can get close to Tabb and help us bring him down."

"Like I say good luck," Paula got up to go, "until yesterday my life was very simple and then you come along and try to change the world. Well girl my life does not need changing so I'll leave it at that. I'll stay out of your way and make sure you don't drag me down with you. In fact after tonight I think it's best that you find somewhere else to stay. Either shack up with Alex whatshisface or make it up with the gym stud."

"Thanks Paula," Jane stared hard, "or should I say Tanya Davis?"

Paula's mouth fell open in shock and she immediately sat back down. "How...How do you know? Who are you really?"

"I'm exactly who you think I am," Jane placed a hand on Paula's arm to comfort her, "I only know about your past and your true identity through the files that The Mole kept on you for Tabb. It was all on Martin Gardner's disk, dossiers on all the staff and the media targets."

Paula shook her head in disbelief, "I just can't believe this is happening."

"Don't worry, your secret is always safe with me," Jane said reassuringly, "but if you can help me find out who The Mole is then you will also be free of Tabb as well. I'll make sure of that."

Paula sat silently and deep in thought for several minutes before standing once more, "can't do it, I'm sorry." She then almost ran out of the café.

"Damn, shit," Jane snarled to herself as the waitress approached with the bill.

As Paula walked back towards The Globe's offices, tears were streaming down her face. The memories of her past life and the trouble in Thailand were sharply ingrained in her mind as the shrill tone of her mobile phone rang out. Paula instantly recognised the personalised ring tone, it was Tabb.

"Three O'clock review, my office, wear no underwear," Tabb barked his monotone order before hanging up.

Paula closed her eyes in frustration. First of all the business with Jane and now she had been summoned to shag Tabb. This was turning out to be one shit day.

51

Julie Ingram had driven DI Parker to a remote village some forty miles south of The Yokel pub, having persuaded the cautious detective to leave his own car behind. Ingram had not given Parker any clues as to who they were going to visit although the suspended policeman had gathered from the lengthy phone call that their soon to be erstwhile host had taken a great deal of convincing to offer any assistance. Finally Ingram stopped the car on the outskirts of the very small village of Didkam.

"So where to now?" Parker enquired, "are we meeting someone here?"

"No, time to get out and stretch our legs," Ingram got out of the car and swiftly moved to open the boot. "Good job I always keep these battered old shoes in case of emergencies." Ingram swapped her stylish high heels for some mud splattered black ankle boots, "follow me."

Parker did as instructed and tailed behind Ingram as she made her way down a barely trodden mud path lined with thick bramble bushes on both sides. The thought momentarily crossed Parker's mind that he was being led into a trap and that Ingram was all part of the conspiracy. Despite his concern and general curiosity, Parker remained silent as the pair walked in single file for about half a mile. Finally they arrived at an old weather beaten six foot wooden gate, flanked and dwarfed by large leylandii bushes. Ingram pushed aside a stubborn branch and revealed an intricate intercom touch pad on which she immediately punched in a code.

"Come on in and I'll put the kettle on," a young cocky male voice shouted before an electronic buzzer sounded and the wooden gate swung open. Ingram moved on through closely followed by Parker as he glanced around trying to make sense of his surroundings. The bang of the gate as it shut behind him made Parker jolt as his frayed nerves kicked in. On the other side of the gate was a path that led straight to a bungalow. Leylandii once again flanked the path all the way up to the building, casting the long narrow garden into darkness. Ingram made her way confidently down the path and entered the bungalow.

From the outside the bungalow had the appearance of an old age pensioner's house but inside it was modern in the extreme. The white walls and minimalist furniture presented a clinical space age feel.

"Jules my dear it's been a long time," a young ginger haired man wearing bright red rimmed glasses and an army camouflage shirt and trousers appeared in the doorway of a side room. Parker thought that he could be no more than twenty years old.

"Hi Edgar, thank you for this," Ingram gave the strange looking geek a big hug.

"And I take it this is the Rozzer who's career I'm going to save," Edgar held out a hand which Parker shook without speaking.

"This is Detective Inspector Jack Parker," Ingram did the introduction.

"Whatever," Edgar huffed, "let's get down to business." He turned on his heels and led his guests over to a large, and consistently very white, room furnished with a white desk that ran the entire length of the main facing wall. The desk was covered in computer screens. Edgar jumped into a wide black chair set on four small wheels and instantly glided down the laminate floor to the other end of the room, where he nonchalantly punched with precision onto a convenient keyboard.

"So what have you got for me?" Edgar swivelled back round with great enthusiasm.

Ingram put her briefcase up on the desk and pulled out a large wad of paper, which included the files printed from Nick Ford's computer and Parker's own notes on the Anderson case.

"I don't want to seem ungrateful or come across as paranoid but can someone please explain what the plan is here?" Parker was feeling decidedly uneasy. Edgar rocked his head back and laughed, "so Jules what do you want to tell Mr Plod? I'm prepared to bet money that computers are not his bag."

"And you'd win that bet," Parker confirmed instantaneously, "I'm still a pen and paper on the beat copper, and always will be."

"Jack, I'll make this brief," Ingram leant back on the desk resting on her hands. "The people who have conspired to bring you down by sullying your name have done so by using and manipulating technology. In plain terms they can hack their way into any system at will and stack the odds in their favour. Now the evidence purports that Nick Ford is the main man and instigator in this regard. Ford may be crap at many things but when it comes to computers he's basically a genius. The powers behind whatever conspiracy or plot is going on are using Ford for his system access and expertise. You were getting close to them and so Ford was told to bring you down. He subsequently hacked into the right systems to make you look dishonest, or bent. Meanwhile he would have had other contacts ready to tee up the so called wrongly accused, i.e. Jess Anderson or most likely her friends and relatives. They would have been presented with some new evidence that supposedly had just come to light and advised how they could use it to their advantage and make you the fall guy in the process. Anyone who reads a story or hears a news item about a miscarriage of justice can be very quick to judge. You have already been condemned in most households as guilty; I even made that judgement myself at first."

"Simple as that," Parker was dumbfounded and a little shaken.

"Simple as that," Ingram echoed, "and you see Martin Gardner's skill was also in computers. I am guessing that he died because of this and he most likely stumbled on something he was not meant to see. Most likely through hacking and I told you when you first came to IBEX that we suspected Martin was up to no good. He may have then shared some information with Stephen Howard, his best friend, which signed Stephen's death warrant as well. Stephen was not as capable with computers. It would be very interesting to find out what Martin found and what the wider picture is but the first thing is to clear your name. That's where Edgar comes in."

"Da da," Edgar made a grandeur trumpet sound as he held his arms aloft.

"If you take what Ford can do on a computer and add it to Martin Gardner's expertise, you will still come nowhere near this man's genius." Ingram gushed as she pointed straight at Edgar.

"Oh you build me up too much," Edgar said mockingly before adding, "actually no you don't. I am really that good."

"Yes and you've never been modest with it," Ingram blew an imaginary kiss at Edgar.

"How do you two know each other?" Parker enquired.

"Through IBEX, where else," Ingram replied as though it should have been obvious. "Edgar used to be a programmer there and it soon became obvious that he was way in advance of any of his colleagues. Like a lot of guys with his particular skill set he used to play around on the system and we are talking IBEX's own system. It was mainly initiating various juvenile practical jokes at others expense, like altering pay slips by inflating them by millions or reducing them to pence or issuing P45's, etcetera etcetera. Real rib tickling stuff but that's how he came to my attention. Unlike a lot of the computer geeks that come before me, I actually liked Edgar. There was something infectious about him. So I gave him some careers advice on how to use his skills more productively and contacts in the technology community. He got out of IBEX in no time and is now best described as an Internet entrepreneur.

"So you've made money from illegal hacking?" Parker did not disguise his law abiding disappointment.

Edgar once again laughed loudly, "no not at all. My business is completely legit and above board. I just make the best use of the Internet to buy and sell goods because there is a huge global market out there. I was even listed in The Sunday Globe's top fifty young entrepreneurs. Let's just say I do surf my way around different sites and systems to gather information which assists my business endeavours, but purely supply and demand you understand. I'm also known to still play the odd practical joke as well, depending on my mood. The recent panic over the Great British chocolate shortage was one of mine."

"So what can you do to help me?" Parker was starting to feel more at ease.

"Well let's start by you talking me through what all these papers are about," Edgar thumbed through the two piles on the desk as placed by Ingram.

"The pile on the left is a set of documents taken from Nick Ford's office this morning that depicts altered and fabricated evidence against Jack. The pile on the right is the true account of events as recorded by Jack, with pen and paper of course, at the time." Ingram cast a wry smile towards Parker.

"And what are the key elements that differ?" Edgar speed read some of Nick Ford's documents, "where's the main concentration?"

"Jack," Ingram prompted for Parker to answer.

"Having read the new fictional account and compared it to my own notes, there are now two key and damning suppositions that turn the case on its head. Quite rightly if this had been fact then Anderson would never have been convicted. But this is not fact and here's the proof." Parker leant over two piles of paper and cross-referenced the conflicting reports, "number one and most absurdly there is an accusation that I purchased and planted the murder weapon. The new account suggests they have a statement from some shopkeeper and receipt of a knife registration entry. I mean I would have to be completely dumb to go through this process to plant evidence."

"Absurd but damning," Edgar confirmed.

"My notes reference the fact that I found the knife in the presence of two officers and that we followed routine in bagging and tagging prior to forensics," Parker ran a finger along his own notes. "Now number two relates to a supposed concrete alibi, which was known to me at the time but my notes confirm this was easily dismissed as the female in question, one Dot Matthews, was proven to be lying and was not in Jess Anderson's company at any time during the whole evening on which the murder took place."

"So let's take these in order," Edgar swung back to face his computer. "If we take a look at the Knife Registry, an obscure database that few shopkeepers actually use but the purpose is to record the sale of dangerous sharp knives in case they are subsequently used to maim or kill. It sort of absolves the shopkeeper of any negligence. Now this conscientious shopkeeper reckons he sold such a weapon to you but has only just twigged that it was related to a murder case and has come up with a receipt of sale dated two days after the murder. Now of course this is easy to falsify and would not stand up on its own so it would basically come down to your word against his. The crunch comes with our knife database as supposedly you can only make an entry on the day of purchase and not retrospectively as there is a protected audit trail. If we look here at the entry made by our erstwhile shopkeeper it clearly records selling a knife to a policemen by the name of Jack Parker on May Fifth, Two Thousand and Six."

Parker looked over at the computer screen to see a picture of a knife identical to the one he found in Jess Anderson's flat alongside the handwritten entry of Parker's name, address and occupation. "How did you get into this database so readily?"

"Piece of piss," Edgar scoffed, "but as a man of the law it's best you stay in ignorance. But the thing is that our man Nick Ford would have entered the same site with the same consummate ease and voila we have this incriminating evidence against you."

"Can you just remove it?" Parker almost pleaded.

"Well," Edgar paused as he tapped away at the keyboard, "I have a better idea to show this up for the ludicrous plot that it is. Give me a few seconds." Both Ingram and Parker watched intently as Edgar moved swiftly between several different websites and search engines across multiple computer screens before dramatically thumping a final key and stopping. "Done, what do you think?"

Parker moved even closer to the main screen and could see straight away that the principle picture of the murder weapon had been replaced by a photograph of a child's plastic toy sword and the description had been amended within the type label to reflect the same.

"So what will this prove?" Parker did not get the joke.

"It will prove that the whole substance of point one is unfounded and show up your accusers to be amateur cheating bastards." Edgar looked very pleased with himself, "when they present their evidence under Knife Registry reference six nine seven one, it will be proven to be for a plastic toy. They will not be able to amend it or add another entry as I've put in my own protection for that whole week. Point one will now be thrown out as a farce and the prosecution, if that's what they are, will now be discredited."

"Very nice, I like it," Ingram nodded in appreciation.

"And what about point two?" Parker was less impressed and would rather have just seen the entry erased all together.

"For point two you say that the so called alibi, Dot Matthews, was not with Anderson all evening. Where was she then?" Edgar said sternly.

Parker exhaled loudly, "Dot Matthews was a well know local Tom, sorry prostitute. We know she was working the street all night and had the CCTV footage to prove it."

"Lets' have a look at that footage then," Edgar again manipulated his computer keyboard with consummate ease and skill. Within a few minutes he brought up a CCTV archive database, "at which town and street did our Tom work?"

"Rose Street in Carnbourne, which is on the other side of town from Jess Anderson's flat. You need to look for May Third last year from around nine pm, the rough time of the murder." Parker was now almost blasé about Edgar's ability to hack into any site he wanted.

Within a few minutes Edgar brought up the footage of Rose Street as requested. The street was well lit by numerous lampposts and the pavements were crowded with local prostitutes. Every so often the camera would pan in on a small group, clearly picking out their faces. "So which one's our Dot?" Edgar beckoned for Parker to come closer.

"None of them," Parker replied instantly in shock, "but that's just not right. I remember viewing the film very vividly. Matthews was clearly identified and she does not get a pick up until about ten fifteen, she wasn't the prettiest on the block."

Edgar wound the film on until ten fifteen at which point Parker once again shook his head. "Still no Dot but this just can't be. I even got two officers to verify as shown in my notes."

"They can easily suggest you conned the two officers somehow. Oh Jack my boy how nice it must be to have so much ignorance of the power of modern technology," Edgar looked up at the DI like a mocking child. "Once again our cyber raiders have used a simple technique. Basically they pasted a loop from another evening when our Dot was not working the streets and repackaged it as the film for the night of the murder. To put it right I can simply find another loop for another night with Dot very much present and prominent and use the very same technique."

"But that will be a false record," Parker sounded affronted.

"But so is what is already there and at least ours is closer to the truth," Edgar was beginning to lose patience.

Parker just nodded in reply before quietly assisting Edgar in finding suitable footage of Dot Matthews to transfer. She walked the street most nights and so it did not take long to find appropriate film that also fitted the required timing relative to the prostitute being present at the time of the murder. Once again Edgar expertly transposed a new record over the incriminating one before adding his own editing protection.

"Where did Dot Claim to be when she was supposedly with Anderson at the time of the murder?" Edgar was not finished.

"According to the notes from Nick Ford she was at the pictures watching a Hugh Grant flick," Parker shrugged as if it was now inconsequential.

"Which Cinema and which street?" Edgar pressed further.

"The Carnbourne Odeon on Canal Street," Parker read directly from the notes.

Edgar again moved through the CCTV archives until he found footage of the cinema on the night in question. He fast forwarded through the film up to early evening and asked Parker to keep an eye out for Matthews and Anderson. Sure enough they both appeared at seven thirty and joined a queue for the eight o'clock showing.

"This is crazy," Parker was now laughing nervously, "I take it that this is using the same trick as before?"

"Oh yes and if we push it on to about eleven when the film would end, voila," Edgar pointed to the two friends exiting amongst a larger crowd. "Our dynamic duo obviously had a night out prior to the fateful day and our hackers have utilised the footage. Probably swapped it of course and I will now do the same within a few minutes." Edgar once again corrected the evidence against Parker, ensuring he adjusted the constant date stamps in the process.

"So Jack my man, you can now clear your name. Just get your lawyer to counter their claims with our own new evidence and you're back on the beat whilst Anderson stays in jail."

"Thank you," Parker said softly with muted admiration, "this has all been rather unusual but I appreciate what you have done within a world I think I will never fully understand or ever really want to be part of."

"No worries my man," Edgar stood up and gave Parker a playful slap on the back, "but don't thank me as I can really do all that with my eyes closed. Thank Jules here as she persuaded me to help you."

"Yes thank you Julie, I really am indebted to you," Parker turned towards the pretty Personnel Manager.

"Don't mention it," Ingram blushed.

"You two should get it on. Cup of char before you go?" Edgar moved out of the room leaving his guests to face an awkward silent moment.

52

Alex Hart was looking forward to getting some fresh air as he endured another journey across London in Brian Harris's old banger of an Allegro. After escaping the clutches of The Assassin once again, Alex's natural instinct was to keep on running but he knew he had a duty to himself and to Jane, who he had embroiled in the whole saga, to see it through. Harris himself seemed completely unfazed by the recent turn of events and was extremely determined to resolve the missing link to the Genealogy puzzle. In doing so he would discredit both Robert Jameson and Raymond Hilliard and that would make Harris's life complete.

After ensuring that The Assassin's black Mini was not on their tail, Harris had stated categorically that he was going to head for the National Archive Centre down in Richmond. He felt sure he could find the answer to the whereabouts of the elusive Marie-Claire Magne and succeed where Jameson had obviously failed.

Harris's confidence rubbed off on Alex, although he was pleased that even the bullish Genealogist was not stupid enough to head back to his own office to continue the research. As they had made their way slowly and uncomfortably down to the National Archive Centre, Alex made a call to Jane Coker to fill her in on the full facts he had learned as well as recent events. Jane sounded pleased without being ecstatic at Alex's success in unearthing the secret of Martin Gardner's disk, although she ultimately seemed more concerned about the safety of her work colleague, Paula Davenport. More alarmingly Jane did not feel comfortable in returning to The Globe's offices and had decided to call in sick. Instead she had arranged to meet a friend who was a Television Journalist at the International Broadcasting Corporation (IBC). Jane needed to talk to someone she could trust and who could in due course help her. It would also bide time prior to her meeting with former MP James Harkness and whilst Alex hopefully finalised the evidence to gatecrash Tabb's world exclusive. Alex agreed to call again once Harris had concluded his research and they would all meet up with Harkness that evening to plot the next move.

"Of course we can get most of the info held here on-line, but this place is like a cathedral to me. This is what it is all about," Harris enthusiastically strode towards the main entrance of the National Archive Centre.

"I'm not questioning your undoubted skills as a Genealogist but do you really think we can succeed?" Alex tried to keep up with the long striding Harris. "I mean it seems really odd that Tabb with all the resources at his fingertips has not been able to trace this girl, who ultimately may be of no significance anyway. Is there any chance that the authorities are already protecting her, which would hopefully foil Tabb anyway?"

"As I say to my clients, until you look you just don't know what's there." Harris charged through the revolving door spinning the glass panes behind him so fast that Alex had to pause before following.

Harris swiftly strode across the reception area with the occasional nodded greeting to passers-by that he obviously knew.

"Hello Brian, long time no see," a middle aged frumpy Receptionist almost gushed.

"Doreen, any length of time without seeing you is a tragedy in my book," Harris replied jovially. "Any chance I could grab the terminal for some research?"

"Well," Doreen checked her computer, "You know that the terminal to which I think you are referring is not meant for general use. You really should have booked ahead for a standard booth and the waiting time is currently about two hours."

"I've just remembered that I promised you that meal at La Gondola. Are you free at seven-thirty this Saturday?" Harris leant on the counter and looked amorously at the very plain looking woman with her hair in an old fashioned bun.

"Oh yes," Doreen sighed, "and terminal sixty-five is all yours as usual. I'll expect your call to confirm for Saturday."

Harris blew a kiss and led a slightly gob smacked Alex away.

"So you're a smooth old sod on the side," Alex was bemused, "a pin-up to Librarians the length and breadth of the country no doubt."

"There is life beyond Genealogy you know," Harris grunted as he almost brushed people aside in make a beeline for terminal sixty-five. It turned out that this was a strategic terminal for staff use only but Doreen had pulled some strings.

"Right let the hunter see the rabbit," Harris sat down and stretched his fingers like a concert pianist preparing to deliver a virtuoso performance.

Alex pulled up a chair as Harris logged on. After requesting and inserting the Gardner disk, Harris quickly began trawling through the various public records within the archive database. Now and again he would cross reference to Robert Jameson's records and the new Royal Family Tree. "A black coffee would be nice, four sugars. There's a machine around the corner," Harris did not take his eyes of the screen.

Alex happily obliged as he could add no value to the seemingly tedious search. He took his time in collecting the coffee to allow Harris some space in which to work. When Alex eventually returned it was to the sight of Harris thumping the desk in frustration. He sussed that all was not going well.

"No joy I take it," Alex handed over the thick black and overly sweet coffee.

"You take it right," Harris grunted, "the fact is that I can follow the path the crook Jameson has taken but I'm hitting the same bloody brick wall and it makes no bloody sense."

"Show me," Alex was intrigued.

"Right well it's very easy to track the tree up to the birth of our elusive Marie-Claire Magne as the donkey work has already been done by Jameson. Despite the very French name she was actually born in Aberdeen, Scotland. This place houses all the central records for England and Wales but the beauty of this particular terminal is that it has access rights all over Europe."

"So if she was born in Scotland, how do you know she's not still there or is that too simple?" Alex asked with some trepidation.

Harris stopped and looked straight at Alex like a teacher about to chastise a pupil for giving the wrong answer. "Another simple lesson for you. You will hopefully be familiar with the process of Census, well in Scotland this happens every ten years and the last was in Two Thousand and One. Our Marie-Claire Magne was born in Nineteen-Fifty Seven, the offspring of Laurent Magne and Sally O'Brien. The Nineteen Sixty One Census shows Mister Magne was involved in shipping, hence his presence in a foreign land. For romantic reasons let's assume that Laurent met and fell in love with local shop girl Sally. At the time of their marriage Laurent was the last of a particular hereditary line drawn back to Mary Seton's beloved brother, George. The Magne family remained in their family home right through to the deaths of Laurent in Nineteen Seventy Five and Sally, who died only last year in Two Thousand and Six. Marie-Claire was their only child. Their presence end eventual deaths are recorded publicly for all to see. Everything also fits with Marie-Claire, who is clearly shown as being resident with her mum and dad until the Census of Nineteen Eighty One. She would have been Twenty-Four and you would expect her to leave home by then but there is no clue as to what happened to her. Certainly no records of her death, of marriage, of emigrating or moving within the United Kingdom. This lady simply vanishes."

"Maybe she was murdered by her father?" was the only suggestion that Alex could muster.

"Maybe and that would make sense in some ways. I mean she has never been shown to have been reported as a missing person or to have changed her name by deed poll. Mind you if the father had killed her surely the mother would have eventually shopped him after his death, which would have also created a record somewhere." Harris rubbed his chin thoughtfully.

"Then I really have no clue," Alex was still surprised that his murder suggestion was even given serious thought.

"We need to take a good look at events in Aberdeen between the Censuses of Nineteen Seventy One and Nineteen Eighty One to see if we can find any clues as to what happened to our missing girl." Harris appeared almost beaten, "it's the last hope."

Alex felt deflated and tired, "we need to hook up with my friend. She has arranged a meeting with an MP or at least he used to be. He wants to see the disk and may be able to help us."

"A helpful politician," Harris sneered, "well there is a first time for everything."

53

Paula Davenport was still inwardly seething as she made her way up in the lift to see Arturo Tabb for her appointment. A regular rendezvous that reduced Paula to the level of common Call Girl, or at least an expensive Escort as she would make herself believe. And Paula always got through it and reaped the rewards both financially and with her ultimate freedom. Then along came Jane Coker, who in two days had turned Paula's world upside down and now she had real concern for her immediate future. It was not just for herself that she feared but also the life of her protégé, the young vibrant and confident girl who reminded Paula so much of herself. That was why Paula was seething, because she knew Jane was right and that she should have agreed to help. The fact that she had not had left Paula feeling more vulnerable and alone than ever before.

Paula trembled slightly as she took the walk down the long dark corridor up to Tabb's office. His PA sneered knowingly and Paula was positive the stuck up little cow knew the score.

"Mister Tabb is expecting you," the PA announced condescendingly, "I will ensure you are not disturbed."

Paula did not look the woman in the eye but instead shakily knocked on the door before entering. The office was in semi darkness as per standard, with Tabb sat behind his desk engaged in a telephone conversation. He cupped his hand over the mouthpiece and simply said "sit" like a master ordering his pet to obey. Paula knew what was expected and took a seat directly opposite

Tabb. As she did so he increased the brightness of the lamp on his desk to illuminate the surrounding area. Paula was in the spotlight. Delicately she uncrossed her long bare legs from beneath a micro short white skirt. As instructed she was wearing no underwear ready to perform Tabb's favourite scene from Basic Instinct. As Tabb continued to conduct his business call, Paula was expected to cross and uncross her legs slowly several times. On each occasion Tabb would grin and simultaneously drool as he looked directly up Paula's skirt. Before she had almost laughed the ritual off but today Paula was openly nervous and continuing to tremble. Finally Tabb finished his call with a gruff and barked order to some unfortunate employee.

"You seem different," Tabb finally took his eyes away from scanning up and down Paula's long legs, "like a frightened mouse."

"I…," Paula almost gagged due to an incredibly dry throat, "I'm not feeling too well."

"No problem, I shall make it quick," Tabb stood up without showing any sympathy, "take your skirt off and bend over the desk."

Paula did as she was told, bracing herself firmly on the desk whilst her legs continued to shake. She heard Tabb move up from behind before feeling the sudden thrust of his penis as he took her roughly from behind. He then violently began to shag as he banged Paula's weak and helpless body against the desk. She was consenting because she had no choice but this felt like rape. Paula would normally blot out the ordeal but today Tabb was rougher than ever before and her eyes welled with tears.

Thankfully Tabb was true to his word and the whole sordid event was soon over. Paula remained bent over the desk for several minutes to compose herself as Tabb redressed.

"You can go now," Tabb said gruffly, "I have an important meeting."

Paula turned around and did not look at Tabb as he mercifully dimmed the lights once more. Paula put her skirt back on and simply headed for the door.

"Just one thing," Tabb's voice reverberated out from behind his desk, "what do you think of Jane Coker?"

Paula stopped and took a deep breath before turning to face her boss, "great, she seems very capable."

"Good," Tabb said simply, "find out more about her. Find her weak point, her skeleton…you follow?"

Paula knew exactly what Tabb was after and decided there and then that she had to get Jane to quit. She had to get Jane away from Tabb's clutches and it was now the time for Paula to run too.

Paula walked back down towards the lift being careful to avoid any conversation with the smug PA. Just as she went to press the button to call the lift it arrived anyway and the doors slid open. Harry the Sandwich Boy walked out.

"Hell darling, where's the usual pretty smile?" the chirpy Cockney winked. "Need me to show you a good time and cheer you up? Just say the word and I'll be there as Michael Jackson once sang."

"You're alright Harry," Paula managed a smile at Harry's persistent cheek. "But thanks anyway. What are you doing up here?"

"The old boy loves my sandwiches too you know," Harry nodded towards Tabb's office. "A special delivery."

"Very good, see you soon," Paula stepped into the lift.

"Sweet," Harry replied just before the doors promptly shut.

Paula's mind was suddenly in a spin triggered by Harry's parting words. She tried in vain to dismiss the very notion but her instinct would not let go. When Paula had inadvertently spoken to The Mole she had agonised on the fact that she had recognised something in the voice. "Sweet," he had swiftly said. "Sweet," Harry had said in exactly the same way and the very same voice. Tabb had said he had an important meeting and yet it was the Sandwich Boy who had turned up and noticeably without any sandwiches. Just who exactly was the real Harry?

The lift doors opened and Paula moved quickly back to her desk. Excitedly she searched for a piece of paper with Jane's mobile number on it. Jane had handed it to Paula earlier and now she had no idea where she had put it.

"Shit," Paula snapped at herself whilst trying to remember what she had done with the note. Finally she remembered scrunching the paper and throwing it in the bin. Paula emptied the contents of the small waste bin on to Jane's desk and rummaged through until she found the screwed up purple notelet. Triumphantly she picked up Jane's desk phone and called.

"Jane listen to me as I need to be quick," Paula spluttered breathlessly, "I know who he is, I know who The Mole is. I need to meet you, say my flat at six o'clock but tell nobody else; I repeat keep this to yourself. Jane this is mind-blowing and ridiculous. All I will say is you were right, he is a creep." Paula rang off before Jane could question her further and allowed herself a satisfied smile.

Up in Tabb's office, Harry was sat facing the Globe's fearsome owner minus his usual constant chirpy grin.

"I tell you it's in the bag; we've done it, pulled off the big one. I had my doubts but we did it. This weekend the world will finally accept that there is nothing that Arturo Tabb cannot achieve. Your place in history is assured by altering history itself and the whole fabric of British society." Harry spoke with a calmer, more serious but ultimately familiar Cockney accent.

"I don't like loose ends and we still have loose ends," Tabb retained a grim air.

"Nah," Harry laughed dismissively, "just some chancer local hack with nine lives I grant you. But at the end of the day who's going to help him? A bearded eccentric buffoon who has no chance of tracking down our elusive

Scottish descendant. If Jameson could not do it then nobody will find the binty believe me."

Tabb sat in stony silence and opened his eyes wide, "I would still prefer it if The Assassin completed his job but we must now move forward. The world awaits and expects our exclusive on Saturday. To not deliver would make me a laughing stock. I will give the green light for The Shadow Team to move south tomorrow."

Just as Harry went to speak Tabb's phone rang. He responded by selecting the speaker option, "tell me."

"Mister Tabb," an officious voice resounded out of the speaker, "we bugged Miss Coker's telephone as you requested. A few minutes ago we picked up a conversation that you will want to hear."

"Continue," Tabb looked back over at Harry with brusque concern.

"OK," the man on the phone replied, "although I must stress that the call is not instigated by Miss Coker herself."

After a slight pause Paula Davenport's voice came through the speaker as Tabb and Harry listened to a replay of Paula's recent revelation that she knew The Mole's true identity. As the tape ended Tabb instantly rang off before dialling out. "Listen carefully, I have another job for you. You must not fail you follow?"

The Assassin sat in his black Mini parked outside of Brian Harris's house, "I follow" he said as he listened to his orders through a Blue Tooth headset before starting up the car and driving away.

54

"You look like you've just seen a ghost," IBC reporter Clare Johnson scrutinized her friend's reaction after she had received a phone call. The pair were sat on a park bench enjoying the mid-afternoon sun.

"Yeah, something like that," Jane Coker was slightly dumbstruck after taking the hurried and garbled call from Paula Davenport.

"So what's going on? What's happening in the life of the always resplendent and interesting Jane Coker?" Clare pressed cheekily, "the girl who always finishes on top."

"Oh that's not true," Jane quickly conceded.

"Oh yes it is," Clare responded again in typical pantomime fashion, "let's think back to college. Student of the year…Jane Coker; Most Original Dissertation… Jane Coker; Top exam results…Jane Coker. You even won the bloody annual table tennis tournament and whipped the guys at pool. And who else could take a couple of years out and then land a job a job at The Globe, the UK's top newspaper."

"I'm just lucky sometimes, or at least I was. Not sure if The Globe job has turned out to be the golden nugget you might think it is." Jane looked on glumly.

"Well you certainly don't seem to be the normal bubbly Jane I remember," Clare moved closer to her friend, "what's wrong?"

Jane suddenly felt very tearful and wiped her moist eyes with her sleeve, "sorry…so much has happened recently and I've just had to keep moving along. It's all just caught up with me."

"Is it man trouble? Are you still with that hunky gym guy?" Clare quizzed.

"Josh, no we've recently split up but that's not the problem," Jane tried to recover her composure.

"Pregnant?" Clare sat agog in anticipation.

"No," Jane snapped back angrily, "I'm caught up in something and it is really big. Although it did start with an old flame of sorts. Do you remember that writer's conference a few years ago up in Birmingham. We all got really pissed on Tequila and I got off with a good looking trainee journalist called Alex."

Clare thought back momentarily, "that's right, you got paralytic and went all the way didn't you. Again you get a shag and I pulled the guy who threw up the moment he walked into my hotel room. I still to this day cannot believe he regurgitated that much chilli, I mean there was enough to feed the entire conference."

"Anyway," Jane stated with marked irritation, "I met up with Alex again by chance a couple of days ago. I was researching a feature with my buddy writer at The Globe. Her name is Paula Davenport and that's who just called me."

"So what's happened?" Clare dropped the jokey and chatty persona.

"In short it's all to do with the world exclusive that The Globe will announce on Saturday. All I will tell you at the moment is that people have died so others could protect the story. Alex is a local journalist who became embroiled in a situation and ultimately due to our chance meeting I am also up to my neck in it." Jane shrugged as she waited for her friend's reaction.

"As a friend I'm very concerned right now and as a journalist I'm bloody intrigued," Clare grasped Jane's hand tight to offer support, "go on."

"I will fill you in on the world exclusive once I have all the definite facts. Alex is currently working on the finer points and we are going to need your help to expose this whole damn mess. I think it's safe to say that my position at The Globe is no longer assured." Jane spoke with more self-confidence, "what do you know about Arturo Tabb and The Mole?"

"The Untouchable and his man of mystery," Clare responded immediately, "we call Tabb the Untouchable at the IBC because he looks and acts like Al Capone. Think of the Robert De Niro portrayal in The Untouchables and he thinks he is just that…untouchable."

"I get the point and it sounds like this is not a new subject to you," Jane was intrigued, "and don't forget that Al Capone was eventually brought to justice. Tax evasion proved to be his Achilles heel and Tabb must have a similar weak point somewhere."

"He may well have but you need to be able to get close enough to find it. At the IBC we're not allowed to go anywhere near investigating him or even criticising him. He's just too powerful and with too much influence in high places, even the satire shows are told to lay off. He even seems to know when something might be targeted at him and somehow steps in before it happens. Tabb has some kind of hold over the IBC but I don't know how or through whom," Clare slumped back on the bench. "Do you mind if I eat something, I'm starving and have not stopped all day." Clare pulled out a tuna mayonnaise baguette in a paper bag wrapping. Down the side of the bag was written Harry's Sandwiches.

"Carry on," Jane was feeling hungry herself, "Harry's Sandwiches, that's' the firm that delivers to The Globe. A real cocky sod that runs it."

"You've met Harry alright," Clare chuckled as she wiped some mayonnaise from her top lip, "he's got it tied up really. Fronts his own business with a very exclusive franchise, delivering to just a few select companies in London. He must have a very good and dedicated team making the sandwiches and he just sticks to the sales. They're bloody nice though."

"Anyway we digress. If I was able to bring down Tabb and expose The Mole in the process, would you be able to run the story?" Jane almost pleaded. Clare thought for a couple of minutes, "yes I'll find a way. I'm a bloody journalist after all. This could ruin me but at the same time it could make me. I have to take the risk."

"Thank you," Jane almost whispered,"

"No problem, life was getting dull anyway which can never be the case when you're around. Now come on let's go and grab a coffee, we're sitting here like it's the middle of summer." Clare pulled her coat together as the sky clouded over and the temperature dropped sharply.

55

Within a short time of facing a ruined career and a potential jail sentence, DI Parker's life was suddenly on the up. After meeting the extrovert Edgar, who had nonchalantly revised the evidence against Parker as if just flicking a light switch, the suspended policeman was easily persuaded by his new companion, Julie Ingram, to her join her for dinner. It was true that her fifteen year old son would be present and the venue would be Ingram's own house but the fact was that she had proven to be a single parent and wanted to cook for Parker. He had liked her since the first time they had met but dared not think that their relationship could develop to another level. Instead Parker maintained a purely professional attitude at all times and ensured he did not contemplate any other type of rapport that would lead to him dropping his guard and showing emotion. The fact was that it was getting more difficult with every moment he spent in her company.

Parker had never married and after passing his Fortieth birthday resigned himself to the fact that he never would. Like a lot of single focussed coppers he was married to the job, spending every waking hour concentring on whatever case he was working on. It had all been too much for the very few women in his life and sadly the force had always won the day when Parker had been forced to choose his priority. Parker loved being a policeman, especially a detective. It was all he had ever wanted but now he had been slapped in the face for simply doing a good job. Parker would certainly have been left out to dry if it had not been for Julie Ingram.

"Did you get through?" Ingram asked as she laid the table in a small pristine dining room.

"Yes," Parker confirmed as he sat down having returned from making a phone call. "Anderson's lawyers have stated they will present the evidence to the CPS at eleven o'clock tomorrow morning."

"That's good, why don't I open up a bottle of wine and make up the spare room. You will have plenty of time to go home and change in the morning and I would imagine you could do with some company," Ingram seemed elated.

"Yes as long as you don't mind," Parker felt like a teenager who had been asked out on a date. "I mean how can I ever repay you, you've saved my career and given me support when I was totally out on my own."

"Just don't slag off my cooking," Ingram shouted as she moved across the room to select a bottle of Merlot.

"Don't worry, I'll do it for you," Ingram's son shouted from the lounge, where he was watching TV.

Parker could not help but snigger, "I promise to keep my comments to a minimum but I'm sure it will be fantastic."

"How did you bring up the fact that you could counter the Anderson claims tomorrow?" Ingram poured out two glasses of wine.

"You know me by now, too honest for my own good. I just levelled with Graham Stone the force lawyer that I had been made aware of what was going to be presented but could not reveal how. He laughed and said it was about bloody time that I played the game. He's going to prepare to counter with the corrected records as designed by our friend Edgar. Of course I did not mention any of that," Parker relaxed as the effects of the wine kicked in immediately.

"Good for you, cheers and here's to tomorrow and the future," Ingram raised her glass.

"Don't suppose I can have one?" Ingram's son interrupted the moment.

"Half a glass Peter if you leave us alone," Ingram responded, "what are you watching?"

"The news," Peter collected a glass.

"That's a first, so what's so interesting on the news?" Ingram looked totally surprised.

"It's all about this big announcement coming on Saturday by some newspaper. They keep showing clips of that big fat rich guy who looks like a gangster. They reckon that they've got a UFO and caught some aliens. Well cool if it's true, the teachers have been talking about it at school." Peter moved back into the lounge.

"So there you go," Ingram said dismissively.

"Actually it is quite intriguing. I was watching the news this morning and the whole thing is causing a lot of speculation. Thankfully it dwarfed the press conference about my supposed corruption. And guess which newspaper it is…The Globe, employer of our snoop and the parent company and client of IBEX itself." Parker moved back into police mode.

"You don't think…" Ingram stopped dead.

"Julie, after today I am ready to consider anything."

56

Jane Coker's meeting with her long time friend Clare Johnson had given here a newfound resolve and inner strength. With Clare's position at the IBC there was now a real chance to blow the whole Arturo Tabb saga out into the open. And now Jane was hoping for the icing on the cake as Paula revealed The Mole's true identity. Jane was confident that it was all coming together at the right time and allowed herself a wry smile on the way to the tube station. The fact that Alex and his new Genealogy buddy had failed in their search for the missing link to disprove the fabricated family tree was of no immediate consequence. That evening Jane would hook up Alex and Harris with James Harkness and the serious plotting could begin. The end of Arturo Tabb and The Mole was surely in sight. Jane was already plotting the bestseller she would sell off the back of this adventure not to mention the speech upon receiving the Booker prize.

Jane arranged to meet Alex and Harris by the Houses of Parliament at eight-thirty without revealing her mission to meet Paula and solve a massive piece of the jigsaw. It was only when Jane passed on Harkness's telephone number, and told Alex to call him directly if she should not show up at eight-thirty, that the nerves began to kick in again. What if Tabb had got to Paula and Jane was walking headlong into a trap?

The final call before heading underground to catch the train was to Harkness himself, during which Jane explained her plan to bring together the key conspirators. Harkness was grateful at the chance to view Martin Gardener's disk and to be able to hear the first hand account of the underlying Tabb plot. This was tempered with the former MP's perceptiveness as he questioned Jane as to why she could not meet any earlier. It did not take much pressing for Jane to confess that she had a rendezvous with Paula and would soon know The Mole's identity. Harkness insisted that he would be there to pick Jane up after the meeting and took down the address. Jane gave the impression that she was parting with the information reluctantly but deep inside she had a great sense of relief that there was now an escape route if the whole thing did turn out to be a trap. Despite supposedly betraying her friend's confidence Jane at least now had a form of safety net. To approach it any other way could just be plain suicide.

As Jane rode the underground she was overcome by paranoia, viewing every single passenger in her vicinity with caution and mistrust. At least whilst she was sat in the carriage there was some comfort in the confined public space. It was when she had to change lines that Jane's heart really raced with the effects of nervous adrenalin as she scurried along constantly checking over her shoulder. On the platform itself Jane stood well clear of the edge, conscious of the fact the she could become an easy target and a familiar Underground statistic as a short sharp push would catapult her in front of an oncoming train. Just like the suicide victim that Paula had reported on earlier that week. Jane questioned in her mind whether the girl was really a suicide victim at all. She had no concept of what to believe in any more. And to top it all every station and linking walkway had posters of all sizes advertising Tabb's biography, I Am The News. It felt like he was watching her every move.

The tube journey to South London seemed to last an age but a check of the watch confirmed that Jane was on time for her meeting with Paula. She was grateful that Spring was around the corner and that the long Winter evenings had gone to be replaced by a prolonged afternoon blue sky. The sun had come out again and was shining brightly. If it had been any other way Jane would have waited for a cab but Paula's apartment was only around the corner and with an extremely long taxi queue she decided to walk.

It was when Jane reached Paula's plush apartment block that her rollercoaster nerves hit another peak. At first she looked up at the large lounge window hoping to see her friend waving to welcome. Instead there was nothing. Jane took a few steps forward and rang the intercom bell and almost instantly heard the click as the system activated but there was no welcoming voice. "Hi Paula it's me," Jane said timidly before the main door clicked open. There was not even a "come on up" to confirm to Jane that all was OK. She knew this did not feel right and every natural instinct was telling her to back away. Jane looked back down the street and plotted an immediate escape route in her mind before slowly pushing open the communal front door that gave initial access to the five penthouse apartments in the block. The expensively carpeted staircase was very well lit by a number of chandeliers which gave the courage for Jane to step inside, albeit tentatively. As she did so Jane heard a muffled scraping noise on the next floor; the same level as Paula's apartment.

"Paula are you there?" Jane shouted loudly, semi hoping to get the attention of a nosey neighbour in the process.

The question brought only a heavier and louder movement from the floor above. Jane moved over to the bottom of the staircase after wedging the front door open with a free ads paper that was lying on the floor.

"Paula are you OK?" Jane craned her neck to look up at the main landing and caught sight of a shadow illuminated by a bright ornate chandelier that hung nearby. The light from the multiple chains of bulbs dazzled Jane for a second and impulsively she went to rub her eyes. As she focussed back on the stairs it was just as a body came hurtling down towards her. With no time to move aside Jane instinctively put her hands up for protection only to be immediately hit with great force. Within a second she was on the floor with the body covering her. Jane felt a sharp pain rip through her back but found the strength to push the body to one side. Jane slowly stood up and looked down in absolute horror at the lifeless stricken body of Paula Davenport. A constant trickle of blood ran from the corner of Paula's blue lips as her head tilted at an obtuse angle. Her neck had been savagely broken.

Jane felt the urge to vomit over her dead friend as her eyes watered profusely. Abruptly Jane's own head was yanked backwards as two strong hands grabbed her from behind. Without a word the overpowering captor squeezed Jane's body into an all embracing lock and began to frogmarch her up the stairs, almost lifting her feet from the ground. Jane felt it become increasingly hard to breath and began to mentally prepare for the end. Any effort to wriggle free was proven to be futile against her captor's superior strength.

A rush of wind somehow swept up the stairs as the communal entrance door flew open. Thankfully the man's grip on Jane loosened as he turned in surprise. Almost immediately Jane was released altogether and she crumpled to the floor, falling down the few stairs that she had been forced to scale. As she tried to climb to her feet once more another man moved past her at speed and hit the captor with a mighty punch. Jane rubbed her sore neck and gasped for air as another figure moved over and embraced her. She swung round to see the friendly face of James Harkness. On the stairs stood a tall muscular black man with a familiar face. At his feet lay the prostrate unconscious figure of The Assassin.

"Jane Coker allow me to introduce you to Luis Carter, former Heavyweight champion of the world," Harkness announced as he propped up the distraught journalist.

"Pleased to meet you Jane, despite the circumstances," Luis said with a gentle voice and coupled with a sincere smile.

57

Arturo Tabb sat solemnly in his dimly lit office as his desk lamp emitted just enough light to highlight his stern features. The computer was logged off and the triple glazed windows and sound proofed walls ensured total silence. A single tear trickled down over Tabb's right cheek but he remained motionless, resisting the urge to wipe it away. Finally he reacted with a violent slam of his fist down on the heavy thick desk. It landed with a full blow and echoed with loud resonance. The target was a photograph taken of Jane Coker on her visit to the IBEX complex. Tabb picked up the picture of the pretty smiling blonde employee and screwed it up with real venom before throwing it with accuracy into a nearby wastepaper bin.

58

Jane Coker felt a shiver run down her spine as she was chauffeured back into the heart of London by James Harkness. She had barely spoken since being rescued from the hands of The Assassin after regressing to effects of severe shock after seeing Paula lying dead. Her cheery and friendly work colleague had been murdered violently and without mercy. The final image of her horror stricken face would haunt Jane for the rest of her life. Coupled with this was the fact that Jane was already experiencing survivor's guilt and the whole notion that she was to blame for Paula's death as if she had been the one to snap her neck and throw her over the balcony. Jane stared in a trance out of the passenger window in the front of Harkness's distinctive Jaguar. Behind her sat Luis Carter, her rescuer, who shyly and humbly remained silent to allow Jane some personal space to grieve.
"We'll soon be back at the apartment," Harkness spoke softly to break the silence, "you'll need to call your friends so they can meet us."
At first Jane did not move or reply but then slowly and tearfully she turned towards Harkness, "sure…and thanks. I owe you my life."
"Believe me you owe me nothing and it was Luis who ensured that you did not come to a grim end." Harkness glanced quickly back at the gentle giant of a boxer behind him, "just wished we could have saved your friend too."
"Yes," Luis said in a whisper, "this has been a horrible thing all round."
Jane turned to acknowledge, "thank you Luis, thank you so much."
"Luis is the bodyguard I mentioned earlier and I'm sure there is none better," Harkness tried to crack a smile, "And the thing is that Luis contacted me. The Globe, thanks to The Mole, had ruined his career as well as his life. And the thing about Luis is he is very smart as well as being a fighter, a boxer who has not had too many punches landed on him to destroy the old brain cells. So Luis decided to fight back but found this opponent to be too powerful. The more he tried to let the world know the truth, the more virulent the lies circulated by The Globe became. That's when he sought me out, realising

that I too had been a victim of the UK's number one newspaper. So far we have really only just been able to empathise with each other and made little headway in our fight. And then along came Jane Coker."

"So you're not a rapist or a barroom brawler?" Jane turned to face Luis head-on.

"Not at all," Luis shook his head in disgust at the suggestion, "I'm quite the sucker when it comes to a beautiful woman and The Globe has played on that. So much so that I have no trust in any women anymore. As for the brawl, I was attacked and forced to defend myself. But that's not how The Globe reported it."

"Shit…the bastards," Jane almost spat with real venom, "we have to bring them down, we have to."

Harkness drove on to meet up with Alex and Harris at an agreed location. After quick introductions and the initial shock of Alex meeting his former idol, Luis Carter, Harkness led Harris in his battered Allegro to the city apartment. Harris was forced to park his car in the street as Harkness could not gain him entry to the secure underground car park.

"So this is how politician's live eh?" Harris boomed as he walked into the luxurious and spacious two-bedroom apartment overlooking the Thames. "All paid for with taxpayer's money no doubt."

"As is the lesson for us all Brian, don't believe everything you read," Harkness spoke warmly, "make yourselves at home and I'll fix some drinks." Alex moved over to Jane who was standing by the window staring aimlessly down at the river, "are you OK?"

Jane did not answer but instead turned and instantly fell sobbing into Alex's arms.

"I'm afraid that Jane has had a terrible experience," Harkness announced as he returned with a tray holding a decanter of whiskey and several glasses. "I think we all need a shot of this."

Jane found the courage and voice to tell Alex what had happened. He shuddered at the thought of The Assassin trying to kill Jane and briefly recounted his own experiences at the hands of the hired killer, which on the last occasion had ended with Harris head butting him to the floor.

"Well Luis here also flattened him this evening so our man should have a very sore head," Harkness restrained a chuckle.

"Did you just leave him?" Alex was grateful for the kick of the whiskey as he drank whilst continuing to comfort Jane.

"Yes in a word, had to get out of there without any questions asked. He was flat out and so with luck the police will tie him up with Paula's murder." Harkness moved over to his computer, complete with nineteen inch monitor, "so does someone want to show me what we've got?"

"Over to you Brian," Alex handed Harris the disk, "you all better get ready for a history lesson."

Harris was in his element as he once again explained the theory behind the Genealogy plot.

"So if I'm understanding this correctly, Tabb is looking to discredit the current Royal Family by suggesting they have no real claim to the throne," Harkness rubbed his chin as he mulled over the facts. "But surely they have no real proof without the actual letters?"

"Ah but the power of suggestion is an amazing weapon if used properly and dressed up correctly," Harris almost shouted. "The facts are that some historical documents were found in Rhiems and they were analysed by Raymond Hilliard. Now this eminent Historian took copies of the documents and will testify they are genuine. They are of course master forgeries and the one thing that could have betrayed them was their age. Now no longer a problem as this concern went up in smoke with the rather convenient fire. So if you take the amazing find through the content of the letters, Hilliard's testimony and Jameson's power to manipulate family trees and then add Tabb's media power…well the Queen will no longer be sitting pretty on her throne."

"Sounds like they've left no stone unturned," Harkness was greatly concerned.

"Almost," Harris wagged his finger in the air and returned to demonstrate his theory on the computer screen by selecting the Seton family tree compiled by Jameson. "There's one thing that could destroy this otherwise meticulous plan and that's a missing girl. A descendant of the Seton family who may or may not hold the key to exposing the whole scam."

"Very tenuous though," Alex chipped, "the chances are that if she can be found it may be that she will be of no help at all."

"Except that…" Harris looked perplexed, "I think that they are aware of the existence of something, most likely other documents but genuine. Ultimately evidence that will destroy their plot and the fact that they cannot find it has caused panic. There has always been talk amongst Historians of enlightening letters written by Mary Queen of Scots, which is probably where they got the idea for this plot from. They have to ensure that Marie-Claire, our missing girl cannot produce such evidence. If you think about it, The Globe goes out to the world with its amazing exclusive on Saturday and then bang she comes out of hiding and brings the whole thing tumbling down."

"We can but hope," Jane finally spoke up, "we must find her."

Harkness busied himself in preparing the two bedrooms and large lounge sofa for his guests to comfortably spend the night. "I suggest a top and tail in the master bedroom whilst the guest room has two single beds. Jane. I think it best you have one of those and a discreet male of your choosing takes the other."

"I'll take the settee," Harris shouted without taking his eyes off the computer screen. "Reckon I'll be sat here most of the night so it will be easier for me to just crash out when I need to."

"I'd like Luis to take the other bed in my room," Jane said in an almost giggly voice, "it will make me feel safer with those muscles nearby."

"Looks like you and me for the top and tail then Alex," Harkness winked jokingly.

"Hang on a second," Alex spluttered with great indignation, "don't you think it would be wise if I slept in your room Jane. You don't even know this man and well what about his history with women?"

Luis stood up abruptly and solemnly stared at Alex before retreating to the kitchen to avoid any confrontation.

"You twat," Jane exploded before following after the former world champion boxer.

Alex went to go after her but was gently restrained from doing so by Harkness. "Best leave them be Alex. I'm guessing you have a soft spot for Jane and understandably so but the fact is that Luis is a good man who has been badly wronged. Don't let your feelings for Jane cloud your judgement of him. He's on our side."

"Obviously you need to learn a bit about dealing with the ladies young man," Harris laughed loudly. "Should take a leaf out of my book."

Harkness raised his eyebrows in mock derision, "come on let's go and order some food. You can square it up with Luis later."

Alex conceded with a slight nod before moving over to review a pile of takeaway menus.

"I'm really sorry about that. Alex was not thinking straight," Jane slowly moved over to a very grave looking Luis, who was pouring himself a glass of mineral water.

"Oh it's OK; I'm very used to most of the world thinking of me in that vein. I just have to make sure I somehow keep turning the other cheek and hope one day all this mess can be resolved." Luis sat down on a stool and rested his long arms on the high granite breakfast bar before beckoning for Jane to also sit down. "I do appreciate your vote of confidence, I mean picking to share a room with me to show that you do not believe the stories."

"You saved my life Luis and believe me I am a very good judge of character most of the time," Jane threw a warm smile. "Well ironically not really when it comes to picking men but that's another story."

"Me and women snap," Luis clicked his fingers in punctuation before offering and then pouring Jane a glass of water. "So what's the story with you and Alex? I take it he's not your man."

"No, although he is a nice guy but just impetuous. We do have an ancient history, but that's all it is," Jane stated with marked insistence.

"Not sure he sees it that way," Luis replied jovially.

"Yes well I can't worry about that now. If you don't mind me asking why do you think The Globe decided to ruin you?" Jane quickly moved the subject on.

"An easy target I guess. A guy who became too big for his boots. I went from your humble and gentle giant with a sweet innocent girlfriend to world heavyweight boxing champion with all the trappings that fame and fortune bring. I let down my childhood sweetheart big time and became a big time Charley, although in the public eye I was mister popularity. Attending all those parties and being invited on all those TV shows; it really did all go to my head. And then came all the Globe accusations and then prison and ruin. The only bright point from it all was that it gave me time to think and bring me back to good old humble boy next door Luis. Still have to right the wrong though." Luis shrugged.

"Mmm, hardly your average boy next door I would say," Jane bit her lower lip seductively.

Jane and Luis continued to sit chatting about their respective backgrounds until Harkness interrupted them when the takeaway food arrived.

"Look man, I'm sorry. That was very insensitive of me," Alex offered a handshake as Luis returned to the lounge.

"No problem," Luis grabbed his hand and yanked Alex towards him before embracing him in a big bear hug.

Alex was almost crushed within the giant fighter's arms. "Cheers, you used to be my bloody hero you know…in fact you still are."

After the food was eaten, Harris returned to his mission in trawling through the local news archives in Aberdeen. Both Alex and Harkness initially tried to offer assistance but instead only served to irritate the impatient and belligerent Harris. They instead retired to bed to get some much needed rest. Jane and Luis did likewise after Luis had chivalrously allowed Jane to settle herself down first. Harkness provided her with an old blue shirt by way of an improvised nightdress. Jane felt extremely comfortable in the soft expensive bed as Luis entered the semi dark bedroom.

"Excuse me madam, you may just want to avert your eyes as I'm very shy you know." Luis whispered.

"Of course," Jane obeyed and turned on to her side to face the wall before curiosity got the better of her and she glanced back over to see the muscle laden Luis stood within a ray of moonlight and dressed only in a small pair of underpants. Jane exhaled heavily as the view momentarily took her breath away before Luis jumped into bed.

It did not take Luis long to fall asleep but despite the extremely traumatic and tiring day Jane found that her brain was strangely wired. She could not switch off and go to sleep and so decided to give up the fight and see how Harris was getting on.

"Any joy?" Jane winced in the highly illuminated lounge as she approached Harris who was huddled at the computer terminal.

"Not really. Aberdeen sadly seems to be a very dull place when it comes to news stories." Harris glanced round to see Jane's shapely bare legs protruding from Harkness's blue shirt, which only just reached the top of her thighs. Underneath she was wearing a skimpy pair of white knickers. "Oh my dear are you trying to push my blood pressure through the roof?"

Jane giggled and moved next to the large bearded Genealogist, "so show me what sort of things you are looking at."

Harris was immediately softened and far more receptive to Jane than his previous male helpers. "I'm looking for something unusual in the news about a young woman that could help explain why our Marie-Claire has disappeared. The closest I have got it is an account of an unidentified body of a young female found floating in the harbour. The age and timing all fit but the question is if this is our girl why she was not reported missing or identified. And of course if it is our girl then bang goes our trump card."

"Could support Alex's theory if her parents had something to do with the death as macabre as that might be," Jane suggested. "You look totally shattered so why not let me take a look. Make us both a coffee and I will have a go. I am a trained researcher you know."

Harris offered no resistance and allowed the pretty blonde to take his place at the computer. As he went off to make the coffee Jane began reviewing various newspaper stories on-line with renewed zest.

Harris returned after a few minutes with two steaming mugs to find Jane looking curiously exited. "I think I may have something," she said simply causing Harris to quicken his step and almost spill both coffees in the process.

"Look, on August the fourteenth in nineteen eighty, which fits the timing of the disappearance of Marie-Claire, there was a big court case against a group of highly influential local gangsters. A sort of Scottish equivalent to the Krays by all accounts. The key prosecution witnesses were two girls both aged twenty-three, which also fits. Both girls were working as maids in a hotel and witnessed the Nutini brothers, our gangsters, kill a number of rivals. The brothers were sent down for life to Barlinnie jail whilst the girls were placed under a witness protection programme."

"My word that must be it," Harris dramatically slapped his thigh in triumph, "witness protection, new identities and you disappear off the face off the earth. That's the bloody explanation."

"Only problem is, how the hell do we find her if she's under witness protection?" Jane sighed in apparent defeat.

"Oh bugger," Harris said bluntly.

59

Royalty? Lucy's Just An Essex Girl – She's the newest and grandest
Royal, yet the woman who is to become the Duchess of Northumberland, and
who takes great pride in her blue blooded roots, is in fact an Essex girl with
ancestors who died as paupers. Months of painstaking research by top
Genealogist Robert Jameson has shown that Lucy Stillman's ancestors
include thieves, servants and chimney sweeps (Full Story Inside)

News reporter Clare Johnson tucked the Friday edition of The Globe under
her arm after allowing herself a wry smile at the front page column that
openly slated the latest young edition to Royal circles. Like many Brits, Clare
had not really taken to the pretentious airs and graces of the Duchess in
waiting, Lucy Stillman. That should put a different slant on her forthcoming
wedding she thought.
Clare re-focussed back on her meeting with Jane Coker the day before. She
pulled out her mobile to check for any texts or messages, but there were
none. Clare went to press speed dial for her friend's number but remembered
the express instruction not to call and that Jane would find a way of
contacting her. The waiting made Clare nervous. So much so that she nearly
relented on her two month abstinence from cigarettes. Sheer will power
dragged her past the small confectionary and tobacco kiosk in the IBC lobby.
 "How's my favourite news reporter then?" the chirpy welcome of Harry the
sandwich boy somehow took her by surprise.
"Harry, a bit early for you isn't it?" Clare said pleasantly.
"Very true my dear but I'm here on other business, know what I mean?"
Harry tapped the side of his nose with an index finger like an old fashioned
spiv.
 "Sure, might catch you later then," Clare hurried by waving as she went.
"Maybe and maybe not," Harry said quietly but sternly to himself.
After opting for a strong black Americano coffee, Clare rushed into the main
IBC newsroom and made a beeline for her desk. Despite the routine "hi's"
and "good mornings" from her colleagues, Clare somehow felt strangely
paranoid this morning. This was not helped by the unusual and eerie silence
around her as she sat down to read through the printed news articles on her
desk.
"Slow news day?" Clare finally shouted over to Darren Street, another
reporter.
"Yeah," Darren moaned, "although we do have a murder. A female reporter
at The Globe was found strangled in her apartment block last night."
Clare's blood ran cold, "what was her name?" She demanded.
"Paula…" Darren checked his notes, "Paula Davenport. Looks like she was a
bit of a fox from her press picture. A real shame."

Clare sighed in semi relief whilst instantly remembering that Paula Davenport was the name that Jane had given as her buddy writer at The Globe, "Any idea who killed her?"

"Nah," Darren rocked back in his chair, "police are keeping tight lipped at the moment and nobody has been arrested yet."

Clare's mind was a whir. What if Jane was also dead and they had not yet found her body. Surely she now had to make that call despite what Jane had said.

"Miss Johnson, can you spare some time in my office please." Colin Valentine the head of the news department was stood by Clare's desk and acting even more of an officious uptight prig than usual.

"Yeah sure," Clare got up and followed the rotund balding manager as the eyes of the newsroom pursued her.

60

On a clear bright day the Scottish Highlands fully bloomed to encapsulate the complete scenic beauty that stretched beyond the still lochs for as far as the eye could see. The contrasting colours of heather and thistles stood out against the shining brown weather-crafted rocks around the long stretches of blue water. Mary stared for several minutes at the breathtaking landscape from the side of a single track road that despite being manmade also blended in to form part of the aesthetic surroundings.

The order had come from London earlier that morning for the Shadow team to move the girl south to Edinburgh. Mary was then to continue by plane to London with the young arrogant woman in her care. At least the ordeal was now nearly over, although having to stop with a puncture to one of the Land Rover's front tyres only ten miles into the journey had proved highly frustrating. Nerves were frayed despite the light at the end of the tunnel for all concerned. The girl had bawled Mary out as if the puncture was her fault and so Mary had taken time out to enjoy the superb view that her homeland offered. Just another twenty-four hours thought Mary and then the girl would be someone else's problem. She would then take her well earned money, excessive as the amount was, and put it to good use. Mary had taken a great risk in accepting this job and would not be squandering the money on holidays and frivolity like the other members of the Shadow team. Her cause and reason was of the highest value and significance.

61

Jane Coker felt greatly reinvigorated as she took a hot shower in the luxury bathroom suite at James Harkness's Thames apartment. The events of the day before were still playing on her mind but were coupled with the determination to look positively to the future. Somehow the newly formed alliance she had brought together had to find a way to destroy Tabb. She owed that to Paula at the very least.

After her shower Jane had no option but to dress in the same clothes that she had worn previously. This instantly made her feel dirty despite the cleansing of her body under the soothing jet of water. She once again was reminded of and sensed the stench of death and despair that was so prominent in the immediate past. Her mind was made up, after breakfast she hoped to buy new clothes.

"Hi Jane, feeling better?" Harkness maintained a sunny disposition.

"Yes thanks," Jane replied whilst appearing downbeat.

"Brian has filled us in on your research last night," Harkness now frowned, "this is one hell of a barrier. Witness Protection is not something that can be penetrated. As you would expect they cover every angle to make sure that nobody can breach the system."

"Looks like Marie-Claire will remain hidden," Alex conceded. "And even if she sees The Globe exclusive she's not going to want to risk revealing her own identity. We did some checking on the Nutini brothers, very nasty and their family influence still runs deep today. There is no doubt that Marie-Claire's life is still under threat."

"All sounds a bit Hollywood to me, are you sure?" Jane was not convinced. The others glanced silently at each other as if there was more information. Harris finally spoke, "as Alex said I continued to look through the archives this morning. Six years ago a girl under Witness Protection made the mistake of attending her Grandmother's funeral. The next day she was murdered and the killer has never been traced. Her name was Tracy Stevens and come and take a look at this."

Jane followed Harris over to the computer. On the screen was a black and white picture of a school hockey team taken in the Nineteen Sixties. "I found this on a school website. The smiling dark haired young lady in the back row is Tracy Stevens and the pretty girl next to her is Marie Claire Magne."

"Oh my god," Jane slapped a hand across her mouth.

"Yes it looks like the two girls were inseparable school friends and of course this confirms that Marie-Claire must be the other girl under Witness Protection," Harris spoke softly.

"Poor girl," Jane shook her head, "having to lead an isolated life looking over her shoulder and all just for having the courage to be honest."

"Yes and of course we know that is where Marie-Claire is bound to stay," Harkness chipped in. "Jane we can still fight Tabb even if we can no longer ridicule the exclusive. One point of attack has to be The Mole himself. Is there anything that Paula said to you that could help unmask him?"

Jane sat down and thought hard, "well she clearly found out who he was but I do not know how. All she said was I was right about him and that he was a creep. This of course implies that I know him."

"So who did you think was a creep?" Alex asked simply.

"Most of the Globe male reporters to be honest," Jane shrugged, "although I don't think I singled out anyone to Paula with any real vitriol."

"Are you sure? Was there nobody who really got under your skin?" Harkness now pressed hard like a legal counsel quizzing a witness in court.

"Well Tabb himself obviously," Jane paused as she ran through the other reporters in her mind and her conversations with Paula. "Nobody else springs to mind apart from…no that would be ridiculous."

"Ridiculous can sometimes be the most plausible," Harkness said in support.

"Shit," the colour drained from Jane's face, "and now I think about it this really could fit. The guy turned up at the Commons yesterday and I know for a fact that he goes to the IBC as well. It's the perfect cover."

"Now you've got me really excited," Alex gesticulated for Jane to continue as Luis Carter sat silently observing.

"Harry…Harry the sandwich boy, although there's no disguising the fact that he's no boy, early thirties at least. I actually referred to him as a creep and it's crazy because he's the last person you would suspect and of course that makes for the perfect cover." Jane slumped back notably exhausted.

"Right it's time to do some research on Harry the sandwich boy," Harkness took a seat at the computer. "I always thought he was a cocky wide boy and now I know why he was always popping by for a chat on his rounds. He was casing me out as a Mole victim. Let's find out who he really is."

The others gathered around to watch as Harkness accessed a website called Johnson Infosource. He selected a free hour trial option given prior to the offer of taking up a subscription. The access then allowed him to check basic company records. Harkness typed in 'Harry's Sandwiches'.

"Let's see what we have then," Harkness speed read the single page of data in front of him. "The company is officially listed as Harry's Sandwich Services Limited. The Director is shown as one Gustav DeRuet," Harkness clicked on the Director's details, bringing up a short biography under an old passport style picture of a very serious looking grey haired man.

"Well that's certainly not Harry," Jane chipped in.

"No and this write-up tells us a great deal. It states that Gustav is acting as what is called a Ghost Director, which in layman's terms means his name is shown in a role for which he does no work at all. His real job is running a European media corporation out of Brussels. And the owner of that corporation is would you believe Arturo Tabb."

"So Tabb owns a sandwich business," Alex chuckled, "very rock and roll."

"Very clever," Harkness had moved back to the main company structure detail. "If you look at the next line of management we find more stooges acting in a ghost capacity. And so it goes on until we reach the so-called workers of which there are apparently two. A lady called Fiona Elliott in charge of catering and labelling, and from what I can gather her job is to order in food from an outside caterer and then label it. Finally we have a marketing and sales officer by the name of Oliver Vance."

"Are we saying that this is Harry?" Jane was stunned.

"There is no picture or biog but we can learn a great deal from the company financials," Harkness opened the respective financial records page and sat back open mouthed. "This is incredible, the company is running at a major loss. Last year sales equated to no more than ten grand, whilst expenses were over a million pounds. They offset the difference by profit funding from a sister company. If you take out the minimal figure for the purchase of the produce and it would seem that the wages for our workforce of two account for the rest of the expense. How nice to be paid nearly a million pounds a year to be a sandwich seller eh?"

"Can we find out more about Oliver Vance?" Alex stated earnestly.

"Allow me," Harris stepped forward as Harkness made way for him to control the computer. "Thankfully the name is not that common, assuming that it is not an alias. If we start with a Census search in the London area and see where it takes us. Now this is where you lot would hit a block as officially Census records can only be published if they are over one hundred years old, so it's lucky I know where to go unofficially so to speak"

Harris typed with great dexterity as he viewed various Census records at speed before finally honing in on one particular declaration. "I think this is our man, although Oliver is shown to be his middle name. This record is for a Thomas Oliver Vance born in Nineteen Seventy in Romford."

"So let's see if Mister Vance has a colourful history," Harkness nodded for Harris to continue.

Harris selected to check local news archives against Thomas Vance and it did not take him long to find a wealth of information. "Well it would seem that Tom has something of a past. The man is a master burglar with a high success rate in the East End running over many years. It would seem that he had a particular skill in breaking into the mansions of the wealthy, bypassing the most sophisticated alarm systems and cracking any safe to order. He was finally caught following a tip off and sentenced to five years in Maidstone Jail."

Harris brought up a local newspaper article on the court case, complete with a picture of Thomas Vance. It was very obviously a younger image of the man Jane knew as Harry, with only his much longer hair and younger features betraying any real difference.

"That's Harry the creep alright," Jane confirmed.

Harris continued his research and quickly arrived at more enlightening and valuable information, "now this ties it all together. Here's another article about a reformed character serving time in Maidstone jail, who used his time inside to study and pass many exams with distinction. The prisoner was Tom

Vance and his chosen subject was Computer Science. And to top it all the article appeared in The Globe."

"That's it then," Harkness uttered in triumph at solving the mystery. "Tabb must have read the article in his own newspaper and cooked up the notion of The Mole. With Vance's all round skills and a prestigious array of clientele, Tabb could gain access and manipulate at will. Whist every one tried to solve the mystery of the elusive and shadowy journalist, the cocky wide boy sandwich seller wore the perfect mask. But now we can remove it once and for all."

62

Clare Johnson did not have the look of someone fearful they were about to be sacked as she sat facing Mark Alford, head of News and Current Affairs as well as departmental manager, Colin Valentine. The two men opposite her in stark contrast had the grave look of an executioner about to deliver the final blow.

"Miss Johnson, I have to say that I am astounded by your attitude," Valentine blustered as his face turned a light shade of red. "To my mind the evidence is damning and you could at least have the common decency to show some professional decorum."

Alford took a more passive role, silently observing Clare's reaction as Valentine went through the accusations against her. On the desk in front of them were a number of printed emails supposedly sent by Clare to a contact at the Cooperative Television Network, CTN. The contents of the mails revealed detailed inside information on a number of key stories being investigated by the IBC's senior journalists. All were exclusive in nature and the divulging of the information would both seriously dilute the impact of the news items as well as giving potential competitive advantage to the IBC's main rival.

"Well I'm sorry if I seem so blasé Colin but excuse my French, it's all bollocks and if you can't see that well…that's nuts." Clare at last showed some fight.

Valentine went to reply aggressively but was halted by his superior Alford holding up a hand.

"Clare," Alford's serious frown softened into a smile as he took a more gentle approach. "If, as you say, this is all bollocks, why do you think anyone would want to set you up like this? I mean they have gone to amazing lengths to do so."

Clare sat back in her chair looking pensive as she pondered on her response. "It's difficult as I do know the reason; well at least I'm ninety-nine percent certain. The fact is that yesterday I was made aware through a source of a headline story. This source is also a journalist and is risking her life to uncover the truth. In fact she may already be dead and her evidence may have gone to the grave with her.”

“So this story that you have stumbled on,” Alford maintained a pleasant approach, “if the people or person it is targeting got wind of it, they would have the power and influence to frame you through forged email correspondence?”

“In a word yes,” Clare replied immediately.

Valentine snorted loudly and shook his head, readily dismissing Clare’s explanation as pure fiction.

“Why then did this source come to you?” Alford continued to take the lead, “with all due respect you are a junior and not very well known reporter. Why did this woman not contact a senior colleague if the story is so big?”

“Because,” Clare sighed heavily,” the woman is my best friend.”

“I’m sorry Mark but I have heard enough of this piffle,” Valentine could contain himself no longer. “You have been caught banged to rights young lady. In fact I’ve always had my doubts about you and the quality of your work. The truth is you knew that your career would be short lived here and so went after a quick buck, besmirching the good name of your employer in the process. The evidence is here in black and white and I’m sure your bank records will show that you received just reward if you want us to pursue that particular avenue. But I say let’s just cut the crap as I don’t want to listen to any more of this Jackanory. I’m giving you the chance to resign now and walk out with some dignity intact.”

Alford completely ignored Valentine’s rant and ultimatum, “Clare why do you think your friend’s life is in danger?”

“Because this morning I saw a news item on her buddy writer, a lady by the name of Paula Davenport, who was brutally murdered yesterday evening.” Clare looked intently at Alford with wide open eyes.

Alford exchanged glances before looking up at the ceiling as he considered what to do, “OK this is what’s going to happen.”

63

Jane Coker sat at the computer in James Harkness’s apartment. She was busily re-reading the encrypted word documents that she had spent the morning compiling. The first, written with Brian Harris’s assistance, had detailed the key facts behind the forthcoming Global exclusive on the Royal Family Tree. The second recorded all the pertinent details needed to unmask Thomas Vance, or Harry, as The Mole.

It was agreed by all to put together a written dossier of all the known details to at least prepare to steal Tabb’s thunder by telling the world what the exclusive was the day before it was announced. Their case could still not be essentially disproved but at least the impact would be diluted. On a secondary level it was now at least possible to reveal The Mole's identity to effectively end his career and continued web of lies and falsehoods.

The information was to be sent to Clare Johnson, Jane's friend and contact at the IBC. The proviso was that Clare could go live with the report that evening, allowing time for Jane and her alliance to either find a way of discrediting the fabricated plot or of linking Arturo Tabb directly to the recent murders. Both tasks were viewed as nigh on impossible due to the meticulous detail and planning afforded by Tabb to protect himself and the story. As Jane sat reading through the full extent of the research, the rest of the team philosophically discussed both what Tabb was about to achieve in running the story as well as trying to spot a potential flaw that could be exploited.

"With Tabb this is all some warped idea of fun, nothing more and nothing less," Harkness provided the summary. "It does not matter that he cannot produce the actual historical proof of the existence of the letters as he has set the framework to make people believe they are real. The public admire and love the whole ethos of Tabb and The Mole. His biography has been a bestseller for months and everyone looks to The Globe to expose all us rotten to the core public figures. So the forgeries are good, as Brian has attested, and he has expert backing that is unquestionable. By sowing the seed Tabb will create chaos and doubt in everyone's mind. Look at all the conspiracy theories that still roll on today from Roswell to the death of Princess Di. Time and time again the theories are discredited but they can never disprove. The most gullible believe Elvis is alive and kicking somewhere while millions read and quote the Da Vinci Code as pure fact."

"So you are saying that is does not matter that everyone believes the story?" Alex chipped in, "the objective is just to stir things up?"

"That's what Tabb is all about and what he does best," Harkness confirmed, " I actually read his biography out of curiosity where he freely admits to torturing small animals as a child to watch them suffer. He also constantly played his classmates against each other to create anarchy at every public school he attended. Now he's successfully destroyed the career of the likes of me and Luis by twisting reality at will. Now he's doing the same with history."

Luis sat nodding in silent agreement.

"And the only way to expose him is to prove him categorically wrong to the world and to do that we really need to produce the hard evidence, but when that evidence goes back over hundreds of years… well the haystack becomes enormous." Harris said dramatically. "They've got the hop on us and have seemingly covered every angle. All we have is an opinion and the chance to expose and destroy their man of mystery. Beyond that we move into the realms of libel with only one eventual winner."

Jane pressed 'send' to deliver the email to Clare Johnson, shuddering slightly as she did so. Both documents were encrypted separately to ensure that only

Clare would be able to read them. Jane had instructed Clare to think of her unusual pin-up choice from their University days. The idol of whom Clare had a large poster on her bedroom wall. Document one was opened by his christian name (Julian) and the second by his surname (Clarey)

64

"That's good news Jack, but of course totally expected," Julie Ingram was ecstatic as she took a phone call form DI Parker in her office at IBEX. "What was the reaction from Anderson's solicitors?"

"Total shock if I'm honest," Parker was calling on his mobile from outside Carnbourne police station where the hearing had been held. "The force lawyer played a blinder. He just calmly countered every bit of false evidence presented and made the whole meeting resemble some kind of stage farce. Anderson's lawyers soon realised that they were on a very sticky wicket and retracted the case against me. I've already been reinstated and the garden leave has been cancelled."

"So what now?" Ingram asked eagerly.

"I need to somehow take care of unfinished business. I cannot just let this lie," Parker spoke with real determination. "There's been a major development overnight. You know the snoop from The Globe who you uncovered at IBEX the other day, well last night she was apparently murdered. I say apparently as the thing is it's not actually her. I mean she is the owner of the blue Mazda and her name is Paula Davenport and she did work as a journalist at The Globe. But the photograph of the dead woman is not our snoop."

"So what does this all mean?" Ingram was intrigued.

"I'm guessing that the dead woman was working in partnership with the actual snoop. She must be a journalist at The Globe as well. The question is why had Paula Davenport been murdered and what does this mean for our snoop?" Parker spoke rhetorically.

"What are you going to do?" Ingram asked with notable concern.

"I'm heading to the train station now. I managed to convince my guv that there was local interest in the murder. Going to hook up with the Met and then see if I can track down the snoop." Parker started walking towards the train station, which was conveniently situated at the end of the road.

"Listen, be careful, you know what their people are capable of," Ingram spoke sincerely. "Give me a call later to let me know you are OK."

"I certainly will," Parker felt a strange sensation of someone genuinely caring for him. "And when I get back we must arrange a date for me to return the complement and cook you one of my infamous lasagnes. Peter will be invited too of course."

"Oh no we will pack him off with his mates somewhere," Ingram was overjoyed, "and invite accepted by the way."

Ingram placed the handset back on the receiver before holding both arms aloft in victory. "Yes," she shouted. Her mind was reeling with recent events as she immediately found it hard to concentrate on any mundane work tasks. Instead she got up and decided to take a walk and maybe take a coffee break. As Ingram strolled down the principal atrium she decided to continue past the open plan café. Curiosity had got the better of her and she decided on a whim to make an impromptu visit to see Nick Ford.

"Is he in?" Ingram almost shouted to Ford's PA as she strolled into her small annexed office.

"Yes…but," the PA had no time to effectively respond as Ingram gave a sharp knock to the door and let herself in to Ford's office.

Nick Ford was sat at his desk taking a phone call whilst his face betrayed extreme concern. "Yes that's taken as read; I will get to the bottom of this. I just don't know what could have gone wrong. Listen I need to go as I have a visitor." Ford promptly hung up.

"Bad news?" Ingram pointed at the phone as she tried not to gloat.

"Um…nothing that cannot be sorted," Ford instantaneously looked to change the subject. "So to what do I owe this honour Julie, I mean you could have just sent me a meeting invite."

"Listen, let's cut the niceties. You don't like me and the reason you don't like me is that I sussed you from the moment I first met you." Ingram leant forward on Ford's desk adopting an aggressive stance.

"Oh I'm sure we could get along," Ford tried to maintain a friendly and calm position, "so why the sudden openness? Have I done something to upset you?"

"Let's just say I know a little about your extra curricular activities," Ingram walked over to stand by the window. "So if I was you I would either watch my back for every second of the working day or I would ship out."

Ford was visibly stunned, "Julie if you are talking about what I think you are talking about then I have some advice for you. Stay well clear and do not under any circumstances stick your nose in or interfere. You are a mother with a son who needs you. Take no risks with things that are well out of your league and do not concern you."

"Are you threatening me?" Ingram turned back to face Ford straight on.

"No I'm just advising you. Do not get involved with me as there will be only one winner," Ford now stood up and pointed with severity at Ingram.

Ingram now felt vulnerable, "well maybe it's too late for you already, I mean your bosses can't be too happy that your latest little plan was foiled. Could be that I've already won."

"You stupid cow," Ford now snapped as he realised the significance of Ingram's confession, "You have no idea what you have got involved in, now stay well away or else I will destroy you, and yes that is a threat."

"Bye," Ingram waved contemptuously and threw a mocking grin. As she moved out of Ford's office and shut the door behind her, Ingram instantly regretted going to see Ford on impulse. She now thought of her son with real concern that she had endangered him.

Nick Ford sat back down at his desk and picked up the phone, "it's Ford, I have solved the mystery concerning DI Parker. We have a problem and I need guidance."

65

Arturo Tabb was keeping a very deliberate low profile. It really went against the very nature of the infamous tycoon who was now recognised the world over thanks to the power of his own media empire. Having teased the world with the prospect of his forthcoming exclusive, Tabb had taken up residence in his own office in The Globe building. Secreted behind a thick oak panelled wall was a small bedroom and en-suite bathroom. Whilst the rest of the world's media tried to second guess the full extent of the scoop that The Globe would announce at Saturday's glitzy press conference, Tabb sat back and waited and watched. He had played his final dice to bring his most daring game to a conclusion. To Tabb that was exactly what this whole affair was, a game. In his mind there could only ever be one winner. Tabb never lost at anything.

Tabb sat on an exquisite black leather sofa in his bijou bedroom flicking through all the news channels on the TV as the speculation grew to fever pitch. Every station headlined the item with Tabb's picture appearing on every newsroom backdrop. Journalists had tried and failed to track him down since Tabb had made his planned and very deliberate announcement at the Global Media Awards. His absence now simply added to the mystery and confused conjecture. Everything was going to plan. Tabb chuckled to himself like a child reacting to an immature joke as he considered the full impact his latest project would bring. At the very least it would introduce a conspiracy debate that would never be resolved. Beyond that Tabb had even made allowance for a split in the British monarchy and holding power over a new Scottish Queen. Only Arturo Tabb had the power to make that happen.

Tabb poured himself a small glass of cognac as he sat smirking and wallowing in assured victory. A loud buzzer interrupted the moment. Tabb pressed a button on an intercom speaker by his side, "tell me."

"Andrew Clark is here to see you Mister Tabb," the PA announced shakily.

"Send him in," Tabb replied without any pleasantries.

Tabb muted his television and headed back into his large and intimidating office. Andrew Clark was his very able Project Manager and the only person who was able to speak with Tabb that day. Tabb took his usual place behind his desk as Clark walked in. His name befitted his appearance as the man now standing before Tabb looked like a typical lowly stereotypical office clerk with a cheap suit, slicked back greasy hair and old fashioned thick rimmed glasses. To most, including Tabb, Clark was a slimeball with no morals or scruples. He would shop his best friend, even his family, for the right price and showed no compassion for anyone or anything. It was never worth playing any political games with Clark as that was his forte. He always won through by cunning and conniving. On top of it all his high degree of intelligence, photographic memory and attention to detail made him Tabb's perfect stooge.

"Tell me," Tabb barked his familiar welcome.

"OK Arturo, I'll start with the good news," Clark spoke cockily and was the only employee to dare address his boss by his first name. It always made Tabb cringe but he let it ride; it would soon be time to dispense with the services of Andrew Clark. This would be his final project and he would be considered a loose end if allowed to live. "The shadow team is on the move and is back on schedule to reach Edinburgh by late afternoon. The Assignment will arrive in London later this evening. Robert Jameson and Raymond Hilliard have both been fully briefed on their respective roles at tomorrow's press conference. They are word perfect. As an aside the little teaser with Jameson's name on it in today's Globe led to over a million Google hits, further substantiating his credentials. The conference room is already being prepared for tomorrow and the worldwide audience is expected to exceed one billion. The press packs have been compiled and bound by a small guarded and isolated team who will be kept in their secret location until Sunday. Delivery will be made overnight under the tightest security.

"Excellent," Tabb snarled, "and any concerns?"

"The bad news," Clark paused as he looked at Tabb for a reaction, "or let's call them annoying irritants. Firstly Nick Ford has raised a concern about a manager at IBEX. He feels that she may be a threat to him but not the project."

"Tell him to scare her off and to use the policeman. That's what he was signed up for, to protect the IBEX interest." Tabb spoke casually, "continue."

"Of greater concern, but no less fixable, we have tracked down the Genealogist's whereabouts. This is the one who had hooked up with Alex Hart, the local journalist from Dartcombe." Clark stopped as Tabb reached out for a file on his desk.

"Ah yes, Brian Harris," Tabb had picked up Harris's file, "he did concern me but Jameson has assured that there is no way he can find the missing link. I am also given surety that the likelihood of this elusive woman having the letters is more than slim. Their existence is purportedly on a par with the Holy Grail and even if they do exist and she has them then to come out in the open will cost her dearly. She cannot harm the project as we will be the first to know about it and will eliminate her."

"Quite right, although of greater curiosity and amusement it would seem that Harris and the journalist have hooked up with the MP, James Harkness. We have found Harris's car parked near the MP's London residence." Clark paused again as Tabb burst into laughter.

"Harkness, this just gets better and better. I mean what do they think they can discover or actually do to harm me. It's laughable," Tabb was highly amused and unconcerned.

Clark's face now betrayed his main concern, "actually it would appear there is another in their party and we have intercepted evidence that they know a great deal." Clark moved forward to present a collection of loose papers.

"These documents were sent by Jane Coker to a contact at the IBC. We took the precaution of tailing Coker yesterday before her meeting with Paula Davenport. Once the IBC journo was in the frame we took steps to eliminate her as a threat. We also tagged her phone and email list. We know from The Assassin that Coker was rescued by the boxer Luis Carter last night, who has been in cahoots with Harkness for sometime. Now we can tie all the threats together in one place and as one team. The mail sent by Coker is proof that she is working with Harris. As reported by Raymond Hilliard, Harris has worked out the nature of the project but all they can do is attempt to spoil the party. If Coker goes out to any other news agency we will intercept."

"Are you sure that nobody else at the IBC got to read these documents?" Tabb showed signs of concern.

"Positive, Coker encrypted the files even though she is strictly an amateur. She gave a clue for the passwords and we were able to solve them in seconds using the Fostex system. It feeds in a thousand combinations a minute and once we had worked out the male Christian name for the first file it was simple to solve the linked password for the second." Clark was extremely pleased with himself.

"I don't care how you get to the results as long as you get them, you follow?" Tabb was impatient and unimpressed. "Now what does this second file reveal?"

"Ah this is of more concern and if I'm honest quite impressive," Clark coughed nervously. "Somehow our band of renegades has worked out The Mole's identity."

Tabb sat pondering the facts for several minutes as Clark shuffled nervously. "Well if our friends have such an interest in The Mole, let's not disappoint them. Time to get rid of this annoying irritant don't you think" Tabb reached for his phone inanely laughing at his own acute cunning.

66

As DI Parker made his journey by train to London it was very noticeable how the weather gradually deteriorated from West Country Spring sunshine to dark rain laden skies over the capital. By the time Parker was picked up by a panda car at Waterloo Station the heavens had opened and the streets were awash from a constant and heavy downpour.

It was mid-afternoon by the time that Parker arrived at the Chelsea apartment that had belonged to the late Paula Davenport. The whole block was cordoned off with the standard crime scene bright yellow tape and the local CSI unit was evidently still scanning the location for clues. Parker was led over to the principal investigating officer, DI Sam Ross, sheltered from the rain courtesy of the panda car driver's umbrella.

DI Ross was stood at the front of the communal staircase, a few feet from where Paula's body had been discovered by a neighbour returning from work. An intricate forensic search was taking place around the ground floor area and on the stairs.

Ross nodded a subdued greeting to Parker, "so what's the angle for your boys then?"

"The deceased was recently in Dartcombe, which is on my manor as you boys say up here." Parker paused for a reaction to his witticism but none came, "she, and a journalist colleague, were both involved in a minor crime. They basically used deception to gain information."

"Interesting," Ross pursed his lips, "and do you know this colleague's name?"

"No although I do have her photograph," Parker pulled out the security photos taken of Jane Coker at IBEX from his briefcase.

Ross looked through the photos quickly, "very interesting as that's our girl."

"Sorry?" Parker took the photos back.

"Well it would seem that both ladies were more than colleagues at The Globe. We have been presented with evidence that they were running some sort of Escort agency on the side. Obviously do not get paid enough to be a journalist these days," Ross scowled. "Anyway it looks like Miss Davenport's unfortunate demise was something to do with a client. The lady in your picture goes by the name of Jane Coker. Her employer, The Globe, has been very helpful. The paper had got wind of what the pair was up to in terms of extra curricular activity and they both were up for the chop. The shame or otherwise has probably sent Miss Coker underground and she is the key to this murder."

"How was Paula Davenport killed?" Parker looked over at the marked area where Paula's body had lain.

"Strangled and thrown over the balcony. Nasty eh?" Tests have already shown that she had taken part in sexual intercourse within the hours prior to the attack." Ross shrugged as if to say that's it before adding, "the neighbour found the body by itself and there are no signs of any break-in. We are now checking all the many fingerprints against the residents and a couple of officers have conducted a house to house for witnesses. We do have a possible suspect as a result but I will let you go and speak to my officers as I need to make an urgent call."

Parker took one more glance around the crimes scene as he sensed he was getting the brush off, "thank you I'll go and have a chat with the officers now."

Parker stepped back out into the rain and made his way over to two uniformed policemen who were in deep discussion as they sat in the back of a police van with the back doors wide open.

"Hi, DI Ross asked me to see you regarding the progress made with potential witnesses," Parker flashed his ID badge.

"Yes Ross warned us that a country copper was on his way," a very tall policeman replied, "and to answer your question on the whole nobody saw anything. That is apart from a very frail old lady who lives in a granny flat opposite. Said she saw a girl matching the description of the victim's flat mate, I quote, rushing to a posh car with a large black man and a man in a suit. Luckily for us the lady's eyesight is very good and she wrote down the registration number. It is a personalised plate, H4 ARK. The car belongs to one James Harkness, the disgraced MP. We've already sent a car to his country estate but nobody home.

"Thank you," Parker made his way back to the panda car and his waiting driver. The whole case seemed to fit neatly for the murder motive, and was surely the final nail in the coffin for James Harkness's once illustrious career. However the one thing that Parker had learned this week was not to take things at face value. This was just too neat, almost as if it had been planned. Parker took a lift back to the local police station to report in and to undertake some research. Thankfully he was given a desk and computer and left to his own devices. His first action was to call The Globe in order to find out more about the two renegade female reporters. The Globe's Press Officer painted a very disparaging picture, particularly of Jane Coker, whilst still expressing regret at the death of Paula Davenport. According to the very direct female Press Officer the two reporters made an unauthorised visit to the Dartcombe area, fiddling their expenses in the process. After assuring Parker that The Globe would cooperate fully with any police investigation, the Press Officer abruptly ended the call.

With his limited knowledge of the Internet Parker found it impossible to build up any meaningful profile of Jane Coker. Police records did not show any previous brushes with the law. Instead Parker began to research James Harkness, on whom there was a wealth of information to be found. It did not take Parker long to find The Mole's exposé in The Globe that ended the once popular MP's career. Parker was now extremely agitated. He knew he was on the verge of something but could not find the final pieces to the jigsaw. One thing was certain and that was whatever way he looked at recent events, The Globe was always the common denominator. It had to be the catalyst.

Finally Parker had a breakthrough. He found a personal profile on James Harkness in which it was detailed that he had two principal residences. The main residence had already been checked by the local force as his listed address. His second, described as a city crash pad, was easily traced with the information available to Parker. Subversively the out-of-town detective printed the details before informing his designated driver that he was going to take a break and see the sights. As the local cops shared a joke at his expense about country bumpkins being slow and lazy, DI Parker made his way to a nearby tube station as he chose to go it alone.

Parker timed his journey well in getting ahead of the main rush hour. The tube journey was relatively quick and thankfully the rain had desisted by the time he took the walk by the Thames along to Harkness's apartment block. As he stood by the main entrance Parker hesitated before pushing the intercom button.

67

The sharp buzz of the intercom alert startled all of the occupants of James Harkness's apartment, including the MP himself. Sheepishly Harkness moved over to the main control and monitor as Jane Coker and Alex Hart followed in his wake. On the screen was a stocky middle aged man in a cheap dour brown suit.

"Yes can I help you?" Harkness spoke confidently into the microphone.

"I hope so," DI Parker replied, "am I speaking to James Harkness?"

"You are," Harkness confirmed, "and who are you?"

"Mister Harkness I am a police officer," Parker flashed his badge to the screen, "Detective Inspector Parker of Carnbourne CID."

"Carnbourne?" Alex frowned heavily at Harkness, "a bit off his patch is he not?"

"Why do you need to speak to me?" Harkness kept it simple.

"I need to ask you some questions about The Globe. I think we can be of mutual benefit to each other," Parker looked directly into the mini camera. Harkness looked around at Jane and Alex, perplexed by the comment. "It could be a trap," Alex offered.

"I don't think so; Tabb would not be so obvious. I think we'd better let him in," Harkness pressed the door release. "Come up to the third floor and knock on the door of apartment 3A."

Parker made his way up the stairs as he rehearsed his most appropriate line of questioning to use with James Harkness. The choice of going it alone had ruled out the option of making an arrest. He could just see the local force having a field day with the fact that he failed to share pertinent information related to a murder enquiry. The decision had been made more on a gut feeling than a logical play it by the book approach. Parker was going against every ideal of his character and he felt like a caged bird released.

Parker knocked on the door with confidence and was greeted by a hesitant James Harkness who eventually welcomed him in. As the Detective walked into the lounge the realisation that he had got it right was immediately confirmed.

"You have to excuse me Detective Parker as I was hosting some friends. If it's OK with you we can talk in the kitchen," Harkness beckoned Parker toward the kitchen.

Parker did not move but visibly scanned the others seated in the lounge, "I think it best if we speak in here as this very much involves your friends."

"I'm sorry," Harkness looked extremely puzzled.

"Well let's see," Parker put down his briefcase and began picking out the others present, "firstly we have Jane Coker, who I believe had a very eventful time in Dartcombe recently with the late Paula Davenport."

Jane reeled in shock as the others looked her way.

"Then we have Alex Hart, a local Dartcombe resident and erstwhile fugitive. Sergeant Etheridge would no doubt send his regards. And unless I'm way off track I would hazard a guess that Jane and Alex make up the couple reported as trying to burgle Nick Ford's house."

Nobody spoke as Parker moved his focus around the room. "Next we have the famous figure of Luis Carter, who I am also now fitting into being the rather large black gentleman spotted during the getaway from Paula Davenport's apartment block last night."

Luis nodded shyly to confirm.

"Finally I have to admit that you have me at an advantage," Parker looked straight at Brian Harris.

"Brian Harris, I'm a Genealogist," Harris introduced himself.

"So Detective Parker," Harkness retained a calm air, "it would seem that you have done your homework and have us all at a disadvantage. I take it you have back-up waiting and we are all to be arrested?"

"Do you mind if I sit down and I would love a cup of tea if there's one going," Parker moved over towards an armchair after getting a nodded approval form Harkness.

Harkness soon returned with a cup of tea as the others waited in anticipation for Parker to speak.

"Nice cuppa, I always think that fine bone China makes such a difference," Parker made idle chat as he almost teased those present. "Now first of all I am here alone and I make that confession to hopefully gain your trust. Since the unfortunate deaths of Stephen Howard and Martin Gardner I have been working on solving the motive behind the two deaths after concluding they were intrinsically linked. This involved trying to track down Alex initially and then Jane following her appearance at IBEX, a company that seemed to be at the centre of the murders. Through my investigations I started to touch a nerve of those behind the killings and as a result they tried to end my career by what I have been told is called cyber framing. Thankfully I have a contact who was able to clear my name through an equal level of cunning and technological expertise."

"Yes I saw your case on TV," Alex interrupted, "and that whole Dartcombe case was handed over to Etheridge, who I have to tell you is a bent copper up to his neck in all of this."

Parker looked knowingly over at Alex, "yes so I have gathered."

"So how did you track us down?" Jane asked.

"Well with a bit of luck and an oversight by the Met if I am honest. Although it might not remain an oversight for long so I best be brief," Parker now spoke directly to Jane. "Following your escapades at IBEX I had two leads to go on. The first was a photograph and the second was the registration of the blue Mazda in which you were seen travelling. I traced the registration to a Paula Davenport, journalist at The Globe newspaper. The assumption was that the photograph, taken by IBEX security cameras, was also of Paula. Once the case against me was dropped I was notified of Miss Davenport's death and was sent her picture, but it was not of the IBEX snoop that I was looking for. There were enough grounds for me to travel to London where I discover that Miss Davenport shared her apartment with journalist colleague Jane Coker. Not only that but I am informed that they were running some kind of high class escort service, which provided a convenient link to a murder motive. Throw in the sighting of the famous but disgraced MP, James Harkness, at the scene and the Met think they have already wrapped up the case."

"The truth is," Harkness now spoke up, "I was there last night with Luis. We saved Jane from the hands of the real murderer. Luis knocked him spark out but I am assuming he made his escape before Paula's body was discovered."

"Correct and very noble of you Mister Harkness, and Mister Carter of course," Parker said sincerely.

"Thank you," Luis said humbly.

"And the escort service bit is all crap too," Jane showed her annoyance, "I'd only spent one night in Paula's apartment which hardly makes me a flatmate."

"I believe you," Parker responded sympathetically, "right so I've told you my side. Who's going to tell me what the bloody hell this is all about?" Parker now spoke sternly.

"Do you have any notion at all?" Jane asked.

"Only that The Globe and IBEX have something to do with it all," Parker confessed.

Alex was prompted to initiate the account of events from his involvement with the Martin Gardner murder and the discovery of the stolen files on the disk. Jane then took up the baton describing how she became embroiled, leading to the eventual death of her colleague, Paula Davenport. After

Harkness and Luis gave a brief description of how they had both been wronged it was left to Brian Harris to once again explain the Genealogy plot behind The Globe exclusive.

"A few days ago I would have struggled to believe any of this," Parker exhaled loudly. "But through my own recent experiences it all makes sense now. The trouble is we do not have the concrete proof needed to bring the perpetrators, especially Tabb, to justice. The one thing we know for certain is that Tabb has a powerful network that can smear and manipulate at will."

"Our one real chance is to find the missing link from the Seton family tree. Tabb has put great credence in finding her so there must be a significant concern on his part." Alex showed his frustration. "The bet is an outside one but to place it we need to get access to the witness protection records. I don't suppose as a policeman you would have that power?"

"No not at all I'm afraid," Parker acknowledged.

"It is impossible then," Jane was ready to admit defeat, "I mean if all the technology brains and tools at Tabb's disposal through IBEX cannot crack it, what chance do we have?"

Parker suddenly jerked forward as he was struck by an idea, "actually I do know of someone who just might be able to help us."

68

The Assassin stood waiting patiently, occupying his time by staring across the Thames as the grimy brown water stirred up vigorously. A strong wind picked up as the rain clouds moved away to leave a constant grey sky stretching to the horizon. The Assassin re-buttoned his long black trench coat before flexing his fingers within a pair of tight black leather gloves. A quick glance over his shoulder confirmed that a short smartly dressed man was approaching.

"Hi," Harry (The Mole) said cheerily, "I'm guessing you're my contact. Description fits although I still reckon you could have worn a red rose in your lapel or something."

"From now on you listen carefully to what I say and only move or do anything on my instruction," The Assassin spoke curtly. "Firstly hold these for me, I need to check my messages," The Assassin handed Harry a large thick brief case and a leather document file.

The Assassin quickly checked his mobile before retrieving the objects from Harry, "right this mission is very simple. Intelligence shows that within this apartment block is a group dedicated to destroying Tabb. They have already gathered enough information to expose your true identity and are now regarded as a major threat."

"Fine," Harry looked continuously around the area but he was alone with The Assassin. "But one thing to make clear I am not getting involved in topping anyone or assisting in the topping of anyone. Is that clear?"

"You are here because of your supposed skills to get me into the building. The plan is to frame the conspirators without having to kill any of them. The latter would be too messy and hard to cover." The Assassin pointed over the apartment block, "over to you."

Harry strolled over to the back of the building and examined the electronic shutter at the entrance to the underground car park. "Piece of cake," he confirmed as he pulled out a pair of brown leather gloves whilst checking for any CCTV cameras. There were none. Slyly Harry moved into the shadows and pulled out a small pack of precision tools. Within a few minutes the shutter raised a couple of feet off the road. Harry fell to the floor and rolled under and in, closely followed by The Assassin. Once inside, Harry moved swiftly to the main stairwell at the other end of the car park. Again he quickly cased the immediate area before working on the lock on the stairwell door, opening it in seconds. He ushered The Assassin to enter first, "now what?" Harry whispered as he followed the sinister figure dressed in black up the stairs. The Assassin did not reply but made his way swiftly to the third floor. He then stopped by the door that led to the landing and over to flat 3A, belonging to James Harkness.

"What's the plan then big man?" Harry asked breathlessly as he bent forward slightly from the exertion of traversing the stairs.

The Assassin reached into his pocket and pulled out a semi-automatic pistol complete with silencer.

"Hey hang on a second, the agreement was that you killed none of them," Harry went white with fear. "What are you planning to do, burst in and take them all out?"

"No, I gave my word that I will not be killing any of them," The Assassin looked directly at Harry, "Tabb asked that you be involved for the very skills you have just demonstrated. That and for me to pass on the message that The Mole is no more."

"What is he pensioning me?" Harry laughed, albeit nervously.

The Assassin aimed the pistol at Harry's chest and shot twice into his heart, "happy retirement."

69

"Will this guy take a lot of persuading do you think?" Alex Hart looked nervously at his watch.

"I hope not but let's just say he's quite eccentric," DI Parker was also getting anxious as he glanced over at James Harkness's phone, willing it to ring. He had made the call to Julie Ingram some thirty minutes ago and she had promised to call Edgar straight away. Parker had explained that he needed Edgar's undoubted skill without going into the full nature of the challenge. "Thing is, and I'm not being funny, but time is really against us," Alex continued to moan. "The drive from here to Didkam including going across London will take four to five hours and the train will be no better."

"Actually I can help there," an unusually subdued James Harkness snapped back into action. "There's a small heliport not far from here where I keep my own helicopter. I'm a fully trained pilot. Once Detective Parker's friend gives us the green light, I can call ahead to get the helicopter prepared and then we can get down to Didkam in no more than an hour. Just need a field to land in."

"Plenty of them near where Edgar lives," Parker confirmed just as the phone rang loudly. Parker quickly moved to take the call. It was Ingram confirming that she had brokered Edgar's assistance, who apparently agreed after being told it would be the ultimate challenge of his skills. Parker confirmed that they would be travelling down by helicopter after getting the thumbs up from Harkness.

Harkness took the phone from Parker and made the arrangements for the helicopter to be prepared for the relatively short journey to the West Country. "I suggest I take Detective Parker, Alex and Brian with me," Harkness stated with a great sense of urgency and excitement as the others stood-up ready for action. "Luis, can you look after Jane? We need someone to stay in London and I suggest you go back to your house in case the police turn up here."

"What about transport?" Luis asked.

"Good point," Harkness pondered, "I have a second car in the basement and best not use the Jag because of the number plate. It would waste a lot of time to drop you off."

"Take my car champ," Harris threw the keys to his Allegro over to Luis. Just as the group were about to go there was a loud knock at the door, causing them all to freeze on the spot.

"Police," Jane surmised.

"No," Parker shook his head, "they would have buzzed from the pavement or smashed their way in."

Harkness moved over to the door and peered through the small magnified peephole. "Nobody there," he confirmed and proceeded to open the door. Parker rushed over to his side.

The landing was empty bar a small briefcase and leather file lying on the floor right in front of the door. After glancing around for the person who had made the delivery Harkness reached down to pick up the items. "Nooo," Parker screamed, causing the former MP to stop in his tracks. Parker looked frantically around the landing as other residents appeared in their doorways, stirred by the commotion.

"It's OK, nothing to worry about," Parker flashed his police badge and urged Harkness's neighbours to go back into their apartments. "Do you have any gloves?" Parker directed the question to Harkness as he crouched and looked over the items on the floor.

"Only washing-up gloves," Harkness replied slightly embarrassed.

"Perfect, can you get them and any plastic bags you might have," Parker remained on his haunches.

Harkness soon returned with a pair of bright yellow rubber gloves and several large department store carrier bags. Parker put on the gloves as if he was a surgeon about to perform a tricky operation. Delicately he then lifted the file and placed it in one of the bags. Hidden underneath the file was a pistol, complete with silencer.

"Oh dear," Parker lightly bit his lower lip, "this is not looking good." Parker placed the gun delicately in another of the bags. He then slowly opened the briefcase to reveal it was full of bundled ten pound notes.

"What the hell is going on?" Alex finally spoke in total bewilderment.

Parker shut the briefcase and carried it back into the hallway with the other two bagged items. "The trick is an old one. The idea was for one of you to handle these objects and thereby incriminate that person and probably the group."

"For doing what?" Alex persisted.

"Lets' see," Parker retrieved the file and opened it. Inside were a number of documents which the Detective quickly scanned. "It looks like we have a complete dossier here detailing various illegal activities for financial gain undertaken by James Harkness with the full assistance of everyone in the room, bar myself. The main crux of your plotting is revealed through supposed original and authentic attestations and account records. It would seem that you have all been guilty of defrauding the general public through some kind of financial scam. I'm sure under close scrutiny that this set of records would provide proof to dishonour and convict you."

"And doubtless our personal accounts have already been credited to reflect our pilfered wealth or a new account opened up in our name for such a purpose." Harkness now realised the objective. "This has Tabb written all over it. His aim is a slur to us all and unfortunately it proves his intelligence has already confirmed that we are a team and where we are holed up. But why the delivery? Is he warning us off with a payment but then why the gun?"

"Oh he's not just warning you off he's looking to finish you," Parker moved back out on to the landing as the others followed. "I think the case of money is there to imply that you were being blackmailed by someone who had uncovered your so-called scam and this person was looking for a payoff."

"Who though?" Jane stayed close to Luis, "and why just leave the money behind? And the gun?"

"Yes the gun," Parker moved over and opened the stairwell door that led to the car park. Lying dead on the floor was The Mole. "He didn't take the money because you shot him."

"Harry, oh my god," Jane threw a hand to her mouth in shock. "So if we had picked up the gun we'd have been implicated in murder as well. And of course it all adds up. Who better to set-up as we had worked out his identity and he would have course been the perfect foil as someone who uncovers such public scams."

"Exactly, he's fulfilled a final use to Tabb," Parker shut the door to conceal The Mole's body once more. "We now have to move quickly and stick to our original plan. Tabb has doubtless arranged for the police to make an imminent appearance, with the notion that you are all still trying to work out what is going on without probably discovering the body."

"And what about Harry?" Jane said anxiously as the group moved back into Harkness's apartment to collect coats and keys.

"We leave him," Parker replied coldly, "although we will take the supplied evidence. He held up the two carrier bags and briefcase whilst still wearing the yellow gloves, "just hope I don't get arrested now. I'll die of shame if nothing else."

Within minutes the group split in two as Jane and Luis made their way down in the lift to collect Harris's car from the street. Harkness led the rest down the stairwell to the car park, with each stepping over the hapless body of The Mole. Parker kept the gloves on until he could place the briefcase and bags in the boot of Harkness's second car, a silver Lexus. The gloves were then also thrown into the boot. Harkness drove swiftly out of the car park emerging into daylight from the dark underground recess. Thankfully the nearby traffic lights were on green and he was able to move unhindered into his short journey, whilst noting with relief that Harris's Allegro had gone from its parking bay, and therefore Jane and Luis with it.

Some five minutes after Harkness had left in a flurry, several police cars with blue flashing lights appeared at speed before coming to an abrupt halt outside of the apartment block.

70

As the day moved on Arturo Tabb was becoming more and more agitated. He felt like a footballer on the eve of playing in the World Cup final or even at a more base level like a child with the highest expectations on Christmas Eve. Such was the desire of Tabb to reveal to the world his closely guarded and meticulously created secret. He had always known that at this stage the plan was to stay in hiding to add to the mystique. Despite an endless array of Su Doku and crossword puzzles, Tabb's mind could not stray from the fact that he was about to complete his most complex and daring plan to date. It was not a unique plan and Tabb had studied in detail the efforts of Gerd Heidemann to bring to the world the so-called Hitler Dairies in Nineteen Eighty-Three. The German journalist and his partner in crime, Konrad Kujau, superbly fooled the world but only for a few days. They failed because they tried to dupe an eminent Historian into authenticating the diaries rather than bring him into the plan. Their research was poor and the diaries were full of historical inaccuracies. Finally, and unforgivably in Tabb's eyes, they left themselves wide open by producing the diaries made of modern paper and written in modern ink. Tabb still had to admire the effort as Kujau made a career out of his notoriety even upon his release from jail; such was the power of media celebrity even back then. Tabb had covered all the mistakes made by Heidemann.

Tabb was even getting bored watching the endless TV newsreels debating his forthcoming opus. Since the elimination of Paula Davenport he could not even use sex as a distraction. The services of a call girl would prove too much of a risk. It was therefore with relief that Tabb was once again interrupted in his annex bedroom to receive a status report from Andrew Clark. The confirmation of the downfall of those who plotted against him would prove a satisfying tonic at least.

"Arturo," the very forward Andrew Clark leant on Tabb's desk as he looked him in the eye, "I'm going to level with you from the off. The plan to eliminate Harkness and his band of merry men was implemented to perfection. However we are advised that the group fled before the police could make any arrests, By all accounts they took the evidence with them and left The Mole's body in situ."

"How can you say something is perfect when it has failed?" Tabb banged a fist down hard on the desk, "I will not tolerate failure." Despite receiving confirmation of The Mole's death, Tabb did not even feel the slightest tinge of remorse or sadness.

Clark jerked backwards in fear, "yes understood and we will succeed in eradicating the threat."

"Do you know where Harkness has gone?" Tabb was already longing for the day when he could dispense with Clark's services once and for all.

"Yes I was about to inform you," Clark could feel his stomach churning as his nerves were pushed to the limit. "Our intelligence has learned that Harkness had booked to fly his helicopter from London to the Dartcombe area. He has logged to take three passengers with him. His objective is unclear."

"Three passengers?" Should there not be four?" Tabb was concerned.

"We think the missing one is Harris as his car has gone. We are watching his home." Clark felt a bit more at ease.

"This is good," Tabb laid his palms flat to the desk, "with our main conspirators all in one place and making such a dangerous journey it would almost seem inevitable that accidents will happen."

"Understood," Clark turned to go. He knew what to do and the project would then succeed. It would then be time to unofficially resign and make his escape. That was a plan even more meticulous in the making.

71

The journey to the heliport took less than twenty minutes, much to the relief of a very edgy Alex Hart. Alex had expected to either be stopped by the police at any moment or come under attack from The Assassin. Even on getting out of James Harkness's car, Alex felt himself stooping ready to avoid a sniper's bullet.

Harkness had his own reserved parking bay at the heliport as he was such a frequent traveller. He had explained during the journey that what had started as an infrequent hobby was destined to become almost an obsession. The more Harkness had been given the opportunity to fly a helicopter the more his passion had grown. His expertise was now so renowned that the former MP even flew at various air shows under the pseudonym, The Kestrel. His fee always went to charity although it was a part of his life that was never publicly reported.

DI Jack Parker decided to move the gun and the folder from Harkness's boot, whilst covering and leaving the case of money behind. Carefully the plastic bag containing the pistol was wrapped in a picnic rug to conceal it. With Harkness's full agreement, the weapon was then stashed away in his personal locker along with the folder.

It was apparent that Harkness was very well known and liked throughout the small heliport. Calmly he explained at the main desk that he was taking a party down for a bit of a boy's holiday in the West Country, which was readily accepted by the two female attendants. Harkness then led his motley crew out on to the tarmac and over to a slick looking blue helicopter. He explained that it was a Bell 206 B2 and was capable of speeds of up to one hundred and fifty mph. Alex and Parker both nodded nervously as they contemplated the prospect of flying so fast in such a flimsy looking machine. Neither had flown in a helicopter before, although Parker had declined the opportunity on several occasions by delegating to a more junior officer to sample the delights of the force's one machine. In comparison Brian Harris showed no nerves at all and almost bulldozed his way on board eager for the off.

Alex and Parker were more than happy to let Harris join Harkness in the front cockpit whilst they tentatively strapped themselves to the white leather seats at the back of the machine. Harkness quickly made some last minute checks before starting up the rotors. At full speed the sound pulsated loudly making the two backseat passengers feel slightly nauseous. Harkness could see they were nervous and turned to offer reassurance that after the initial speed and sensation of take-off, everything would settle down and they could enjoy the ride.

Alex and Parker braced themselves by gripping hard on the seat as Harkness finally took the machine up and away. Just as Harkness had promised the two nervous passengers soon became accustomed to the speed and general motion allowing them to relax and feel more comfortable. Alex still kept his eyes firmly fixed on the front screen after finding his view a bit too panoramic. At least the noise has eased off slightly although conversation was conducted by semi-shouting.

"So how easy is it to fly one of these things?" Harris's normal booming voice sufficed to be heard.

"Like driving a car really, as simple as that." Harkness shouted back.

"Can I have a go?" Harris eyed up the controls.

"Not now Brian," Harkness chuckled as he noted Alex and Parker's anxious reaction, "I promise to give you a lesson when this is all over."

Harkness expertly moved the machine over the delights of the English countryside, although dusk was beginning to fall as the green fields and trees darkened in colour by the minute. Alex tried to find enjoyment in the journey but still yearned for the prospect of being back on terra firma. Parker now felt brave enough to appreciate the view as he contemplated how his life had changed so dramatically in the short space of one week.

Harkness made good progress down to the West Country, "should be there in about half an hour," he shouted as the darkness of early evening finally took hold.

"Is that another copter over there?" Harris pointed to a faint flickering light moving ever closer.

Harkness studied the view for a second and checked his small radar, "yes and it seems to be coming to greet us."

"Police?" Alex queried.

Harkness took another look, "not unless the boys in blue have started flying Apache Attack helicopters. Not standard around here are they Jack?"

"No," Parker replied apprehensively as the other machine came very clearly into view.

Hold on tight," Harkness took his machine down and in an arc before accelerating at full throttle. The Apache followed instantly releasing a missile from under one of its wings. Harkness jolted his machine to the left and the missile missed by a couple of feet.

From his seat in the Apache, The Assassin was surprised that his first shot had not hit home. As a former Army pilot this was his realm and it would only be a matter of time before The Assassin would finish the job. He knew it would have to be completed fairly quickly whilst they were over sparsely populated countryside with little chance of any witnesses. The Assassin would ensure his prey did not reach urban safety.

As Harkness moved forward at speed he began to slalom his machine causing Alex and Parker to feel sick. Alex now just closed his eyes and waited for the worse to happen. Surely it would be over quickly when the inevitable happened. The Apache fired another missile which again Harkness somehow avoided.

This time The Assassin cursed loudly; he'd not expected such a high level of pilot competency. It was time to move in for the kill. The Assassin accelerated the Apache towards the tail of the fleeing helicopter. Soon there would be no room for it to manoeuvre once in range.

"I think we've had it," Harris looked around at the chasing machine, "he's coming in close to finish us off."

Harkness did not reply but he knew that Harris was right. The end was looking unavoidable now. He took a final desperate option to move the machine even lower and follow the dark and choppy River Darcot. The Apache reciprocated and closed in as The Assassin readied his finger to fire. Harkness looked up and could just make out the huge structure of Darcot Bridge coming into view. It presented him with one final roll of the dice. Harkness jolted the machine several times to keep The Apache at bay. It only served to make The Assassin even more determined. Harkness pushed the throttle to the maximum but could not shake off his opponent. The chance of survival was extremely slim as Harkness finally pulled his machine through a sharp trajectory. The Assassin reacted and followed, primed and ready to deliver the killer shot. His finger moved over to the button as Harkness rose sharply again almost touching the underbelly of the solid towering bridge. With only a few feet to spare, Harkness somehow moved under and up once more. This time The Assassin could not react as the Apache's rotors clipped the edge of the bridge. His machine abruptly span out of control, plummeting to earth at high speed. Within seconds it was a fireball on collision with the river bank.

High above the River Darcot, Harkness levelled his machine and slowed to a moderate speed.

"Nice flying sir," Harris said simply.

"Oh my god," Alex was hyperventilating, "this is just too much."

"Well I think that we can say the threat is over," Harkness commented calmly without betraying his utter relief.

"Well done," Parker added.

"Sort of poetic justice really," Alex looked back as a plume of smoke rose high above Darcot Bridge, "that's the bridge they threw me off."

72

Julie Ingram took the call from DI Parker on her mobile as she was rushing out of the IBEX office complex. She had hoped to have been at Edgar's by now to greet Parker on arrival but was called in to see Bob Eubank, IBEX's CEO, at the last minute. Apparently the office rumour mill was circulating a story about the friction between Ingram and Nick Ford. Ingram did her best to appease the situation by inferring it was just a friendly professional disagreement that had already been resolved. Unfortunately Eubank took a lot more time and effort to fully convince than Ingram could afford. To top it all Eubank then insisted on giving one of his professional mentoring speeches which went on and on. Ingram was only able to finally escape after Eubank received a call from his wife. As he took some strict domestic orders Ingram quickly moved to the door in hasty retreat. Cursing Ford's PA, a well known office gossip, Ingram collected her coat and raced out of the building. Parker sounded unusually flustered, which he explained was due to a frantic and eventful journey. Ingram told Parker to take his friends over to meet Edgar as he was expecting them. She then clicked off her mobile and headed for the car.

"Excuse me Mrs Ingram," a voice rose above the general chit-chat generated by the crowd of departing workers.

Ingram turned to be greeted by Sergeant Etheridge in full uniform, "yes Sergeant how can I help you?"

"I'm afraid I need you to come with me," Etheridge moved closer, "there's been an incident."

"An incident?" Ingram echoed, "I'm sorry but unless this is critical I am very late for an appointment."

"The incident involves your son, Peter, Mrs Ingram," Etheridge said solemnly.

Ingram froze to the spot, numbed by the thought of something horrible happening to Peter, "what has happened? Is he OK? Is he hurt?" Ingram now spluttered in panic.

"It is best you come with me," Etheridge put his arm on Ingram's shoulder to comfort before guiding her towards the panda car. Ingram followed with tearful apprehension.

"Please tell me he is OK." Ingram repeated her plea as she got into the back of the car.

"He's fine Mrs Ingram but he's got himself into a fair amount of trouble. Nothing that we cannot get sorted out very quickly with your help."

Etheridge started up the car and drove out of IBEX, waving to the security sentry as he went.

Ingram felt a great sense of relief that Peter was at least safe but was now concerned as to what trouble he was in with the police. Peter was such a good boy and just not they type to commit a crime. It could only be high jinks at worst or maybe she did not really know her own son. It was then it hit her. At the Yokel Pub Parker had stated that Sergeant Etheridge was somehow involved in the conspiracy. He was Ford's collaborator. Ingram was now certain she had walked headlong into a trap. She was in trouble and even worse it would appear that Peter was in trouble as the bait to catch Ingram.

"Where are we going?" Ingram now spoke with more assuredly.

"To see Peter," Etheridge replied without flinching.

Ingram sat back in her seat as the panda car moved out into the countryside. She felt trapped and alone. Slowly Ingram moved her mobile out of her coat pocket, coughing as she pressed the mute button and at the same time keeping the small delicate handset from view. Whilst keeping a close eye on Etheridge, Ingram tentatively typed in a text message.

SOS wth Etheridge thy hv Peter.

Ingram picked out Parker's mobile number in her address book and pressed send before securing the phone back in her coat pocket.

73

James Harkness had managed to land his helicopter with consummate ease in a large field alongside Edgar's secluded property. Alex Hart felt like falling to his knees and kissing the ground such was his relief to be still alive.

After making the call to Julie Ingram, DI Parker led the others over to meet the young eccentric Edgar after once again passing through the odd but effective security set-up. Edgar buzzed for them to come in, stating that he was in the last room at the end of the corridor. Just as Parker had been on his first visit the others followed him with curious bemusement as they walked along the clinical white hall that led to a large network of rooms inside what had supposedly been a quaint country bungalow. As they neared the end of the long corridor the shout of "in here Copper" resounded from the final room with its door slightly ajar. Parker moved on into the room which was an extremely spacious recreation room. Various games consoles were lined up along each main wall whilst in the two far corners stood a pool table and bar football table respectively. Up on the wall was a fifty inch LCD television on which Edgar was playing tennis through a Nintendo Wii console.

"Gents may I introduce Edgar," Parker announced with a smirk.

The others all stepped forward to introduce themselves and shake Edgar's hand, with Alex nearly tripping over his own feet as he perused the room with both admiration and envy.

"Shall we go to the computer room so we can explain our conundrum?" Parker offered.

"Where's Jules?" Edgar ignored the request and continued to swing the Wii handset.

"I've just been speaking to her, she got held up but is on her way," Parker replied. "It is best if we continue and explain the nature of our challenge."

"All in good time Copper," Edgar grinned as he placed a back-to-front baseball cap on his head. "First I want you to give me a game of tennis. And if you don't I won't help you and your friends."

"Fine," Parker scowled as the others looked at each other in bewilderment. "I'm afraid nothing is ever straightforward with Edgar gentlemen." Parker put his coat to one side and took and handset from Edgar, "so what do I do?"

After a quick demonstration Parker found himself playing a game of Wii tennis as his new friends watched in silence, whilst generally growing impatient. Harkness was wondering if the treacherous journey from London had been worth while. As Edgar proceeded to thrash Parker, the Detective's mobile chimed to announce the arrival of the SOS text from Julie Ingram. All those in the room were oblivious. Thankfully the game was short and sweet with Edgar taking great delight in easy victory.

"Anyone else fancy a game?" Edgar shouted to the erstwhile spectators. Alex was tempted to accept before Brain Harris spoke for them all, "I think that playtime is over as we have serious business to conduct."

"Have it your way big man," Edgar put the Wii handset down and beckoned for his visitors to follow. The group was led back to the main computer room in which Parker had previously seen Edgar manipulate and change the evidence against him. Edgar jumped onto a chair on wheels and slid down the entire length of the room, halting by a principal keyboard. "OK shoot, what's this so-called challenge?"

"This is very impressive," Harris strode around looking at the various pieces of computer hardware on offer, "The amount of research I could do if I had all this."

"The challenge," Harkness ignored Harris and did not disguise in his voice his initial first impression contempt for Edgar's character, "is to retrieve information on somebody shielded by Witness Protection."

Edgar burst out laughing, "are you serious man? Why not tell me to hold my breath under water for an hour or jump off the roof and see if I can fly. I have more chance of achieving those."

"Looks like you were wrong Jack," Harkness turned to Parker, "the kid's no more than an average computer geek."

"Oh I see, play the psycho babble. Put me down until I rise to the challenge." Edgar jumped out of his chair to stand toe-to-toe with Harkness.

"Well what's it to be then, rise to the challenge or wimp out?" Harkness stood his ground.

Edgar grimaced, "I like you Harky, you remind me of my dad. And because I like you and PC Plod over there I'll have a go."

"Bloody glad to hear it," Harris shouted before producing a file full of papers printed from Harkness's computer. Harris explained to Edgar that they were looking for Marie-Claire Magne and how she had become part of the Witness Protection programme.

After studying the files Edgar logged on to his main computer and began surfing various websites and databases. In the process he also fired up two other systems and gave Harris and Alex specific instructions of information he wanted them to find. Edgar's demeanor was now deadly serious.

"Harky or Plod, make yourself useful and go and make some coffee. This is going to be some bloody haul," Edgar did not take his eyes from the screen. "And find out where the bloody hell Jules has got to. Too much testosterone in this room for my liking."

Parker went to check his mobile and realised he had left it in the recreation room. "James, I'll go and fetch my phone and we can make the coffee."

Parker directed Harkness into the state-of-the-art kitchen before going to retrieve his phone. He quickly spotted his coat and went straight for a pocket to check if there were any messages. There was one unread text from Julie Ingram.

74

Julie Ingram vaguely recognised the route that Sergeant Etheridge was taking but was not sure enough to pinpoint where they might be heading to.
"Is it much further?" Ingram leant forward.
"Nearly there and then all will be revealed," Etheridge replied smugly.
"And of course this has nothing at all to do with law and order does it Sergeant?" Ingram was angry, "what sort of justice do you work for?"
"You're a very bright and perceptive lady Mrs Ingram," Etheridge's voice remained unaffected. "Justice is a very simple concept and if we all abide by the rules then we need not fear it."
"And what about Peter?" Ingram was now once again on edge as she feared for her son's safety, aware of what these people were capable of.
"Peter is fine," Etheridge spoke reassuringly, "and will remain fine I'm sure. You will see to that. Here we are now and you'll be pleased to see a familiar face to greet you."
Etheridge took the panda car down a bumpy grassy lane, at the end of which was a number of bleak derelict industrial buildings. Ingram now recognised the spot and once again covertly retrieved her mobile. Despite being concerned at seeing no acknowledgement from Parker to her original text, Ingram proceeded to type again. She typed 'Tin Mine'.
Once the message was released Ingram again concealed the phone in her coat as the panda car came to a halt. Standing outside was Nick Ford.
"Julie how nice to see you out of work," Ford opened the rear passenger door as Etheridge got out of the car.
"You don't frighten me Ford," Ingram climbed out clutching her coat.
"And I would not want to," Ford continued in a smarmy and patronising vain before gruffly speaking to Etheridge, "take her coat and make sure she has no phone."
Etheridge did as instructed as Ingram found some relief from sending her earlier messages to Parker. Her only hope was that he had received and worked them out.
"Come this way and let's go and see Peter shall we," Ford returned to his sycophantic pitch, "lovely boy by the way, just like his mother."
Ingram wanted to physically attack Ford but showed restraint, "if you have harmed him Ford I will kill you."
"Ooh these modern female managers can be so vicious Sergeant. Real equality of the sexes these days don't you know." Ford led Ingram and

- 176 -

Etheridge over to a large warehouse type building before opening the door and illuminating the interior with a torch. Ingram stumbled a couple of times on the odd piece of machine debris lying on the floor. Etheridge remained silent as Ford led them over to another door and into a large annex.

"Here he is," Ford shone the torch into the corner of the dingy and dusty room. Peter was sat tied and gagged on an old wooden chair looking petrified and tearful.

75

SOS wth Etheridge thy hv Peter.

DI Parker held up his phone so all could see the message. In his mind there was now only one goal and that was to rescue Julie Ingram and her son. It was because she had stuck her neck out for him that Ingram was now in trouble. Parker was still determined to remain rational and not panic. To apply a common sense approach had served him well in all his years in the force. He had to detach himself from the emotion of the situation and retain professional focus.

"Etheridge," Alex almost spat, "the bastard. We have to find him and quick."

"Are you alright Jack?" Harkness looked over at the solemn Detective deep in thought.

"Yes," Parker replied after a pause, "I just wish I had more to go on."

With perfect timing the second text from Ingram arrived.

"Tin Mine," Parker read it out, "but where? Which One?"

"Could be The Hippodrome," Edgar shouted.

"Sorry?" Harkness shot a disgruntled look.

"No he has to be right," Alex butted in, "the old Nixon Family mine. It has been deserted for years and became a bit of an attraction for local teenagers holding parties and raves, hence the nickname of the Hippodrome. Then some kids fell down an old shaft and safety became a big issue when the story hit the national headlines. The police now patrol it and it's bang in the middle of Etheridge's patch."

"I know the one, it has to be our only shot," Parker became animated as he pleadingly looked over at Harkness for help. "James, as much I hated the experience I think the only way to get there in time is by your helicopter."

"Let's get going then," Harkness took no persuading, "Alex you best come with us so we can find this place."

"Yeah right," Alex' stomach immediately knotted at the thought of another high speed ride.

"Brian, can you stay and help Edgar?" Harkness took on the role of leader. Harris simply acknowledged by holding a hand aloft as he continued to scrutinise some data on his computer screen.

"Hurry back for tea and medals," Edgar whooped before adding, "seriously copper bring Jules back safely."

"Will do," Parker replied before charging out of the bungalow with Harkness and Alex.

Within five minutes the helicopter was airborne. Parker knew that he had to make the rescue official and made a call to his DCI, Andy Burton. Choosing his words carefully and relying on the trust that the pair had built up in working together for fifteen years, Parker relayed that a kidnapping had taken place and hostages were being held at the Nixon Mine. He strongly requested that squad cars were sent to the location but without police broadcast. The caveat was that Parker would explain all, including why he was flying around the West Country in a helicopter rather than sitting in a London hotel room. The objective was to save Julie and Peter and then Parker would need to think on his feet. Burton agreed to lead the squad to the mine himself, containing his bewilderment at the recent turn of events.

76

"So now what?" Julie Ingram stayed composed as she comforted her son, now released from his shackles.

"Well do you remember that great quiz show from the Eighties called Bullseye?" Nick Ford paced in front of his hostages in the torch illuminated but gloomy annex room. Sergeant Etheridge stood guard by the door. "The host of that show, Jim Bowen, used to have this really nifty catchphrase for the show's losers. It was let's see what you could have won."

"And what's your point?" Ingram snapped impatiently.

"My point is that despite this cruel aspect of showing the poor losers what they could have taken home, it was all very cleverly geared toward causing embarrassment to the contestants and in so doing increasing the viewing figures." Ford continued in full dramatic flow, "now as an experiment it would have been interesting to turn it around a little and show the contestants up front what they could win. Would they have raised their game to perform that much better? And you see that's the opportunity I'm giving you."

Etheridge had moved over next to Ingram and instantly grabbed and pulled Peter away. At the same time Ford pulled out a gun and pointed it straight at Ingram.

"Julie, this is how it's going to work. You're going to play my version of Bullseye." Ford produced a pad of paper from inside his jacket, "the rules are very simple. To win you just need to come outside with me and write your own resignation letter from IBEX. Then you and Peter can go home as winners and start a wonderful new life."

"And if I refuse?" Ingram began to feel sick.

"Then it's a question of here's what you could lose," Ford nodded at Etheridge who started to drag Peter towards a small covered trapdoor. "You see the Sergeant here has to patrol this place because of the many hazards and dangers that come with a derelict old mine building. Would you believe there have even been fatalities of adventurous youngsters falling down the numerous inspection shafts, just like that one over there. Tragic really."

"You'll never get away with it," Ingram sneered, "and what if I sign the letter and then just rescind it tomorrow?"

"Number one," Ford came up close to Ingram, "are you really going to call a long serving and trusted officer of the law a liar and murderer? And number two, you rescind the letter if you wish but always look over your shoulder and remember what you could have won or in your case what you will undoubtedly lose."

Peter desperately tried to wriggle free from the Sergeant's strong grip but without success. Ford simply held out the pad of paper and a pen.

"Can you hear something?" Etheridge shouted over to Ford, "we might have visitors."

Ford listened intently and could just hear the faint buzz of a helicopter, "nothing to worry about. Keep the boy in here whilst me and Julie go and play for Bully's star prize."

Ingram reluctantly followed knowing that she had no choice. Her only hope now remained with DI Parker.

77

James Harkness hovered his powerful helicopter above the grim looking industrial site that once served the local tin industry. DI Parker and Alex Hart scanned the area below for any sign of people. It was Parker that spotted Etheridge's panda car slightly obscured by a tree but picked out by the helicopter's limited spotlight. "It's got to be him," Parker shouted.

Harkness took the helicopter down to land in a former loading bay generating a large cloud of dust in the process. Just as he touched down, Nick Ford appeared holding a gun to Julie Ingram. Both were startled by the sudden noise and appearance of the helicopter. Ford instinctively grabbed Ingram tight to his body whilst pushing the gun barrel into her rib cage. He was panicking inside now as the odds seemed against him.

As the dust settled DI Parker stood alone to face his adversary. At the same time Ford was joined by Etheridge at his side, still clinging hard to the struggling Peter.

"Detective Inspector Parker, I congratulate you. I never thought you had it in you." Ford made it clear that he was holding a gun against Ingram.

"So what now Ford? I would say it's over for you and Etheridge so why not just let Julie and Peter go?" Parker moved tentatively forwards, maintaining a calm pose and tone.

"You see I'm bound to win because I have the more powerful friends. It's like being in the best gang at school," Ford was now mocking.

"Where are the others?" Etheridge looked around with concern.

"Waiting for their moment Sergeant," Parker replied.

"Let's just call it quits then. We'll hand over Julie and Peter and then make our way out of here like nothing happened. Because it never did," Ford said cheekily before being distracted by the sound of a convoy of cars coming down the track. Flashing blue lights heralded the arrival of a fleet of police cars, although the usual sirens were muted. Seizing the moment, Ingram stuck the full force of a high heel shoe into Ford's shin and pushed him to the ground. Alex and Harkness appeared from the shadows to grab Ford before he could react. Parker moved over to confront Etheridge.

"Time to retire Sergeant," Parker squared up to the corrupt officer.

"Oh very Inspector Morse you boring has-been," Etheridge said with venom as he eyed for an escape route.

Parker threw a powerful right hook to catch Etheridge full in the face, sending him reeling to the floor and releasing Peter in the process. "I see myself as more of a Bruce Willis sort of cop these days so yip-e-ki-yay motherfucker. Always wanted to do that."

Peter moved over to his mother as Etheridge got up and tried to make a break before Parker blocked him and the two policemen began to wrestle. Simultaneously Alex was struggling to hold Nick Ford down as the police cars finally arrived. A loud shot rang out.

DCI Andy Burton came running over to the gathered crowd. Sergeant Etheridge was lying lifeless and bleeding on the floor.

"Where's Parker?" Burton shouted.

"Apprehending the kidnapper," Harkness replied. Neither Ford nor Parker could be seen.

Ford had run back into the main building and was scrabbling desperately in the dark, tripping several times but clutching on tight to his gun. He was aware of being pursued and the need to make good a quick escape. Looking over his shoulder, Ford pushed on through into the small annex in which Peter had been held captive. From nowhere he was hit by a charging rugby tackle as Parker powerfully knocked him to the floor. The gun fell from his grasp and skidded across the floor. Ford tried to pick himself up but was grabbed by Parker, who proceeded to drag him over to the shaft opening. The drop below was some forty feet. Parker pushed him to the edge.

"What are you doing? You're meant to be a policeman," Ford screamed in desperation.

"It is very simple, I chased the kidnapper who just shot a policeman and he fell down the shaft. No loose ends you see." Parker held a strong resolve.

"I didn't mean to shoot Etheridge, it should have been you. You can't do this, I demand you release me." Ford gulped in fear.

"Fine but mind your step," Parker loosened his grip as if he would let Ford fall. Ford cried out loud fearing the end. Parker looked down on him with menace, "all I want is a name. Who's your contact at The Globe?"

"I can't tell you," Ford screamed as Parker loosened his grip again.

"Time's running out," Parker lowered Ford into the hole as running footsteps approached.

"OK I'll tell you, it's Andrew Clark," Ford spluttered as he gasped for breath. Parker pulled Ford back up as DCI Burton arrived with several men. "I've got him Andy, the gun's on the floor somewhere."

"Well done Jack, looks like you can add cop killer to kidnapper. Etheridge is dead." Burton ordered his officers to take the bewildered Ford away.

"So are you going to tell me what's going on Jack?" Burton looked serious as he waited for a reply. The two detectives walked back outside as the covered body of Etheridge was being taken away.

Parker took his boss to one side, "Andy to go through everything could take all night and unfortunately I do not have that time to spare as Ford and Etheridge are not the end of it."

"Etheridge?" Burton grimaced, "are you saying that he is part of whatever is going on?"

Parker paused before answering carefully, "yes he and Ford were in cahoots to protect certain information that was acquired through IBEX. Julie Ingram uncovered the plot and nearly paid dearly for it."

"And the Gardner and Howard deaths, I take it they link in somehow?" The perceptive senior detective easily put the pieces together, "and of course the odd events around straight as they come Jack Parker being exposed as a bent copper."

"That's it Andy, but Ford and Etheridge are just the foot soldiers. There are far bigger fish to fry," Parker glanced over at Harkness and Alex waiting by the expensive and impressive helicopter.

"Jesus Jack, I feel like I've suddenly got James Bond under my command." Burton paced a few steps as he mulled over what to do, "right I'll take care of things here. All I ask is that you are careful and if you get in trouble keep me out of it."

"Nice one Andy, I won't let you down." Parker moved away to comfort Julie Ingram before stopping halfway, "and just one favour, can you keep the kidnapping from going public for twenty-four hours?"

"OK you've got it," Burton instantly agreed despite a shake of the head, "but Jack make sure you play it by the book."

Parker turned and smiled through the darkness, "only way I know Andy."

Parker marched over and immediately embraced Ingram as she watched a kindly policewoman comfort her son. His hollow offer to stay and protect the shaken couple was rejected by Ingram. She knew that Parker had to close out

the case and gave assurance that she would stay with her sister that evening.
Just as Parker turned to run to the helicopter he instinctively stopped in his
tracks and ran back to kiss Ingram.

"Still on for dinner?" Parker said smugly after Ingram had offered no
resistance and willingly participated in a full blown snog.

"You bet," Ingram giggled before helping to lead Peter away.

Within seconds Harkness's helicopter was airborne once more.

Jane Coker lounged on the luxurious black leather sofa in Luis Carter's
stylish and tastefully furnished lounge. For the first time in a couple of days
Jane felt extremely relaxed as she sipped on a glass of Merlot. Luis was busy
preparing a meal as a Katie Melua CD played melodically in the background.
The smell of chicken and onions wafted from the kitchen and stirred Jane's
taste buds as if she was waiting in anticipation on some special date.

"How are you feeling?" Luis appeared in the doorway, "and fancy a top-up?"
He nodded towards the wine glass.

"Fine although a little woozy from the wine," Jane giggled before holding
out her glass for more.

"You'll be safe here," Luis said reassuringly as he filled Jane's glass,
"although I hope the others are OK. No word as yet."

"No but that's to be expected. We will hear something soon enough," Jane
smiled sweetly up at the big handsome and muscular boxer.

Luis returned to his cooking duties after seeming embarrassed at Jane's
attention. Jane stood up and took a closer look at the array of family
photographs that adorned the mantle above the impressive log fire. It was
clear that Luis was a warm and loving son as he shared several scenes with
his mother and father along with his sister. The happy and content smiles
radiated from each portrait.

"I haven't seen or spoken to my parents in over a year," Luis confirmed with
a heavy heart as he stood in the doorway. "Only my sister will support me
now. Even my own mum and dad believe the lies that The Globe told about
me."

Jane looked on in shock, "that's terrible. Surely they knew you well enough
to know it was all lies?"

"My mum said she thought I had been changed by fame and she was right.
The thing was that it had not changed me into the monster that The Globe
portrayed. All the accusations had a profound effect on me and I became
even more distant and estranged from the ones I loved most. I withdrew into
a shell as I tried to cope with the embarrassment of my unwanted fame. It
was only the support and love of my sister, Felicia, that saved me from

complete ruin. She made me see the need to fight back and so here I am," Luis had finally opened up.

"You have a very special sister Luis. I'd love to meet her when this is all over," Jane put an arm around her towering host. "We will make sure you are reconciled and reunited with all your family."

Jane followed Luis into the kitchen as he finished preparing their meal, which was subsequently enjoyed with another bottle of wine. The couple soon lost themselves in conversation as they both willingly shared stories from their past. It was only when Luis went to make some coffee that reality came back to hit Jane.

"Luis can we go and put the IBC News Channel on?" Jane stood up expectantly, "my journalist friend should have aired The Globe story by now. I need to check."

The couple once again retired to the lounge and Luis selected the News Channel on Digital. Although there was still a great deal of coverage of the forthcoming Globe exclusive, including intense speculation about the subject of Saturday's press conference and conjecture around the whereabouts of Arturo Tabb, there was no mention of Jane's fed information to Clare Johnson. Luis even checked the TV Text for breaking news.

"Maybe it will come out later," Luis said philosophically.

"No something's not right, Shit I just hope Clare is OK." Jane looked extremely worried.

Luis limply put an arm around Jane's comparatively slight figure and pulled her close for comfort. Jane immediately felt her concern waver as she turned to face Luis. Within seconds they kissed and fell into each other's arms. As The Globe debate continued on the TV the mismatched couple found a needed passion in each other. Finally Luis stood whilst picking up his beau and carrying her like a small doll into the bedroom. As the door shut behind the TV news reporter switched to a breaking news item.

"Now just in, news of a helicopter crash close to Darcot Bridge in the West Country. It is understood that there have been fatalities but at this point it is not known how many or why the accident occurred."

79

"So what's the story with you and Jane?" James Harkness made small talk with Alex Hart as both sat in the background in Edgar's computer room.

"There's a bit of history between us if you know what I mean," Alex replied with a cocky laddish tone. "We still have an obvious lust for each other."

"Great," Harkness nodded unconvinced, "she's a very nice girl with a strong personality."

Edgar and Brian Harris were still frustratingly searching multiple databases and websites as they continued the seemingly impossible hunt for Marie-

Claire Magne. The hours of fruitless concentration finally told on Edgar as he slammed his keyboard with a fist and jumped to his feet in a rage.

"Come on boys let's take a break and think about this," DI Parker added a calmness to the proceedings.

Edgar did not speak but moved over to the corner of the room whilst rubbing his eyes.

The long silence that followed was eventually broken by Alex, "if I was under witness protection I would still find someway of contacting my family."

"But she has no family as her parents are both dead," Harkness retorted.

"Right but she's an only child. Now I'm an only child and by default I have acquired and got close to my other relatives like my cousins, even my Godparents. Believe me it's a typical trait." Alex looked around at the others.

"Worth a go," Edgar marched back over to his computer and began tapping away frantically once more.

"What are you checking?" Alex looked on with curiosity.

"I'm checking on Marie-Claire's aunties and uncles and for any Godparents." Edgar continued unabated. After some twenty minutes he finally spoke, "the bad news is that her mum was also an only child and her dad's only brother died as an infant. However the good news is that she does indeed have a Godmother who would seem to be very much alive and kicking and living in an old people's home in Inverness. Even better it would seem that the kindly nursing staff have set-up a Hotmail address for Ninety Three year old Rebecca Young."

"Can you access her mail?" Harkness asked with some concern that it could be that easy.

"Oh yes already done it," Edgar confirmed his fear as the others gathered around to view. "Well it would seem only one person ever writes to old Becky and this is someone by the name of Mary Stone. If you read these loving letters it would seem they are very close and eureka, this one even starts Dear Godmother. Thank you lord." Edgar punched the air.

"And of course Stone is an anagram of Seton" Harris chipped in smugly.

"So how do we trace Mary Stone?" Parker asked.

"First we look for more clues in these very lengthy and helpful emails," Edgar stated as he retained a deep concentration. "It would appear that Mary lives in Edinburgh….she has a daughter of sixteen, called Sally. Oh dear the daughter was involved in an accident last year that has left her paralysed. She fell of a horse during some kind of event. Mary has taken on the role of full time carer."

"So the daughter has taken Mary or should I say Marie-Claire's mother's name," Harris confirmed.

"This is very interesting," Edgar continued oblivious, "the last mail mentions that Mary has been offered an incredible job opportunity and that she would not be able to contact Becky for some time as she will be strictly incognito. It mentions that Sally will be cared for whilst Mary is away and that she will soon be able to give her daughter a chance to live again whatever that means. This mail was sent over two months ago."

"So we're buggered then? "Alex shrugged.

"No, oh no, we're too close now," Edgar gritted his teeth with determination. "Let's see if we can find out where the daughter is."

Once again the others stood around aimlessly as Edgar trawled various hospital records before eventually shouting out "found her" after a matter of minutes. "And it's even better than that," he added.

Edgar sat back to allow his audience to clearly see the information on the computer screen. "All I did was go back to the daughter's doctor and found a medical tracker on her whereabouts for any treatment administered. Good old Mary was never going to take a chance on Sally's health and this tracker brings us right up to the present. Young Sally is currently residing in an expensive private hospital in London called True Hope. It specialises in spinal injuries.

"Excellent, we've found the girl but how do we find the mum?" Sit and wait for her to turn up to visiting time?" Harkness was not convinced.

"In a word yes," Edgar laughed, "and although mummy has not been to see her daughter for over two months, would you believe that Sally is being discharged at eight o'clock tomorrow morning. Guess who's coming to collect her?"

80

Mary Stone's job was nearly complete. She had arrived safely in London with The Assignment and chaperoned the brash young woman to the five star luxury hotel as instructed. After the tedium of the last few weeks and the unenviable task of caring for the tetchy and pompous so called heir to the throne, Mary could see the light at the end of the tunnel. Since taking sole care of The Assignment after leaving Scotland, Mary had actually found the girl easier to deal with. She still despised her pretentious character but could now sense a nervousness and vulnerability in her mood as the realisation that the plan was about to come to fruition. Living off the prospect of being named the true Queen was one thing but to be finally revealed to the eyes of the world in that role was another. The curtain was about to go up and the leading lady had stage fright.

As Mary peered out of the window from the exclusive fifth floor guest suite and watched the traffic pass by below she allowed herself a wry smile. First thing in the morning she would be free once more and the young girl who supposedly had the world at her feet would be in the hands of the various PR Consultants and Behaviour Coaches. Mary would take the ridiculous excessive pay-packet and go to the only person who meant anything in her life. Now a tear trickled down Mary's cheek.

81

After it was decided that Harkness would fly his crew back to London at the crack of dawn, Edgar passed around cans of beer in celebration at finding Marie-Claire Magne. Brian Harris was convinced that she was the key to disprove The Globe's exclusive despite his companions still having doubts. For now they would enjoy the moment as the alcohol eased and numbed their weary bodies.

"Cheers Edgar, I knew you could do it," DI Parker sat next to the geeky looking computer boffin. "And thanks for putting us up for the night."

"No worries and party on," Edgar clashed his beer can against Parker's, "and well done on the dramatic rescue of the lovely Jules. Not your ordinary sort of day eh?"

"Edgar, any chance we can use the Wii?" Alex shouted over.

"Be my guest," Edgar pointed towards the games room door with his beer can.

"Actually whilst they go off and play can I ask one more favour?" Parker cornered Edgar and spoke in a semi-whisper.

"Sure copper whatever," Edgar replied after a slightly startled pause.

82

The End Of The Mole – The celebrated Investigative Journalist, The Mole, has announced his retirement. The decision comes on the eve of the maestro's greatest achievement, which will be revealed at The Globe's earth shattering world exclusive later this morning (Full Story Inside).

There was a very cold chill in the early morning air as DI Parker rang the doorbell at Luis Carter's London residence. In fact he had to ring it several times before Luis finally appeared in the doorway after checking on who his visitor was through the security peephole. As soon as the door opened Parker signalled to Harkness, who was waiting in his car. The former MP simply waved back in acknowledgement before driving off, chauffeuring Alex Hart and Brian Harris.

"Jack, wow!" Luis stuttered as he came to his senses, securing the tie-up belt around his dressing gown as he did so. "Come on in."

Parker entered clutching an early edition of The Globe in one hand and carrying a briefcase in the other. "Sorry for the unearthly hour, but we have a lot of work to do.

It was six-thirty am.

Jane Coker stood at the top of the stairs wearing one of Luis's old training sweatshirts. The garment completely swamped her, reaching down over and beyond her knees.

"Morning Jane," Parker said cheerily.

"Hi," Jane replied as she ruffled her unbrushed blonde locks.

"Glad that you are both safe. Maybe we could get some coffee and I will fill you in on the events of last night and then our proposed battle plans for today." Parker sounded extremely gung-ho.

Jane joined Parker in the lounge feeling both tired and slightly guilt ridden about the events of the previous night. It was not guilt for the moment of passion but rather the fact that she had not contributed any further to the fight against Tabb. Thankfully she had to make very little small talk with the Detective before Luis returned with a tray of coffees.

Both Jane and Luis sat agog as Parker relayed the details of the helicopter ride and the rescue of Julie Ingram and her son.

"Mercifully the journey back this morning was much less eventful, although I'm sorry to say that Alex was sick both before take-off and on arrival." Parker chuckled, "the result of one too many beers I hasten to add."

Jane tutted loudly, "figures."

Parker went on to explain how they had managed to track down the missing link to the Genealogy puzzle, Marie-Claire Magne.

"So now to the plan," Parker leant forward as if not to be heard. "We have two missions. Number one is for James, Alex and Brian to track down Marie-Claire and see if we can provide evidence to totally discredit The Globe's exclusive. This would of course be a major victory in itself."

"And number two?" Jane now hunched forward, "I take it this involves us?"

"It does," Parker replied with some reluctance, "I have a plan to destroy Tabb once and for all beyond humiliation. In the process we will clear the good names of both Luis and James by giving him some of his own medicine. I will understand if you do not want to help me."

Jane and Luis glanced at each other. "I think we will do anything," Jane responded for the pair.

"Good, then I will explain all," Parker could not hide his excitement.

83

Arturo Tabb put on his most exclusive and expensive Italian suit, made to measure with the finest cloth from Milan. As he postured and admired himself in the full length mirror Tabb felt every bit the victorious winner. The human cost was of no consequence as only the result mattered. That would be confirmed and revealed to the world in a matter of hours when the name of Arturo Tabb would be spoken of and revered around the world once more.

Tabb had been up since five am which was a standard to ensure he enjoyed each day in full. This day would be the most special of all. A quick check of his one hundred grand Cartier watch confirmed it was nearly seven. Andrew Clark would soon be arriving for the final briefing before the countdown could really begin. Tabb would then claim his prize and associated accolades before plotting the next chapter. It was a future that would not include Andrew Clark. The Assassin had already been replaced and his first mission confirmed. Nobody was indispensable or irreplaceable in Tabb's eyes, with only the present company excluded.

84

James Harkness drove to the True Hope hospital in good time and parked nearby. There was still over two hours to go before Mary Stone was due to arrive to discharge her daughter. The first and only contact with the hospital was made by Alex Hart as he made subtle enquiries to ensure that Sally Stone was still a patient. This was done under the cover of being a distant cousin who wanted to arrange a gift delivery. Alex managed to suitably charm the Receptionist who was happy to confirm that Sally was a patient. As he stood in the main reception area Alex also checked out the general layout of the hospital. From the shining expensive ceramic floor to the gleaming white flawless walls, it was a place that exuded wealth. Every level of staff from porter to nurse to doctor was smartly dressed and there was a complete calmness about the surroundings in contrast to the hustle and bustle of a National Health hospital.

Alex reported back to Harkness and Harris, who were waiting patiently in the car.

"One thing is for certain, Marie-Claire has come into some money," Alex confirmed. "Just think exclusive Harley Street and you'll get the picture."

"Well it can't be a pay-off from Tabb or he would not still be looking for her," Harkness pondered, "or did he finally find her?"

"We can only hope not," Alex was also having doubts, "so what is the plan now?"

"We take different positions," Harkness stated with a military air, "Brian can take the rear of the building and I will watch the entrance. We all have a photo courtesy of Edgar and a mobile phone. At the first sighting we will gather as a group to agree the best approach."

"So what's my role?" Alex was looking perplexed as Harris just nodded in agreement to the plan.

"A floater," Harkness smiled mischievously, "you can move between the two of us as the youngest and fittest team member. Reconnoitre the wider area."

"OK," Alex just shrugged.

"Fine and first duty is to fetch some coffees. White, two sugars for me," Harkness instructed as he got out of the car, leaving Alex dumbstruck.

85

Sally Stone was propped up in bed supported by several thick orthopaedic pillows. As a nurse busied herself checking a couple of charts and prescription lists, Sally remained focussed on the TV news. The speculation was reaching fever pitch in relation to The Globe's forthcoming press conference. The world's media was already gathering at The Globe's London office, with many journalists eager to try and sniff out a spoiler before the main event. To gain an insight now would bring instant fame and notoriety for the hack and their employer. But still there was only speculation and no concrete confirmation of the actual story. What was certain was that the whole world was watching and waiting in anticipation. Even the nurse kept glancing up from her work to listen to the IBC reporter. Sally was curious too but today was even more momentous for her as she was to be soon reunited with her mother.

"And so in around two hours time the world will finally get to know what Arturo Tabb and his Globe newspaper has uncovered that will stun the world. With the revelation this morning that the infamous Mole has retired, supposedly reaching the pinnacle of his career with this story, just how big will this exclusive turn out to be or will it simply fail to live up to all the hype? This is Clare Johnson for the IBC at The Globe offices in London."

86

If Jane Coker had stayed for another five minutes to continue watching the IBC coverage of The Globe exclusive she would have seen her friend Clare Johnson taking the central reporting role. Instead she had left with DI Parker and Luis Carter to instigate the first part of the detective's plan.

Luis chose to drive Brian Harris's old Allegro, which Jane found far from comfortable. Graciously Parker had opted to sit in the back but it then became unclear if his peaky disposition and quiet demeanour were due to the car's bumpy suspension or if he was nervously contemplating what he needed to do. In fact it was a combination of the two. Parker was starting to have doubts about the odds of success but knew he had to persevere and press on. He had to try whatever the consequences.

Luis drove until he reached a street a couple of blocks away from The Globe's office. It was from there that Parker would move on alone, aiming to rendezvous back with Jane and Luis in half an hour.

Parker nodded a slightly nervous farewell to the newly bonded romantic couple before pushing up the collar of his long grey coat and heading towards the crowds milling outside The Globe office. Parker did not join the expectant throng of eager reporters and curious spectators but instead moved around to the side of the building. Above him a large screen had been erected to transmit the conference to those outside who did not have the vital invitation and pass to enter.

"I'm sorry no access without valid ID," an extremely large security guard stepped in front of Parker.

"I'm on official police business," Parker growled as he flashed his badge.

"Oh right," the guard stuttered as he considered what to do.

"Well you can try and stop me and I will arrest you for obstruction," Parker snarled menacingly.

The guard stepped aside and Parker moved swiftly on in to the main building, his heart beating fast as he marched with purpose across the foyer to the lifts. Joining several staff members he selected floor three as if he was a regular visitor. On exiting the lift he continued down the corridor before veering off and walking straight into a nearby office.

"Sorry who are you and what do you want?" A flustered and indignant man said from behind his desk as he looked up at Parker.

"Detective Inspector Parker and I want you Andrew Clark," Parker moved to confront Tabb's project manager with a real swagger.

87

Mary Stone felt strangely subdued on the day she was to relinquish control of the Assignment and then be reunited with her daughter. It was as if she was getting a vibe that the day was not going to go to plan. After months of focus and planning for this very day, Mary was living on her nerves through fear of failure.

The first concern came with the call that instructed Mary to call a cab and bring the Assignment to The Globe building. The idea was to keep the arrival as completely low key, which made sense but the original directive was that a car would pick the Assignment up and Mary would then be free to go, with the job of escort taken up by another. At worst she would now be delayed in getting to the hospital but at least she had confirmed that full payment had already gone into her bank account.

The Assignment herself seemed almost pleased that Mary was to continue to accompany her. The young girl needed a touch of familiarity after spending most of her waking hours nervously vomiting down the toilet. As the cab took the two women across London Mary began to feel anxious for the pale ashen faced pretender to the throne. All the gutsy bravado had now gone and Mary knew that the girl was nothing more than a political pawn. Despite the very rich rewards Mary could not help but feel the guilt that came with the job she was about to complete.

The cab arrived in good time despite the heavier than usual London traffic, with the driver dropping his fare away from the ever growing crowd. As instructed Mary gently led the young girl towards the side of the building. Suddenly she stopped dead as a number of cameras flashed nearby. A TV crew began running towards them. Instinctively Mary put up a hand to cover her face and began to run pulling the Assignment along as she went. It was only when Mary reached the door and glanced nervously back that she realised the TV crew were tracking someone else.

"What the bloody hell are you doing?" Andrew Clark scowled from the doorway, "I said inconspicuous arrival. And what's with covering your face? It's the Assignment that needs protection; nobody is interested in your ugly mug."

"I'm sorry," Mary stuttered anxiously, "I just have a thing about cameras. But no harm done."

"No," Clark said dismissively, "well I guess you can go. The money's in your account and I never want to see or hear from you again. The consequences would be beyond severe."

"Yes I understand and that's fine. Thank you," Mary said bowing with humble subservience before quickly turning on her heels and leaving.

"Stupid old binty," Clark sneered, "good job she has no bloody idea what this will really mean. Come on let's go and get you ready for the show."

Clark led the tearful and frightened young girl away.

Mary scurried out of sight from the crowds, desperate to find a taxi to take her to the hospital and the reunion with Sally. She was still in good time. In the process Mary ran straight into a couple walking towards her. The shock sent her reeling.

"It's alright love," the large black man said with calm assurance.

Mary glanced up to acknowledge. "Sorry," she uttered before rushing off once more.

"Poor woman, obviously a lot on her mind," Luis Carter glanced over at Jane Coker.

"Haven't we all," Jane was uninterested, "let's go and find Detective Parker."

88

As Jane Coker and Luis Carter neared the front of The Globe building both instinctively bowed their heads through fear of recognition. Luis for his celebrity, and he had chosen to wear a thick scarf under his coat to disguise his distinctive features. For Jane it was fear of being seen by someone on Tabb's payroll.

The gathered crowd now resembled a mass of football fans eager to get into the stadium and watch the match. Up above the large screen flickered into action, showing a montage of news reports from the various newscasters present. As all eyes fixed on the screen, Jane and Luis anxiously scoured the scene for DI Parker. He was nowhere to be seen.

"Shit, I've got a bad feeling that something has gone wrong," Jane stated with great concern.

Luis reluctantly nodded in agreement as he continued to look around. It was then that Jane heard a voice that she recognised, but it was booming out through large speakers across the main square. Up on the screen was Clare Johnson reporting for the IBC as she stood barely a hundred yards across the street.

"That's my reporter friend I was really worried about," Jane almost shouted with some relief, "come on let's go and find her."

Luis had no option but to follow as Jane almost sped away. After managing to push through a mass of people, Jane timed her arrival perfectly as Clare was just wrapping up her mini report to camera. Without hesitation Jane moved straight over to confront her friend.

"Clare what's going on?" Jane spoke under her breath.

"Jane!" Clare was clearly startled, "oh my god you're OK." Clare led Jane to one side as the camera crew took a break. "I thought you were dead when the news came in about Paula Davenport. Where have you been? Why didn't you contact me?"

"We've had to be very cautious using any phones but I sent you an email. Did you not get it?" Jane said emphatically.

"In a word no," Clare shrugged, "mind you there's been a lot going on. Someone tried to frame me. They must have somehow linked the two of us and if they were on to me they've probably intercepted my mail."

"How did you get out of it?" Jane moved closer with curiosity as Luis stood guard.

"It was all down to Mark Alford, the head of News and Current Affairs. He believed and trusted me when nobody else would. I'm afraid I had to divulge the detail of our conversation. He was brilliant and even wanted me to take the lead reporter role here in the hope that you would get in touch. You have to meet him." Clare looked around for a sign of her boss.

"Yes all in good time," Clare glanced around apprehensively. "First we have to go and find someone, do you still have the same mobile?"

"Yes and is that the boxer, Luis…Luis Carter?" Clare had just recognised Jane's companion.

"It is but I'll save the introductions for later. Once you are in the press conference it will be good if I can text you with some feeder questions to ask of Tabb's cronies. It would be a major help and give you some great credibility on your first major assignment."

"Look I can get you in, Mark can pull some strings. He was so sure you were still alive and would turn up. The man is brilliant I tell you." Clare was still scrutinizing for a sign of Alford.

"Thanks a lot but we have a friend in possible danger," Jane ushered Luis away. "Keep your phone on and I'll be in touch."

Clare stood on the spot feeling deflated as with ironic timing Mark Alford appeared next to her. With a beaming smile she confirmed that Jane had made contact and that they had forged a plan in respect of the conference. Alford seemed annoyed and was insistent that Clare alerted him the instant she next heard from Jane. He then moved away to make a phone call, "This is Alford, Jane Coker is in the vicinity."

89

Alex Hart was bored of continually pacing backwards and forwards between James Harkness and Brian Harris. He wanted some action and yet the time of Marie-Claire Magne's supposed arrival had come and gone. He was starting to think it was a no-show and all the recent effort had been in vain. Alex had come so close to completing that major article for his portfolio, as his Editor Dan Goodman termed it. But Goodman would also say that conjecture was not proof. There would be no chance of a Booker prize without a concrete ending.

Distracted by the shop window across the street, displaying several very large plasma TVs, Alex ambled over to take a closer look. He was immediately startled by a black cab sounding its trumpeting horn as it sped down the inner lane reserved for taxis. Alex stepped back quickly almost tripping over his own heels. In typical fashion the driver gesticulated with a raised fist as his female passenger sat still and unmoved. The woman briefly turned to look at the errant pedestrian. That look sent a chill down Alex's spine. In a split second he realised he was looking at the face of Marie-Claire Magne.

"It's her, she's here," Alex shouted at the mobile phone after excitedly punching in Harkness's number. "A black cab should be with you any second now; Marie-Claire is the passenger."

Harkness agreed to call Harris as Alex began jogging towards the hospital. He soon met with Harkness and Harris lumbered behind. The trio watched from a hundred yards away as Marie-Claire paid her fare and entered the hospital.

"OK over to you Alex," Harkness looked straight at the energized Journalist. "The hospital already sees you as a relative and we need you to use that position to get to see Marie-Claire. Make sure you use the name Mary Stone and just make sure you do not blow it. All we want is some time to talk to Mary and we can then leave her be."

Alex was lifted by his bestowed responsibility and marched over to the hospital with a steely determination to succeed.

Mary Stone could not hide her glee any longer as she beamed a smile at the hospital Receptionist. She almost wanted to sprint past the desk and rush to hug her beautiful but helpless daughter.

"You can rest assured Miss Stone that Sally has been absolutely fine and has been responding very well to her prescribed treatment. You can be very proud of her," the Receptionist reciprocated the happy vibe. "I do know that she is so excited that you are coming to collect her today."

Mary thanked the bubbly middle-aged woman before heading off towards her daughter's private room.

"Oh Miss Stone sorry to delay you but I nearly forgot to mention, one of Sally's cousins came in earlier. I think that a surprise delivery may be on its way." The Receptionist tried and failed with a dramatic wink.

"I'm sorry…I mean you must be mistaken," Mary's heart sank as she contemplated just who could have tracked her down. Had the renowned connections of the Nutini brothers finally hit the jackpot or was she about to be discovered and unmasked by Arturo Tabb's people.

"No Mary the lady is correct, although to be fair it's you I need to see." A young unshaven but good looking man stood in front of her.

Mary moved over to him and spoke softly, "who are you? What do you want with me?"

"My name is Alex Hart and I'm a journalist. Basically I just need your advice as I think you may be able to help bring down a murdering crook by the name of Arturo Tabb." Alex dispassionately stood his ground.

"Tabb? Are you connected to Tabb? But how did you suss me?" Mary had now led Alex away from the curious and prying ears of the Receptionist.

"I know a lot about you and no I have no connection with Tabb apart from needing to destroy him." Alex looked coldly into Mary's eyes, "Mary or should I say Marie-Claire, are you willing to help me? All I ask is that you speak to me and my friends. There's a café over the road and we promise not to keep you very long as we know how important it is for you to be with your daughter."

"Sounds like I have no choice really," Mary slowly nodded as she relented, "I will give you fifteen minutes and no more."

Mary assured the Receptionist that she just had to step out briefly with Sally's' cousin and that she would return shortly. Alex then led her out of the hospital and across the street to meet the two other men.

"Allow me to introduce my friends," Alex announced in triumph.

"Well one I know already," Mary sighed.

"I suppose that scandalous MPs do tend to get their photo bandied around a fair bit," James Harkness reached out to shake Mary's hand.

"Oh yes come to think of it I do recognise you too. Harkness isn't it?" Mary stated assuredly.

"Please call me James." Harkness shot Harris a puzzled look.

"And it was you Brian Harris that I initially recognised. The infamous Genealogist, I've been to a number of your lectures. Always very entertaining and very good."

"Charmed I'm sure," Harris kissed Mary's hand.

"Let's go and get a coffee," Harkness pointed to a nearby café, "we can then explain what this is all about."

"I think I already know," Mary announced.

Alex found a secluded corner table whilst Harkness collected four mugs of coffee.

"So Mary tell me, how on earth can you know why we are here?" Harkness cut straight to the chase.

"Well Alex mentioned that you wanted to bring down Arturo Tabb. In tow you have a renowned Genealogist. It could only mean one thing," Mary leant forward feeling as if she was in total control. "You know about the story behind Tabb's exclusive and the plan to unveil a young lass as the long lost, or buried, pretender to the throne. But the most impressive thing of all is how you managed to place me in the equation and then actually find me."

"You know about Tabb's plot?" Alex almost shouted, "is that why you've been away and come into some money? Has Tabb paid you off?"

Mary rocked her head back and laughed, "och Tabb has paid me alright and a ridiculous amount of money at that. But let's just say he has no idea of who I am. He was desperate to find me and all the time I was hidden right under his nose."

"Mary you have our undivided attention," Harkness spoke for the stunned trio.

"I am assuming by the fact that you somehow tracked me down that you are aware of my real past and the fact that I have lived most of my adult life under Witness Protection." Mary smirked in acknowledging the three nodding heads. "To be honest I really struggled to find a new identity, even though I was allowed to still live in Scotland. I was initially sent to the Highlands, where after many years of living as a recluse I thought I had at least found the man of my dreams. The man who was to be the father of my beautiful Sally. He turned out to be a violent wife beating bastard and with the help of Witness Protection I was able to disappear and start a third life with my daughter. We moved to Edinburgh away from the bastard's clutches. That was the happiest time of my life. Sally blossomed into a beautiful and very active teenage girl who truly was and still is my best friend. Then the accident changed everything." Mary sat in glum silence.

"The accident?" Alex echoed.

"Sally loved horse riding," Mary continued, "she was never happier than when riding. Then she had a fall and her beloved grey Thoroughbred landed on her. It broke her back and my young girl was to never walk again." Tears welled in Mary's eyes.

"Take your time," Harkness placed a comforting hand on Mary's shoulder.

"Thank you," Mary managed a smile, "anyway from then on I devoted my time to caring for my daughter. Every day my heart was breaking inside but I managed to find a job as an archive librarian that provided some money and a much needed distraction. At least I could follow my other great passion, History. It was through my work that I came to meet Raymond Hilliard and Robert Jameson."

Harris literally ground his teeth as the mention of Jameson's name, "so were they looking to seek you out?"

"They were looking to find a legend and in the process found that I was the missing link with the key. Unfortunately for them they had no idea that Mary Stone was in fact the Marie-Claire Magne their research had pinpointed."

Mary allowed herself a wry chuckle, "Jameson and Hilliard devoted long hours both day and night searching for their grail, which was the so called Historian's Fable that letters existed that were written by Mary Seton, a Lady In Waiting to Mary Queen of Scots. The letters purportedly contain astonishing facts that would rock the monarchy to its core. It was said they were confessional in nature as Mary Seton reached the end of her days during retirement in Rhiems and unburdened her soul to a close relative"

"I have heard of these letters but of course Hilliard and Jameson did not find them did they?" Harris said smugly.

"No they did not but what they did find was enough detail and historical fact to support a scandal. The piece that was missing was the letters themselves. By making sure that the evidence could not be challenged the pair were confident of pulling off a major con trick. Through Jameson's' skill in manipulating family trees they produced an heir to the throne that could be readily controlled .They then planted a set of letters in Rhiems and paid off various people to declare the find. The fabricated letters were in this new theory kept by Mary Seton as a secret record of her correspondence with Mary Queen of Scots prior to her time of captivity in England. It was easy to invent the idea that Mary Queen of Scots had somehow entrusted the letters to Mary Seton in order to hide their dark secret shortly before she was made captive. Hilliard was then of course dispatched to authenticate the find before anyone else could react and a convenient fire left the plotters in check position on the chess board."

"But not checkmate?" Harkness interjected.

"No and they knew that but all of their research came back to me as the only viable relative who could substantiate the truth. Hilliard was so sure that the letters existed and very concerned about his reputation if they became public. Jameson assured him that if their employer, Arturo Tabb, could not find

Marie-Claire Magne then nobody could. There was also the caveat of the Witness Protection programme and the risks that would come if I, Marie-Claire held up my hand." Mary paused to drink some coffee.

"So how do you know so much?" Alex was extremely curious, "did Hilliard and Jameson actually involve you in their research."

"They involved me in terms of using me in my capacity of historical librarian in gathering archived documents and files. Of course they had no reason to distrust me or know that I in fact was already an expert in what they were researching. Quite often they would even leave notes lying around which I would copy and read later. They would print off emails on my own printer from a contact at a data centre called IBEX, from where someone called Nick Ford would supply reams of information, both about me and other modern descendents in the Seton line. I was able to piece together the whole plot, right down to the fact that the aim was to cover the story under the guise of The Mole to add further credibility and dramatic effect." Mary relaxed more and more as she shared her secret knowledge.

"So what happened next? Why did you have to go away and then end up getting paid by Arturo Tabb?" Alex's journalistic instinct clicked into overdrive.

"By pure coincidence and chance," Mary rolled her tongue, "Raymond Hilliard took quite a shine to me and even took me out to dinner a couple of times. He was very aware of the situation with Sally and how devoted I was to caring for my daughter. I let it slip that my dream was to one day be able to take Sally to America for what they call plasticity treatment. Through electrical devices patients with spinal cord injuries are able to stand and walk again, but it takes three months training and is very expensive. I had read all about it in an SCI newsletter and the thought of my Sally walking again filled me with hope. Anyway Hilliard took pity on me and I was soon offered a job of chaperoning a young girl for which I would be paid a ridiculous amount of money. All that I and my two male bodyguards knew was that the girl was special and from a royal bloodline. She truly believed it herself and was a total pain in the arse and it was obvious that she had been easily disillusioned and controlled."

"So it was an offer you could not refuse?" Alex could now empathise.

"For my daughter's sake no, although there was the concern at the back of my mind that they could trace Marie-Claire Magne and find she was very close by after all. But I had to take the chance. I secured a sizeable payment up front and was able to find a place for Sally in the hospital over the road. I was then sent to France and then on to a remote cottage in the Highlands. The final task was to deliver the girl to The Globe offices this morning at which point I was to be relieved of my duties, leaving me free to fly Sally to America. The tickets are booked for this evening." Mary sat back as if the story was over.

"What you have told us Mary certainly fits and we now know that The Globe has its star guest ready to make an appearance at this morning's press conference." Harkness paused before taking a direct approach, "the question is do you know if the letters do exist and if so where they are and can they be used to disprove Tabb's fairytale?"

"In a word yes, and that fits all," Mary replied teasingly before taking a more serious approach, "alright enough of the games. I have a letter that has passed through the generations that was written by Mary Seton during her retirement to Rhiems. It was written shortly before her death in Sixteen-Fifteen, when to be honest she was living in abject poverty. It was intended for a cousin but was never delivered and included in a collection of effects after her death. Although the letter is quite mundane in nature it does confirm that Mary regretted never baring children and her writing is very succinct for a lady of seventy-four. If nothing else it will clearly show that the supposed correspondence written to Mary Queen of Scots during her captivity is a forgery. The letter I have will stand up to any testing of authenticity."

"Part of me is delighted that we can call Tabb's bluff but another part of me is totally deflated that this fabled letter contains no more than the final routine diary account of a sad old lady." Harris slouched heavily in his chair.

"Are you saying we can borrow the letter?" Harkness stayed focussed on the main task.

"You can have it. It is held in a safety deposit box near here, which I have already arranged to empty and close today. I will need to go and make preparations for Sally to be transported to the airport and will then collect the letter for you. All I ask is that you never reveal how it was acquired." Mary got up to go, "I will meet you back here in one hour."

"And you will not want it back?" Alex did not hide his surprise.

"Once I leave these shores I aim to begin yet another new life. The letter is part of another past and it is time to move on." Mary made a swift exit.

91

"Mister Tabb, I'd like to introduce you to Sophie Devine," Andrew Clark spoke humbly as he led the frightened young heir apparent into Arturo Tabb's office.

"Charmed," Tabb gently shook the girl's hand after being thrown slightly by Clark's unusual subservient demeanour.

"Sophie is feeling a little nervous, which is understandable," Clark continued in his own uneasy vain, "but I have assured her that she is amongst friends and that The Globe will take very good care of her."

"Of course, of course, you are very much part of our family now. We will ensure you are protected from the world's media. Has Sophie signed the contract?" Tabb glared at Clark.

"Yes she has after we fully explained the benefits it would afford her," Clark did not look Tabb in the eye but kept his head bowed.

"Excellent well then I will allow Mister Clark to take you along to a brief rehearsal of what you can expect this morning and I will then be personally at your side as we reveal who you are to the waiting world." Tabb ushered the couple to the door as Sophie just smiled and nodded.

Tabb did not enjoy being nice to anyone and so was relieved that the niceties were over. His relief was short lived as Clark reappeared, "Mister Tabb, just a small formality but can you come out and countersign the POA on behalf of Globe Enterprises?"

"I suppose so," Tabb growled and marched past Clark and over to his PA's desk.

Clark quickly followed behind, carrying a folder of papers which he handed to Tabb. The media tycoon threw the papers down on the desk before scanning his eye over the main document.

"It also needs to be stamped with the company seal. Allow me to get the stamp on your desk," Clark scurried away holding on tight to his briefcase. Tabb continued to read the Power Of Attorney as Sophie Devine stood nervously at his side. He then quickly signed above the signatures of Sophie and the Company Secretary. "Clark have you not found that stamp yet?" Tabb marched back into his office to find Clark shiftily sitting in Tabb's chair, "what the bloody hell are you doing?"

"Sorry I was just trying to locate the stamp. Thought if I sat down I might spot it," Clark reacted like an employee caught with his fingers in the till.

"Out," Tabb barked as Clark hurriedly jumped up form the chair. The rotund tycoon reached for the stamp conveniently placed in the middle of the desk. "Are you blind? What's getting into you Clark?"

"Sorry Mister Tabb, just not feeling very well but all will be fine. Allow me to administer the stamp," Clark almost ran from the room before hastily returning having stamped and sealed the document. "Thank you and good luck with the conference, I'll be watching from the floor."

"And very soon you'll be no more," Tabb snarled to himself as he stood alone cutting a sinister figure in the semi-dark office.

92

Jane Coker was feeling helpless as there was no sign of DI Parker amongst the milling crowd and the start of the press conference was now less than an hour away. Luis Carter confirmed with a shake of the head that his own recent search had been fruitless.

"That's it, I have to try and call him," Jane said firmly as she flicked open her mobile phone.

"What if they have him and they are waiting for your call?" Luis held up a cautious hand.

"The alternative is to do nothing," Jane went to dial but her phone rang for an incoming call instead,. "Hi…no there's a problem. We've lost Parker, just can't find him anywhere. I'm going to try and call him."

Luis watched as Jane listened intently before acknowledging that she had made contact with IBC Reporter, Clare Johnson. After diligently listening to more instructions, Jane meekly rang off.

"That was Alex; they've got a copy of a letter written by Mary Seton. They are due to pick it up in about half an hour, about quarter past nine, and then hotfoot it over here." Jane seemed far from elated.

"What about Jack?" Luis still looked around in hope.

"Harkness has said that I must not call him as if he is held captive it could somehow lead them to us. Instead he wants me to tee up Clare for their big arrival. If the pick-up is nine-fifteen then they will not get down here until the press conference is underway. They want Clare to set up a big entrance," Jane shrugged with sarcastic enthusiasm.

"I'm sure Jack can look after himself," Luis put an arm around Jane to comfort her.

"Thanks," Jane gazed up at her gentle giant, "but it's more than that if I'm honest. This letter will certainly embarrass Tabb but his media empire will help him squirm out of it. Jack's plan would have finished him and I needed to do that for Paula."

After contemplating her position for a moment, Jane made a call to Clare Johnson. She explained that they now had the evidence to shoot down The Globe exclusive and they needed the IBC to give them the voice to be heard in the press conference. Clare said she would need to run it by her boss, Mark Alford.

Jane only had to wait five minutes for the return call, just as the invited journalists began to make their way into The Globe building for the start of the press conference.

"Well OK if that's what he wants then that's what we will have to do." Jane looked confounded as she listened to Clare, "I will meet Mark at the front of the MYEX exchange bureau as soon as our friends arrive. Understood."

"What's going on?" Luis was impatient.

"Seems that Clare's boss will only play ball if he can meet me and see what we have. Clare's going into the conference and so as soon as the others arrive with the letter I need to go and meet this wonderful Mark over at that foreign exchange bureau across the road." Jane nodded over at a tall narrow building with long luminous sign spelling MYEX. "Apparently he's so excited about what we have, even though he has no idea what it is, that he is willing to miss the first part of the press conference to help us."

93

Mary Stone's reunion with her daughter Sally was every bit as emotional as Mary had envisaged it would be. The strong emotionally hardened Scot was once again reduced to tears as the sight of her stricken girl. It only required the sweet welcoming smile as the pretty Sally finally saw her mum again after so long apart.

After several long and lingering hugs, Mary explained that they would soon be starting a new life in America, where Sally would once again know the joy of walking. The hospital staff helped pack Sally's belongings and collected her specially designed wheelchair. Mary then explained that she needed to make some final arrangements for their trip and that she would return for Sally in about half an hour. The staff were so friendly that a trainee nurse said she would willingly keep Sally company until Mary's return, whilst the senior doctor said he would even arrange for hospital transport to take Mary and Sally to the airport.

Mary once again caught a cab for the short ride to the bank holding her safety deposit box. As well as the Mary Seton letter, Mary had also deposited various other documents, including Sally's passport, the flight tickets and some treasured photographs of her parents. The bank proved to be extremely efficient as Mary did not have to queue or wait long for her box to be brought out. She secured the majority of the contents in a holdall bag before requesting a large envelope from the bank assistant. Mary then carefully held the very old letter concealed in a thick plastic protecting wallet. It was still in extremely good condition after surviving over several centuries. Mary gazed at the piece of history before her and then concealed it for the last time.

As agreed Mary made her rendezvous with the recently acquainted renegade male trio. It was just after nine-fifteen. All three had been anxiously glancing at the café door willing for Mary to appear as they also kept an eye on the small TV screen fixed to the far wall. The picture showed the interior of The Globe conference room as the world's media waited for the show to begin. After several well intended hugs, the trio all wished Mary the best of luck among the thanks for helping their cause. Within seconds they had gone, hotfooting their way to Harkness's car which was now conveniently parked on the street outside. Mary sighed with contentment as she looked up at the televised scene at The Globe, which had the café clientele captivated. She then calmly, and completely unnoticed, walked away.

94

At exactly nine-thirty the lights of the packed auditorium in The Globe building dimmed. A hush of anticipation followed amongst the gathered media invitees as two unfamiliar men walked out and on to the small platform before taking a seat behind a table shrouded in a bright blue tablecloth. Both looked nervous and uneasy in the spotlight.

"Ladies and gentlemen," a tannoy announcement boomed out of the multiple speakers positioned around the room, "may I introduce your host, the head of Globe Enterprises, Arturo Tabb."

In comparison to the previous entrance Tabb appeared like a political leader about to deliver a rousing speech at a party conference. With a confident swagger he moved up on to the platform and picked up a microphone.

"Ladies and Gentlemen welcome to your part in history," Tabb looked around arrogantly at those assembled before him. "Because my friends that is what today is all about…history. In a moment I will hand over to our two much esteemed guests to explain the full intricacies of the incredible revelations uncovered by The Globe's premier reporter, The Mole. Both of these gentlemen are experts in their chosen fields and will fully validate what The Globe has discovered does indeed support the incredible conclusions and facts that cannot be ignored. Please be patient and all will be revealed, but first I would like to pay tribute to the career of The Mole. For obvious reasons he cannot be here with us today and has sadly chosen this most auspicious of achievements as the point at which to mark his retirement."

Clare Johnson, like many of the assembled journalists and reporters, was willing for Tabb to get to the point. As Tabb read through some of the highlights of The Mole's illustrious career Clare checked her watch and wondered if Jane Coker had met with Mark Alford. There was still no word of confirmation through her earpiece or via text.

"I give you The Mole," Tabb took a step back as the crowd returned a muted applause. A large projector screen above Tabb's head flickered into action showing the picture of a burnt out building. The lights over the audience dimmed further although the small centre stage remained illuminated.

"May I introduce Raymond Hilliard, a distinguished and celebrated Historian specialising in the reign of the Stuart monarchy." Tabb retreated into the shadows.

Hilliard nervously got to his feet and picked up a microphone. "Thank you, as Mister Tabb has stated I have dedicated a career in reviewing the life and times of the Stuart monarchy. It was therefore a common practice that I am asked to comment on or review significant theories and discoveries from that period in history. The burnt out building that you see on this slide is in fact, or was, a small chapel in the French town of Rhiems. You may have even read in some of the smaller newspaper columns that I had been asked to go to Rhiems to authenticate and verify a collection of documents found secreted in an old stone hidey-hole in this very chapel. I arrived at the chapel late in the evening of February thirteen this year after catching the first available flight. The owner of the chapel refused permission for me to take the documents away and the light in the chapel was poor. Intending to return in the morning I was still able to conduct a number of simple tests on the parchment. The lab results from the tests later confirmed the documents to be around four hundred to five hundred years old. I have included the results of these tests in a press pack that you will all receive at the end of this conference and have the actual paper fragments I removed here with me today.

Hilliard paused and sipped some water as he realised that the crowd would have already worked out that the letters were destroyed, just as he expected and wanted.

"On a secondary level I took a number of digital photographs of the papers, although you will have to forgive their dark nature due to the limited light." Grainy pictures of the letters flashed up on the screen briefly as Hilliard paused once more. "Despite being extremely tired I decided to take a look at the photographs on my laptop that evening. It was then the full enormity of the find hit me. What had been found was a series of letters written in correspondence between Mary Queen of Scots and her loyal and favourite lady-in-waiting Mary Seton. Such letters have been fabled to exist in Historian folklore, with the legend stating that they were entrusted to Mary Seton shortly before Mary Queen of Scots was taken into captivity in England. Mary Seton was to eventually retire in poverty to Rhiems but would never betray her former mistress. These letters are written in Latin whilst carrying the Queen's seal and scribed in her hand as I recognised from famous surviving letters. I am of course fluent in Latin and have since had the handwriting checked and confirmed by experts as being authentic." Hilliard was now much more composed as he spoke expertly on his specialist subject.

"I must confess that as no letters exist written in the hand of Mary Seton I could not verify the handwriting but the age testing of the parchments and the sequential narrative in the chain of correspondence gives absolute credence to the fact that the letters are genuine. That night, as you can imagine, I hardly slept and made my way back to the chapel at first light. It was then I literally fell to my knees in horror. The chapel had been burnt to the ground and the letters destroyed. Was it an act of God? Who knows but I thank my lucky stars every day that something drove me to both test and copy the letters."

Hilliard stopped once again for dramatic effect as he drank some water. In the crowd Clare Johnson was now transfixed to the proceedings.

"And so to the contents of the letters and how I came to entrust the wider scope of the investigation to The Mole and The Globe in uncovering the greatest historical expose of them all."

95

The crowd assembled outside The Globe building were engrossed as the large screen relayed the conference, just as a global TV audience were equally spellbound. James Harkness arrived at the scene having listened to Hilliard's opening gambit on the car radio along with companions Alex Hart and Brian Harris. It was Harris who was clutching tightly to the golden letter secured in a brown envelope as if his life depended on keeping hold of it. Whilst Harkness frustratingly could find nowhere to park the clock was ticking. Finally he made a snap decision to drop off his passengers.

The conference continued with Hilliard disclosing the translation of the contents of the newly discovered letters as he built up to the revelation within that James I was not the natural born son of Mary Queen of Scots and that the true heirs to the throne were the twins supposedly still born to the Queen on the island of Lochleven. Hilliard then added further spice by revealing that subsequent painstaking research had revealed that one of the twins, a girl, had subsequently died in infancy. Now was the perfect time to reveal the Genealogy expert who had made the discovery as Hilliard made way on the stage for Robert Jameson to explain how he had mapped out an intricate family tree all the way up to the present starting from the surviving male twin.

Alex Hart called Jane Coker and was quickly reunited with his old flame, accompanied respectively by Brian Harris and Luis Carter. It was with great reluctance that Harris released the letter into Jane's care. The bullish Genealogist then became even more concerned with the fact that Jane would not let anyone accompany her in her vital meeting.

After making a short call to Mark Alford Jane left her friends feeling nervous and apprehensive as she assumed full accountability for the fight against Tabb. As the smarmy tone of Robert Jameson's voice resonated across the main plaza Jane stood impatiently at the corner of the MYEX building. It was not long before she was confronted by the stylish and confident figure of Mark Alford.

"Hi Jane, pleased to meet you," Alford held out a hand which Jane politely shook, whilst she held on tightly to the letter in her other hand.

"Hi, listen we need to be quick," Jane looked around anxiously.

"No problem let's have a look at this letter and we can get things moving," Alford held out his hand again.

Jane went to give him the envelope before stopping quickly in her tracks, "how do you know I have a letter?" Jane took a step back, moving the document back behind her back.

"A guess," Alford said unconvincingly, "look Jane it will just make good sense to everyone concerned for you to hand over the letter."

"And if I refuse?" Jane started to edge away.

"Stood behind you right now is a man with a gun complete with a very effective silencer. He fires accurately below your shoulder blade and you slump forward into my arms. We both move you back out of sight into the alleyway and all these people with their focus elsewhere are none the wiser. I take the letter and you become a simple crime statistic." Alford spoke with real menace as Jane felt the jab of a pistol barrel in her back.

"So that's it, now it all makes sense," Jane spluttered in frustration, "you did not trust or want to help Clare, you just saw an opportunity to use her to get to me."

"Very perceptive," Alford moved forward, "now I want you to back away very slowly into the alleyway and then hand me the letter."

From a distance the tall figure of Brian Harris could just see Alford and Jane engaged in conversation, whilst the gunman stood back in the shadows out of view.

"Has Jane gone to her rendezvous?" James Harkness marched up to rejoin the group.

"Yes, Brian's keeping a watchful eye," Alex nodded.

"Who is Jane meeting?" Another familiar voice asked. It was DI Jack Parker.

"Jack, where have you been?" Luis excitedly stuttered.

"I had to report into the local station to make my presence and authority here completely kosher, but I ended up getting held up much longer than intended. Had to rely on my Guv, Andy Burton, to give me jurisdiction." Parker spoke with frustration.

"Yeah and I just found him wondering around," Harkness confirmed.

"So who is this contact that Jane has? James has filled me in on the letter, which is a real result," Parker was genuinely surprised.

"Some senior guy at the IBC, her friend's boss. Reckons he can help us crack this," Alex replied.

"Yeah his name's Mark Alford," Luis confirmed.

Parker's face grimaced with concern as he snapped, "where are they meeting?"

"They are just over there," Harris pointed towards the MYEX building, "or at least they were. Bugger, they've gone."

"Shit," Parker almost screamed, "Mark Alford was one of the key names that I got out of Tabb's crony, Andrew Clark."

Without hesitation Luis began running towards the MYEX building, knocking people out of the way as he went. Alex led the others in hot pursuit. Luis bludgeoned his way through and ran blindly into the alley as his friends struggled to keep up. Instantly he spotted Alford holding the envelope containing the letter as Jane cowered in the presence of a stranger nearby. Luis simply sprinted and jumped at Alford knocking his stunned target to the ground. Jane reacted quickly and grabbed the letter as it slid unattended across the floor. After throwing a single knock-out punch to Alford's jaw it was then that Luis looked up to see the barrel of the Hitman's gun. Alex had now led the charge of the others to the scene. The Hitman looked up and started to back away before instinctively aiming his pistol at Jane. Luis hastily realised his intent and within an instant the gun was fired. But the former boxer had used very ounce of his athletic ability to throw himself forward and into the line of fire. As the Hitman retreated it was the body of Luis Carter that lay motionless on the floor.

A short eerie silence was broken by Jane's scream as she saw blood seeping from Luis's chest. The Hitman had turned to go but was bravely caught by a scything rugby tackle from Alex. As both men then grappled on the floor the inexperienced Hitman tried desperately to turn the gun towards his opponent's head. Just as the barrel moved into line a swift kick from the boot of DI Parker sent the gun spiralling through the air. With his weapon gone the Hitman was quickly restrained as Parker called for police back-up and an ambulance.

Jane tearfully cradled and rocked the limp body of her hero boxer as the others watched helplessly. Harkness finally reacted and used his jacket to staunch the blood, with the movement instilling a reaction as Luis drifted back into consciousness and his eyes flickered open. The stricken fighter managed a weak smile towards Jane.

"Hang on in there Luis," Alex encouraged.

"Will do," Luis managed a faint breathless response, "just promise me you will all finish the job." The boxer then relapsed into a coma once more.

An ambulance crew arrived just before several armed police officers. Parker was busy checking the prostrate body of Mark Alford. "DI Parker," he shouted flashing his badge from a crouched position. "Arrest that man over there for attempted murder and then I want you to retain this piece of shit for aiding abetting." Parker jerked Alford's body with his knee causing the newsman to mumble as he came to his senses.

"What's this all about?" The senior police officer demanded, "what authority do you have here?"

"I'll give you my DCI's number to ratify my authority. In the meantime you need to keep these two in custody until I complete my investigation." Parker barked his orders with assured authority.

"And what about these others?" The senior officer was highly suspicious.

"I need their assistance to foil a major crime," was Parker's simple response. The senior officer insisted on making the call to DCI Burton before letting Parker go, as the DI allowed himself a sardonic chuckle as his boss received yet another unusual call from the Met.

Luis Carter had once again regained consciousness as he was placed on a stretcher, "Jane please see this through."

"But I need to be with you now," Jane said tearfully.

"No," Luis insisted as he winced in pain, "go ahead with the plan. You owe it to Paula."

Jane hesitated before Harkness volunteered to go in the ambulance with Luis. At the same time the police finally led the Hitman and Alford away as the IBC man loudly protested his innocence.

"What are you going to pin on Alford?" Alex said as an aside.

"I'll think of something," Parker smirked, "in the meantime let's go and kick some ass." The DI held up an official press badge and conference invitation taken from Alford's jacket pocket.

96

The majority of the press conference audience sat open-mouthed in disbelief as Robert Jameson explained how his extensive Genealogy research had drawn-up a family tree line of inheritance dating back to the supposedly genuine surviving offspring of Mary Queen of Scots. For the final piece of the jigsaw credence was given to the modern research of The Mole in tracing and then finding the true heir to the throne. The final statement drew an audible gasp from those assembled in the hall.

"And so ladies and gentlemen," Jameson announced triumphantly, "I give you our true Queen…please meet Sophie Devine."

Arturo Tabb led the blushing young pretender into the room, linking arms for both comfort and show. The room remained in stunned silence.

Clare Johnson knew that whatever was revealed was going to be a falsehood but there was still no direction as to how Tabb could be challenged and disproved. Then came the signal that she had been waiting for: a text from Jane Coker.

'look out for 2 men with a brown envelope. 1 very tall with beard. Jane'

Clare instantly looked to the back of the room just as Brian Harris and Alex Hart entered. Harris was certainly tall with a beard and was clutching a brown envelope as the duo made their way to the front.

"Ladies and gentlemen, we do have time for limited questions before we release today's press pack containing all of the pertinent information and records. It will give you all the evidence you will need to digest and report on this historic day." A Globe compere now assumed responsibility for proceedings.

Clare Johnson intuitively held up her 'table tennis' bat sign emblazoned with IBC, whilst beckoning Harris and Alex over.

Robert Jameson and Raymond Hilliard had now spotted the arrival of Harris but were powerless to stop the compere from handing over the floor to Clare as a microphone was hastily delivered.

"Clare Johnson, IBC," Clare stated clearly and succinctly, "allow me to pass the microphone to a subject matter expert in this field."

Harris thankfully took the mic, "Brian Harris, Genealogist, and this is all bloody poppycock, made up bunkum, fairytale fiction." His voice boomed through the speaker system with some feedback distortion.

"It is you that is the fake," Jameson retorted mockingly, "so where's your proof man?"

Harris held up the brown envelope, "I have here an actual letter written by the hand of Mary Seton. It is very straightforward in nature, although does mention her regret in never marrying or having children. I put this forward and stand behind it for date testing and handwriting testament versus your badly photographed and now unfortunately destroyed letters. With the undoubted confirmation that this letter is genuine, what can we deduce about this fantastical find in Rhiems? Without genuine confirmation from Mary Seton, where is your story?"

All eyes in the auditorium were now trained on the imposing figure of Brian Harris. Arturo Tabb shot an angry glance at Jameson and Hilliard as the compere faltered in trying to bring order. Tabb finally took the mic himself, "very interesting Mister Harris. It looks like we have a stalemate for now but I'm extremely confident that once the relevant tests and reviews are carried out the conclusion of truth will lie with The Globe. Our integrity has always been undisputed. For now ladies and gentlemen we will take no more questions but I assure you that a follow-up conference will be arranged once Mister Harris's noble claims have been clearly refuted." Tabb ushered the others from the platform to the exit firmly believing Harris and the letter could subsequently be discredited.

The auditorium floor now erupted into a cacophony of noise as members of the audience got to their feet shuffling chairs and shouting questions in the process. As Tabb led his people away a line of security guards blocked any approach. Instead the audience now moved in on Brian Harris and Alex Hart, who were more than happy to field any questions.

97

"Where's Andrew Clark?" Tabb bellowed to his PA as she stood nearby. "He asked if you could meet him in your office," the PA replied frankly. Without any acknowledgement Tabb stormed towards the lifts leaving a bewildered Sophie Devine with Robert Jameson and Raymond Hilliard. Within minutes Tabb was marching into his office, where he found a very edgy and apprehensive Andrew Clark. "Tell me, and this better be good," Tabb growled.

"They somehow found the missing link," Clark confessed, "but it's even worse."

"Tell me." Tabb rose up menacingly.

"We believe that they have evidence linking you to a murder and our intelligence says it is watertight," Clark was almost hyperventilating.

"Then bury this bloody evidence," Tabb was ready to punch his cowering project manager.

"No chance of that Tabb," a female voice announced from the doorway.

Tabb spun around to be confronted by Jane Coker with a gun in one hand and a file of papers in the other.

"You," Tabb rocked his head back and laughed, "a naïve trainee journalist. Do you think that you can outwit me?"

"Move over there behind your desk," Jane waved the gun at Tabb. "You stay there," she spoke directly to Clark.

Tabb moved back with a confident sneer, "So Miss Coker what do you have on me?"

"This file has concrete evidence of your part in the death of Thomas Vance; also known as Harry but better known to you as The Mole." Jane held up the relatively thin foolscap leather file.

"May I see," Tabb held out his hand whilst remaining totally unflustered.

"Fine but of course all the information is copied and filed," Jane handed the file over. As she stepped backwards Andrew Clark immediately lunged forward and grabbed her locking both arms firmly across Jane's shoulders. Both began to grapple frantically but it was Clark who wore his weaker female opponent into submission. Tabb reacted by swiftly pulling a gun from the top drawer of his desk.

"Let's calm this down Miss Coker," Tabb aimed the barrel straight at his intruder.

Jane easily relented and Clark took away her gun.

"What now Tabb? You have me but the evidence will still prove damning," Jane tried to remain composed.

"Evidence can be changed and challenged as I am sure you have come to realise, and by removing you from the picture should makes things even simpler." Tabb grinned before turning to Clark, "you know what to do and make sure nobody else disturbs us."

Clark made a hasty exit whilst still carrying Jane's gun.

"So what did you hope to achieve by confronting me? Did you really expect your pound of flesh?" Tabb was enjoying being back in the ascendancy.

"I owed it to my friend, Paula Davenport. You had her killed and I wanted to see you squirm in person," Jane spat with aggression.

"The lovely Paula Davenport, I do truly miss her. Best shag I ever had," Tabb mocked as he wagged the gun at his hostage. "Well it would seem that our meeting is about to be called short as I believe I can hear the insufferable Clark returning with some very nice gentlemen who will take good care of you."

Jane glanced over her shoulder to the doorway but it was not Andrew Clark who came into view but DI Parker, flanked by several armed policemen.

"Put down your weapon," the leading policeman with a rifle shouted.

Tabb meekly complied.

"Looks like the game is up at last Tabb," Parker moved forward holding up his badge as one of the policemen carefully removed Tabb's gun.

"Detective Inspector Parker, would you kindly explain to me what is going on? And no just calling your DCI for authority on this occasion will not do," DCI Paul Fletcher of the Met spoke sharply before Tabb could respond.

"Yes now I can tell you exactly what is going on sir," Parker remained totally relaxed. "The original reason I was sent up to London was to trace this young lady here, Jane Coker a junior reporter on Mister Tabb's newspaper, The Globe. Jane was a colleague of Paula Davenport, who was murdered at her home two days ago. A crime that was being investigated by one of your own men, DI Ross. Jane was a potential witness and maybe even a suspect in that murder along with the disgraced MP James Harkness. After making several enquiries I was able to track down the possible whereabouts of Mister Harkness. I followed my hunch and went to his London apartment where I also found Jane Coker."

"So what does this have to do with me? Why not just arrest this girl who had trespassed into my office with a gun with the intention of killing me. That is the only reason I used my gun, to defend myself." Tabb sat back in his chair.

"Continue," DCI Fletcher ignored Tabb as he nodded towards Parker, "and first explain why you went to confront Harkness without notifying or consulting me or DI Ross."

"I was unsure I would find Harkness at the apartment as it really was just a pure hunch. It was whilst I was at the apartment block that a major incident occurred, in which I became embroiled." Parker looked over at Tabb for a reaction but did not get one.

"I take it you mean the murder of a sandwich delivery boy by the Thames where witnesses claim a mystery policeman was also present." DCI Fletcher had been briefed on the killing.

"Correct and yes that policeman was me" Parker came clean, "but this was a complex case. Both Harkness and Jane Coker had been expecting the visit of the sandwich boy as you so eloquently put it, but he was not delivering any snacks. Miss Coker had been assisting James Harkness in revealing the identity of The Globe's mystery reporter, The Mole. For Harkness this was to unravel what he believed to be an injustice carried out by The Globe against him in the paper's series of scandal exposes. Jane Coker along with her colleague Paula Davenport had uncovered a number of illegal practices undertaken by their employer, which included collusion with the IBEX data centre which is also owned by Mister Tabb. Paula Davenport paid for this knowledge with her life."

"Oh really this is crazy, we are in the realms of pantomime. Do we really need to continue with this?" Tabb pleaded.

"Jane Coker and James Harkness joined forces along with another wronged by The Globe, the boxer Luis Carter." Parker ignored Tabb, "and Miss Coker finally managed to unmask The Mole through her job as a reporter for this newspaper."

"Are you saying that The Mole was this sandwich boy?" DCI Fletcher tried to jump ahead as Tabb roared with laughter at the suggestion.

"The records will show the victim to be Thomas Vance who simply used the pseudonym of Harry and the sandwich business as a front. Vance was a former petty criminal on the payroll of Arturo Tabb and yes he was The Mole. His career was coming to and end and agreed to sell key records that proved both James Harkness and Luis Carter were framed by The Globe. The Mole was shot and killed and the file of evidence removed whilst I was at the apartment block. We did not see the killer but the Mole's dying words were simple… Arturo Tabb."

"Enough," Tabb banged both hands down hard on his desk, "this is preposterous. Are you trying to say that I shot this sandwich boy? Where's your proof man? I am Arturo Tabb and my every move is public. The world is my alibi."

"The proof is here in this room and the reason I believe Miss Coker came to see you." Parker pointed at Tabb's desk, "if I am correct that file contains the information that The Mole brought to give to James Harkness yesterday. I would like it removed for fingerprints in relation to Mister Tabb and the dead man."

DCI Fletcher gave the OK for an officer to remove the file for forensic examination.

"Now I put forward that Mister Tabb came back from his press conference to discover Miss Coker and pulled a gun on her. Miss Coker told me she was going to find the file and I immediately arranged for armed back-up as a precaution as I believe him to be The Mole's killer."

"She pulled a gun on me," Tabb sneered.

"So where is this gun Mister Tabb?" Parker moved up close, "and I am sure you realise that we will have ballistics check your gun against the bullet that yesterday killed The Mole. Finally where have you been for the last few days? Not on TV, not in the papers, nowhere."

Tabb realised he had been meticulously set-up, "you cannot do this. This is not possible." He jumped up and grabbed Parker by the lapel.

"Take Mister Tabb away and book him," DCI Fletcher ordered.

Tabb still shouted his innocence as he was led away.

"Parker, something does not add up here," DCI Fletcher scowled. "Your DCI reckons you are a real old school play-it-by-the–book copper but this is just too smooth. If I find anything that does not fit here I will come back and after you."

"It will be watertight believe me," Parker said confidently, "and then you can say a good old slow country copper closed out a major case for the Met."

DCI Fletcher marched off leaving Jane Coker and Parker alone. Both stood in silence for a few minutes before Jane finally moved to embrace the scheming DI whilst breaking down in tears.

"Well done Jane you did it. For Paula, Luis and all of Tabb's victims justice will be done," Parker felt psychologically exhausted.

"What about Andrew Clark?" Jane was still in shock that the plan had run like clockwork.

"Ah yes Andrew Clark. He was the key to the plan and was a willing helper after I explained his future had three potential paths; I had enough evidence to send him down for a long time or there was the fact that Tabb had already put out a contract on him. The final option was to help us nail Tabb using his own dirty tricks and then get out of the country. Once he had planted the gun by swapping it with Tabb's own and set you up with Tabb, he was free to go. He handed me your gun and made a beeline for the airport and we should never see his snivelling face again." Parker winked.

"And the final bait was to deliver the Mole's actual file complete with some new evidence, am I right?" Jane looked serious.

"Yes, well deduced. The new information was created by my new Techie friend, Edgar. Let's just say that Edgar has helped correct a number of lies by crafting some manufactured records of his own, with my artistic input." Parker seemed very pleased with himself, "there is a saying that if you want to defeat your enemy, sing his song. We just put a new hymn sheet in a file already given to us by our enemy. The new records will also fully exonerate both James Harkness and Luis Carter."

Jane's face turned to a grimace, "Luis," she cried out with concern.

Epilogue
(One Month Later)
i

Tabb To Stand Trial – Arturo Tabb, the multi millionaire media magnate, is to stand trial for murder. Tabb, owner of The Globe Newspaper, is accused of assassinating his former premier reporter who was known by the alias The Mole. It is believed that The Mole, real name Thomas Vance, had agreed to provide former MP James Harkness with evidence that the newspaper's allegations about him and former boxer Luis Carter were falsified. It is claimed that Tabb shot Vance and retrieved the file of evidence at Harkness's London residence. It was only due to the diligent investigation by Detective Inspector Jack Parker, working on secondment from Carnbourne police, that the murder was linked back to Tabb. With the assistance of former Globe journalist Jane Coker, DI Parker was able to ensnare Tabb with both the gun and file of evidence in his possession. The tycoon is expected to receive a life sentence but maintains that he has been the victim of an elaborate plot. (Continued Inside)

"Welcome to the Sunday show," the smartly dressed male TV presenter held up a copy of The Sunday Chronicle, a popular broadsheet, to camera. The front page article is accompanied by a picture of an irate looking Arturo Tabb flanked by several police officers.

"Arturo Tabb always maintained that he was the news and if we look at all of today's early editions it is fair to say that he is dominating all the front pages as well as the bulk of the inside cover pages too. Apart from the high profile murder charge, many of the tabloids concentrate on the now laughable attempt by Tabb to dismiss the Queen's right to the throne. Both the murder and the fraud were only exposed thanks in part to the tenacious work of two journalists, Alex Hart and Jane Coker. I'm glad to say we have them both here this morning and they are talking to our very own Clare Johnson."

"Alex Hart and Jane Coker, welcome to the Sunday Show," a very smartly dressed Clare Johnson beamed warmly at her two high profile guests as they sat on a very garish orange sofa with a backdrop of the London Eye behind them. "Alex if I could start with you. Originally a fugitive from justice, you were able to piece together an historical jigsaw with the help of Genealogist Brian Harris to very publicly expose and disprove Arturo Tabb's attempt to re-write Royal history and con the world. Not a bad bit of work for a local journalist more used to covering village fetes," Clare shot Alex a mischievous look.

"Yes thank you Clare and it is fair to say that I have covered the odd fete in my time. There is a genuine innocence and honesty in local journalism which can naively lead you to believe that all journalists write nothing but the truth. My old colleague at the Dartcombe Herald, Richard Kay, had seen both sides of the coin and would often lecture me on it being a big bad world out there.

But it was my old Editor, Dan Goodman that maintained that every journalist has a big story in them through a good old sincere hack's instinct. To be honest this story found me but I would like to thank Dan for all his guidance and support whilst also paying tribute to two young men, Martin Gardner and Stephen Howard, who both died so that The Globe could protect its exclusive."

"He was never a bad lad," Richard Kay muttered as he sat watching the small portable TV in Dan Goodman's office, "reckon he's going to go far."

"Let's face it he's achieved what we always dreamed of, he's got the portfolio and nobody can take it away from him." Goodman exuded pride.

"It was the tragic murders of these two young men that led to your life as a fugitive after you were actually implicated in the Stephen Howard killing," Clare continued in more sombre mood.

"That is correct. It was the information that Martin Gardner and Stephen Howard uncovered at the IBEX data centre that was the basis of The Globe's attempt to fabricate a new royal line of succession. IBEX is owned by Arturo Tabb and one of its employees is due to stand trial for his part in the murders." Alex shivered at his last memory of the stricken Stephen Howard.

"So Alex tell me, however did you and Jane get together?" Clare returned to a jovial interviewing style, just suppressing an inside knowledge wink at the last moment.

Alex blushed, "we had met several years ago at a writer's conference and fate brought us together once more. I was able to confide in Jane."

"Moving over to you Jane, what was your reaction after running into Alex and then hearing this incredible story?"

Jane tried not to look her friend in the eye but kept focus, "mind blowing and very intimidating if I am honest. I had only just started my job at The Globe which gave me a good opportunity to do some research. With the help of my friend and fellow journalist, Paula Davenport, I was able to uncover the fact that The Mole was a front for fabricated attacks on public figures. Paula was to pay for this knowledge with her life," Jane paused for a moment. "It was through our research that I traced two of The Mole's high profile targets, former MP James Harkness and the boxer Luis Carter."

"Luis Carter was shot and badly injured as the truth came out. How is he?" Clare already knew the answer.

"Luis is fine," Clare announced with a beaming smile, "a little sore but recuperating at home with his loving family. He has had literally thousands of get well wishes from fans."

Luis Carter grimaced as his sister, Felicia, hugged him tightly on the couch in their parent's lounge. The boxer's chest was heavily strapped with bandages. His proud mother and father sat nearby.

"And this whole saga really did take a very sinister turn for you Jane with both the deaths of Paula Davenport and The Mole." Clare slyly signalled for Jane to continue.

"It was horrific but thankfully at this stage the police had begun to probe more deeply into Paula's death, which led to Detective Parker tracking me down along with Luis Carter and James Harkness. It was actually whilst he was with us in James's apartment that The Mole was shot. From his vast experience Detective Parker was able to track down the weapon and with it the killer. As you know there is soon to be a very high profile trial as a result." Jane knew she could not say too much due to the pending court case. "Detective Parker of course has been held up as a role model for good old fashioned honest police work in contrast to the modern hi-tech times we live in," Clare alluded to a number of recent tabloid articles and TV documentaries.

"Of course," Jane said simply.

Down in Villamoura, Portugal, Jack Parker and Julie Ingram were enjoying a relaxing stroll as they walked hand in hand around the marina, totally carefree and away from the media spotlight.

"Coming back over to yourself Alex," Clare shifted her body position to face her male guest head on. "Whilst Jane assisted Detective Parker you were now focussed on a bygone age. Through detailed research you assisted Brian Harris in finding and validating the original letter written by Mary Queen of Scot's loyal lady-in-waiting, Mary Seton. It was this letter that in one blow exposed The Globe's revelations about the Royal Family Tree as nothing but a tissue of made-up lies. Where on earth did you manage to get the letter?"

"To reveal the source of the letter would betray a trust but let's just say that the evidence was literally with The Globe the whole time," Alex remained succinct.

"Intriguing and of course I was fortunate enough to be the one to give you the floor at the conference to challenge The Globe's experts, Historian Raymond Hilliard and Genealogist Robert Jameson. Hilliard has now famously confessed to his part in plotting the scam in contrast to Jameson, who is still professing his innocence. Can we really believe he was conned and really just a victim? And as for Brian Harris, he has become something of a celebrity. We see him as a regular on the chat show circuit and it is rumoured that he has just signed up for his own Genealogy show on this very channel."

"Yes can't wait to watch that one," Alex commented with obvious sarcasm.

"One person who really seems to be enjoying her fifteen minutes of fame is Sophie Devine. If she had become Queen I'm not sure how pictures like this would have gone down at the palace," Clare held up a Sunday paper centrefold spread that showed Sophie lounging in black underwear and stockings under the headline 'How I Was Duped'.

"Quite," Alex visibly exhaled at the sight of the sexy scandal piece.

"The network that supported this elaborate sting was far reaching as we know, with even the IBC playing its part as the former head of News and Current Affairs, Mark Alford, is due to face corruption charges. But out of it all like a Phoenix from the flames it has been confirmed that James Harkness has been appointed by the government as special envoy to the Middle East." Clare referred to yet another newspaper article. "And it would seem that some papers are even touting and supporting Harkness as a future Prime Minister."

"The very same papers that once joined in the witch hunt to destroy him. How quickly a life can be changed," Jane spoke with pointed bitterness.

"So what next for you two?" Clare asked jovially.

"I'm now writing a weekly column for a major newspaper called 'From The Hart'. An honest journalist's view of the world and all that." Alex was revelling in the freedom of his new job.

"And I am to take up a position as a lecturer in journalism at a university in America," Jane was overly excited about starting a new life in New York with Luis.

The interview now drew to a close and the camera moved back to the main presenter, who provided the link introduction to a film report on changes in modern teaching practices.

"Thank you guys," Clare was relieved that her first major TV interview was over. "That went well, so how does it feel to be the new champions of open and sincere journalism?"

"Papers still need to be sold and headlines made attractive. People do not want to read about the mundane and so things will never really change. The truth can always be sensationalised with careful editing," Jane shrugged.

Alex picked up one of the Sunday papers to prove a point. An article was headlined 'I Saw Two Men Shoot At Dodi and Diana's Car'. "Grab's the attention doesn't it, but do you believe it?"

Clare considered for a moment but did not answer, "how about breakfast? My treat."

"I'm sorry but I have to get going," Jane glanced at her watch before hugging Clare.

"Who said anything about you? My offer was to this gorgeous man here," Clare linked arms with a flattered and slightly flustered Alex and led him away.

ii

In the early hours of the morning in a small bijou house on the outskirts of San Diego, Mary Stone was finding it hard to sleep. She decided to give up the fight and got up to have a glass of milk.

"Mum are you OK?" Sally's voice echoed from her large bedroom.

"Hey darling did I wake you?" Mary came and sat on the edge of her daughter's bed.

"No, I've been lying here thinking," Sally blinked her eyes as Mary switched on a bedside lamp.

"What about?" Mary asked softly.

"I was trying to understand what you told me about where you really came from and how you were able to help some people right a wrong because of your past. One day will you tell me more about when you were young and about Granny and Grandad?" Sally innocently appealed.

"Of course my darling," Mary leant forward to kiss her daughter's forehead with a tear in her eye. "Now you get some rest."

Mary switched off the lamp and wandered back into her own bedroom as the first rays of daybreak began to beam through the blinds. She headed straight over to a grey fire proof security box that sat by the side of a computer desk. Mary unlocked the box and slowly pulled out a collection of old papers which she placed carefully on the desk in front of her. Although extremely yellow and withered in nature, the print was clear and written by the hand of Mary Seton. "You are not quite ready for the truth of who you really are my darling and neither is the world."

Printed in Great Britain by
Amazon.co.uk, Ltd.,
Marston Gate.